Dear Target Reader,

I'm overjoyed that Targe
for its Diverse Book Clul
also learned a lot: about myself; about people who've experienced things I never have; about places I've never lived; and about how important love and friendship are for all of us.

The Proposal starts with . . . well, a proposal. A very public one. Nik Paterson is at Dodger Stadium with her boyfriend of five months and all of his friends, and he surprises her with a proposal over the JumboTron. She's both stunned and horrified, and when she says no, her now ex-boyfriend storms out and leaves her there to deal with the aftermath. Carlos Ibarra—who some of you may remember as Drew's best friend from my first book, *The Wedding Date*—is sitting right behind Nik, and he helps her get out of the stadium before the camera crews descend on her.

I got the idea for this book after what felt like an epidemic of public proposals, all of which made me cringe. No matter if you're an introvert or extrovert, no one wants to be forced to make a major life decision with the whole world watching. Talk about a trap: there's no good way to say no in that situation, and if you do, everyone will think you're the bad guy. Nik uses both rage and humor to recover from this experience, and she leans on her friends and Carlos, who laugh and yell along with her. And in the process, she and Carlos—both of whom are staunchly anti-relationship for very different reasons—accidentally fall for each other.

The Proposal deals with love and grief, family and friendship, tacos and cupcakes, and anger and forgiveness. Writing this book made me laugh a lot, made me grateful for my loved ones, and made me very hungry. I hope all of you who read the book have the same experience.

Thanks for reading, and I hope you love *The Proposal*!

Jasmine

P. S. I love to hear from readers! Find me on Twitter @thebestjasmine or facebook.com/jasmineguillorywriter and tell me all about your own proposal story!

TITLES BY JASMINE GUILLORY

The Wedding Date

The Proposal

The Proposal

....

Jasmine Guillory

JOVE
NEW YORK

A JOVE BOOK
Published by Berkley
An imprint of Penguin Random House LLC
375 Hudson Street, New York, New York 10014

ISBN: 9781984804884

First Jove trade paperback edition: October 2018
Jove trade paperback Target Book Club edition: October 2018

Printed in the United States of America
1 3 5 7 9 10 8 6 4 2

Cover art and design by Vikki Chu
Book design by Kristin del Rosario

To my dad, Paul Guillory.

You have always believed in me.

Thanks for raising me to believe in myself.

ACKNOWLEDGMENTS

Throughout this publishing process, I've been overwhelmed with gratitude for so many people and their kindness, generosity, and willingness to help. I've gotten advice, assistance, and support from countless people, without whom this book wouldn't exist.

I couldn't have dreamed of finding as wonderful a publishing home as Berkley. Cindy Hwang, thank you for being a fantastic editor and champion. Kristine Swartz, Megha Jain, Jessica Brock, Fareeda Bullert, Jin Yu, Erin Galloway—thank you for everything you've done for me and my books. I'm grateful for you every day. Marianne Grace, Emma Reh, Vikki Chu, and Rita Frangie, thank you for making sure my books look amazing, inside and out. Lauren Monaco, Andrew Dudley, and the entire Berkley Sales team, you're all superstars. I'm thrilled to work with all of you.

Everyone should be so lucky as to have an agent as good as Holly Root. Thank you so much to you and everyone at Root Literary.

So many writers have shared their time and knowledge with me. Amy Spalding and Akilah Brown, your guidance has been invaluable to me. Thank you for responding to all of the texts and IMs and emails, for talking me down and for pumping me up. I will forever be grateful for Roxane Gay, Heather Cocks, Jessica Morgan, Ruby Lang, Sara Zarr, Melissa Baumgart, Tayari Jones, Robin Benway, Caitlin Cruz, Nicole Cliffe, Daniel Ortberg, Laura Turner, Jami Attenberg, Stephanie

Lucianovic, Samantha Powell, Nicole Chung, Rainbow Rowell, and Alexis Coe. All of you have helped me in countless ways.

Rachel Fershleiser and Margaret H. Willison, your enthusiasm for books in general, and my books in particular, is the absolute best. Thank you for being you.

My friends are the most wonderful people in the world. Janet Goode, I love you so much. Melissa Sladden and Jina Kim, thank goodness we found each other. Simi Patnaik and Nicole Clouse, I have no idea what I would do without you both. So many others have loved and supported me in so many ways: Jill, Katie, and Sally Vizas, Lisa McIntire, Sarah Mackey, Julian Davis Mortenson, Nathan Cortez, Kyle Wong, Ryan Gallagher, Sarah Tiedeman, Toby Rugger, Leslie Gross, Kate Leos, Lyette Mercier, Joy Alferness, Nanita Cranford, and Laurie Baker.

I owe so many thanks to Wellesley College and the entire Wellesley community, but especially to Colleen Richards Powell, Korrie Xavier, and Marthine Satris.

I would be nothing without my family. My parents, Paul and Donna Guillory, filled our home with books and taught me by example the joy of reading. My sister, Sasha Guillory, who I read to and who read to me. My grandparents, aunts, uncles, and cousins, who love me to pieces. Thank you for everything.

Natalie Stewart Cortez, I hate that you aren't here to read this book, but I try every day to live up to your memory. You found joy and laughter in life, even during the hard times, you fought for what you believed in, and most of all, you loved and loved and loved. May we all have people to love us as much as the world loved you.

Chapter One

Nik Paterson looked around at the perfect Los Angeles day: clear blue sky, bright green baseball field, warm sun shining down on the thousands of people with her at Dodger Stadium. There was only one thought on her mind: *when can I get out of here?*

Fisher was next to her, his blond man bun golden in the sun, laughing as he drank warm beer to celebrate his birthday. He and his buddies were talking about lifting, or their latest auditions, or their upcoming car purchases—all of the things his friends always talked about, all of the things Nik couldn't care less about. If she'd known this birthday outing was going to include a bunch of Fisher's friends, she would have at least gotten one of her girlfriends to come along so she would have someone to talk to.

Although to be fair, it was possible Fisher had told her his friends were coming and she hadn't been paying attention. She tended not to pay that much attention when Fisher talked, but then, she hadn't been dating him for the past five months for his conversational skills.

Nik looked back up at the scoreboard and sighed. It was still only the fifth inning; she probably had at least an hour, maybe an hour and a half, more of this.

She didn't have anything against baseball, exactly. It was just that she'd rather be spending this beautiful spring day at home with her laptop and a glass of bourbon on the rocks than outside at a baseball stadium with a warm beer. But when the hot dude you were sleeping with wanted to go to a Dodgers game for his birthday, you sucked it up and went along with him and his bros.

She sighed again and reached for her phone. Maybe she could get some work done as she sat there.

Just as she was starting to make some actual progress on a draft of an article, Fisher nudged her hard.

"Nik! Put your phone down, you can't miss this!" He threw his arm around her and kissed her on the cheek. She pressed save and tucked her phone back in her pocket. His favorite baseball player must be coming up to bat or something.

She looked down at the field, but nothing was going on there. She followed Fisher's pointed finger and looked up at the scoreboard, just in time to see on the screen:

NICOLE: I LOVE YOU. WILL YOU MARRY ME? FISHER.

She turned to Fisher, her mouth wide open.

"What the hell is going on?"

To her horror, he dropped down onto one knee, on top of the peanut shells that carpeted the concrete, dangerously close to the puddle of spilled beer.

Oh God. He had a ring box in his hand.

"Nikole." He tucked a strand of hair behind his ear and opened the ring box. She averted her eyes. "Will you make me the happiest man in the world?"

Was she asleep? This definitely felt like a nightmare.

They'd only been dating for five months! That he loved her was news to her—he'd certainly never said *that* before—but a proposal? He didn't even know how to spell her name!

She tried to put on a smile, but she'd never had the best poker face—except, strangely, when she was actually playing poker. Not even his best friends would call Fisher perceptive, but even he could tell something was off with his happy moment.

"Nik, did you hear me? You're just standing there. You haven't even put the ring on!"

"I don't . . ." She cleared her throat and tried to talk in a low voice, so the whole damn stadium couldn't tell what was going on. "It's just that we've never discussed this. We aren't really in a place to . . . I didn't . . . I just wish you'd brought this up before . . . before now."

"Are you saying no?"

He was still on one knee, good God.

"I'm saying this isn't really the place to have this conversation."

He just stared at her, wide-eyed.

"Are you saying no?" he repeated.

She took a deep breath.

"I'm trying not to say that out loud so everyone can hear me."

She was still hoping this was some sort of a joke. That any minute, he would reveal this was for a commercial or a reality show or something, and they would all laugh and go back to not paying attention to the game.

"Come *on*, Nik," Fisher said. Why wouldn't he stand up? "We're great together! Live a little! Give us a shot!"

Live a little??? Was he approaching marriage like he would a spontaneous trip to Palm Springs for the weekend?

"Fisher. Don't do this."

"I can't believe *you're* doing this to *me*." He snapped the ring box closed, stood up, and tossed his head. The head toss didn't work as well when his hair was in the bun. "Rejecting me in public! On my birthday! What kind of a person are you?"

He stormed off and ran up the stadium stairs. So she guessed this wasn't a joke then.

She looked at his bros, and his bros looked at her. They shook their heads like they were disappointed in her, turned, and filed out of the row after him.

Which left Nik alone to face the forty-five thousand pairs of eyes on her.

• • • • • • •

Carlos nudged his sister Angela as the blond dude and his bros stalked up the stairs and out of the stadium.

"Now I know what to tell your boyfriend not to do."

Angela rolled her eyes.

"Nice try, but I don't have a boyfriend."

Damn. She consistently refused to let him meet guys she was dating, so he was reduced to trying to trick her into admitting she had a boyfriend. Either he never managed to catch her off guard enough to admit it, or she'd never had a boyfriend since he started trying this. He was betting on the former.

Granted, he never told Angie anything about the women he went out with, either, but that was different. He hadn't dated anyone seriously in years, and none of the women he had minor interludes with these days mattered enough to meet his sister.

"You have one good point," Angela said. "Anyone dating me should definitely not do that." Angela's hand gestures got bigger as she talked. "She said they hadn't discussed it. Who proposes to someone if they haven't discussed it? Especially in public?"

He looked back down at the woman—Nicole—now alone in her row. She'd sat back down and was typing something on her phone. The sun picked out the golden highlights in her dark curly hair. She was doing a very good job of pretending the whole stadium wasn't talking about her.

"I feel so bad for her." He couldn't believe she hadn't jumped up to flee the building. The game had started back up again, but no one was watching. Everyone was looking at her. Including Carlos.

"So do I," Angela said.

Nicole twirled one of her curls around her finger and pretended to watch the game. Carlos realized he was staring at her and forced himself to look away.

He turned to Angela and shook his head.

"I get trying to make a big romantic gesture and all, and wanting a surprise, but . . ."

"Deciding to spend your life together shouldn't be a surprise," Angela said. "It should be something the two of you talk about first!"

"Oh, hey, speaking of," he said. "Did I tell you Drew proposed to his girlfriend a few days ago?"

She laughed.

"Really? That's fantastic. I never would have thought a year ago that your friend Drew would be engaged." She looked up at the JumboTron, and then at Carlos. "She did say yes, right?"

He laughed.

"She did. But then, they'd talked about it first."

Carlos looked back at the woman two rows down, who had *not* said yes. She was aggressively not looking at anyone around her. Her hair moved in the breeze that blew through the stadium, and her dark brown skin glowed in the sun. He'd only seen her face briefly up on the JumboTron, until he'd realized that this real-life drama was going on just ten feet below him, but he'd seen a striking face, with big dark eyes and bright red lips. He wondered how long she was going to stay at her seat. She probably hadn't wanted to leave right away for fear of running into the man-bun guy, which made sense. But if he knew anything about the way things happened in L.A., if she sat here too long, she was in danger of . . .

Yep, there it was. The camera crew.

He poked his sister. She looked down and saw the problem immediately.

"Oh my God, what a nightmare," she said.

"We've got to save her," he said.

"How do you propose to do that? Pun not intended."

"Follow my lead." He stood up and made his way out of their row, Angie right behind him.

He walked down the wide stadium stairs, his eyes on the field. When he got two rows down, he paused and glanced to the side. *I hope this works*, he thought, before he went in.

"Nicole? Nicole, it is you!" he said, loud enough that not only she and the entire camera crew heard but also the other rows around them all turned to look. "Angela, look, it's Nicole! We haven't seen you for . . . my God, how many years has it been?"

Angela took up his prompt as Carlos pushed the camera crew aside to get to Nicole.

"At least five years, Carlos, it's got to be? Nicole, how are you?"

His sister threw her arms around the grinning woman, and whispered something in her ear before the embrace ended.

"It's so great to see you after all this time!" Angela said. She looked around with a huge smile on her face, and appeared to notice the camera crew for the first time. "Oh my goodness, are we interrupting something? I am so sorry, guys!" She smiled at the three men who had surrounded Nicole up until about thirty seconds before, with that wide-eyed look that had never failed to make men fall at her feet. "We haven't seen each other for so long, imagine running into you here."

"Oh wow, how do you know each—"

Carlos stepped in front of the guy with the camera. If the dude got aggressive, well, Carlos was pretty sure he had at least four inches and thirty pounds on him.

"We were just heading to get more beer and Dodger Dogs, want to come with?"

Want to come with? He sounded like one of his sixteen-year-old patients.

"Great idea, I'm starving." Nicole wiggled past the cameraman. "Chat with you guys later!" she called back to them, as she, Carlos, and Angie raced up the stairs.

Hmmm, apparently, sounding like your sixteen-year-old patients was a way to not seem suspicious.

They kept up the pretense on their way up the stairs, all saying things like "Wow, it's been so long!" and "Fancy meeting you here!" and "I couldn't believe my eyes that it was you!" over and over. When they finally got all the way up the stairs and inside, the three of them all leaned against the nearest wall and erupted with laughter.

"Thank you guys SO MUCH for saving me," Nicole said when

she finally stopped laughing. "I was in the middle of trying to remember the martial arts moves I learned twenty years ago, but you rescued me without me having to knock someone down or, more likely, embarrass myself."

"You're not saved yet," Carlos said. He put his hand on her back and grabbed his sister by the arm. "We've got to get you out of this stadium. They'll find you again if you stick around."

"Oh, I can find my own way out. I'm sure you want to get back to the game." She stood up straight and smiled at them. "But thank you again, I really appreciate it."

He was about to say good-bye when he thought of something.

"Did you drive here? Or was your . . . or did you get a ride?"

She shrugged.

"My ride seems to be long gone, but I'm sure there's another way to get back to Silver Lake from here. Isn't there a shuttle or something? Or I can get a ride. I have all of those apps."

He and Angie exchanged glances. He envisioned her waiting in the parking lot at Dodger Stadium for a ride and getting ambushed again. He bet Angie did, too.

"Silver Lake is in our direction," he said. "We can give you a ride back." He could miss the rest of the game. It wasn't like they were playing the Giants or anything.

She raised her eyebrows at him and turned to Angela to shake her head.

"No, seriously, that's okay. You don't have to give up the rest of the game for me; you don't even know me. Plus, you two probably have better things to do than drive a stranger around Los Angeles."

Angela looked confused and then laughed.

"Oh wait, did you think we were on a date? Ugh, no, he's my

brother. Trust me, I'd rather be driving you around L.A. than watching baseball with him."

Nicole looked at Carlos.

"Are you sure? You really don't have to."

He grinned and threw his arm around both women.

"Call it my good deed for the week," he said. "Come on, let's go before those vultures follow you."

Chapter Two

Nik walked across the parking lot with Carlos and Angela. She was grateful the exodus from the game hadn't started yet, so they didn't have to wade through crowds of people. The few they did see gave her dirty looks. That's right, she was the bitch who broke the pretty blond boy's heart, live on the JumboTron.

She shook her head. That really had happened. She had really been proposed to, and then abandoned, in front of the world.

She could not believe Fisher had done that to her. Just that he'd proposed to her in the first place was shocking—she would have been certain neither of them thought their relationship was heading toward marriage. She didn't think either of them *wanted* their relationship to head toward marriage. But not only did he do it, he did it in public. At a *baseball* game? Good God, she was furious at him.

She also felt like a huge asshole. She'd just refused her boyfriend's proposal in front of thousands of people. On his birthday.

All of the people giving her dirty looks hated her for a good reason. She hadn't meant to hurt Fisher! He was a perfectly nice, incredibly boring guy. She probably could have found a nicer way to respond to the proposal, but she was so stunned she couldn't think straight. Plus, diplomacy had never been her strong point.

Thank God she'd gotten rescued by the Wonder Twins here. She should probably be wary of getting in a car with two strangers who had picked her up at a baseball stadium at a low moment in her life, but she didn't have the energy. She should especially be wary of this guy, who seemed way too attractive for his own good, with his tousled dark brown hair, big brown eyes, and that slight Saturday scruff on his cheeks. Normal Nik wouldn't have trusted this guy for a second. Dazed by the JumboTron, Nik had told him where she lived. But at this point, she didn't have the strength to do anything but be relieved she was no longer inside the stadium.

"Thanks again for getting me out of there. I was just sitting there texting my girlfriends about this fiasco and trying to figure out how I was going to get home when the camera crew showed up. I still can't believe any of this happened."

Carlos unlocked his car, one of the fancy red sports cars she was used to seeing around L.A. Ah, yes, of course the kind of guy who would almost knock down the cameraman and smile while he did it would have a red sports car. He opened the front passenger door for her. She shook her head.

"Oh no, I can get in the back."

Angela laughed and opened the back door.

"Don't worry about it, Nikole. I think you deserve shotgun today."

"Nik." She needed to make this one thing clear, even though she was only going to know these people for the length of the car ride to Silver Lake. "Everyone calls me Nik. My first name is Nikole, yes, but it's Nikole with a K."

Angela looked at Nik for a long beat, her hand still on the open back door.

"But didn't the screen spell it . . ."

"With a C? It sure did!"

She got into the passenger seat and put her seatbelt on, and Angela slid into the seat behind her.

"You do not mean to tell me he spelled your name wrong in his *proposal*?" Angela said.

"That's exactly what I'm telling you. Only one of the many things that stunned me about this afternoon." Her pocket buzzed. "Wait, hold that thought, I have to tell my friends my ride is taken care of."

She had forty-three new text messages.

"Shit."

She clicked on her messages and let out a deep breath. Okay, thirty-three of the messages were from the group chat with her girlfriends, first their reactions to her initial texts about the proposal and then their increasingly agitated texts asking her where the hell she was when she stopped responding.

Sorry sorry, camera crew was in my face, some strangers rescued me, getting a ride back to the eastside from them right now, long story. Meet me at the bar within the hour.

She scrolled to her other new messages. Two were work related, she would deal with those after she'd recovered from the hangover she had every intention of having tomorrow morning. Oh my God, three were from people she knew who had been at Dodger Stadium that afternoon and had seen her on the JumboTron. There were more than eighteen million people in the greater Los Angeles area, she knew no more than a few hundred of them, max, and three of those had just HAPPENED to be at Dodger Stadium the one time in her life she was there, just so they could see the craziest thing that had ever happened to her? This was like some sort of sick joke.

And the other five texts were from Fisher.

You fucking bitch, I can't believe

She turned the phone off and dropped it in her pocket. So Fisher wasn't a perfectly nice guy after all. She wasn't even going to think about looking at those texts until she had at least two or three shots of bourbon in her.

"Everything okay?" Carlos asked, glancing over from the driver's seat.

She laughed, even though none of this was really funny. Now she understood what hysterical laughter really meant.

"As okay as anything can get today, I guess. Sorry for zoning out like that, I had a bunch of texts. My friends are very relieved that I got out of there in one piece."

"God, me, too," Carlos said. "When we saw that camera crew coming for you, I was worried that you'd either punch them all and run or burst into tears."

"Believe me, I was contemplating both," Nik said. "Unfortunately, I don't exactly know how to land a punch, and I didn't really want to get filmed crying on top of everything else."

He grinned at her, and she grinned back. It was refreshing to be around a guy who would joke with her like this after months of Fisher, who would only look at her blankly.

"Where to?" Carlos asked. "Do you want us to drop you at home, or at a friend's house, or . . . ?"

She was glad that she'd already made plans to meet Courtney and Dana at the bar, otherwise Dazed-by-the-JumboTron Nik probably would have given the first guy she'd met in forever who had a sense of humor her home address.

"There's a bar on Sunset that has a bottle of bourbon with my name all over it. My friends are meeting me there to hopefully get me drunk enough so that I forget this day ever happened."

"I cannot believe he spelled your name wrong," Angela muttered from the back seat.

"To be fair to him, we'd only been dating for five months, maybe he just hadn't absorbed that bit of knowledge about me yet."

"Wait, WHAT?" She'd thought that Angela was the loud one, but Carlos nearly shouted that. "You'd only been dating for five months, and he proposed? In public?"

If she had to pick a strange man to rescue her, at least it was one who was outraged by the right things.

"Exactly! We'd only been dating for five months, he proposed, in public. And I'm the bad guy for rejecting him on his birthday?"

"You are not the bad guy," Carlos said. "Trust me on this."

She was tempted to text Fisher back, curse him out from here to oblivion, and tell him what she really thought of his acting, but she restrained herself. Barely.

Angela piped up from the back seat. "So, how long have you lived in L.A., Nik?"

She was grateful for the opportunity to talk about something else.

"For about six years, but I've lived in California most of my life. What about you guys?"

"Born and raised on the Eastside," Carlos said.

"Don't let my big brother over here act like he's got Eastside cred; he's been living on the Westside for years and just moved back, thank goodness."

"Thank goodness?" Carlos said. "This is the first I've heard of my little sister being thankful that I'm back on the Eastside. Thank goodness for what, so you can have someone to come over to your house and kill spiders for you in the middle of the night?"

"Exactly!" Angela said. "That, and someone to build my IKEA furniture for me, and to dog sit for me when I go out of town."

Carlos somehow managed to roll his eyes while keeping both eyes on the road.

"You don't even have a dog!"

"But I might! Someday!"

The siblings' friendly bickering kept her entertained for the rest of the ride to the bar. And more importantly, it kept her distracted enough so she didn't text Fisher back.

By the time they pulled up to the Sanctuary, the bar that she and her girlfriends had been coming to for almost as long as she'd lived in L.A., she'd even managed to laugh a few times at the stories that Carlos and Angela told about each other.

"You guys are going to come in, right?" she asked them. "I owe you far more than a drink for what you did for me today, but we can start with that."

Carlos and Angela exchanged a quick glance. It was a look full of wordless communication, but she couldn't tell whether it was "This woman seems crazy, let's get the fuck out of here" or just "I was getting carsick in the back seat, let's get a drink."

"Sure," Carlos said. "I was about to get another beer anyway right when all the action started at the game."

She felt her shoulders relax as soon as the three of them walked inside the bar. The dark, cool interior was such a relief after the unrelenting bright sunlight that she'd been enduring all day. She pushed her sunglasses up to the top of her head, where they would undoubtedly get caught in her hair within minutes, and glanced toward the corner of the room. Her friends Courtney and Dana were right there, waiting for her in their favorite booth.

"I made it," she said as she walked up to them. "Where's my drink?"

"There." Dana pointed behind her. She turned around, and the bartender, who had been pouring them drinks at least twice a week for the past four years, handed her a glass of bourbon with one big ice cube. That was fast. Granted, they were regulars there, but this was a record. Courtney and Dana must have told Pete that something was up.

"Thanks, Pete. Get my friends here whatever they want, please? On me."

As Pete took their orders, she slid into the curved booth next to Courtney.

"Hey," Courtney said. "You okay?"

She leaned her head against Courtney's shoulder for the briefest of moments.

"I'm fine. Just kind of shell-shocked at what just happened, I think." She motioned for Carlos and Angela to join her in the booth.

"Dana and Courtney, meet Carlos and Angela. They saved me in about a dozen different ways this afternoon, and I will owe them far more than my firstborn child. Carlos and Angela, these are my friends Dana and Courtney, who were about to come to Dodger Stadium and carry me away from that godforsaken place, so it turns out you saved them, too."

Just then, the bartender brought two more drinks to the table.

"A toast!" Nik said when the drinks were on the table. "To friendship, both real and feigned."

They all clinked glasses, and Nik took a deep gulp of her bourbon.

"Okay," Courtney said. "We need details. What did that toast mean? He seriously proposed? For the record, I never liked Fisher. He was never nice to me—I don't think fat Korean women were in his target demographic. Where is he now? Did he cry? Tell us everything."

Nik took a deep breath. She still couldn't believe this had actually happened to her.

Dana patted her on the shoulder and shook her head at Courtney.

"Let her finish her drink first! You don't have to tell us the story right now. Are you hungry? Should we get pizza? What kind should we get?"

She definitely wasn't drunk yet, but pizza sounded incredible right now.

"Absolutely. Fisher hasn't eaten carbs in like two years, so pizza sounds fantastic. I don't care what's on it as long as it includes pepperoni and lots of cheese."

Dana pulled out her phone and opened a delivery app.

"Are you two in, too?" she asked Carlos and Angela. They both nodded.

After a few clicks, Dana looked up from her phone.

"Okay, it's on its way here. Where were we?"

She took another sip of her drink. Thank God for bourbon.

"I don't know where we were, but to tell the story backward, that toast was because these two pretended to be long-lost friends of mine to save me from a camera crew. God bless them."

"A camera crew?" Courtney stared at her, then at Carlos and Angela, Nik guessed to confirm she hadn't lost her mind.

"Yep." Carlos nodded. "We were sitting a few rows behind Nik and saw the whole proposal happen. And then when we saw the camera crew walking toward her, we knew we had to do something."

"Where did you even come up with that idea? That was brilliant!" Dana said.

He nodded and lifted his glass.

"Thank you for that; I agree, it was brilliant." He grinned at Nik, and despite herself, she grinned back at him. "But I have to admit, the credit all goes to our cousin Jessie. She told me a story once about a woman in a parking lot doing that to her when there was a creepy guy following her, and I guess it stuck with me."

Angela laughed.

"I was going to let my brother take the credit for that idea, even though I knew he got it from Jessie. I'm just glad to know he pays attention to the women in his family."

Nik couldn't remember the last time she'd seen a man voluntarily give credit to a woman for an idea. That was one of the major reasons she'd gone freelance, all of the men talking over her and pretending they'd come up with her ideas, even when everyone had heard her say them out loud.

"Oh, please," Carlos said. "I pay probably too much attention to all of you."

Nik finished her drink, and within seconds another one showed up on the table in front of her.

"Thanks, Pete," she, Courtney, and Dana said in unison.

"You three must tip very well," Carlos said.

They all laughed.

"That, and Pete's had a crush on Dana for at least two years," Courtney said. Dana grinned and shrugged.

"Okay, okay." Nik took a sip of her new drink and set it down.

"And now for my part of the story. Here is the most important thing: I had NO IDEA that anything like this was coming. I was racking my brain on the way here for where this came from, and I swear, I had no hints."

She'd actually started wondering within the last few weeks how much longer this Fisher thing would last. Not only did he bore her, but she didn't really think he was all that interested in her, either. She didn't look like the models his friends all dated, he didn't even pretend to be interested in her work, and she found his laughable. A great recipe for a marriage!

"Anyway. The game was whatever, fine, boring, sunny, et cetera. And then all of a sudden, Fisher told me to look at something. I thought it was some stupid baseball thing, so I looked at the field, but then he pointed toward the JumboTron. And up there, in twelve-foot-high letters, was something like 'I love you, will you marry me?'"

"You forgot the most important part," Angela said. "It said 'Nicole, I love you, will you marry me?' Nicole with a C!"

Dana and Courtney gasped in unison. The appropriate response.

"He spelled your name wrong in his proposal?" Courtney asked.

"Yes!" Nik said. "But wait, think about that part later, let me get the whole story out first. So when I saw the thing up on the screen, I thought it was some sort of joke or that he was just showing me because that's my name and it was someone else in the stadium, or something like that. He'd never even said I love you to me before—which, if he had, this whole nightmare today never would have happened, because I'd have cut that thing off in a heartbeat, but anyway. Wait, where was I?"

"You saw it up on the screen . . . ?" Dana prompted her.

"Oh, yeah. So I turned to him, and he was down on one knee. With a ring box in his hand!"

"What did the ring look like?" Courtney asked.

"The ring?" Nik paused. She'd been so freaked out at the time she hadn't even looked at it. "I have no idea. I don't think I even saw it. Hell, I don't even remember what I said to him, something about how we should have talked about this before, and then he said something like, 'Are you saying no?' and I told him I wasn't saying that out loud, and then he told me to just live a little. LIVE A LITTLE. Like deciding to get married on a whim is the thing all the cool girls are doing these days. And when I again refused, he got furious and stood up and left and his friends followed him." She turned to Carlos. "Did I forget anything?"

Carlos made a face. Oh shit, what had she forgotten?

"Just that . . . just that there was a camera on you the whole time, so the entire thing was broadcast to the whole stadium. No one could hear what you were saying—I mean, we could, we were just a few rows behind you and your dude talked pretty loudly—but what was going on was probably pretty clear to everyone."

"Oh yeah, right. That part." Nik put her head down on the table. "I think I need to just stay here for the next few days. Throw a blanket over me and just leave me here in the bar, and for the love of God, take my phone with you. Maybe by the time I resurface, everyone will forget that any of this ever happened."

Dana patted Nik on the back and Courtney took the phone that Nik had tossed on the table and tucked it away in her pocket.

Someone pushed her drink against her hand. She grabbed it, lifted her head, took a sip, and put her head back down on the table. Thank God for bourbon.

"Did I forget anything else?" Nik sat up and pushed her hair back.

"I saw the ring," Angela said.

"WHAT?" the whole table said in unison.

Angela looked at Carlos.

"You didn't see it? Oh yeah. He opened the ring box when he first got down on one knee, and the camera zeroed in on the ring. I can't believe you didn't notice."

She knew there was a reason she'd wanted Carlos and Angela to stay.

"Well?" Nik asked. "Don't keep me in suspense. What did it look like? Please tell me you remember."

Angela paused.

"Okay, you know the Kate Middleton ring, right? The Princess Diana one? With the huge sapphire in the middle and diamonds all around it? It looked just like that. Except smaller."

Nik banged her drink down on the table. It sloshed everywhere, but she was past the point of caring.

"Does he think he's some kind of a prince?" She took a deep breath. "Wait, that sounded mean. That was mean, I guess. But . . ."

"But you are not a princess ring kind of person," Courtney finished.

"But I am not a princess ring kind of person!" Nik said. "Nothing against princess rings, but IF I wanted an engagement ring from him—which I absolutely did not—it wouldn't have been a replica of a princess ring. He obviously doesn't know me that well; I'm not a baseball-game proposal kind of person, either. But seriously, a princess ring? For ME?"

"You did get up at four a.m. to watch Harry and Meghan's wedding though," Dana said.

"That was different," Nik said. "Anyway, is there anything else I missed about the proposal?" she asked Carlos and Angela. "Am I remembering the forlorn look on Fisher's face correctly?"

Carlos shrugged. "He looked more outraged than forlorn, really. Like a kid having a tantrum."

Yeah . . . that sounded like Fisher, unfortunately. She mopped up her spilled drink with some of the extra napkins Pete had left on the table.

"Carlos is right," Angela said. "No offense, but he seemed like kind of a baby."

Nik shrugged and sighed. Fisher had been kind of a baby. A baby with beautiful blond hair he constantly admired in the mirror and great abs. So yeah, it made sense that he would yell and storm off when she'd publicly rejected his proposal.

"None taken. He was kind of a baby. But babies can be pretty great sometimes—isn't that why people like them?"

Carlos cleared his throat.

"As a professional baby expert: people like babies because they're cute, they have big heads, and because they're pretty helpless without us. They can scream really loudly, though."

Courtney nodded.

"Yep, that sounds like Fisher. Down to the big—"

"COURTNEY!"

Dana and Courtney giggled and high-fived, and Nik tried and failed to suppress her laughter.

"You two are the worst friends in the history of the world, do you know that?"

They nodded, still laughing.

"We know," Dana said.

* * * * * * *

Carlos coughed. Maybe they needed a reminder that there was a guy at the table with them?

Nope, that just made all four women, his little sister included, glance his way and laugh harder. Excellent. He looked at Nik, who was looking back at him. She winked at him. He grinned and winked back.

One of the friends' phone buzzed. Dana, right? She was the black one who looked like a model. Courtney was the Korean one with pink lipstick on.

"Pizza's here!" she said. A few minutes later, a huge pizza box covered their table, and they all had big pieces of pizza in their hands, the pepperoni oil dripping onto more napkins that the bartender had thrown onto their table.

"I didn't even ask if anyone was a vegetarian or gluten-free or anything," Dana said. He and Angela both shook their heads.

"This is a Los Angeles rarity, to have five people at a table all dig into a cheese-covered, two-meat, gluten-filled pizza without hesitating."

Nik lifted her almost empty glass.

"To new friends and gluten!"

They all toasted and stuffed pizza into their mouths.

"Wait." Nik looked up at him and started to say something, but stopped to finish chewing her bite of pizza. "Did you say a few minutes ago that you're a baby expert?"

His sister just shook her head.

"My brother. Always with the delusions of grandeur."

He had the opportunity to impress three attractive women with his degrees and knowledge—could his sister at least try to be a good wingman here?

"I'm a pediatrician, but to be perfectly honest, I don't see a lot of babies anymore. I'm the assistant director of the teen clinic at Eastside Medical Center."

"Oh." Nik put her pizza down and reached for a napkin. "You're a doctor."

Okay, he'd never had a woman with that look on her face when he'd said he was a doctor. Like she'd smelled something bad.

"Oooh, you brought us a doctor?" Courtney poked Nik.

Nik looked at Dana and rolled her eyes.

"A doctor," Courtney said, presumably to the table at large. "That's a normal job. I didn't think people in L.A. had normal jobs anymore. All of the jobs here are, like, writer, magician, fit model, actor, cupcake baker, dog walker, social media manager, juice shop cashier, and nonsense like that."

"Well, what do you all do?" he asked Nik and her friends.

"Writer," Nik said.

"Cupcake baker," Courtney said.

"Actor," Dana said.

He and Angela both laughed, but they didn't.

"Oh wait. You're serious?"

Nik nodded and sipped at the dregs of her drink.

"It's true. We're a parody of L.A. sitting right here." She turned to Angela. "What about you? You are also probably something normal, like a teacher or a social worker or an accountant."

"Marketing, for one of the studios," Angie said. "I'm also a parody. Granted, I got my MBA first, so I could have done a normal job, but no, I went straight for the L.A. stereotype."

"What kind of stuff do you write?" Carlos asked Nik.

"Lots of entertainment and celebrity-related stuff, and some more newsy journalism occasionally."

"What about Fisher?" Carlos couldn't keep himself from asking. "Was he also an L.A. stereotype, or was he a lawyer or trader or something?"

Nik shook her head. "Actor! I should have known! Never date an actor; you get proposed to in public with a fucking princess ring." She took another bite of pizza and swallowed it. "Sorry, Dana. No offense."

"None taken," Dana said.

Nik sighed.

"Speaking of Fisher . . . he sent me some texts after he left the game. I only saw a glimpse of one of them, but . . . it wasn't so great. I guess I probably need to read the rest, right?"

Ahh, that's probably what she had been looking at when her face shuttered when they were in the car. She probably didn't want to talk about this with strangers around. Carlos caught Angela's eye, and she nodded.

"Ladies, my sister and I should take off. We have a family event that we have to get to and we can't be late."

"Oh!" Nik looked up. Was it just his imagination that her face fell? "If you have to go, I understand. But you guys, I can't thank you enough for today; you two saved me on what was maybe one of the weirdest days of my life."

Angela stood up, and all of the women followed her out of the booth.

"It was our pleasure," she said. Nik threw her arms around Angie and whispered something in her ear that made her laugh. Then she moved over to Carlos.

"Carlos, thank you so much." She gave him a tight hug and a

kiss on the cheek. He almost kissed her back, but stopped himself just in time. She'd probably had enough out of men today.

"Glad we could help."

Dana and Courtney both hugged him, too.

"Thanks for taking care of our girl until she could get back to us. *You* are the prince of the day," Dana said.

He and Angie left Nik and her friends to dissect the texts, something he knew women loved to do.

* * * * * * *

"That was nice of him, to leave just then," Dana said, after the three of them sat back down in their booth alone.

"What do you mean?" Nik said as she reached for another piece of pizza. "They said they had a family thing."

Dana rolled her eyes.

"Sure they did. He wanted to let you show us Fisher's texts without him around, so he made up some reason to leave." She took a sip of her drink. "I don't often say this about men, but I liked him."

Courtney nodded.

"I liked him, too. You know what I think?"

Oh God. Whenever Courtney asked that question, either something great or something terrible was on its way. Sometimes it was a little bit of both.

Nik rested her chin on her hand and closed her eyes.

"What do you think?"

"I think Carlos should be your rebound."

This time it was just terrible.

"Dana, talk some sense into her, please." Nik looked from Dana to Courtney. "Number one, Fisher and I broke up, like two hours ago. Number two, Carlos seems like a very nice guy, but he's a doctor, come on."

Dana looked at her blankly.

"And?"

What was wrong with them?

"*And* Justin was a doctor, remember?"

Dana and Courtney looked at each other, then back at her.

"Yes, Justin was a doctor," Dana said, in her most patient voice. Nik hated that voice. "That doesn't mean that all doctors are assholes."

That's not what she meant and they knew it.

Well, okay. That was kind of what she meant. But still.

"Justin was a surgeon." Courtney took a gulp of her drink and slammed the empty glass onto the table. "That's different than a pediatrician."

Not that different. She hadn't seen or talked to Justin in years, but she remembered him and his God complex all too well.

"Plus," Courtney said, "Carlos is hot. I would go for him myself, but he was staring at you all night."

Nik rolled her eyes and drained her glass.

"That is not true."

"Oh, come on," Dana said. "Even I think he was hot, and I'm a lesbian."

Nik shook her head.

"I'm not arguing that point. Of course he's hot, did you see those forearms? I meant it's not true that he was staring at me all night."

Courtney and Dana looked at each other and laughed. There was no point in arguing with them about this. Especially since she wasn't even sure if she was right.

"You have a rebound with Carlos if you want," she said to

Courtney. "I'm taking a vow of celibacy. Men are clearly not for me at this point in my life."

Dana and Courtney dissolved into laughter.

"No really, you guys. I mean it!"

Their heads were down on the table. Courtney's face was possibly buried in a slice of pizza? It apparently didn't matter, they were still laughing.

"I'm not joking! I need a break. Once you find yourself on the JumboTron with a guy kneeling at your feet with a princess ring in his hand, you start to reevaluate your life, okay?"

Courtney sat up, a piece of pepperoni in her bangs. After that performance, Nik wasn't going to tell her it was there.

Dana gulped down the rest of her drink and waved Pete over for more drinks.

"A pitcher of water, too, please," Nik said to him. "I want to be able to at least somewhat function tomorrow."

As soon as he walked away, Dana turned to her.

"If we say we believe you and your vow of celibacy, can we get back to Fisher's texts?"

"We believe you, we believe you," Courtney said, the pepperoni bobbing up and down as she nodded her head.

They did not actually believe her, she knew that, but there was no point in arguing with them right now. They'd see. She took her phone back from Courtney.

"Here." Nik unlocked the phone and pushed it across the table. "After the glimpse that I saw, I don't know if I want to see the rest."

Dana picked up the phone and Courtney looked over her shoulder. Nik looked at their faces as they scrolled through the messages. After about two seconds, they both looked ready to kill.

"That bad, huh?" she asked.

Courtney's eyes narrowed at the phone. Oh no, it was even worse than she'd thought.

"Okay. What do they say?"

Dana cleared her throat. Thank God neither of them offered to just delete them for her. Her friends knew her far too well for that.

"'*You fucking bitch, I can't believe you did that to me on my birthday.*' That was the first one," Dana said.

"'*I can't believe you would be that stupid. I was the best thing that ever happened to you.*'" Dana looked up from the phone. Nik nodded for her to continue. "'*You're such a*'—I'm not saying that word—'*my friends always said so. I saw your potential when no one else did. You were lucky to be with me, you're never going to get the chance again. No one else will ever love an unfeeling bitch like you.*'"

Well, at least she didn't need to feel guilty about hurting him anymore.

"I don't *want* anyone else to ever love this unfeeling bitch. Something terrible always happens when a man says 'I love you.' First, Justin said it and then he tried to sabotage my career, then Fisher said it and I get put on a big screen and he texts insults to me. If that's what love means, no thank you."

Dana took a sip of her drink and kept reading.

"'*You're going to die alone, and you could have been my princess.*' There are five exclamation points at the end of the word princess. FYI."

At least that made her laugh. Thank God for unnecessary exclamation points.

"Okay, and here's the pièce de résistance." Dana pushed the phone over to her, and she looked at the picture that filled the screen: Fisher, Dodgers cap on backward, middle finger in the air, with the princess engagement ring on said finger.

"OH MY GOD."

Dana and Courtney exploded with laughter. Courtney's head shook so much that the pepperoni finally fell onto the table and she didn't even notice. Nik laughed until tears streamed out of her eyes. They collapsed against the booth cushions, laughing so much and so loudly that even the too-cool-for-school dudes at the end of the bar turned and stared.

"Are you KIDDING me? Is this some collective hallucination? What was IN those drinks that Pete brought us? Since when is Fisher Vanilla freaking Ice?"

"Well." Nik managed to stop laughing and reached for what was definitely her final drink. "I feel better already."

Chapter Three

On Monday morning, Nik stared at her laptop from the other side of the room. It wouldn't stop pinging at her. She'd turned the sound off, she'd moved over to the couch, but she knew it was still happening. It had been almost forty-eight hours since the nightmare proposal, and she was getting hundreds of messages in a constant stream through every possible avenue. She'd had so many texts when she'd woken up the day before that she'd thought her phone had malfunctioned.

Apparently, her JumboTron moment had been on SportsCenter on Saturday night. And then again on Sunday. She'd had no idea that she knew so many people who regularly watched SportsCenter.

To make things even worse, some enterprising person had tagged her on Twitter with the video of the proposal, so she was getting thousands of tweets about it. The bulk of them ranged from insulting to abusive, with a lot of just plain mean thrown in for kicks. A lot of men out there seemed personally insulted that she, a black woman, had rejected a white man. Most of their messages to her used either her least favorite insult for women or her least favorite insult for black people and, in many cases, both.

Until she'd blocked Fisher's number, he'd also kept sending her messages, and most of them weren't as unintentionally funny as the Vanilla Ice picture. The last few had been kind of scary, and she didn't scare easily.

The whole time she had to keep tweeting her way through it, because she used Twitter professionally, and she refused to let on that any of these assholes were upsetting her. Plus, that was her "brand" and all—that kind of sarcastic, witty, tough-skinned woman who nothing could bother. She had to pretend to be laughing with the rest of the world about what a bitch she was, retweet a few stupid memes with her face on them, and make a joke on Facebook about her relationship status changing, when she felt overwhelmed and outnumbered the whole time.

At least she hadn't seen any footage of Carlos and Angela posted anywhere. They'd probably jumped in before that camera crew had gotten anything worth posting. Whatever it was, she was grateful for it. She wouldn't have wanted them to get dragged into this chaos or to get punished by the whole world for their good deed.

Good deeds—plural. Not only had they pulled her away from the camera crew, gotten her away from the stadium of doom, and delivered her to her friends, but as she'd discovered on Saturday night after winning the fight with Dana and Courtney to pay their bar tab, Carlos had already paid for it. And she didn't even know his last name, or how to get in touch with him to thank him.

"Wait a minute, Nikole," she said out loud. She talked to herself a lot when she was alone in her apartment, which was frequently. "You are a journalist. You should be able to find this man in less than five minutes."

It took her about a minute and a half. There he was, Carlos Ibarra, picture and all, on the website of his hospital. Thank God the bourbon on Saturday hadn't dulled her memory. There was no email address listed, but she clicked around the hospital website to see what the other email addresses at his hospital looked like. She jumped over to her email account, opened the "compose" pane, and tried to ignore the dozens of new emails that had come in since she'd last looked.

> **To:** Carlos_Ibarra@eastsidemedicalcenter.com
> **From:** Nikole@NikoleDPaterson.com
> **Subject:** Thanks again
>
> Hi! It's me, your friendly non-princess from Saturday. I just wanted to a) thank you again for everything you did, and b) yell at you for not letting me buy you the drink I owed you afterward. I don't know if you saw, but the whole proposal has kind of gone viral, which . . . is an experience, that's for sure. Anyway, I hope you're well, and thank your sister for me, too!
>
> Nik

She typed the email in a hurry and pressed send before she could reconsider. Her friends would be so triumphant if they knew she'd emailed him. They would think she bought into their stupid rebound idea, when that wasn't at all the case. Obviously she found him attractive—she wasn't made of stone—but just as obviously, it was the wrong time to get involved with anyone. She just wanted to thank him again for saving her, that was all.

Of course it wasn't until after she'd hit send that she thought about the major downside of actually sending an email right now—she'd have to look at her incoming messages to see if he responded.

She couldn't even get any work done. The story she'd been working on at the baseball game was still stuck in the same place it had been when Fisher had told her to look at the JumboTron screen. She'd been halfway through a sentence, and now she had no idea how the sentence was supposed to end. She probably had important work-related emails, but she'd have to wade through the hundreds of other messages to find them. She threw her arms in the air, went into her bedroom, put on the first real clothes she found, and left to go for a walk. Without her phone.

By the time she'd walked the thirty minutes to Courtney's cupcake shop, she felt a little better. Despite herself, the fresh air and the blue sky made her relax, and the physical activity even cheered her up a little. When she walked into Cupcake Park, she didn't quite have a smile on her face, but at least she could tell the scowl had gone away.

"Hey!" Courtney was alone in the shop when she came in, wearing her trademark pink lipstick and a pink polka-dot apron. "You haven't been answering your phone. Dana and I have both been trying to call. How are you doing?"

She groaned and leaned against the counter. Courtney's brightly colored cupcakes, all decorated with frosting flowers or trees, stared back up at her from the other side.

"Coffee, please?" She shouldn't have even bothered to ask.

Courtney had already poured cups full for both of them and set one of each of her favorite cupcake flavors in front of her. "You're the best, thanks."

"We both know that," Courtney said. The bell rang, and Nik stepped aside so that the three teenage girls who came in could see and debate their cupcake choices. By the time they left five minutes later, Nik had finished her lemon cupcake and most of her coffee. Courtney poured her a new cup.

"How did business go today?"

Courtney had opened her cupcake shop just under a year ago, and there had been a number of touch-and-go moments with it, but lately business looked like it was picking up.

"It was great. There was a line out the door for like half the day, and I just got two big orders, including one for a wedding." Courtney looked hard at Nik. "But I know you didn't walk all the way over here to find out how my business is going. How are you? How bad is it?"

Nik groaned.

"It's so bad." She took a sip of coffee and reconsidered. "I mean, I'm not dying or anything, and this should all fade away within a few days. But God, it doesn't feel like that right now. I'm not answering my phone because I had to turn the sound and the vibrate off, and then put it in my refrigerator to chill out, because it feels like the whole world is calling me or texting me. I needed a break."

She could *not* tell Courtney that she'd emailed Carlos. She would do her "I told you so" dance around the whole cupcake shop. Had Carlos replied to her email yet? Ugh, she wished she'd brought her phone, just so she'd know.

Courtney checked the time and walked over to flip the sign on the door from OPEN to CLOSED.

"Do you think all of the proposal brouhaha will blow over?"

Nik grabbed a broom to help Courtney do her end-of-the-day cleaning of the shop.

"I'm sure it will. I just hope it blows over *soon*. The only email I responded to so far today was from the *TODAY* show, telling them no, I would not come on the show to talk about the proposal. I'm kind of worried that Fisher will say yes to them or someone like them, but there's nothing I can do to stop that, and I feel like reaching out to him at this point is a very bad idea."

"Have you heard anything more from him?" Courtney tossed Nik a cloth to wipe down the countertops while she packed away the rest of the cupcakes.

"Unfortunately, yes. I've blocked him everywhere, which probably means he's saying all sorts of shit about me that I can't see, but at this point, that's better than the alternative."

Courtney turned on Missy Elliott to keep them company as they cleaned up.

"Oh, I'll find out what he's saying about you, don't worry about that." Courtney had an evil grin on her face that Nik decided not to ask about. It was probably better that she be ignorant of whatever Courtney was planning to do to Fisher.

"Want a ride home?" Courtney asked her. "Dinner? Leftover cupcakes?"

"No, no, and yes. Or rather, no, yes, and yes. Have I ever said no to leftover cupcakes? But I can walk home. I need to work up my appetite for these."

Courtney filled up a box of cupcakes and put it in one of her pink and white bags.

"Let me know if you need anything else. And if you need company tonight, I can be there at the snap of your fingers; you know that, right?"

Nik walked around the counter to give Courtney a hug.

"I know. Thanks."

Of course, once Nik walked home, she'd started to regret not getting a ride from Courtney. Not because the walk tired her out, but because she wished she wasn't alone. As she approached her building she was on high alert for Fisher's silver sports car in the area.

"You're being stupid," she said to herself on her doorstep. "Also, you're talking to yourself in public this time; you should really save that for *inside* the house, Nikole."

She unlocked her front door, and then hesitated on the threshold. Finally, she grabbed a cast-iron pan from her kitchen and, feeling like an idiot the entire time, looked in every hiding place in her apartment. After finding nothing other than a lot more dirty laundry than she thought she'd had, she tried to relax and sat back down at her laptop to check her email.

Fifty-seven more people had emailed her in the two hours that she'd been gone. And not a single one of the fifty-seven was named Carlos Ibarra.

* * * * * * *

"It was like this, Dr. Ibarra," Luke, his newest patient said. "There was this girl, right?"

Carlos laughed.

"How did I know that that's how this story was going to start? But keep going, all of the best stories start that way."

Carlos listened to the kid's story, took notes, gave him both medical advice—for the sprained ankle that he got from running down the street with the girl (rest, ice, elevation, lots of ibuprofen) and the rash he'd gotten from hiding in the poison-oak-laced bushes behind her house (a prescription cream)—and general life advice (girls who make you go through dangerous situations to prove your worth to them are always exciting at first and then you regret it).

That, of course, made him think about how he'd shoved that cameraman out of the way in order to get Nik safely out of Dodger Stadium. The difference, though, was that was his idea, not hers. But he understood where his patient was coming from—he still felt a rush when he thought about swooping down on Nik and getting her out of the stadium. It was probably just because he didn't do anything dangerous these days other than driving too fast.

He'd had SportsCenter in the background on Sunday morning and was engrossed in the Sunday *L.A. Times* movie section, when he'd heard the announcer say "Can you believe what happened to this poor guy?" He'd looked up at the screen, just in time to see Nik's wide-open mouth and Man Bun drop down onto one knee. He'd been wondering all day how Nik was doing. He wished he'd figured out a way to smoothly get her phone number before he and Angie had left the bar. Maybe sometime he would go back to see if he could accidentally run into her there. She said she and her friends went to that bar a lot, right?

He went back to his office after that appointment, hopefully his last one of the day, unless there was an emergency in the next hour and a half. He typed his notes from his appointments into the online system, making sure to only note the parent-friendly details from the stories that the teens had told him since their parents all had access to their information. With just half an hour to go until his Monday was over, he clicked over to his work email, to see what stupid administrative tasks people had sent him this time.

Nikole Paterson? He clicked on the screen so fast that he accidentally clicked on the email below it first, and had to skim through a message about vaccinations before he realized what was happening and went back.

"I don't know if you saw, but the whole proposal has kind of gone viral." He had, in fact, noticed that the whole proposal had gone viral. She must have heard from everyone she knew, and then some. He had no idea how she'd found his email address, but he was glad she had.

> **To:** Nikole@NikoleDPaterson.com
> **From:** Carlos_Ibarra@eastsidemedicalcenter.com
>
> Hey! Good to hear from you. I figured you'd want to yell at me about the drinks, but I also figured you and your friends already had too much bourbon to figure out a bill. And yeah, I saw you on SportsCenter. Have you gotten emails and texts from literally everyone you know?
>
> –
>
> Carlos

He got an email back right before he was about to leave the office.

> **To:** Carlos_Ibarra@eastsidemedicalcenter.com
> **From:** Nikole@NikoleDPaterson.com

To answer your question, every single other email in my inbox has the subject line "Was that you?" or "OMG that was you!" and I can't bear to look at any of them. So yes, I've gotten texts and emails (and Facebook messages, and tweets, and LinkedIn messages, for the love of God) from literally everyone I know. I have ignored all of them so far and have been hiding in my apartment almost all day, with a brief excursion to pick up cupcakes from Courtney's shop, but I'm going a little stir-crazy.

Nik

Was that a hint? She didn't seem like a hinting kind of person, but maybe?

To: Nikole@NikoleDPaterson.com
From: Carlos_Ibarra@eastsidemedicalcenter.com

If you're in the mood for a friendly face tonight, let me know. About to leave work, want to grab dinner? Text me, I'm at 310-555-4827. I promise I won't say "OMG that was you!"

Carlos

He double-checked his phone all the way to the parking garage, but nothing. Okay, maybe it wasn't a hint. Damn it. It had been a long time since he'd met someone who could laugh at herself the way Nik could, even in the middle of a crisis.

Also, he'd really liked the way she'd looked in that snug baseball T-shirt and those jeans, he wasn't going to lie.

He'd seen way too many accidents in his stint working in the ER to check his phone while he was driving, but he had to fight himself more than once from reaching for it on the way home. But when he pulled up to his apartment and grabbed it out of his pocket, there was nothing other than five group texts about his basketball league.

Just as he walked in the door, his phone chimed.

Going to take you up on that offer for dinner, but this time it's my treat. What time and where? Not a bar, though, I'm still recovering from Saturday.

He was so busy grinning down at his phone that he almost tripped over the Amazon box in his entryway. Worth it.

7:30? Thai? There's a fun place on Sunset, do you know it? Night+ Market?

She did know it. He changed into jeans and his favorite T-shirt, killed some time by replying to all of the basketball messages with trash talk, and walked back out the door.

He put his name on the list and hung out by the door and pretended to be absorbed in his phone. She walked in the door at 7:33, not that he was checking. She stood at the door and peered around the restaurant, a guarded look on her face, her sunglasses again tucked into her dark curly hair.

"Hey!" He waved at her. Her face relaxed into a grin when she saw him. She was wearing jeans and a black shirt that looked better on her than any plain black shirt had a right to look.

"Hey yourself. Thank you for rescuing me yet again. If you hadn't suggested dinner, I would have had a half-dozen cupcakes for dinner, hated myself for it, and then had another half dozen for dessert."

He laughed.

"Thai food is definitely a much better idea. Where'd all the cupcakes come from?"

She leaned against the wall next to him.

"I forced myself out of the house today and walked to Courtney's shop. I hung around until closing and she gave me the leftovers."

"That's convenient to have a friend with a cupcake store." Now that he was looking at her closely, he could see a spot of white frosting standing out against her warm brown cheek and fought his impulse to wipe it off.

"You're telling me. She usually gives any leftovers to the employees at the other shops nearby, as a sort of goodwill/'we're all in this together' kind of thing, but I guess today she thought my need was more important. I certainly wasn't going to argue with her."

They made small talk as they waited for their table, too surrounded by other people to talk about anything important. After longer a wait than he'd hoped, the host finally called his name.

As Carlos walked behind Nik on the way to a table, he admired her shape in her snug jeans. He was pretty sure this woman hated all men at the moment, but he could look, couldn't he?

They both ordered beer before they opened their menus.

"You're going to have to keep me from ordering everything on the menu, I'm starving," he said.

Nik glanced over the menu and grinned.

"Luckily, I heard from you at just the right time before I dove into the box of cupcakes. And I'm glad you wanted to go to this place. I haven't been here in far too long; Fisher didn't like spicy food, so . . ."

He looked up at her with his eyebrows raised.

"Fisher didn't like spicy food, and you went out with him for more than one date? How did that happen?"

She sighed.

"Excellent question, really."

The waitress brought their beers, and she took a sip.

"Never again, though," she said. "I'm swearing off actors. You think you're just casually dating, and then bam, they spring a public proposal on you."

Carlos shook his head.

"Is he a real actor or a wannabe one?"

She laughed.

"You always have to ask that question in L.A., right? A real one, but a terrible one. And that's not even my rage talking; I thought that even while we were dating."

Oof. This woman did not mince her words.

"How did you even meet him?" He shook his head. "You don't have to answer that. You're probably sick of even thinking about this. We can talk about work, or our last vacations, or baseball, or whatever."

She widened her eyes in horror.

"Good God, not baseball, anything but baseball." They both laughed. "As for not talking about this, honestly, I wish I could stop thinking about this. I've probably thought about Fisher more in the past two days than I did in the entire five months that we were dating, that's the wild part. But wait, you probably don't want to hear more about my disastrous love life; you heard plenty on Saturday."

Actually, he'd left right when they'd gotten to the good stuff. And honestly, he was dying to know the details.

“If it helps you to talk about it, I’m happy to listen,” he said. Did that sound magnanimous enough? “I talk to teenagers all day; hearing a story about an adult disastrous love life will be refreshing after their stories, I promise.”

She pushed her hair out of her face and smiled.

“Okay, but you’re going to have to tell me at least one good work story afterward, so I don’t feel like such an idiot. You see teenagers; you must have some great ones.” She glanced down at the menu. “Wait, let’s order first. You already said you were starving.”

The waitress stopped at their table, and they ordered far too much food for two people.

“What did you ask?” she said when the waitress walked away. “Oh right, how I met Fisher.” She sighed. “Last year, I did a profile of Anna Gardiner for *Vogue*. She only really got big, like, last summer. Right before she got the role that led to the Oscar nomination and *Vogue* cover and everything else, she was in a terrible and short-lived TV show. Fisher was her co-star.”

He held up his hand to stop her.

“I’m sorry, but you got to meet Anna Gardiner? Most famous people are no big deal, a dime a dozen in L.A., blah blah, but Anna Gardiner? What was she like? Don’t tell me she was terrible; I loved that movie.”

He was so thankful none of his friends were here to witness him babbling about a movie star—they would make fun of him from here to eternity.

“She was honestly great! Which is the whole reason I met Fisher, actually. Anna and I got along really well, and she ended up inviting me to her birthday party, and that’s where I met Fisher. When he asked me out, I was positive that he just wanted to go out with me because he wanted me to write a puff piece about him for something. I sort of never stopped thinking that, actually."

She shook her head and laughed.

"The funny thing is that whenever I went to industry parties with him, when people I knew through my work saw us together, they would look so confused. A few times, when he was on the other side of the room, they even said to me, 'You're here with *that* guy?' I was never sure if that was an insult to me, or to him."

The waitress set their spicy and sweet wings down on the table, and they both grabbed one.

"Anyway, going out with Fisher was very low-stress, until two days ago. I've had such a busy few months of work and Fisher was just a fun guy I hung out with when I had time. I even felt guilty about saying no to his proposal, because I didn't want to hurt his feelings! That was, until . . . well, apparently, I'm not as good at reading people as I thought I was."

He looked closer at her. He was pretty good at reading people, and she looked really stressed about this whole situation.

"Have you heard from him again? Since his bad texts on Saturday?"

She looked up at him.

"How did you know they were bad?"

He gestured to her face.

"That same worried look that's on your face right now was on your face on Saturday night when you told your friends he'd texted you. I figured there was something in there that bothered you, and since you'd just rejected him in front of thousands of people, I assumed it was something pretty nasty." He held up his hand when she started to protest. "I'm not blaming you for rejecting him in front of thousands of people. As a matter of fact, I was pretty impressed that you were honest with him, instead of being nice to him just to make him feel better. But when I saw that look on your face, I figured he wanted to lash out at you."

She nodded.

"He sure did. Which . . . I like revenge as much as the next person, so I get that, but he didn't have to keep going."

He dropped his chicken and sat up straight.

"Is he still texting you?"

She shrugged.

"I'm not sure. The last text I got from him before I blocked him was 'Watch your back.' I'm sure he's just trying to freak me out. I don't really think Fisher is the violent-revenge-for-rejecting-him type." She shook her head. "But I should know better than to say that there's no such thing as one violent-revenge type; anyone can be like that. I didn't tell Courtney and Dana about that text. They would have freaked out, moved in with me, firebombed his house, and reported him to the police, probably in that order. Unfortunately, he succeeded in freaking me out, if that was his motive."

He sympathized with Courtney and Dana. He would want to do the same if anyone texted stuff like that to Angela.

He reached across the table and touched Nik's hand.

"I'm sorry that happened to you. Are you . . . do you live alone?" He shook his head. "Wow, did that sound creepy. What I meant was, are you okay? Are you worried that he'll come to your house if you don't respond to him?"

She started to shake her head and stopped.

"I wasn't at first. I do live alone—I probably shouldn't tell you that; you're still a stranger, but hey, you have a good sister, you can't be too terrible—and I wasn't worried at all yesterday. But then today, after Fisher's texts, and then all of the tweets and emails from strangers that were way worse than what he said . . . when I walked into my apartment, well. That was another reason I was glad to leave to go to dinner tonight; it was good to get out of there and have some company."

He wanted to ask her what was in those messages from strangers that were way worse than Fisher's texts, but he wasn't sure if she wanted to talk about it. And he wasn't sure if he was ready to hear the response.

Two more platters of food landed on their table. He scooped papaya salad and pork belly onto both of their plates.

"I'm glad I could help, but it sucks that he's made you so anxious about this."

She took a bite of the pork belly and grinned.

"This is delicious, but also it's hot as hell." She squeezed his hand, and he smiled at her. They looked at each other for a long time, their hands still linked across the table. Finally, she broke the eye contact and dropped his hand.

"Okay, please, let's talk about something that isn't me. I deserve your best teen-client story, after that."

He grinned.

"I have a lot of good ones, but my favorite is the kid we nicknamed Santa, because he and his girlfriend tried to hide up the chimney."

She rubbed her hands together.

"Tell me everything."

Chapter Four

When the waitress brought the check to the table, Nik handed the waitress her credit card.

"This one is on me. I'm still mad at you for paying for our drinks from Saturday. I owed you."

He pursed his mouth and considered.

"Okay, fine, but you get all of the leftovers. Deal?"

He said that like it was a punishment. Which, considering how spicy some of their leftovers were . . . he might be correct about that.

"Deal. I can have them for lunch tomorrow, in between all of the cupcakes."

As they walked to her car, he elbowed her.

"Yes?" she said, in answer to his look.

"I know you're pretty nervous about all of the Fisher stuff. Do you want me to follow you home just to make sure everything is okay? I mean, I'm sure everything is fine, I just thought I'd—"

"Yeah," she said. "That would be great."

Why had she agreed to this so quickly, she wondered on the short drive to her house. She usually hated it when men got all protective about her safety, like she was some delicate flower who didn't know how to protect herself.

But that hadn't been what Carlos had done, and she'd appreciated it. After her panic from this afternoon, it would be nice to have backup for those thirty seconds it took for her to walk through her apartment. Plus, not to be shallow, but the way Carlos's T-shirt clung to his biceps . . . she was pretty sure Carlos could take Fisher down easily.

But wait a second. Was she really going to get some dude she hardly knew to do a walk-through of her apartment just because she got a few nasty text messages? That was ridiculous. She was a grown woman; she'd lived on her own for years; she could take care of herself. She should text him right now and tell him that she was fine and didn't need his help.

Yeah, she'd do that. She reached in her pocket for her phone. When she got home, she'd text her girlfriends and tell them how stupid she'd almost been.

Well, she'd text her girlfriends if she was still around to text them.

She could hear Courtney's voice in her head.

What do you have to lose here? Are you really worried about looking silly in front of a man you barely know? Who cares?

She cared, damn it.

But her friends would kill her if she sent Carlos away and anything happened to her.

Okay, fine. She put her phone back in her pocket.

She parked in the lot behind her apartment building and met Carlos on the front steps.

“Thanks for coming inside with me. I feel like an idiot,” she said as she unlocked the door.

“Don’t worry about it,” he said. “I’m a pretty impressive dude; people feel like idiots around me all the time. I’m used to it.”

Despite her rising anxiety, she laughed as they walked up the stairs to her second-floor apartment.

“Did he have a key?” Carlos asked in a low voice.

Nik sighed and stopped on the stairs.

“I never gave him one, but I left my keys around all the time, and it’s easy to get keys copied. And there was one time when I forgot my keys at his house for a whole weekend and had to get my set of extra keys back from Dana. I didn’t think anything of it at the time, but . . . I’m paranoid now, I guess.”

Carlos put his hand on her shoulder, and she relaxed against it.

“Are you ready to go inside? Or do you need a minute?”

She pulled away from him. She never should have done this, but she had no choice now.

“No, no, I’m fine. Let’s go in.”

He took the key out of her hand and unlocked the door. She could have done that herself, but okay. He pushed it open slowly. Why had she turned off all of the lights before she left her house? Energy-saving nonsense. Now she felt like one of those women in horror movies. One of the ones who got killed in the first fifteen minutes.

Wait, no. Those women never had the sense to get someone else to come with them when they had a bad feeling.

Carlos pushed the door wide open and stepped through it in front of her.

“If the demon gets me, tell my mother I loved her.”

Apparently they watched the same kind of movies.

She followed close at his heels as he walked into the living room and flicked on the lights. Everything looked the same as when she'd left it two hours before: her laptop on the desk against her big bay window, her remote on the floor by her coffee table, her T-shirt and—oops—bra on the top of the couch where she'd thrown them off after getting Carlos's text. She saw a smile around his eyes when he turned in that direction, but he didn't let it reach his mouth.

"Is there anywhere to hide in this room?" he asked her under his breath. She shook her head.

She started to walk down the hallway that led to her bedroom, but he put his hand on her shoulder to stop her.

"Let me go first."

He didn't wait for an answer. She stared daggers into his back as she followed him down the hallway. Just because she'd accepted his offer to make sure Fisher wasn't around didn't mean she was okay with him ordering her around in her own apartment. This had been a terrible idea.

When she walked into her bedroom, he'd already flung open the closet doors and was running his hands through the crowded coat side of her closet. He turned around well after she was satisfied that there was no one hiding among them.

"Are all of these coats . . . yours?" he asked her. "You do realize you live in Los Angeles, right?"

"Shut up. It gets cold here sometimes. And I go to New York at least once or twice a year."

He shook his head, with a smile in his eyes.

"Mmm, yeah, that totally means you need twenty coats, absolutely."

She tried not to grin back at him and failed.

He stepped around to the far side of her bed, then went into the hallway and threw open the hall closet. She supposed that Fisher *could* have hidden in there, if he'd been hiding his contortionist talents from her. He glanced at the shelves full of extra bedding, towels, and boxes of sparkling water, and closed the door without a word. He stepped into the bathroom, and she heard the shower curtain swish across the rod.

"All clear in the bathroom, too. Anywhere else?"

She walked down the hall to the kitchen, simultaneously so relieved she was ready to collapse and feeling so stupid she wanted to hide among all the coats in her closet.

"I mean, I suppose if someone was really trying, they could hide in the refrigerator, or under the couch, but I somehow doubt that. I think we're all clear." She opened the refrigerator and pulled out a bottle of wine. "I'm sorry for dragging you along on this wild goose chase. I don't know what got into me. Wine?" She glanced over at him, standing in her living room, and saw him peer under the couch. She smiled and poured two glasses.

"Here." She handed him a glass and sat down on the couch. "Thank you. I'm not usually . . ." She shook her head. "Anyway, thank you. I hope you're not too much of a man's man to drink rosé."

He sat down next to her and picked up the wineglass.

"No such thing." He took a sip of the wine and glanced over at her. "You should get your locks changed."

Okay, that was enough telling her what to do.

"I know I should get my locks changed; I'm not an idiot," she said.

He put his glass down.

"Hey, I'm sorry. Of course you aren't. I didn't mean to suggest that." He looked at her, then looked away. "I'm used to taking care of all of the women in my family, so I have the tendency to go overboard sometimes. I didn't mean to tell you what to do."

She picked up his wineglass and handed it to him.

"It's okay, really. I didn't mean to snap at you." She closed her eyes. "I don't usually give in to fits of paranoia like this, and I hate it. Sorry for taking it out on you."

He smiled at her and patted her thigh. She hated herself for wanting his hand to linger there a lot longer than it did.

"You have nothing to be ashamed of. Every woman needs a big strong man to come and protect her; that's not your fault. It's just because you're naturally weak and helpless, just by virtue of, you know, being a woman and all. You needed a man like me to do the hard work of looking under your bed. I understand that you aren't capable of stuff like that."

She smacked his arm.

"You asshole." She was laughing so hard she had to put her wineglass down. "You had me going for at least five or six seconds there! You were so close to me throwing this wine in your face and literally kicking you out of my apartment."

* * * * * * *

Carlos laughed and relaxed against the couch cushions. He'd been a little worried that she'd get furious at him for that, but he also thought it might break some of the tension. One of the things that he already liked so much about Nik was how independent she was; he should have known that telling her what to do would piss her off. Angela had gotten mad at him just a few weeks ago for taking her car in to get serviced; she'd said she was fully capable of doing it for herself. He'd told her it wasn't that he didn't think she was capable of it, it's just that he'd felt like it was his job to do it. That hadn't made her less mad.

She waved at his wineglass.

"Drink, drink, I promise I won't knock the glass all over you."

He took another sip. He usually made fun of Angela for drinking rosé. She could definitely never find out that he drank it with Nik and liked it.

"But really, don't feel bad," he said. "It's totally normal to freak out about stuff like this. And my stint in the ER during my residency really opened my eyes to how often this stuff happens to women. I mean, fine, he wasn't here and you felt silly that you had me come up, no big deal. But too many women ignore those feelings or don't want to feel silly, and I've seen some of the aftermaths. Feeling silly is definitely better."

She took another sip of her wine and leaned back. When she'd sat down on the couch, she'd sat down right in the middle, so he'd had no choice but to sit right next to her. They were so close they were almost touching.

"I almost called you on the way here and told you I didn't need you, but I knew my friends would have yelled at me and told me not to be a fool." She paused. "I think I've given other people similar advice, now that I think about it. It's always easier to give people advice than it is to take it yourself."

Should he put his arm around her? He really wanted to, but she'd just had a dramatic breakup a few days ago, and she might smack him and order him out of her house. But she was curled up on the couch next to him like that, all cozy with her wine; this seemed like a prime situation for making a move, right?

"Speaking of giving advice," she said, "you said that you spend a lot of time giving advice to teenagers, and I'm totally curious about your job. What does it mean, to be the assistant director of a teen clinic?"

Okay, it seemed like she just wanted to talk, as they sat here shoulder to shoulder in the dim lighting on her couch while holding glasses of wine. Great.

"Excellent question, and one that I'm still kind of figuring out the answer to. I've only been doing it for about six months, but I love it so far. Basically, all of the health care of the kids that the medical center serves—who are in the twelve to nineteen age group—is routed through our clinic. The goal is to recognize that teens are in a special place, both mentally and physically, and to serve their needs as best as we can."

"I wish my doctor's office had had a teen clinic when I was a kid," she said. "I always remember feeling so grumpy about still going to a pediatrician when I was a teenager, surrounded by babies and toddlers."

She took another sip of wine and picked a piece of lint off of his shoulder. He felt lulled by her touch, the warm night air, by her presence.

And also probably the wine.

She stood up to get the bottle of wine from the fridge and brought it back over to the couch.

"You said you'd only been there for six months—where were you before that?"

She tipped the wine bottle toward his glass and raised her eyebrows at him. He nodded. Was she trying to get him to linger? Had the whole "I'm afraid of my ex" thing just been bullshit to get him to come up to her apartment? Would he care if that was the case? He grinned to himself. Would he care if a hot girl made up a story about being scared of her ex-boyfriend to get him up to her apartment? Hell no, he would not care.

"I was at St. Elizabeth's Hospital on the Westside. I liked working there a lot, but this job is different from what I'd been doing there, and it's a lot of fun. Plus, it was great to come back to the Eastside and be closer to my family."

But wait. He didn't know this girl that well, but from his few interactions with her, she seemed pretty forthright and honest, almost to a fault. He didn't really think she'd make up a story if she wanted him in her apartment. She would just ask him if he wanted to come upstairs.

Plus, if someone was pretending to be scared, they would have acted much more scared than she did when they walked in. She hadn't been clingy or crying or any of that stuff. She'd just looked tense and angry. And she even hadn't hinted for him to come over; he'd been the one to offer.

"I spend so much time with L.A. people who are from somewhere else; it's always fun to meet a real local," she said. "Do you have a big family?"

He rested his hand on the couch, right by, but not on, her knee.

"Yes and no—it's a big extended family, but Angie's my only sibling. But we grew up right around the corner from my mom's sister, Tia Eva, and her daughter, my cousin Jessica, who is basically like a sister to me. She's the one I told you about at the bar who I got the 'Is that you?' idea from." He smiled. "That's another reason why this was a good time to move back to the Eastside; Jessie's pregnant now with her first kid, and my whole family is over the moon."

She tucked her hair behind her ears and looked up at him. He liked the way she concentrated on him when he was talking, like she was really listening to what he had to say.

He *also* liked the way the neckline of her shirt kept dipping lower and lower. He had to force himself to not let his eyes linger for too long on her cleavage.

"Are you over the moon about the baby, too?"

Her shirt dipped off one shoulder. He really wanted to reach over and push it off all the way. It took him a minute to remember what she'd asked him. Right, right, Jessie's baby.

"Oh yeah, definitely. You'd think that after being a pediatrician for years now I'd think babies are a dime a dozen, but I can't wait until Jessie has hers. Not that I'm ready in the least to have one of my own, but that's what's going to make Jessie's so fun. Being an uncle is going to be great. All of the fun and none of the responsibility." He laughed. "Plus, this way, my mom will get off my ass about giving her grandbabies because she'll have Jessie's baby to hang out with."

She looked at him sideways.

"Or, she'll be on your ass even more because she'll be so excited about the one baby that she'll want more."

He held his finger up to her lips.

"Shhhhh, don't say that. She knows it's going to be a long time before that happens. I have too many other people to take care of right now. I'm just glad that I'm back on the Eastside. I can be closer when the baby is born, as well as for things like killing spiders—real and imaginary—late at night for Angela."

She took the last sip of her wine and smiled at him.

"She's lucky she has you. I was lucky that I had you around tonight, too." She sat up straight and put her feet on the floor. "Do you have to be at work super early in the morning? It's getting late."

That sure sounded like his cue to go. Damn it. He looked at his watch and barely noticed what it said.

"It's getting pretty close to my bedtime." He put his hand on her arm. "Are you going to be okay tonight?"

Her eyes shot to the door, but she nodded anyway.

"Of course. I'll be fine, don't worry about me."

He'd been on the point of standing up. Instead, he settled back down on the couch.

"Well, when you say it like that, I'm worried about you. Do you want me to . . ." He was going to say, "Do you want me to stay?" but that sounded like he was inviting himself into her bed. And while he'd love to get an invitation there, he didn't want to look like even more of an asshole than he already had tonight. "Do you want me to stay until one of your friends can get here?"

"I feel ridiculous even thinking about doing that, but . . . maybe. Courtney has to be up at the crack of dawn, so I don't want to call her. I can call Dana, though. I don't think she's filming tomorrow. Oh God, that reminds me! Instagram!" She pulled her phone out of her pocket.

He had no idea what the hell that meant in this context.

"Instagram?" he asked.

"Fisher Instagrams his whole life, for 'branding' and his fans or whatever. If he's updated in the last few hours or so, at least I'll know what he's up to."

She typed something into the search bar on her phone while she talked.

"I blocked him on everything, so he can't contact me, but if I'm logged out, I can still see . . . oh my God, Carlos. Look at this! He's in Vegas!"

She turned her phone around so he could see the video of Fisher dancing terribly at some club. He let out a shout of laughter.

"Wow." He scooted closer to her so they could both watch. My God, she smelled good. He wanted to stay this close to her on the couch for a long time. "Is this guy for real? Play it again."

She played his video four or five more times, and they laughed harder every time.

"This is almost as good as the middle-finger ring picture," she said, still laughing.

He raised his eyebrows at her.

"What middle-finger ring picture?"

"Oh my God. I'm so sorry. I didn't show you. You and Angela left before we looked at his texts. Look at this picture he sent me."

She scrolled through her phone and pulled up a photo of a blurry middle finger with a blue engagement ring on it. He recoiled.

"Oh my God. He seriously texted you this?"

As she'd scrolled to the photo, he'd seen flashes of a few of the texts Fisher had sent her after the proposal. That fucking bastard.

"I know. I know." She was still looking at the photo, and not at him. "You don't have to say anything. I have terrible judgment in men; we all know that now, but this is really incredible, right?"

He stood up. He was glad for her that Fisher was out of town, but now he had no more excuses to stay here.

"It's so incredible that I need to go home now to process that. And also because I have to be up, awake, and ready for patients at eight thirty a.m. tomorrow."

She walked him to the door.

"Sorry for keeping you up, and thanks again."

She reached out to hug him, and he pulled her in tight. Her body nestled up against his felt so good. He wanted to hold on for much longer and forced himself to let go.

"Glad I could be here. Good night. And if you want to stack a chair behind that door after I leave, feel free. No one will know about it but you."

She laughed and reached up to kiss him on the cheek.

"I just might do that, thanks."

Chapter Five

Nik shut the door behind Carlos and closed her eyes.

Maybe, she thought, if she stood there for a few minutes with her forehead against this door, it would magically take away the far too many feelings going through her head right now.

She gave it about two minutes, but it didn't work. So she flopped back down on the couch and pulled the blanket over her face.

Why hadn't he offered to stay with her that night, Fisher or no Fisher? She would have said "No, you're too busy, I don't want to inconvenience you more than I have," and he would have offered again, and she would have said, "Are you sure?" and he would have said, "Of course," and she would have said, "You really don't have to, but . . ." and he would have said, "I want to!" and then she would have tackled him on the couch. That would have been a much better ending to tonight than her being on her couch alone feeling like an idiot.

Worse, he hadn't even tried to kiss her! She'd given him every damn opportunity—she had practically shoved her boobs in his face—and he'd been all smiling and talking about his cousin and his patients and blah blah blah. Sure, she'd asked him about those things and hadn't asked him, "Do you like my boobs in this shirt, Carlos? I grew them just for you," but he should have gotten that that was what she'd *meant.*

Ugh, and she hadn't even invited him upstairs on some sort of "come look at my etchings" pretext. She'd wanted him for—gag—protection. When she'd unlocked her front door, she'd been so grateful that he was there. She'd felt actually *comforted* by his presence. Even when he'd ordered her around in a way that she would normally hate, she'd still been so relieved that he was there.

How humiliating. She, Nikole Paterson, who prided herself on being self-sufficient and self-reliant and an Independent Woman, et cetera, et cetera, had caved under the slightest amount of pressure and called on a man to come save her. And she'd almost thrown herself at him in the process.

Okay, this was getting way out of hand. Sure, her fingers were dying to run themselves through his thick dark hair, and her hand had lingered a little too long on his bicep tonight, and every time he curved those inviting lips of his into a smile, she wanted to pull him closer. But a rebound with Carlos was a terrible idea, remember? She neither wanted, nor needed, a rebound with anyone! That was why she'd hinted it was time for Carlos to go home. Men were trouble. She'd learned that over and over again. Plus, Carlos was a doctor, and she was done with doctors. They thought they were better than everyone else.

She'd never forget that time when her digital recorder had failed unbeknownst to her during an important interview and she'd burst into angry tears about it to Justin. He'd said, "Come on,

Nikole. It's just an interview with an actor; it's no big deal. Unlike in my job, no one's going to die because of a little mistake." She was still mad she'd stayed with him for another year after that.

She shouldn't have let Carlos come over in the first place. Even though he'd seemed nice and, yes, she had wished in a weak moment that he'd ended up in her bed, he still clearly thought that she was a helpless woman who needed him to protect her. He'd joked about that, but was it really a joke?

Letting men see your vulnerabilities was always a mistake. There must be better avenues out there to protect herself against creepy ex-boyfriends than calling for the nearest man to protect her.

* * * * * * *

"A self-defense class?" Dana asked. "You want us to go to a self-defense class together?"

The three of them were all out at the bar two days later, partly because she hadn't left her apartment since Monday night, partly so she could share her great idea with them.

"It's a good idea!" Nik said. "They're supposed to be very empowering."

Courtney and Dana both stared at her like she had sprouted a second head.

"'*Empowering?*' Since when do you use words like 'empowering'?" Courtney asked.

She had a point.

"Sorry, I've been looking at too many self-defense class websites. But doesn't it sound fun to go punch some stuff? It'll be a great workout."

Now Dana looked interested. The poor thing had to constantly exercise. She'd gotten a best friend role in a sitcom the year before, which meant she could never get above a size two, and even that was pushing it.

"That does sound fun, but is this one of those classes where everyone is supposed to share some trauma or something and then you punch it to, like, conquer your fear or whatever?" she asked.

"There are a bunch of different kinds," Nik said. "They teach you how to defend yourself, and—"

"Yes, I got that; it's right there in the name," Dana said.

"Shut up, you know what I mean. It'll help us be more confident walking down the street at night or dealing with creepy guys."

"I drive everywhere, and I've been dealing with creepy guys for over twenty years. What else you got?" Dana drained her drink.

"Hmm, will it also help some of us deal with ex-boyfriends who send vaguely threatening messages?" Courtney asked.

She'd sort of hoped that they wouldn't connect the dots about why she was interested in the class. It was a ridiculous hope, though. Unfortunately, she had intelligent friends.

"You didn't tell me that." Dana sat up straight. "What the hell did he say to you?" She pulled out her phone. "I'm texting my roller derby friends—what's his address?"

Nik grabbed her phone away.

"You don't need to text your roller derby friends. It's not like that."

Dana smacked Courtney on the shoulder. "Why didn't you tell me this was happening? He's freaked her out so much that she wants to take a self-defense class?"

Courtney took Dana's phone from Nik and handed it back to Dana.

"Why am I getting yelled at for this?" She pointed at Nik. "She's the one who should have told you."

Dana squeezed the lime into her gin and tonic before she took a sip.

"Oh, don't worry, I'm mad at both of you. But I know you saw her on Monday. You told me she'd blocked Fisher, but not that his messages had gotten her to the self-defense class state. I'm going to that man's house with a pitchfork."

Even when they drove her crazy, Nik loved her friends so much.

"You don't need to go to his house with a pitchfork." She took a sip of her drink and reconsidered. "At least, wait a few days—he's still in Vegas."

Dana opened the calendar on her phone and made a note.

"Look, this isn't about Fisher," Nik said. Her friends stared at her with identical looks of disbelief. "Okay, fine, it's not *only* about Fisher. It was just . . . when I got home on Monday, after his texts and all of the harassment from random dudes, I was so paranoid. I even . . ."

She'd tried to avoid telling them this, but part of her always knew it would come out in the end.

"So Monday night I had dinner with Carlos, and . . . I was so anxious about all of this that I got him to come check my apartment with me. It made me feel so stupid."

Dana put her arm around her.

"Oh, honey. That sucks, but you have nothing to be ashamed about. It's those assholes who made you so worried who should be ashamed of themselves. I'm glad Carlos was there."

Nik leaned into her friend and nodded.

"He cracked jokes the whole time, thank God. If he'd been

super nice and thoughtful and concerned about me, it would have made me throw up."

"Okay." Courtney put her drink down. "I'm also very glad he was there for you, and I'm even more glad he wasn't all weird about it, but what will make me the gladdest is if you tell us you slept with him afterward."

She shook her head.

"No, guys, seriously, it wasn't like that."

Courtney pursed her lips.

"But why wasn't it like that? He's hot, he's clearly into you, he's the perfect rebound, and good Lord do you need one."

Only the first one of those points was correct.

"No, I told you. I have to swear off men for a while. Every relationship I've had with a man in the past decade has been awful. There was Justin and Fisher, and remember that graphic designer I dated last year, who told me he was in an open marriage on the fourth date? I've had enough."

Courtney nodded, like she'd heard this a million times before. To be fair, she probably had.

"Yes, yes, we know, except we also saw the way you looked at Carlos on Saturday night. Maybe you should swear off men for a while *after* you've had your rebound."

Did they not listen to her, or did they just decide they knew better?

"One: I told you guys, starting anything with him, or any man, is a bad idea. Men always think they can make demands on me, and I'm sick of that. Two: Carlos is clearly not interested in me—he didn't make the slightest move on me on Monday night. And three: if I did want to date someone right now, Carlos is absolutely not that someone."

Dana put her hand on Nik's.

"You've got to get over this doctor thing. This guy is not like Justin. Not all doctors are like Justin."

Nik sighed and took a sip of her drink.

"I know he isn't. Like, I know that intellectually. And I've been over Justin for a long time. I really have been. But it took years after I was over him to get past how shitty he made me feel about my writing. I'm just now at the place where I'm proud of both my work and my career, and I don't want anyone to try to fuck with that."

Dana nodded.

"We know, honey. But you're a very different person than you were when you dated Justin. What would you have done two weeks ago if Fisher had pulled a Justin and told you not to take a great new job?"

"I would have laughed at him," Nik said immediately.

"Exactly!" Courtney said. "To take another example from Justin's greatest hits, what would you have done if that Morton dude you dated had read one of your pieces and had told you to give up writing?"

Nik had to laugh. Her friends remembered everything. Well, almost everything.

"Morris, not Morton. And fine, I would have thrown him out of my apartment. I get your point. I'm in a better place in my life, fine. But still."

"But still what?" Dana threw her arm around her. "Have more faith in yourself, Nik. We do."

Nik refused to let herself cry.

"Oh, shut up. It's only because of the faith you two have in me that got me out of the relationship with Justin in the first place, so there."

She pulled both of her friends into a brief hug. As much as she loved her friends, they were wrong about Carlos, though. Everything they'd said about the guys she'd recently dated had proved it: the reason it was so easy to discount them and their opinions was because she didn't like those guys all that much. Carlos, though, she actually liked. Dating someone you found both smart and interesting seemed much harder. Much riskier.

"To get us back on topic: we *were* talking about how Monday night I asked a man who I barely knew to come to my apartment with me because I was feeling helpless. And if there's one thing I hate, it's feeling helpless."

"You also hate raw peaches," Dana said.

"That fuzz against your teeth!"

"And those five-finger running shoes," Courtney said.

Nik shuddered.

"They make your feet look like hobbit feet!"

"Filled doughnuts," Dana said.

"They ooze!" Nik said. "Especially the ones with red stuff inside—it's like there's blood in there."

"When people have the keyboard sound up on their phone," Dana said.

"Okay, but doesn't everyone hate that?" Nik asked them.

"Beaches," Courtney said.

"So much sand," Nik said. "It gets everywhere. And I mean *everywhere.* I don't know why people love them."

"Rompers."

"Carrot cake."

"Mashed potatoes."

"People who don't use the Oxford comma!"

"Don't forget Chardonnay!"

"Okay, okay, fine, you guys can stop now," Nik said. They would have gone on forever if she hadn't interrupted them. "You're both correct. I hate many things, okay? But feeling helpless is high up there. You happy now?"

It was amazing that two women who were so different in both looks and personality could have the exact same smug smile.

"Yes," they said in unison.

"After all that, now you know you have to go with me to a self-defense class, right?" Nik said.

"Oh." Dana looked at Courtney, and they both looked back at Nik. "We were always going to go with you. We just had to make fun of you first. When's the first class?"

Nik grinned.

"Tomorrow."

* * * * * * *

Carlos sat down on the corner of his couch with his dinner late on Wednesday night. He hadn't heard from Nik since Tuesday morning—he'd texted her to check in and see how she was doing, and she'd texted back that she was much better and thanked him again. He'd assumed that was a brush-off and he shouldn't text her again, but now he was reconsidering that. Nik's brush-offs didn't seem that subtle, for one thing. He'd seen that at Dodger Stadium. Maybe he'd text her one more time.

Did those Thai leftovers kill you? I hope you ate them yesterday. They get spicier over time.

A few seconds after he pressed send, his phone rang. My God, was it that easy?

He looked at his phone. Angela. Nope, not that easy.

"Hey," she said. "I just got off the phone with Jessie."

His cousin Jessica had just been diagnosed with preeclampsia, and he'd been fielding calls from his mom and aunt about it all day. He'd finally gotten to talk to Jessie right before he left the hospital that evening.

"I talked to her, too," he said to Angela. "Don't freak out. It's still early, but it's a good sign that her doctors sent her home and had her go on bed rest instead of admitting her."

Part of him wished her doctors had admitted her to the hospital—that way she and the baby would be safe and monitored every day in case of any problems. The thing no one told you about being a doctor was how much you would panic when people you loved had anything wrong with them. Doctors knew way too much about the worst-case scenarios.

"You're telling *me* not to freak out? From what Jessie said, you freaked her out! She said her doctors made her feel less stressed about this, and when she left her doctor's appointment, she wasn't too worried, but after she talked to you, she's all anxious again."

His phone buzzed.

Oh wow, really? Thanks for the news bulletin. That would have been a nice thing to tell me on Monday night, not well after I ate them for lunch on Tuesday and had my tongue on fire for 12 full hours. Now I know why you let me have them.

He tried not to laugh. He didn't want to have to explain his laughter to Angela.

"I'm sorry I freaked Jessie out, but she needs to know when she should go back to the hospital. If her blood pressure gets too high, it can be dangerous."

He texted back.

I don't know what you're talking about. I was just being a gentleman.

"She knows all of that; that's what her doctor is for! We all know all of that now. We have Google, too."

He rolled his eyes at his bowl of lentil soup. It was like Angela wasn't even listening to him.

"I didn't know that because of Google. I know because I'm a doctor!"

They all remembered he was a doctor when they needed him, but ignored it whenever they felt like it.

"I know you're a doctor, but stop making her more anxious about everything! She needs your support right now, not you trying to drive her blood pressure up."

Of course Jessie had his support. Jessie was his younger cousin, but only by a year. She had teased him and played with him and laughed at him and encouraged him and been proud of him his whole life. One of the framed pictures he had in his house was of him at three and Jessie at two, both looking dubiously at baby Angela.

Ohhhhhh, is that what being a gentleman is? Letting the woman absorb all of the pain while you take the glory? Now I understand what all of those men who told me they were such gentlemen were saying.

He had to mute his call so he could laugh at that.

"Look," Angela continued. "I know you're stressed right now, coming up on the five-year anniversary of Dad, but—"

He stopped laughing.

"It's not that," he said. He'd been trying to ignore that the anniversary of his father's death was coming up. "I'm just trying to take care of this family, that's all."

Ever since his father's death, Carlos had sort of considered himself head of his family. He'd never say that out loud to his mother or to Tia Eva, but he assumed they thought the same thing. Jessie's dad had never been around, so his dad had always done all of the car maintenance, yard work, and home repairs for all of them. When his dad died, Carlos had taken over all of that. But it was more than just the physical work: he thought of his family as his responsibility. He wasn't going to have anything happen to Jessie on his watch.

"Look, I don't want to fight about this," he said to Angela. "I'm just trying to take care of Jessie the best I know how. I have to work late tomorrow, but I'm going to stop by to see her on Friday."

Don't tell anyone I told you the gentleman code. The other gentlemen out there will murder me.

"Oh great, I have an idea: before you stop by to see Jessie, why don't you go to the doctor? She would love that, and so would I."

He sighed. Not this again.

"Next topic, Angela."

She laughed.

"Fine, but remember what I said. By the way, did you see the video of that proposal pop up everywhere? Wild, right? Poor Nik. I wonder how she's holding up."

My lips are sealed. I mean, until I write the big exposé about this.

"She's hanging in there," he said, without thinking.

Oh shit.

"Oh, *is she*? How do you know that, may I ask?"

Well he definitely could *not* say it was because he and Nik had been texting throughout this conversation. Anytime he even hinted that he enjoyed a woman's company, Angela was convinced they'd live happily ever after. And while he still didn't know what was going to happen between him and Nik, he knew that wasn't in the cards.

"We had dinner on Monday night. She emailed me to say thanks for Saturday—she wanted me to say thanks to you, too, by the way—and we ended up grabbing Thai food."

"Hmmmm. Weird that you didn't mention that she wanted you to say thanks to me. I wonder how that happened?"

Why couldn't they still be talking about Jessie?

"I've kind of had a lot going on this week, Angie. Between being a doctor and taking care of our whole family, it sort of slipped my mind."

"Well, I liked her, and it seems like you liked her, too, so . . ."

Just make sure you don't use my real name in your exposé. Give me one of those hipster baby names, like Carver or Fletcher or Winston.

He never should have let it slip that he'd even thought about Nik after Saturday night. He needed to nip this in the bud right away. Even if something did end up happening with Nik, it wasn't going to be the kind of relationship his sister kept pushing him toward.

"I didn't like her that much. I only had dinner with her because I felt sorry for her. She was dealing with some harassment after the video went public and was freaked out."

Maybe someday he'd be able to date someone seriously, but it was way too soon since his father had died for that. He couldn't put another woman over his mother and sister—not to mention Jessie and Tia Eva. He needed to be able to race to Angie's house when she sprained her ankle or go furniture shopping with his mom on the weekend or change the tires on Tia Eva's car. All of the things his dad used to do. If he was dating someone, he wouldn't be able to do any of that.

"Mmmhmmm," Angie said. "You felt sorry for her, sure. Like I believe that one."

He shook his head.

"Good-bye, Angela. Talk to you later."

How about Atticus? You seem like you could be an Atticus.

He put his feet up on his coffee table and laughed and laughed.

Chapter Six

"I cannot believe you're making us do this," Courtney said as they got out of the car. "You know I avoid all situations where the correct attire is athleisure."

Nik zipped up her hoodie and ignored her.

"Oh hush," Dana said to Courtney. "I like that outfit on you. I've been trying to tell you for months how much more comfortable you'd be in leggings or yoga pants at work all day."

Courtney shook her head as they walked toward the gym. Nik had almost avoided this class in principle because it was called "Punch Like a Girl," but it was the only class on the Eastside that started in the next few weeks. And it somehow felt urgent for her to do this *now.* It wasn't that she really thought Fisher—or any of the other creepy guys who sent her messages—would actually do anything to her. It was more that she'd realized that she would have no idea what to do if any of them did.

She couldn't wait to tell Carlos that she was taking the class. She was pretty sure he'd get a kick out of it. That was, if she ever saw him again. They'd texted for hours last night, and on and off again today, but that didn't mean anything.

"I don't care how comfortable leggings are; I like my dresses for work, thank you very much," Courtney said. "I spent years dressing in ugly plus-size suits for corporate America. It's a relief to wear A-line dresses in ridiculous patterns. Plus, I run a cupcake shop that I named after myself; dressing like a cupcake is very hashtag on brand."

"I cannot believe you said 'hashtag' out loud like that." Dana pulled her hair up into a ponytail. "You've clearly been doing too much store-related social media lately. We might need to have an intervention."

Courtney pulled her phone out of the pocket in her leggings.

"Are you kidding me? I just hit twenty-five thousand Instagram followers! I'm doing something right." She smiled at a picture of a cupcake before she tucked her phone back in her pocket. "Yes, I know I'm obsessed; you don't have to tell me twice."

Nik pulled out her own phone. Who knows, that source may have emailed her back!

I swear to God, a patient today told me she babysits for a kid named Kaftan.

She hid her smile.

The gym was a big, kind of anonymous-looking building with only a metallic gold sign over the door that said NATALIE'S GYM.

"Where did you find this place?" Dana whispered to Nik. "I've never seen a sparkly gold sign at a gym before."

"Shhh," Courtney said. "I feel more at home at this place already if there are sparkles involved."

Nik ignored them and went up to the blond woman in a pink tank top sitting at the front desk.

"Hi, I signed up online for three of us for the class." She refused to say the name.

"Punch Like a Girl? Fantastic!" The incredibly thin, perky, ponytailed woman beamed at her. "What are your names?"

"Nikole Paterson, Dana Carter, Courtney Park," Nik said, pointing at herself and each of her friends in turn.

"Nice to meet all three of you!" the woman said. "It's a sliding scale, so just let me know what you're comfortable paying. Usually you can pay for one class at a time, but for this class, we like you to pay for the whole six weeks in advance, so we can count you in for the whole run of the class."

Nik handed over her credit card. She'd never heard of a sliding scale gym in L.A. before, especially not a cute one like this. That would have been useful when she was just starting out, but luckily, she could afford to pay the list price now.

"Great!" The woman stood. "You're all paid up and checked in, the locker rooms are through there, and we'll be in Studio A for the class—starts in ten minutes!"

"Great!" Nik said back, and was immediately ashamed that she'd adopted the other woman's exclamation points. This was just like how whenever she went to the South, she started drawling and saying "y'all" after the first five minutes.

None of them needed the locker room, so they shuffled into Studio A. It was a big, brightly lit exercise studio, with shiny wood floors, mirrors covering one wall, and a water fountain in the corner. A big sign by the door told them—in more metallic gold letters—to turn off their phones and put any personal items in the cubbies by the door.

"Are we in kindergarten?" Dana said, gesturing toward the sign. "I don't know about this place, Nik."

Courtney quickly shed her jacket and tucked it and her purse into a cubby.

"I obey any sign that sparkles at me—you know that," she said to Dana. "Have an open mind! You're too used to your high-pressure SoulFit or CrossMethod or whatever the hell it is you do when you work out."

Dana raised her eyebrows at Nik.

"Some sparkly signs and this woman is all in. I've never seen her change her mind so quickly about anything."

Thank God her friends were with her. There were many things in life she would cheerfully do alone—go to movie, out to dinner, on an international trip—but she never would have had the guts to come to a class like this alone.

She took out her phone to turn it off, and what the hell, send one more text.

Now you're just making things up, but I swear I just heard someone at the gym call someone else Sunshine.

At seven on the dot, the blond woman from the reception desk bounced into the center of the room.

"Welcome, everyone!" All of the murmurs quieted down, and everyone turned to her. "I'm Natalie, and I'm so glad to see all of your beautiful faces here today!"

Oh God. This was the kind of person who said "all of your beautiful faces." What had she gotten them into? She saw Courtney and Dana exchanging glances.

"So, as you all know, this is a six-week course to teach women how to fight." She smiled at the half circle of women gathered around her, and they all smiled back. More or less. "Some of you probably signed up for this class thinking about how they do self-defense classes for women in the movies. You know, a man all dressed up in lots of padding, and everyone gets to beat him up and knock him down; we all laugh, right?" They all nodded, more sure of themselves this time. That was exactly what Nik had wanted. To be able to punch a man and walk away from the class confident knowing she could.

"Well, that's not what we do here." Natalie's voice had changed. It was still pink and sparkly, but somehow had steel behind it, too. "We don't want this to be some fake empowering nonsense that lets you leave here after you knock down a man covered in padding, who was unable to move and who'd given you, like, ten minutes of warning that he was going to try to attack you. What the hell good does that do you?"

Hmmmmm. This was getting interesting.

"If we did that, you'd leave after six classes, still completely unable to face whatever it was that drove you to sign up for this class. That's not what I'm about. In my classes, we're going to face those fears head-on. And we're going to teach you how to punch like a girl. Because you know what?"

Beyoncé's "Run the World (Girls)" suddenly blasted from the invisible speakers in the room, and the whole class jumped, then laughed, then sang along.

"That's right. We run the world, girls. Don't ever let anyone forget that." Natalie beamed at them. Nik suddenly noticed the size of her biceps. She had definitely misjudged this woman by her blond hair and cheerful voice, that was for sure.

"I know, I know, you're all looking around for the punching bags and boxing gloves. That's next week. Today we're going to start with loosening up and learning some form." She smiled at them, a smile that felt like a hug. How did she do that?

"Okay, everyone!" Natalie bounded to the front of the class and faced them. "Now, we're going to learn proper form. We have to get your hands, your arms, your shoulders, your back, and your legs all in order." She demonstrated a punch, her ponytail swinging. "That's what you are all going to look like before the end of next week's class. Now, let's talk about how you stand. That's the most important part."

Nik imitated Natalie's stance. She already felt stronger. She bet if Carlos saw her now, he wouldn't think she was some sort of weakling.

Well, okay, she still didn't know how to throw a punch, but she would very soon, which was the important part.

"We get to use punching bags next week, you guys!" Courtney said as the three of them walked out of the gym an hour later. They were dripping with sweat and had huge grins on their faces. "I can't wait."

Nik looked over at Dana.

"What did you think, D? I know this one became a convert as soon as she saw the sparkles, but you were more skeptical. You going to keep going with us?"

Dana jumped into the front seat of Nik's car.

"Absolutely. Now that I think about it, I've always wanted to know how to punch someone in the jaw."

"Same here," Nik said.

* * * * * * *

Carlos woke up extra early on Friday morning and went for a run. The hell with apples; it was a run a day that kept the doctor away.

He was so tired of Angela bugging him about going to the doctor, and lately Jessie had been doing it, too. They'd started bringing this doctor thing up over a year ago when he made the mistake of letting it slip that he hadn't been to the doctor in years. He knew it was because they were just paranoid about something happening to him like it had happened to his dad, but he was fine—he kept telling them that. He knew his own family history all too well; he didn't need to go into detail with someone else about it. And he already knew everything he needed to do for his health, and he didn't need some other doctor bugging him to cut carbs and exercise more, blah blah blah.

He'd planned to take a few hours off on Friday afternoon, so when he left work early, he drove down to Los Feliz to the bookstore he liked there, Skylight Books. He'd promised Jessie that he would pick up some books for her to read while she was on bed rest. He was pretty sure that Jessie was more stressed about having preeclampsia than she'd let on to him. Books would help her relax, no matter what she was reading.

"Looking for anything in particular?" a voice next to him said. Oh thank God, someone on the staff to give him advice.

"I am, and I need some help." He turned around to find Nik standing next to him, that worried look on her face from Monday night replaced by a grin.

"Hey! What are you doing here?" he asked. He pulled her into a hug. He'd been on the point of asking her to get a drink last night, but she'd gone radio silent on him for a few hours, and when he heard from her again, it would have been way too late.

"I'm here all the time," she said. "Today there's no particular mission other than seeing if I can find a book I'm in the mood for. I have stacks of brand-new books at home, all of which I was excited to read when I bought them, but now . . . none of them seem quite right to me."

He nodded.

"Yeah, I know how that is. All of the books that you have are sad books when you're in a happy book mood, or vice versa. Or dense when you want a page-turner."

She smiled up at him. Her skin almost glowed in the warm light, her hair bounced as her head turned, and her huge smile made him feel warm inside. He couldn't help but to smile back at her.

"Exactly! All of the books I have right now are either very smart nonfiction books about very important issues that I would rather jump in front of a moving train than read right now or novels where all of their *New York Times* reviews said the writing was 'beautiful,' and I don't have the patience for beautiful writing right now. What are you looking for?"

They walked a few steps together, away from the woman who seemed to be bothered by their above-a-whisper-level conversation.

"I'm shopping for my cousin who's on bed rest, and she's obsessed with true crime. Books like that stress me out, but she can't get enough of them. But since I can't read them without having nightmares, I have no idea what I should get her. Plus, she's a librarian, so I'm always terrified to buy her books."

Her eyes lit up.

"It's your lucky day because you're looking at Southern California's true crime book expert. I'd call them my guilty pleasure if I believed in guilty pleasures. I can give you as many recommendations as you have bookstore dollars to spend."

Well then. It was his lucky day for more than one reason.

She picked up a book from the shelf they were standing in front of and paused.

"Wait, is this the same pregnant cousin you were telling me about the other night? What happened?"

He'd forgotten that he'd told her about Jessie. He was impressed that she'd remembered.

"Yeah, Jessie. She has preeclampsia. We found out this week." He tried not to let on how anxious he was. "She'll be okay, we think—it's not the most serious kind, but it's going to be a long twelve weeks for her."

She squeezed his arm.

"Oh God, that must be so stressful." She turned back to the shelves, her hand still on his arm. He resisted the urge to flex. "Okay, this just means we've got to get her some excellent books that will make her happy to stay on the couch. Do you know what she already has?"

They walked out of the bookstore forty-five minutes later, a bag of books in each of his hands.

"Can I buy you some coffee to thank you for your help?" he asked her.

"Absolutely not, I owed you this favor," she said. "But I can buy you coffee to thank you for your help on Monday night."

He laughed.

"Okay, how about I buy you coffee and you buy me coffee then?"

She steered him down the street.

"Deal."

They ended up at a coffee shop with outdoor seating a few blocks away and sat down at a shady table with their iced espresso drinks.

"Preeclampsia can be scary, right?" she asked. "How is your cousin doing?"

Thank God *someone* understood that.

"It can be really scary, yeah. I think Jessie's doing okay, but I'm not sure if she's taking this seriously enough. She's only twenty-eight weeks, so we're all just hoping the baby stays put for at least another two months."

He'd been terrified when he got the first text from Jessie. Thank God it wasn't as bad as he'd initially thought, but that terror hadn't completely dissipated.

She touched his clenched fist. He forced his fingers to relax enough to clasp her hand without breaking it.

"What's making your face do that?" she asked him.

He scrunched up his face at her, and she laughed.

"My face do what? What is my face doing?"

She touched his cheek with her free hand.

"You have a dimple in this cheek right here. All afternoon and evening on Saturday, I saw it winking at me. The same thing happened when we were in the bookstore just now. But as soon as we sat down, the dimple disappeared. And lines appeared up here." She drew a line across his forehead with her finger. He closed his eyes at her touch. She dropped her hand, and he opened his eyes.

"Remind me not to go to Vegas with you," he said. "You'll let everyone know all of my tells!"

"Oh no." She shook her head. "I'm an excellent Vegas buddy. I'll tell YOU everyone else's tells."

He laughed and sighed. His face was probably doing that thing again, but he couldn't help it.

"This early in her pregnancy, for her to get this diagnosis—there's a lot that could go wrong. I don't want the rest of my family as anxious about this as I am, so I'm trying to be calm about this when I talk to them. I'm just worried."

"Where's her spouse in all of this, or is she single?"

He shook his head.

"No, she's married, her husband's great. But Jessie and Angela and I grew up together, she doesn't have any siblings, so I'm sort of her big brother, as well as Angie's." It had always been his job to take care of Jessie and Angie. And since his dad died, he'd made an effort to always be there for them, even when he'd lived all the way over on the Westside. Jessie was still his responsibility, Jon or no Jon.

"Anyway, I was supposed to go out of town this weekend, but I'm going to have to cancel. My best friend Drew got engaged last week and he and his fiancée are having an engagement party in Berkeley. I was supposed to fly up tomorrow morning, but I can't leave Jessie now. I still have to cancel my flight and call Drew and tell him I'm not coming."

He sat up straight and tried to shake all of this off. Why had he just let all of these stupid emotions out to this woman who barely knew him?

"Sorry for spilling all of that. I'm sure you didn't come get coffee with me in order to hear all about my family drama."

She shook her head and squeezed his hand.

"Well, you didn't go get dinner with me in order to become my private security guard, so I'd say it's about even." Her face lit up. "Ooh, here's a thing that I bet a pregnant woman on bed rest will love: cupcakes. Courtney's shop is just a few blocks away. Want to walk over there?"

Chapter Seven

Nik shook her head when she saw the pink and white polka-dot Cupcake Park sign. What was she doing bringing Carlos here? She would never hear the end of it from Courtney. But he'd looked so sad about his cousin. Cupcakes were the first thing she could think of that might cheer him up.

"Hey!" Nik said to Courtney, who stood behind the counter with a smirk on her face. "I brought you a customer."

Courtney waved as she carefully placed an assortment of cupcakes into a box for the woman standing at the register.

"Hey, Carlos, good to see you again. Welcome to Cupcake Park. Nik can give you the rundown of all of the flavors while you wait. She knows them almost as well as I do."

Nik gave him a wry smile as they went up to the counter.

"As much as I hate to say this, she is correct. I curse the day one of my best friends opened a cupcake shop so close to my apartment. And unfortunately, it looks like business is booming, so she'll be here for a while, tempting me with her delicious sugary treats. I think she did this to get revenge on me for something."

Courtney and her customer both laughed.

"I can't tell if you're the worst possible advertisement for my store or the best. I guess time will tell."

The customer picked up her bag containing two big boxes of cupcakes.

"Get the strawberry ones," she said. "Those are my favorite. Those and the coconut-lime ones. Ooh, and the matcha ones!"

Nik shook her head after the customer left the store.

"All of those are very good, but she's wrong. He should get the confetti ones and the lemon ones."

Carlos smiled at Courtney.

"Those flavors all sound great, but I need to start with some red velvet. These are for my cousin, and those are her favorites."

Courtney smirked at Nik, and Nik put her head in her hands.

"What did I say?" He turned from one to the other.

"When I was opening this place, I insisted that I needed to have red velvet cupcakes. Nik argued *strongly* against them. She said my whole shop was going to be about unusual and interesting flavors, and that red velvet cupcakes weren't good enough for me."

"They taste like nothing!" Nik said. "They're just a vehicle for cream cheese frosting, but you can put cream cheese frosting on other cupcakes!"

"I guess I can see who won this argument," he said, and gestured to the case full of red velvet cupcakes.

"A good cupcake shop has got to have some crowd pleasers," Courtney said.

Courtney was always so happy that she'd been right about red velvet, damn her.

"You're shopping for your cousin?" Courtney asked Carlos. "Any special occasion, or a just because cupcakes are great?"

He smiled at her, but he had that sad look in his eyes again.

"Sort of. She's pregnant and newly on bed rest, so I wanted to bring her some cheer."

"Oh no, your poor cousin. Okay, some cheer, coming right up. How many do you want?"

Carlos put his bags of books on a chair.

"A dozen. At least. If I know my family—and I do—everyone is going to be coming by her house in the next few days, and they'll all eat one, minimum."

"Okay, got it." Courtney pulled out a big pink box. "Here, I'll put together an assortment of Cupcake Park's greatest hits, and Nik can take you into the back to show you my kitchen, aka my pride and joy. One question: how do you feel about spicy food?"

He looked at Nik and they both laughed.

"I feel great about it. Why? Do you have a spicy cupcake?"

Courtney grinned her slightly evil grin.

"Nik, you tell him all about my spicy cupcake while I put together this box of treats, okay? And yes, yes, I'll give him some of the confetti cupcakes."

Nik led Carlos through the door marked employees only and tried to ignore Courtney's knowing look. It was like she thought the whole reason Nik had brought Carlos here was for Courtney to start up the rebound refrain again.

To be fair . . . she'd been thinking a lot about that moment on the couch the other night. Maybe too much about it. If Courtney *did* start up the rebound refrain again, she might be somewhat more receptive. Maybe.

"How long has this place been here?" Carlos put his hand on

her lower back to steer her around some cardboard boxes stacked on the floor.

"Just over a year." Would he slide his hand up her back to put his arm around her shoulders? Come on, give her this one thing. YES. YES, HE WOULD. She leaned toward him and tried not to let her smile show her triumph.

"Did she have another bakery somewhere else?"

Nik shook her head. How could he expect her to have an actual conversation with his arm around her like that, and his warm body right next to her?

"No, she used to be an investment banker, isn't that wild? But she'd saved up a ton of money and had always loved baking. About a year and a half ago, she saw this place for lease and took the plunge."

"Wow," he said as they walked through the kitchen. "That's inspiring."

She nodded and looked up at him.

"Agreed." She wanted to touch his hair so badly. It was slightly too long and a little messy from the wind. If she could just brush it back with her fingers . . .

She felt a buzz from his pocket, and they both jumped and pulled away from each other. He shook his head and reached for his phone.

"That was Jessie, wondering when I'm coming over. I should probably . . ."

She nodded.

"Yeah, let's go get your cupcakes from Courtney."

They emerged back into the store. Courtney's smirk was in full bloom. Nik glared at her, but it didn't make the slightest impact.

Carlos pulled his wallet out of his pocket and handed her his credit card. "Thanks so much for the cupcakes. I'm sure Jessie will love them."

"My pleasure." She ran his card and handed him the receipt. "Thanks for coming by, and I hope this isn't the last time. And make sure you warn everyone about the spicy chocolate cupcakes; they're the ones with the chili pepper on top."

He laughed and waved good-bye as they left the store.

"Thanks for bringing me here," he said to Nik as they walked to his car.

They stopped in front of his car, parked just a few doors down from Cupcake Park.

"Keep me posted," she said. "About how she liked the cupcakes, and how she's doing."

He opened the trunk and put the books and the cupcakes inside.

"I will," he said. "And about how she likes those fucked-up books, too."

She laughed.

"Please do."

He opened his arms for a hug.

"Thanks for all of your help today. With the books, and everything else. Now I definitely owe you a drink. Next week?"

She let the hug linger and kissed him on the cheek when she eventually pulled away.

"Absolutely. Text me and let me know what works for you."

She pulled out her phone as soon as he drove away, certain about what she would find.

Sure enough:

If you don't get your ass back to my store, I'm going to murder you with my bare hands.

Nik grinned and walked back to Cupcake Park.

* * * * * * *

Why did Jessie have to text him right then? He'd been about two seconds from kissing Nik, and unlike Monday night, he'd been pretty sure she would have kissed him back. And then the damn text from his cousin had to get in the way.

He was already mad at Jessie for how nonchalantly she was treating her preeclampsia, and she had to go and do this to him, too? Now she was in for it. That was, if he could concentrate on anything other than how good Nik smelled, and how soft her skin was, and how he'd wanted to pull off her clothes right there in the bakery kitchen.

Jon opened the front door almost as soon as he knocked. Carlos walked in, carrying the bookstore bags in one hand and the cupcake bag in another.

"Hey, man, how're you holding up?" Carlos asked him. Carlos had been very suspicious when Jessie had introduced him to the skinny, white, bearded English professor she was dating, but now he liked Jon a lot.

"Okay, except for your cousin over here trying to kill me." Jon smiled at Jessie with so much love and worry in his eyes that Carlos had to look away.

Jessica was reclining on the couch like a pregnant Cleopatra. Her long dark-brown hair and big brown eyes added to the resemblance.

"Carlos!" Jessie smiled up at him. "I was wondering when my good-for-nothing cousin was going to stop by."

He set the bags down on the coffee table and leaned in for a hug.

"What's your blood pressure right now?"

Jessica pulled away.

"Come on, Carlos. This is your cousin, not your patient. Take a deep breath."

He knew she was his cousin. He wouldn't be half as worried if she were his patient.

"Don't give me that 'take a deep breath' nonsense. Come on, what's your blood pressure?"

Jessie reached for her bottle of water and took a swig.

"Now that we're on the topic, what's your blood pressure, Carlos? When's the last time *you* went to the doctor?"

"Oh my God, Jessie, don't do that right now. This is serious!" Jon shot a look at him, and he realized that snapping at his pregnant, sick cousin probably wasn't the right move.

"Yes, yes, I know it's serious. Can we get to that?" She pointed at the bag on the coffee table. "What'd you bring me? Wait, I mean . . ." She arranged her face into a perfect fake look of surprise. "For me? You didn't have to bring me a present, Carlos! No really, you didn't! Okay, fine, if you *insist*." She grinned at him. Despite his irritation with her, he couldn't keep from grinning back. "How'd I do? Did I look just like Taylor Swift?"

"Fantastic, you were perfect. No one would have known the truth." He gave up on the medical questions for the moment and handed her the carefully wrapped stack of books. "Here, dig in."

She squealed and tore into the wrapping paper. He had to remember to thank Nik for getting the bookstore to wrap the presents. He would have just handed Jessie the bag.

"Oooh, I've been wanting to read this book! I didn't know it was in paperback, awesome." She tore through the books, and when she looked back up at Carlos, he was surprised to see her eyes full of tears.

"You asshole. These are all so perfect. Thank you."

She reached her arms up, and he hugged her again, longer this time.

"I know how you feel about being bored, so I thought some reading material was in order. I'll be around all weekend, so if you get tired of reading, I can come entertain you."

She narrowed her eyes at him.

"What do you mean you'll be around all weekend? Angie told me you were leaving tomorrow to go up to Berkeley for Drew's engagement party."

He had forgotten he'd told Angie about that. Damn it, why did she have to tell Jessie everything?

He shook his head.

"Oh no, that's not this weekend. She must have heard me wrong. That's in a few weeks."

Would she buy that?

"I always know when you're lying; you know that, right? I refuse to let you miss out on your best friend's engagement party. I'll be *fine*. I have Jon here, and Angie is fifteen minutes away, and my mom and your mom and God knows how many doctors. You can't hover over me like this for the rest of my pregnancy."

There was no way he could go; she knew that.

"Jessie. Come on. I can't leave now; you know that."

She set her mouth in that stubborn way she'd been doing ever since she was a toddler.

"No, I don't know that. As a matter of fact, here's what I do know: if you try to come over this weekend, I'm not even going to let you in my house. So you might as well go to Berkeley because you're not going to see me if you're here."

He turned to Jon, hoping he would talk some sense into her.

"You know she'll do it," Jon said.

Unfortunately, he did know.

"Fine." He shook his finger at her. "But I swear to God, Jessie, you had better text me if anything happens. Promise me."

She rolled her eyes at him.

"I promise. Are we done with that?"

He nodded.

"Now!" She pointed to the cupcake bag, just out of reach. "What's in the pink bag?" He sighed and pushed it toward her. Leave it to Jessie to keep her mind on her presents.

"Oooh, it's heavy. Hmmm, what place did my hipster cousin discover?"

"I'm not a hipster!" he yelled. This is what he got for his pains.

"Carlos. You hang out in Silver Lake. Come on."

"I have a perfectly normal haircut! I don't have a beard or Warby Parker glasses! I *never* wear a hat."

She laughed harder and looked at Jon.

"I love doing this to him. He gets so mad every time!" She pulled the cupcake box out of the bag and opened it. "Oooooh. Red velvet cupcakes! And . . . is that Funfetti? Gourmet Funfetti cupcakes?" She took a cupcake from the box and took a bite. "Oh my God. If this is what hipsters eat, I've changed my mind about them; I want you to be the hipsterest hipster in all of Los Angeles if you're going to bring me baked goods like this. Jon, you've got to try one."

He grinned at the look on her face and at the frosting on her nose. He was so glad he'd been able to make her happy, even though he was still furious at her. The cupcake store had clearly been a good idea. Another thing to thank Nik for.

"So I heard you picked up a girl by using my story. You're welcome."

Angela *really* told Jessie everything.

"I did not 'pick up a girl.' I just helped someone out of a difficult situation, that's all."

Jessie took another bite of her cupcake.

"Mmmmhmm. Just one question: have you seen this girl since you helped her out of that one difficult situation?"

Thirty minutes ago, and I was this close to pushing her up against a wall to kiss the hell out of her until you texted me and interrupted us, he didn't say.

He picked up one of the spicy cupcakes to play for time. After one bite, he had no idea why Courtney had warned him about the chili powder.

"As I'm sure you already know from my chatty little sister, I met up with her for dinner a few days later, but it was no big deal."

When should he text Nik about going out for drinks? He'd said "next week" so he should probably wait until then to ask. But he could text her tonight about what a hit the books and the cupcakes were.

Jessie pursed her lips at him.

"You always say things are no big deal, but I don't believe you anymore."

How had their conversation become all about him? Time to turn this back to Jessie.

"Do you know what IS a big deal? Preeclampsia, that's what's a big deal."

Jessie and Jon both went into peals of laughter. He glared at them.

Wait. There was the chili powder. Oh wow, it kind of snuck up on you, didn't it? He mentally apologized to Courtney for doubting her.

"Oh, Carlos, thank you for that. I haven't laughed so hard in at least a week."

He made a face at her.

"Hah hah hah, I'm glad that you found that amusing, but seriously, Jessie . . ."

She held up a hand to stop him.

"Seriously, Carlos. I love you, but you are not my doctor. You're not even an OB. I know what I'm supposed to be looking out for here. Please relax so that I can relax. Go on your trip. Celebrate with your friends. Drink lots of champagne, since I can't. And chill out."

He didn't think he was going to be able to relax until she'd safely delivered the baby, but he figured telling her that at this point was probably not a good idea.

"Fine. Can I make you some dinner, then?"

As soon as he got home from Jessie's, he called Drew.

"Hey, man, how's it going?" Drew asked when he answered the phone. "Ready for the party?"

"Very. I always told you that you crazy kids would make it."

"Yeah, yeah, yeah," Drew said. "You told me so, I know. I'm never going to be able to ignore your advice again in my life, am I? Anytime I try, it's going to be 'Hey, Drew, remember that time you almost let Alexa—you know, the love of your life—get away from you?' and I'm going to have to give in. What a nightmare."

Carlos laughed.

"Yes indeed, your life seems like a total nightmare. I feel so bad for you."

"You should," Drew said. "You absolutely should. I had to

make pancakes this morning. Me! Making pancakes! I spent hours on the couch afterward to recover."

"What a tough life."

"It's terrible and I love it. Speaking of, what's going on with you? Any women I should know about?"

He flashed back to that moment with Nik in the bakery.

"If you're trying to get me to settle down like you, dude, it's not happening. You know that's not me. But are you at home? Do you have a second?"

Drew's voice got serious.

"What's up? Something wrong?"

Carlos walked into his kitchen to see if he had any beer in his fridge.

"You remember my cousin Jessie, right?"

Oh thank God, there were two bottles in the back.

"Yeah, of course. Is something wrong with the baby?"

Drew knew him too well.

"Jessie has preeclampsia."

"Oh." Drew paused. "How far along is she? When did they find out?"

"Twenty-eight weeks, and just a few days ago. Her doctor isn't that worried, and she's on bed rest, but . . ."

They went over the details of Jessie's case, like they'd done together about other patients hundreds of times, back when they worked together and would bounce questions and ideas off each other. Turning Jessie into a patient, and not his cousin, gave him some of the distance he needed.

"Okay. I feel a little better. Thanks." He wished Drew still lived in L.A.

"No problem, man. Let me know if there's anything I can do. We'll miss you this weekend, but I totally understand that you can't leave Jessie now."

Carlos opened his second beer.

"Oh no, you're stuck with me. Jessie refuses to let me stay in L.A. this weekend. She said if I don't go up there and go to the party, she won't allow me in her house. Thank God I already told you I'd cook stuff for your party. I'm going to need to keep busy the whole time."

Drew laughed.

"That sounds like your family. We can go to the store after I pick you up from the airport tomorrow morning."

He already had some snacks in mind to make for the party. Fancy pigs in a blanket would keep him occupied for a while, for starters.

"Perfect. Hey, on a different topic: did you see the thing about that failed proposal at Dodger Stadium last weekend?"

Drew groaned.

"Did I ever. Thank God that happened after I proposed to Alexa; otherwise I would have totally lost my nerve."

"Yeahhhh, so, funny story. I was sitting right behind them when that happened."

"What? Are you kidding me?" Carlos heard some commotion in the background, and then Drew clearly talking to Alexa. "That proposal I told you about! Carlos was there. He was sitting right behind them." Drew came back on the phone. "Alexa is dying over here and says you have to tell me all the details."

"Put him on speaker!" Alexa shouted in the background.

Carlos laughed and told the story, with all of the details he could remember. After spending all day talking about scary topics, it was fun to tell them about how he'd met Nik.

"Wait, so after you threw this unsuspecting, traumatized woman into your car—and then drove her through L.A. in that terror mobile, you and Angela went out drinking with her?" Alexa asked.

"I can't believe you would say something like that about my car! Is this what happens when people get a ring on their finger and stop being polite?"

"The entire world knows you're terrifying to be in a car with," Drew said. "Finish the story."

"Some friend you are. But, yes, that's pretty much exactly what happened. Except we weren't just with her, we were with her and her two best friends. It was me and four very angry women. I was just grateful I got out of there alive."

The three of them cracked up, and Carlos wished again that they all lived in the same city.

He would tell Drew the rest of the Nik story sometime when Alexa wasn't also there. Nothing against Alexa, but this was a guy kind of conversation. Maybe soon, he'd have more than an almost kiss to tell him about.

"Okay, guys, I'd better run."

"Talk to you soon," Drew said. "Keep me posted on Jessie, okay?"

Carlos nodded, even though he knew Drew couldn't see him. "Will do, buddy. Thanks."

"Anytime."

Chapter Eight

When Carlos left work on Wednesday, all he wanted was a very strong drink. His day had been full of minor disasters: a patient's dad had yelled first at the patient, then at Carlos; he'd called a patient by the wrong name, and then had called her by a different wrong name when he tried to apologize; a nurse had dropped a tray of urine samples on his shoes. Thank God he'd had an extra pair of shoes in his office.

Well, there was one other thing than just a strong drink that would put him in a better mood . . .

"Oh hell, why not?" he said to himself and scrolled to Nik's name in his phone.

Hey, you in the mood for that drink?

They'd been texting on and off since they'd seen each other last, but until now neither of them had mentioned getting together again. He kept almost bringing it up, but each time it was either so early in the day that it would look too premeditated or so late in the evening that it would look like a booty call. Now seemed like just the right time, but with his luck today, she'd be out with another guy already.

He drove toward the grocery store while waiting to see if she'd answer. He could stop for gas at the station next door. And if she said no, or even worse, didn't answer, at least he could splurge on some good bourbon.

Just as he pulled into the grocery store parking lot, his phone buzzed.

I am absolutely in the mood for that drink, but I can't tonight. Courtney's in the midst of a cupcake crisis; we have to deliver a zillion cupcakes up into the hills, her help bailed on her and her car broke down so we have to do it all in mine.

Apparently, Courtney was having a day like he was.

Oh, the hell with it. He had no other plans tonight but to sit on the couch and yell at his TV screen.

Do you need help? I'm not far away, and my car is 100% functional.

He got her text back within seconds.

Are you sure? That would be a lifesaver, but seriously, if you're busy, it's no problem.

Did he really want to spend his evening driving cupcakes around? No, of course not. Did he have an ulterior motive for volunteering to help? Obviously.

On my way.

When he got to Cupcake Park, Nik was standing in front waiting for him.

"You're our hero. Drive around the back into the alley, that's where we can load up. Just FYI, Courtney is freaking out, so don't be surprised when you see her."

He waved and drove on into a narrow alley around the corner.

He pulled up when he saw a rack full of cupcake boxes and parked behind Nik's car.

"Carlos!" Courtney came running to the car, with many colors of frosting all over her pink and white apron. "You're a hero and a saint, and I'll find a way to thank you but I can't do that right now because we're in a time crunch. Help us load up."

Carlos jumped out of the car.

"Aye aye, captain."

They very carefully loaded what felt like hundreds of boxes of cupcakes into the two cars, while Courtney ran back and forth bringing more boxes out.

"Only on the floor!" Courtney shouted. "No boxes on seats! They'll fall off at the slightest hit of the brakes and disaster will strike."

He couldn't look at Nik, otherwise he knew he would laugh out loud.

"See what I meant about her freaking out?" Nik said as soon as Courtney went back inside.

He nodded.

"You weren't kidding about a cupcake crisis."

They unceremoniously tossed all of the crap that had been in both his and Nik's trunks into the back room at Cupcake Park to maximize the space for the cupcakes. When they were all loaded up to Courtney's specifications, she programmed the address of the place they were going into Nik's phone, and took Nik's car key out of her hand.

"I'll take your car and meet you two there." She pointed her finger at Carlos. "No crazy driving, do you hear me?"

He turned to Nik.

"Why would she say that to me? I'm an excellent driver."

Nik laughed at him and got in the passenger seat.

"You'd better drive like you're transporting a tiny baby. If a single one of those cupcakes arrives with even slightly smashed frosting, Courtney will murder you."

He pulled out of the alley and zoomed toward the freeway.

"I'm offended that you would even feel the need to tell me that. I've been driving on L.A. freeways since I was practically a toddler. Those cupcakes will arrive in perfect condition, mark my words." He revved the motor at a stoplight, and Courtney, in the car next to his, looked over at him in horror.

"You just woke up the baby in the back seat, and it's pissed," Nik said.

He sped through the light when it turned green and laughed on his way to the freeway entrance.

"I was in a terrible mood, but that look on Courtney's face just cheered me right up. She might kill me, but it'll be worth it."

"Oh, she will definitely kill you, but she'll kill you after you get her cupcakes to the event." Nik relaxed into his passenger seat. "Speaking of babies, how's your cousin?"

He ran his hand through his hair and sighed.

"She's hanging in there, thanks for asking. Oh, she told me she tore through that Jamestown book and loved it. I'm not sure if that's because she was anxious or bored, but either way it helped, so thanks for the recommendation."

"My pleasure." He glanced back in her direction just to see her smile. "It's always good to find people who seem nice and normal and share my love for this genre. It makes me feel less evil to be so into such terrible stories. Wait. Your cousin is nice and normal, isn't she?"

To be honest, he'd always kind of thought that Jessie's love of true crime showed the evil side to her, but he probably shouldn't say that out loud.

"I guess that depends what you're comparing 'nice and normal' against," he said.

Nik laughed.

"Well, you and your sister both seem . . ." She looked sideways at him. "Nah, I take that back. Your sister seems nice and normal, maybe. You, I don't know."

He shook his head.

"See, this is what happens when you go out of your way to help people—they spend the whole time insulting you."

Nik patted him on the thigh. He wished she would leave her hand there, but no luck.

"But seriously," she asked, "did you have to go far out of your way to come help? Where do you live, anyway?"

He pretended he was checking to change lanes just to look over at her. He would have driven from clear across the city just to see the way she looked in that tank top.

"Atwater Village, not too far from here. But I was even closer, because I was at the Vons in Silver Lake when I got your text."

"Oh wow, Atwater Village is such a great neighborhood," she said. "How long have you lived there?"

Her hair was back in one big ponytail. His fingers ached to pull it out and run them through it.

"Let's see, it's the end of May? Almost six months. I bought it in January, which is a terrible time to move, especially with a brand-new job. But it was all kind of a fluke. I lucked into it. The seller had just gotten a new job on the East Coast and had to sell fast, so I got a good deal."

"Congratulations, that's fantastic," she said.

"I still can't believe I'm a homeowner." Sometimes when he looked at his house keys, it still blew him away that the place was all his. "It's tiny, but it works for me."

He pulled onto the freeway exit.

"Oh look, there's Courtney in my car," Nik said, gesturing to the car in front of them at the light.

"Have you been friends for a long time?" Carlos asked.

Nik nodded.

"We went to Stanford together. We lived next door to each other junior year. One night she got locked out and knocked on my door, and we've basically been friends ever since."

He and Courtney both turned to head up into the winding roads into the hills. He hoped that none of the cupcake boxes moved while they went around curves. As much as he'd teased both Nik and Courtney on the way here, he really did want the cupcakes to arrive looking perfect.

"Is that how you met Dana, too?"

She nodded.

"Yeah, but not in the dorms. I met Dana through a theater group on campus. One night, the director hit on Dana in a pretty gross way, and Courtney came with me to rescue Dana." She shook her head and laughed. "Long story short, that guy woke up the next morning with spray paint all over his beloved car. I'm not going to say how it happened, because no one ever found out. I'll just say that Courtney is a really good person to have on your side."

He'd be sure to keep that in mind. He loved his car too much not to.

"Did you move to L.A. together?"

She shook her head.

"No, Courtney moved here right after graduation and has been here ever since. I moved to New York after graduation, but I couldn't stay away from California too long."

He had always fantasized a little about moving to New York, but both the weather and the distance from his family had always held him back.

"Do you think you're going to stay here?" he asked.

One of her curls had escaped from her ponytail. She tucked it back in.

"Oh yeah. I've been in L.A. for six years, and it's home now. I can't imagine living anywhere else."

He nodded.

"Granted, I've lived in L.A. most of my life, but I agree. Also, how much farther?"

Nik looked at her phone for the directions.

"Only half a mile."

He grinned at her.

"How much do you think Courtney is freaking out now?"

Nik leaned back against her seat and considered.

"Well, she'll definitely be calmer now that we've got your help, but she's always hyped up before she does an event. She'll be in drill sergeant mode when we get out of the car; I'm going to prepare you for that now."

Just then, the GPS told them that their location was up ahead on the right. Courtney was already there. She jumped out of the car right when they pulled up and came straight over to his car, already talking.

"Listen to me very carefully. Do not take a single box out of this car without my supervision. Open the trunk and all of the doors, but don't touch anything yet. I'll go inside to see where we should unload, I'll be right back."

She pulled her apron off to reveal an identical clean apron underneath, flipped her head upside down and redid her ponytail, and walked up to the house. Carlos got out of the car and obediently opened his back two doors and the trunk. He and Nik leaned against the car, almost, but not quite, touching.

He looked down at her. That rogue curl had escaped her ponytail again. He couldn't resist tucking it back in. She smiled her thanks at him.

"Hey." She put her hand on his arm. "Thank you so much for helping us. We could have done this ourselves; it just would have been much more stressful for both of us, especially Courtney."

He slung his arm around her shoulders.

"Does this mean that I get free Cupcake Park cupcakes for life? Because I think that would be an appropriate token of gratitude."

Nik relaxed against him.

"I don't know about for life, but I'm pretty sure you're going to get quite a few free cupcakes out of this. Just make sure to say—"

Courtney came racing out of the door, flanked by two waiters.

"We have reinforcements! Okay, everyone. I'm going to hand the boxes out of the cars to each of you, and we'll all walk inside carrying a box and put them on the designated table in the kitchen. Nik and Carlos, follow Andre and Kevin here once you have your cupcakes. We'll do this until we get them all unloaded."

* * * * * * *

As the five of them went back and forth from the cars to the kitchen, Nik shook her head at herself. Most people who had the hots for the sexy doctor nearby would ask him to get a drink, or would text him increasingly suggestive jokes until he got the hint, or would "injure" themselves and call him in a panic, preferably while wearing a casually elegant sundress and a sexy bra. No, she'd asked him to come help her and her panicked friend drive dozens of cupcakes up into the hills and then carry them as gently as they would bombs about to detonate. And she was wearing an old tank top and torn jeans. And not the artfully torn kind.

Courtney owed her big for this one.

"Okay." Courtney glanced at the clock after the four of them had stacked all twenty boxes on the table. "I need to set up my trays and arrange the cupcakes, but I don't need help for that; I have plenty of time. Thanks to you two. You can go."

Nik turned to Carlos and hugged him.

"Thank you so much. Go and have your relaxing evening." She turned back to Courtney. "Where should I wait for you?"

Courtney looked at her like she was an idiot.

"You don't have to wait; you can go, too."

Nik returned her look.

"You don't have a car, remember? I have to drive you home."

Courtney pointed at Carlos.

"He can drive you home. I'll bring you back your car tomorrow. If you're waiting around for me, it'll stress me out."

Nik looked at Courtney. She saw the glimmer in Courtney's eyes. Ohhhhh. Courtney was trying to throw the two of them together. Nik looked away.

"I can drive you home, no problem," Carlos said.

Courtney looked victorious. No one ever called her subtle.

"Are you sure? I'm not really on your way, am I?" Nik asked

him. Why was she asking him that; what the hell was wrong with her? Just get in the damn sports car with the hot man, Nikole.

He shrugged.

"No, but you're not that far out of my way."

Courtney winked at her and turned to open the cupcake boxes.

"Thanks for your help, Carlos. Your next dozen cupcakes are on me."

"Are you sure she doesn't need us to stay and help?" Carlos asked as Nik got back into the passenger seat of his car.

Nik shook her head and put her seat belt on. Okay, this was it, right? She didn't remember how to do this kind of thing. She hadn't been at all interested in the past few guys she'd dated until well after they'd asked her out . . . and sometimes, not even then. Should she ask him if he wanted to get that drink after all, on her? Should she just invite him up to her apartment when they got to her place and pounce on him? Or should she just wait to see if he made a move?

"Oh, she definitely doesn't need us. Courtney is the ultimate micromanager when it comes to her cupcakes. She only let us carry the boxes tonight out of sheer necessity."

Carlos nodded and turned the car on.

"Well, she's done a great job so far doing it all herself," he said. "I get the impulse."

She could put her hand on his leg or something? Why was she so bad at this? She was usually *great* at flirting with men. Had she lost her mojo?

"I do, too, but I wish she had more reliable help. Thank goodness I live close by and could race down to the store today."

Carlos touched her hand.

"You're a good friend. She's lucky to have you."

Nik felt her cheeks get warm.

"Oh, well—"

His phone rang, and he pulled it out of his pocket.

"Oh shit. I'm going to have to take this. Sorry about that." He pulled over under a clump of trees and turned the car off.

"Hey," he answered the phone. "Is something wrong? What's your blood pressure?"

Really? His cousin, right now? She tried not to let out a frustrated sigh. She was pretty sure this meant the universe was against this whole rebound idea.

She sat there silently, trying not to listen. Which was impossible because he was two feet away from her. She pulled out her phone to text Dana so she wasn't too obviously eavesdropping.

Sitting here, next to Carlos, I think I've forgotten what to do with men, all I can talk about are cupcakes and I keep laughing too loud, help—erase erase erase erase. Just because he was facing out his window didn't mean he wouldn't turn around at any moment and be able to see everything she was typing.

"Don't give me this 'I just wanted to talk to my cousin' bullshit—you know I'm going to worry whenever you call me from here on out. And I already told you that engagement party was fun, and that I think two of Alexa's friends secretly have the hots for each other. Did you forget that phone call? Oh! I get it! You're bored stiff. You're used to talking to people at work all day and now you're stuck at home. I get it, bed rest would bore me to tears, too. We have to find more ways to entertain you. What about those books I got you?"

Carlos turned to her and smiled, and she smiled back. He reached up and tucked that annoying curl that kept falling out of her ponytail behind her ear. God, she loved it when he touched her like that.

He moved his hand down from her head to her shoulder. His fingers moved gently, up and down her bare shoulder. She sighed.

Suddenly he let out a bark of laughter. It made her want to laugh along with it.

"You've read how many?" He looked down at Nik with a huge smile on his face. "Which was your favorite?"

Oh good, she could stop pretending she wasn't listening.

"You loved them all?" He held eye contact with Nik, and his smile got even bigger. She could feel a matching smile spread across her own face. "I'll be sure to tell my friend who recommended them how you felt about them.

"I guess I'd better buy you some more. In the meantime, I've heard there's this thing called Netflix. You should look into it."

He kept smiling at Nik. It took all she could to resist leaning against him. His eyes crinkled with the laughter she could tell he was holding in.

"As a matter of fact, people *do* tell me that I'm funny. I'll bring more books on Saturday, okay?"

He hung up the phone and tucked it back into his pocket. He pushed his hand through his hair and smiled at her.

"As you heard, Jessie loved the books."

She bit her bottom lip. Good Lord, this man was more attractive by the second.

"I'm glad." She leaned toward him and willed him to start playing with her hair again.

A car shot past them on its way up the hill, and they moved away from each other.

"We should get you home."

He turned the key and gunned the motor to get them back onto the roadway. The engine sputtered and stopped.

"Uh-oh." Carlos turned the key again, and nothing happened. "Shit."

"Did you run out of gas?" she asked him.

"What? No, that's impossible. I never run out of gas. I went to the gas station tonight, right after I went to the grocery store . . ." He trailed off, then looked at her in horror. "I didn't go to the grocery store. I didn't go to the gas station! I was on my way to the grocery store when I got your text. Shit. I did run out of gas."

She patted him on the shoulder.

"It's okay; it's no big deal. We can call Triple A. You do have Triple A, right?"

He nodded, but made no move toward his phone or wallet.

"I never run out of gas! I can't believe I let this happen to my car. I never even get down below a quarter tank, but this week has been so busy and I let it go way longer than usual."

Nik narrowed her eyes at his steering wheel.

"Didn't you notice your gas light go on?"

He refused to make eye contact.

"The thing is . . . I always keep my gas tank at least a quarter full, so the gas light in this car has never gone on before. So . . . yes, it went on, but I was preoccupied, and I'd never seen it before so I didn't . . ." She held her laughter in so well, even when he finally turned to look at her, but something in her eyes must have betrayed her. He frowned at her. "The gas light in this car is in a weird place, okay? Are you laughing at me?"

She shook her head and rubbed her hand up and down his arm.

"No, I'm not laughing at you. I'm desperately trying not to laugh at you, here."

She knew how touchy men were about their cars. He would probably get mad at her for that, but she couldn't help making fun of him.

But he grinned at her.

"Okay, fine, I will admit that this is a little funny." He put his arm around her shoulders and lowered his voice. "You have to promise to never tell anyone about this, though. I have a reputation to uphold."

She nodded and turned so her lips were almost touching his ear.

"Cross my heart; it's our secret. Just one question: do you think you maybe want to call Triple A to get us out of here?"

He pulled his wallet and phone both out of his pocket.

"Right, of course."

He made a face at her when he got off the phone.

"They're on their way, but it'll be a while. Apparently, 'out of gas in a safe spot in the hills' is low priority."

Nik took off her seatbelt and leaned toward him.

"We might as well get comfortable while we wait for them." She looked around the car. "How long have you had this car, anyway?"

He closed his eyes for a moment before answering her.

"Almost five years."

His car had confused her, ever since she'd gotten to know him a little bit. He didn't seem like the kind of guy to be obsessed with his bright red sports car, but from his reaction when the car had run out of gas, that seemed like exactly what he was. Granted, people in L.A. tended to care about their cars more than anywhere else she'd ever been, so maybe it was just that.

"Why did you buy it?" she asked. "A celebration of a new job or something?"

He shook his head, but didn't say anything. He ran his fingers down the steering wheel. The silence went on so long that she didn't think he was going to answer her at all. She opened her mouth to ask him another question when he finally spoke.

"My dad died. Almost five years ago, my dad died."

Oh God. Leave it to her to ask the asshole question.

"Oh Carlos, I'm so sorry. You don't have to . . ."

He shook his head and kept talking.

"My parents didn't have lots of money—they always managed to give us all of the important stuff, but they were both school teachers for thirty years; they were never flush. But it turned out that he had a ton of life insurance. Some in my mom's name, of course. But some in mine, and some in my sister's. After he died and I got this enormous—to me, at least—check . . ." He paused for a second before continuing. "Well, I didn't know what to do with it. I deposited it in my savings account, and just let it sit there for a while. I was going to use it to pay off some of my med school loans. I probably *should* have used it to pay off some of my med school loans. But then one day, I took a different way home from work. I saw the sun gleaming off of a bright red sports car with a big price tag on the windshield. I turned straight into the lot and bought that car an hour later. My dad always liked flashy things. Sometimes I feel like that was a stupid way to use his legacy, but . . . I think he'd like this car a lot."

She pulled him into a hug. His head dropped down on her shoulder, and they sat there together for a few minutes, breathing with each other.

"Thanks for telling me," she said.

"Thanks for listening," he said.

His hands moved up and down her back, and then gently through her hair.

She turned her head and kissed his jaw. His cheek.

He pulled back to look at her. She looked back at him: his kind big dark-brown eyes; his thick almost-black hair that she was dying to touch; his warm skin, with stubble already visible along his jawline; that hint of a dimple in his cheek; his lips, a dusky pink, not quite smiling, but looking like they would smile at any minute.

He lifted his hand from her shoulder and stroked her cheek, and she smiled.

He slid his hand around to the back of her neck and pulled her toward him. And finally, *finally*, he kissed her. Soft, at first. Not tentative, but slow. Gentle. Tender. She hadn't realized just how much she'd wanted him to kiss her until just this moment. She kissed him back the same way, happy to let him take the lead, as long as he stayed here in this car and kept kissing her.

Her hands went up into his hair, that hair she'd been wanting to touch for so long, and she sighed with some combination of relief and lust.

That sigh seemed to signal something to him. He pulled her tighter against him, and his hand ran down the side of her body. His lips, his tongue, got stronger, and she met his urgency with her own. He pulled away, and she almost moaned in frustration, but then he trailed his mouth down her neck, kissing and biting and kissing again, until her hands gripped his hair and she gasped.

He raised his head.

"You liked that?" he asked, as he nuzzled her ear.

"God, yes," she said.

"That's what I was hoping," he said. She turned her head and kissed him again.

"I've been wanting to do this ever since I met you," he said.

"Oh my God, me, too," she said. She didn't realize how true that was until she said it out loud.

They looked at each other and laughed. He brushed her hair back from her face and smiled at her. That same smile that had made her trust him at Dodger Stadium. She pulled his face to hers and kissed him again and again.

She started to pull away to say something witty, but he ran his tongue around her lips, so she had no choice but to open them and meet his tongue with her own. His hands kept moving, this time up and down her torso. He lingered beneath her breasts and then started making long, slow, circles around them that got progressively smaller and smaller.

"I like that, too," she said, breathing hard.

"Good. I hoped you did. Because I really like doing it," he said as he reached her hard nipples. He leaned forward to keep kissing her as he touched them. Why had she held off kissing this man for so long?

"Are we . . ." He touched her in a way that made her gasp and lose her train of thought for a second. "Are we going to get in trouble if someone finds us like this? We are up in the hills, after all. I don't know if a lot of people who look like us live up here."

He pulled back, but his hands lingered on her breasts.

"You're right. I definitely don't want some rich dude who lives up here to call the cops on us. I haven't made out in a car since . . . my God, since I was in high school, I think." His hands slid down to her thighs. "The problem is, and the thing that I'd forgotten is . . . making out in cars is really hot."

She glanced down and saw the clear evidence of how turned on he was.

"Mmmm, it is, isn't it?" She put her hand on his knee. "Do you know that this is the first time I've ever made out like this in a car?" He watched her fingers trail up and down his thighs, never getting quite where she knew he wanted them to be.

"Never? How is that possible?" he asked, not raising his eyes.

"I have no idea, but I was clearly missing out." Her fingers did little loops on the insides of his thighs, and he let out a breath.

"Uh-huh. Is your first time everything you wanted it to be?" He raised his eyes to hers.

"Everything and more." She leaned forward to kiss him and to move her hand higher.

HONNNNNNNNK.

They sprang apart and looked up at the mechanic's truck parked in front of them. Carlos's cheeks got red and he bent down to reach for his wallet.

"You the one who called about running out of gas?" The guy was at the window, a leer on his face that Nik wanted to smack off of it. Maybe after a few more self-defense classes she could.

"That's me." Carlos got out of the car and handed him his driver's license and AAA card.

Nik looked out the car window without seeing a thing. Holy shit, this really seemed to be happening. Was she sure she wanted to do this? She'd *felt* sure while Carlos was kissing her. But she still felt hesitant. Something about Carlos seemed different than the guys she usually went out with. She didn't know if it was different good or different bad. The uncertainty made her nervous.

After far too much chatting, the mechanic poured a gallon of gas into Carlos's tank and gave him a screen to sign. He winked at her before he got back in his van. She rolled her eyes.

"Oh my God." Carlos got back in the car and shook his head. "I haven't gotten caught in a car making out with a girl since I was seventeen. And then it wasn't even my car! I'm twice that age now; at least the car is a lot better." He wrapped his arms around her. "And the girl is, too."

Okay, hearing that was almost worth getting checked out by the mechanic. She lifted her face to him, and he kissed her hard.

Chapter Nine

Carlos stopped at the gas station at the bottom of the hill.

"I should fill up here, even though it's like twenty cents more expensive than it is near my house." He leaned over to kiss her. Now that he'd started kissing her, he couldn't stop. She kissed him back so hard it was a struggle for him to pull away and get out of the car.

Had he made it weird when he brought up his dad to Nik? Did she think his reason for getting the car was stupid? Some people had, which is why he never told people the real reason anymore. He just let them think he was one of those L.A. dudes who liked sports cars. He didn't know why he'd told her.

When he got back in the car, they grinned at each other and both leaned in for another kiss. He felt like a horny teenager. He loved it.

Finally he turned the key and pulled out of the gas station. Within seconds, they were both singing along to Beyoncé as they shot down the freeway. She smiled at him as she sang along, and he sent silent thanks to Courtney's flaky employee, her broken down car, and the entire concept of running out of gas for getting him here.

A few songs later, and they'd pulled up in front of her apartment. She ran her hand from his knee up his thigh and smiled at him.

"Are you going to come inside?"

He tried not to grin as big as he wanted to, but he was pretty sure he failed. His terrible day had officially turned around. He couldn't wait to pounce on her as soon as they walked into her apartment.

As she unlocked the door to her building, he thought of something.

"Did you get your locks changed?"

Fuck. Why did he ask her that? She'd snapped at him once for bringing that up. What was wrong with him?

She held up a brand-new key.

"Last week. I felt stupid for doing it, but then I remembered what you said about how feeling silly is better than the alternative."

Oh thank God, she wasn't mad at him.

As they walked up the stairs to her apartment, she smiled wryly.

"I also convinced Courtney and Dana to take a self-defense class with me. Well, it's really more of a boxing class, actually."

Well, he hadn't expected that.

"Wow, that's great. How was it?"

She stopped at her front door to unlock it with the new key.

"It was surprisingly fun. There's only been one so far, but I'm happy I'm taking it."

"That's awesome. I'm impressed."

He was also glad that she'd trusted him enough to tell him she was doing it. And flattered that she'd gotten her locks changed at least in part because of something he'd said.

When they walked into her apartment, he was ready to throw her down on the couch, but she walked into the kitchen before he could reach for her.

"Do you want some wine?" she asked him.

Hmmm. He couldn't be wrong about why he was in her apartment, could he? He had been here before, and nothing had happened then.

No, this was different. She'd seemed like she'd wanted to pull his clothes off in the car. Maybe she was just nervous now that they were back at her apartment? He wasn't sure what was going on, but he'd better take her lead on this.

"Sure." He sat down on the couch. "More of that rosé, maybe?"

She laughed and opened the refrigerator.

"I *think* you're making fun of me and my rosé, but I don't even care, because I love it. As a matter of fact, yes, I do have another bottle of rosé open now—though this time it's a different one—and I'm going to pour us both glasses of it, take that."

She came over to the couch with glasses of wine for each of them. Okay, she sat down right next to him; she was clearly not keeping her distance. He put his arm around her and pulled her close.

"I have to confess I have been known to make fun of my sister for her love of this wine, and it kills me that I actually liked the one you gave me last time because now I might have to eat my words to Angie." He took a sip. "Actually no, there's no way I'd do that. But this is terrible—I definitely like this wine."

He let his fingers drift into her hair, and she relaxed against him.

"Oh no, you've discovered a kind of *wine* that you like, and it happens to be *pink* wine. What will you ever do with yourself?" She swatted his thigh. And then left her hand there. "You can't possibly let a *woman* know that she was right about wine; that's impossible."

He shook his head. He finally pulled that ponytail holder out of her hair and let her curls spring free.

"No, that's not it. I'm happy to let women know they're right about many things. My boss was right about the diagnosis of the kid I saw today. You were right about the books I bought for Jessie. Jessie was right when she told me I'd get into med school. It's just that I can't ever admit to my *little sister* that she was right about something I've been teasing her about for years. Come on now."

"Mmmm." She looked up at him. "I'm an only child; it's possible that I don't get all of the big brother–little sister relationship nuances, so I'll that one go." She rested her head on his shoulder. "Oh! What did Jessie say her favorite of the books was?"

He was trying to concentrate on what she was saying, but between her fingers gently massaging his knee and feeling her sigh as he stroked her hair, his mind was in many places.

"Um, what did she say? Oh! She said her favorite was the Jeffrey Dahmer book. I don't understand either of you. If I read those books, I would have nightmares for weeks."

She set her glass, still half full, on the coffee table.

"People have said that to me. Maybe I just don't have very vivid dreams." She brought her hand up and drew it through his hair. She plucked his glass out of his hand and put it on the coffee table next to her own. "Or maybe I just dream about other things."

He smiled. The preamble was apparently over. He turned to face her and pressed her down onto the couch until she was underneath him.

"Yeah? What is it that you dream about?"

She grabbed the bottom of his button-down shirt and pulled it over his head.

"This." She pulled him against her and kissed him.

Mother of God. He thought he liked kissing her when they were making out in the front seat of his car, but that was clearly only an appetizer. There, she'd seemed enthused, but still tentative. Now, she was both passionate and forceful, as if to make it clear she was all in. Her hands moved under his T-shirt and up and down his back, pressing him harder against her. He moved his attention to her neck, kissing her smooth brown skin.

"Do you dream about that, too?" he asked her.

"My God, yes," she said.

He blew gently over her skin and kissed the cool spot. He did it again lower, and then again lower. He loved the way her fingers tensed on his back. He drew his hand up and plucked her nipple. She arched her back and moaned. He kept kissing her neck and playing with her nipples until he thought both of them were going to explode.

"We both have way too many clothes on." He pulled her tank top off, to reveal her black lace bra underneath. "Mmmm, this is a very pretty bra. But right now, it's in my way." He reached around and unsnapped her bra and tossed it over the couch. He sat back to admire her.

"That's better."

She shook her head.

"You said we both had too many clothes on, but I didn't see you take any off."

The woman had a point.

He stood up, tugged his pants off, pulled his T-shirt over his head, and stood in front of her in his boxer briefs.

"Is *that* better?"

She smiled and nodded, her eyes roaming all over his body, but coming back to focus somewhere right around his waistband.

"Much better."

She didn't bother to get up, but pulled her jeans off and threw them on the floor next to his clothes. He took a long look at her curvy body. Holy shit. He climbed back on top of her.

* * * * * * *

Oh thank Athena, Aphrodite, and all the other gods for the many crises tonight that had resulted in Carlos in her bed. Okay, it was her couch, but this wasn't the time for details. She was very glad she'd gotten over her weird—and stupid, in retrospect, now that she'd seen him without clothes on—anxiety about this guy. The way that he looked at her body . . . well, that kind of look was exactly what she needed after this past week and a half. He looked at her like her body was a joy to behold, like he couldn't wait to touch her, kiss her, like he was lucky to be here with her without any clothes on. Damn right he was.

She was feeling pretty fucking lucky herself right now. This man definitely knew how to touch a woman, that's for sure.

"We need to get these off of you," he said, caressing her sensible black cotton underwear. She'd had no idea she was going to be having sex later when she'd left the house that day, okay? At least they were bikini cut. She lifted her hips to give him better access.

He shook his head.

"No, not that way." He got up off the couch, pushed her coffee table back out of his way, and turned her around until she was sitting forward. "Okay, now." He hooked his fingers in her underwear and pulled them to the floor. Then he pushed her legs apart and knelt at her feet.

"Mmmm." He stared straight in front of him with a hungry look on his face. "That's even better." He reached back and pulled her toward him. Well, maybe he tried to pull, but she was so eager for what she knew was coming that she fairly launched herself at him.

Good *Lord*. She lay back on her couch pillows, gasping for air. She thought she liked it when he kissed her mouth, that was nothing to what those lips and that tongue—dear God, that tongue—could do to other parts of her body. It felt so good she wanted it to go on forever. She thought there was no way for it to get any better. And then he added his fingers to his lips and his tongue, and she came so hard she saw black spots floating in front of her eyes.

"Holy shit," she said as soon as she could talk. And then she did something she'd never done after an orgasm before: she started giggling uncontrollably.

"What's so funny?" He sat back up on the couch, and she leaned against him until they were laying down again, her tucked into the curve of his arm.

"Nothing," she choked out. "This was just not at all how I expected my day to go. I didn't even . . ." she tried to catch her breath. "I didn't even have my good underwear on!"

He glanced at the clothes littered across the floor, then back at her.

"Who cares about what kind of underwear you had on when you have that body underneath it?" He ran his hand down her torso, the side of her hip, her thigh. Something inside of her melted.

"You jackass."

"What?" He froze. "What did I say?"

She shook her head.

"You can't say shit like that when my condoms are all so far away in my bedroom. Because now I want you to fuck me right this second."

He jumped into a runner's stance.

"Where are they? I can run fast. Especially when I'm motivated."

"Top drawer of the nightstand. Go."

She relaxed back on the couch and laughed as he raced to her bedroom. She could feel the shit-eating grin on her face. Ahhhhh, that butt in motion was fantastic.

He was back in less than thirty seconds, true to his boasting. He dropped his boxer briefs to the floor and ripped open the condom packet. Thank God enough lights were on in her living room so she could see he really was as big as she'd thought he was. Sometimes touch could be deceiving, especially with layers of clothes in between, but boy was this not one of those times.

He was back on the couch and on top of her as soon as he'd rolled the condom on. She wrapped one leg around him to bring him in closer, and he groaned in her ear and moved faster. So she did it with the other leg and he bit down on her shoulder.

He took her hands and moved them to the arm of the couch behind her.

"Hold on."

She obeyed him and was glad she did. She held on for dear life and met him thrust for thrust as he pounded into her, faster and faster, until he finally roared and collapsed against her.

He lifted himself up a little while later and kissed her cheek.

"I'm never going to make fun of rosé again if that's the result." He stood up and went over to the kitchen to throw out the condom. "Pink wine, man. Who would have thought?"

She laughed and curled up in the corner of the couch.

"There's more in the fridge." She pulled the blanket that hung on the back of the couch over herself.

He opened the fridge and took out the bottle.

"Look, lady. Some of us need a little bit of a break before we have more *rosé*, okay? Let a man breathe for a minute."

Oh, she would let him breathe as long as he wanted if he did it with that grin on his face and that swagger in his walk.

"I'm just glad I introduced you to the glory that is rosé, that's all. You take your time. I don't want to rush you."

He topped up both of their glasses and carefully pushed the coffee table back to its normal spot before getting under the blanket with her.

"You know what would look great on that table?" he asked her, nodding at her coffee table.

"What?" She stared at the table, trying to figure out what he meant. It was just a chestnut wood coffee table, nothing fancy, but the perfect height for propping her feet up to watch TV. What did he think would look good on it, coasters or coffee table books or something?

"A large pizza. With everything. That much rosé makes me hungry."

She shook her head.

"Not everything. No blue cheese or olives. Everything other than that."

He reached down to the floor for his pants and pulled his phone out of the pocket.

"I can live with that. Large pizza with almost everything coming up."

He called some pizza place she'd never heard of and ordered a monstrosity of a pizza. As soon as he listed the toppings on the phone, her stomach rumbled. Apparently, that much . . . *rosé* . . . made her hungry, too. Well, that, and she hadn't eaten since lunchtime.

* * * * * * *

"I've never ordered from this place before, but this sausage is great," she said as she picked up her second piece. Carlos was already on his third.

"Look," he said, when his mouth was no longer full. "You don't know me that well yet, but one thing you should know is I'm very good at ordering food. I know you didn't trust that this pizza was going to be good. I could see it in your eyes when I ordered. I'm not even going to make you admit that you were wrong, because that's the kind of guy I am. But that should be the last time you ever doubt me on food matters."

She reached for her wineglass to wash down the delicious grease.

"Noted. Does that mean you're a good cook, too?"

He shrugged, but that cocky grin was still on his face.

"I mean, yes, I'm a fantastic cook, but I try not to brag about it." His grin widened and she laughed. "I don't do enough cooking these days, though, what with work and everything else."

"How did you learn to cook?" she asked.

He took another bite of pizza.

"Originally, from my mom. She taught both me and my sister all of her specialties, and then I taught myself how to cook other stuff. First, when I was a poor student, and then when I realized that cooking was meditative for me, a way to relax and take a break and be alone with my thoughts."

He shook his head and was silent for a moment.

"In med school I used to make huge pots of chili for my roommates, and we would all eat it for a week. My buddy Drew and I met when we were in this fellowship together. It was so stressful and exhausting. We both happened to have the same day off one week, so I invited him over to eat enchiladas and watch the game. We were so tired that we both fell asleep on the couch after we ate and woke up just as the game was ending." He laughed. "We've been friends ever since."

She laughed, too. She and her friends had bonded over revenge; he and his friend had bonded over food and a nap. That sounded about right.

Speaking of sleep . . .

"Hey, what time is it?" she asked him.

He checked his phone, on the coffee table along with the now almost empty pizza box and wine.

"Ten thirty." He put his wineglass down. "I hadn't realized it was so late. I'd better be going."

"Oh." She put hers down, too. "Oh, okay. You probably have to get up early, I guess."

He stopped halfway through standing up and sat back down.

"Didn't you . . ." He paused for a few seconds, shrugged, and continued. "Just to be clear—do you want me to go? Because if you do, it's no problem, but if not, I'm happy to stay."

"No!" She shook her head and put her hand on his knee. "I mean, no, you don't have to go. Sorry, that must have sounded like a hint, that's not what I meant. I was just thinking it was about time we left the couch. We haven't even made it into my bedroom yet, and we finished the bottle of rosé, so . . ."

He took her hands and pulled her up off of the couch with him. "Lead the way."

Chapter Ten

Nik woke up the next morning significantly later than she usually did. As a writer who worked from home, she generally had to keep herself on a pretty strict schedule or she would get nothing done. She almost always forced herself to keep to that schedule, even though everyone she knew—including Fisher—had made fun of her about how rigid she was about it.

But when you woke up in the wee hours of the morning because a big, warm, strong man was kissing you awake, and then you spent the next hour doing delicious things with him in your bed before he had to leave to get to work on time, it was only natural that you'd fall back asleep and not wake up until . . . holy shit, it was nine thirty.

She stretched luxuriously in her big empty bed and smiled at her rumpled sheets. She felt like the queen of the world. She liked this feeling.

She stumbled into the kitchen, naked and pleasantly sore. She'd forgotten to set up her coffee maker the night before—she had been a little distracted, okay?—so she tossed out yesterday's coffee filter and turned her coffee grinder on. She hummed as she scooped coffee into the machine, measured out the water, and got her favorite coffee cup down from the cabinet. While the coffee brewed, she went back to her bedroom for her robe. Not that she minded being naked, but she'd left the windows open overnight, and the morning air was chilly.

Would she see Carlos again? He didn't seem the type to sleep with her and then disappear, but you never knew with men. She hoped she'd see him again, though. The sex was fantastic, and he made her laugh. That was a pretty rare combination in her experience.

She sat down on her couch with her coffee and dug into her bag for her phone to check her email. She took one sip and laughed at herself. Check her email, what was she thinking? If she knew her friends, and she did, she would have many text messages to respond to first.

Sure enough, Courtney had texted her and Dana early this morning.

Nik, I have your car, let me know if I can come pick you up this afternoon and get it back to you. Also DID YOU BANG CARLOS I AM BETTING THE ANSWER IS YES BUT I NEED TO KNOW IMMEDIATELY.

Then Dana:

Wait, what? I thought she was still being all wishy washy about it? What happened? I need details, how did I miss this?

Courtney filled Dana in, Dana responded with many exclamation points, the two of them had a nice long chat about her long before she was awake.

Good morning, friends. I'm around anytime today for a car exchange. Also, yes.

She couldn't resist teasing them a little.

She hummed as she checked her email. Okay good, she'd gotten the go-ahead from the studio to do a profile of the up-and-coming black female director, her piece on that school teacher in Fresno who had taken in ten of his students as foster kids was going to run in the *Times* Sunday magazine in a few weeks, and the editor she hated working with was resigning and moving to New York for a magazine she also hated. What an excellent morning.

Yes? YES??? We get a hell of a lot more than fucking yes.

She laughed out loud at Courtney's text.

Nik will give us the details as soon as she wants to give us the details.

Dana was always the nice one.

However. She had better want to give us the details within the next two minutes, or I'm never going to let her borrow my shoes again.

Not that nice. She'd better respond.

I don't know why Courtney even asked the question, she orchestrated the whole thing! Don't worry, you'll get all the details tonight after class. Long story short: it was excellent, you both were right, he left a few hours ago, and I'm exhausted and very smug. I probably won't get any work done this morning but I don't care. I have no idea if I'll ever see him again but it was still worth it. Happy?

She went to the kitchen for a refill on the coffee and heard numerous texts come in as she poured it.

From Dana: We have to go through an hour and a half class with you doing your "I Just Had Sex" face before we hear the details? I'm going to kill you.

From Courtney: Yesssssssssss. I think this is worth skipping class for, don't you??? Wasn't one class enough?

From Dana: No, we have to go, we already paid for the whole six weeks.

From Courtney: I hate you so much. Can't we get the dish before class, then?

From Dana: I'm filming all afternoon and I won't allow you to hear about this before I do.

From Courtney: Ugh fine fine, that's a legit excuse, but still, I'm dying over here. And N: I would bet you're going to see him again.

And, right as she read that one, another text jumped onto her screen:

I hope you got back to sleep this morning after I left. You going out of town for Memorial Day weekend, or are you free Friday night?

She took another sip of coffee with a big grin on her face and texted her girlfriends.

Apparently you'd win that bet. See you both tonight. She set her mug down on the coffee table, stood up, and danced in her living room for a full minute before texting Carlos back.

Friday night works for me!

Wait, no. Right before she pressed send, she deleted the exclamation point. She was all for being straightforward and not playing games with guys, but he didn't need to know a text from him literally made her dance.

She also didn't need to tell her friends how right they were that a rebound had been exactly what she needed. They would be sure to tell her that themselves.

When Nik walked into class that night, Courtney and Dana were both already there. And both glaring at her.

"I texted that I got out of work early and we could meet up before class. Why didn't you answer?" Dana whispered.

Oops. She'd put her phone in lockdown mode this afternoon to get work done and had forgotten to take it off. She had gotten a ton of work done, so that was a positive. A negative was that her friends were going to kill her.

"Sorry, I was working, and my phone was off," she said. Their expressions did not change. She couldn't help but laugh, which just made them glare all the more. "Okay, I will tell you one small detail to get you even more excited for the full story: we didn't even make it out of his car before we started kissing."

Dana high-fived her.

"I'm still mad at you, but also, I'm thrilled at how unlike you that is."

Dana was wearing a very cute hot pink sports bra, and that brand of workout leggings that looked amazing on tall, willowy people like her, but terrible on anyone else. Nik looked down at her own old Stanford T-shirt and comfortable yoga pants and sighed. She'd been paranoid for years after moving to L.A. that Dana would decide to ditch her and Courtney for other actress/model types. There was something about being in this city, where looks were so important, that made you doubt everything you'd been confident about, including your friends. Dana had never wavered, though. Now Nik was ashamed that she'd ever doubted her.

"Hi, class!" Natalie said. They all immediately switched their attention to the front of the room. Today her hair was up in an impossibly high topknot.

"I'm super excited about our class today! Today you all get to use . . . punching bags!"

The whole class applauded, even though the punching bags had been already hanging up throughout the room when they walked in, so it was kind of self-evident they were going to use punching bags today.

Carlos had seemed so surprised and pleased when she'd told him about this class. He was always cracking jokes, so she'd steeled herself for him to make fun of it, but he seemed almost proud of her.

"Remember, punching bags are pretty big and heavy, so you're really going to feel it when you punch them. But before we get to the bags, let's go over the form lessons we learned last week. Did you all practice like I told you to?"

There was faint applause from the class. Nik had definitely intended to practice. She'd gone home all hyped up and ready for it, and she'd thrown a few punches at imaginary people in her apartment that night. But then, she got sore. And busy. And after a few days of not practicing, the idea of practicing sounded intimidating, and it sounded much easier to not practice, so that's what she did.

Dana was clapping with energy, though. Overachiever. She'd probably practiced every day.

"Not as many as I hoped, but that's okay. Practicing by yourself can get a little scary, right? Don't worry, we'll get you guys over that hump today." "Stronger" by Britney Spears blared out through the speakers. This woman was magic with the music. "Now, watch me." She stood in the stance she'd taught them the week before and did a fierce one-two punch at the air. "Remember, that's a jab. Now you guys do it. Make sure you're a good distance away from each other, and I'll walk around the room and check in on you."

Nik imitated her and punched the air. OW. All of those hours of athletic sex made turning that way pretty painful. She wouldn't give up a second of it, though. She grinned, stretched, and punched the air again.

"Good job, Nik!" Natalie was suddenly behind her. "Remember, elbows in and keep those feet planted, okay? You've got some real power behind that punch—keep it up!"

Why did she usually hate people who spoke like cheerleaders, but somehow when Natalie did it, it actually did inspire her to keep it up? Maybe because it actually seemed sincere coming from her.

"Excellent, Dana. I can tell how much you've been practicing. Keep that thumb secure. Great work!"

Nik turned around to make fun of Dana for being the teacher's pet, but Dana was beaming so hard she didn't have the heart to do it.

"Other side!" Natalie shouted to the class. They all turned and kept going as she finished her loop around the room.

"Okay, everyone! Great job. Now you all get boxing gloves. And look, I know that in a real situation you're not going to be able to pull out your boxing gloves before you can defend yourself or a loved one. But we have to protect ourselves as we learn how to do this, don't we? You learn how to punch these punching bags hard with these gloves on, and you'll be able to break a man's jaw with your bare fist. I guarantee it."

Ahh yes, that's the other reason she didn't mind Natalie's sugar-sweet attitude. Because every so often, she could see the cyanide hidden in there.

Natalie walked them through wrapping their hands with tape and putting on gloves. Nik held her fists up in the air. She nodded at them with a triumphant smile. Her whole body felt stronger, just with these on.

There were two rows of punching bags hanging in the room, one on each side. She, Dana, and Courtney were all in a line.

"Okay, great! Everyone is ready. Now, remember everything I told you, remember your form, and start punching!"

Nik stood back, paid attention to her form, and sent her fist flying into the punching bag.

Holy shit. Natalie wasn't kidding. That thing was like a brick wall. But it was pretty satisfying to see it swing from her jab. She threw another punch.

After a few minutes, Natalie was at her side.

"Nik! You're doing so, so great today—just look at you."

She grunted, tried to make her form perfect, and punched again.

"Oh, that was a good one. Excellent job. One question: why did you sign up for this class?"

Nik looked at the punching bag instead of at Natalie.

"Eh, I thought it would be fun to come with my girlfriends, you know."

Natalie patted her on the shoulder and smiled.

"Of course! Okay. Now tell me the real reason."

Nik turned to look at her, and Natalie was smiling back, as bright as could be. Nik sighed.

"My ex-boyfriend was a real asshole." She realized that could describe more than one person. "Actually, too many of my ex-boyfriends are assholes."

"You aren't alone there!" Natalie stood behind the punching bag and held it still. "Okay, now picture their faces on this punching bag. And then punch the hell out of it."

Nik took a step backward, stared at the bag, and let her fist fly. It felt great.

"Fantastic!" Natalie said.

Nik grinned.

"That was fantastic, wasn't it?"

By the time they made it to the bar after class, all three of them were high on pure adrenaline.

"Did you see me punch that bag?" Courtney asked the other two. "By the time we're done with this class, I'm going to have it flying across the room. I promise you."

"I'm going to be so fucking sore tomorrow, and I don't even care." Nik made a fist and flexed her just visible muscles. "My biceps hurt right this second, and I'm not even mad about it. That was awesome."

Dana said nothing; she just beamed at the damp table.

Pete dropped their drinks off at the table, and they all thanked him.

"Now do I get to say 'I told you so' about this class? Aren't you guys glad you did it with me?" Nik asked them.

"I am *very* glad we did it with you," Dana said.

Courtney shook her head.

"Sure, fine, the class is better than we thought, but Dana and I have a much bigger 'I told you so' coming up."

She'd walked right into that one, hadn't she?

"What did we sayyyyy?" Courtney said to Dana, her hand raised high in the air. Dana high-fived her, with a small, but just as smug, smile on her face. "We told you that you needed a rebound, didn't we? I can't believe we've waited this long. Tell us everything."

Nik couldn't keep the smile off her face as she told them the story—or most of it, at least.

"Thank God we convinced you to get over that whole bias against doctors thing," Dana said.

"Oh, I still don't like doctors, but in the end I couldn't help myself," she said.

The three of them all laughed.

"Wait." Nik had a terrible thought. "What if Carlos doesn't realize that this is just a rebound? What if he's a serious relationship kind of guy? I don't want to accidentally get into another Fisher situation."

"Oh, come on." Courtney laughed. "This is Los Angeles. There is no such thing as a 'serious relationship kind of guy' in this city. You don't know this because you aren't looking for one, but I promise you, men like that don't exist here."

Nik shook her head and drained her drink.

"That can't be true. Remember all of those cozy little couples holding hands at brunch last time we went? Also, one of the supposedly mythical serious relationship Los Angeles men *just* proposed to me, remember?"

Courtney rolled her eyes.

"Fisher doesn't count. Everything about that proposal was fucked up. And all of the couples we saw having brunch were there after their third successful date, but they'll move on to someone else within three weeks to three months, maximum. Serious couples don't go to brunch; they stay home and cook for each other. Everyone knows that."

Courtney liked making bold pronouncements about what "everyone knew," most of which just made Nik laugh. But this time . . . Nik's mind flashed back to some cozy brunches she'd made for Justin. She gratefully took her new drink from Pete.

"Okay, but what about all of the married people? You're not going to claim that there are no married people in all of Los Angeles, are you?"

Courtney sat up straight and winced.

"I think I'm already sore from that damn class. Yes, of course there are married people in L.A. People arrive in L.A. in serious relationships or already married, that's the only way it happens. No one meets a spouse in L.A., except for celebrities, and those relationships are all fake, anyway."

Dana, who had been rolling her eyes throughout all of Courtney's decrees, nodded.

"Our cynical friend over here is wrong about everything except that last thing. Celebrity relationships are all fake."

Nik narrowed her eyes at Dana.

"Wait, you can't mean *all* celebrity relationships. Even I know in my heart that John and Chrissy—"

"Back to Carlos," Courtney said. "I knew he was worthy. You told me how much he liked the spicy cupcake. And I believe we all remember that Fisher did not."

All three of them nodded.

"Excellent point." Nik waved at Pete and pointed at their drinks to request another round. "I feel like, in the future, all you need to say is 'Fisher liked that' to steer me away from someone, or 'Fisher didn't like that' to steer me toward them."

Pete put their drinks down on the table to a flurry of thank-yous.

"However." Nik took a sip of her gin and tonic and smiled. "I do have to thank Fisher for one thing: if he hadn't proposed to me at Dodger Stadium, I never would have met Carlos. And after last night, well, that would have been a real shame."

The three of them clinked glasses.

• • • • • • •

Carlos walked into his apartment on Thursday night with an enormous grin on his face. He should be exhausted, after getting barely any sleep at Nik's place last night, then racing home just to shower and change and head to an extra-long work day, but he didn't remember when he'd felt less tired. He was ready to go back to Nik's tonight to keep going. If only.

He was very glad he'd texted her this morning about Friday night. He'd almost waited, in the interest of being chill about everything, but then he remembered how much he'd hesitated to ask her out for drinks in the first place, and how ridiculous that felt now.

He walked into his kitchen to see what he could scrounge up for dinner. When his phone rang, he was certain for about a second it was Nik calling him. He glanced at the screen and shook his head at himself.

"Hey, Angie."

"I heard you talked to Jessie last night."

"I did." He'd almost forgotten about that. It had happened right before he realized he had run out of gas. "She sounded good, but bored. She said I have to get her more books. I'm going to try to do that tomorrow or Saturday."

When he'd suggested Friday night to Nik, he'd had no real plan in mind other than to see her again. But then she'd texted him back asking him what he was in the mood to do, and he felt like the answer she was looking for was not "sex on your couch, then pizza, then more sex was pretty great last night— we could do that again?" The guys she tended to go out with were probably "fancy pizza place in Silver Lake where you had to stand in a long line" kinds of guys, and nothing against guys like that, but that wasn't him.

"Jessie told me you yelled at her. You have to stop doing that! It's going to make her blood pressure worse, I already told you that. And I looked up preeclampsia, and—"

"Angela. Are you really trying to tell me something about medicine you found on the Internet right now? Seriously?"

But also, he had to come up with an idea for something to do with Nik—before they got to the good part—that made it clear this thing wasn't on a path to a proposal. He liked her a lot, and the sex had been great, but he was not on the hunt for a girlfriend, let alone a wife. All he wanted from Nik was to have someone to blow off steam with every once in a while, whether that was more great sex or more great sex plus a few drinks or more great sex plus some joking around, et cetera.

"I'm just saying, if you want Jessie to relax, you're going about it the wrong way. The books were great and so were the cupcakes. Keep doing things like that. Stop hounding her about her blood pressure."

Why did his family always say things like this to him? He wasn't "hounding" Jessie; he was just trying to make sure she was taking care of herself. He wished he had some of Nik's rosé right now. Hell, he wished he had Nik with him right now.

"Fine. I just wanted to make sure that she's taking this seriously. I don't want anything to happen to Jessie or the baby."

He walked over to his pantry, his favorite room in this house. He hadn't had time to cook for a few weeks, and he'd missed it. All of the chopping and stirring and puttering around relaxed him after a long day. He put a big pot of water on to boil.

"I know," she said. "She knows that, too. Just try to be more gentle about it with her, okay?"

"Okay, okay, I promise. Satisfied?" he said to his sister. Nothing else would get her off the phone.

He hoped Nik understood that he wasn't looking for a girlfriend. He thought so. Because after everything that had happened with Fisher, both at the Dodgers game and afterward, he was pretty sure Nik was in no mood to get back into a relationship. But was there a way to make that clear to her without acting like he assumed she'd fallen in love with him or something?

Oooh. Here was an idea. He put his phone on speaker so he could text and keep talking to Angela.

What's your feeling on Mexican food? Any interest in checking out my favorite taqueria?

There. A date at a taqueria should say "fun, but not serious" right on the label.

"Hey, speaking of medical stuff." Angie's voice got really casual. Too casual. "Have you thought any more about making that doctor's appointment? Just you know, with Jessie having these issues, and our family history and all, it's good to . . ."

"Angela." He grated cheese harder than necessary into a big bowl. "Stop. Don't worry about me, I'm fine."

"I know that's what you say, but what does it hurt to get a few checks?"

He was so tired of this conversation. He didn't want to go to the doctor, and he didn't need to go to the doctor.

"Angela. I'm fine. I eat healthy, I run, I get enough sleep, I'm making myself a salad for dinner right now. Relax. Channel your worry about Jessie in a more productive way than bugging me, like knitting or chopping wood or something calming."

He reached into the back of his pantry and found his pepper grinder. He ground a bunch of pepper on top of his mountain of grated cheese.

He checked his phone, just to make sure he hadn't missed Nik's text. Not that he assumed that people would always text him back immediately, but this morning when he'd asked Nik if she wanted to hang out on Friday night, she'd texted back pretty quickly.

"Knitting? Chopping wood? Have you never met me before? I tried to knit a scarf once and ended up almost cutting off the circulation in my fingers. And do you think I live in a cottage in the woods and have an ax? I live in Los Angeles, remember? The way we do stress relief here is yoga classes, acupuncture, and weed."

"Okay, great." He added salt and a handful of dried spaghetti to the now boiling water. "Go to yoga, go to acupuncture. As your older brother, I cannot advise you to do that last one, but if you do it, maybe you'll stop bugging me, and we'll all be happier and more relaxed!"

Maybe Nik was offended that he was only suggesting a taqueria. Maybe she wanted him to be one of those "standing in a long line for fancy pizza" kinds of dudes. Maybe she was standing in one of those lines with another guy right now.

"Yes, well, I'll see what I can do."

He pulled his tongs out of a drawer and stirred the pasta with them.

"Hey, have you talked to our friend from Dodger Stadium lately?" she asked. "I told you I liked her, didn't I?"

Maybe she'd said yes this morning just to pacify him but he'd never hear from her again, and his text would be just out there in the universe, unanswered, forever.

"Nope. Anything else you need to nag me about tonight?"

"Shut up and go eat your salad. Talk to you tomorrow."

Ten minutes later, he sat down at his kitchen table with a big bowl of cacio e pepe. Okay, yes, it wasn't a salad, but man couldn't live on lettuce alone, could he? Plus, he'd worked off a lot of calories with Nik the night before.

His phone buzzed.

Come on, I've lived in California way too long not to love Mexican food, what an insulting question. If I get over the insult, which I'm not sure I will, checking out your favorite taqueria sounds great.

He laughed at his phone and put down his fork.

A thousand apologies. But who knows, you may not like everything at this place. Some of it might be too spicy or too weird for you.

He took his first bite.

Want to bet?

He grinned.

Chapter Eleven

Nik woke up on Friday at her usual eight a.m. and immediately thought about her date with Carlos that night. Okay, it wasn't a *date* date. It was just a glorified hook up, with food first—she was pretty sure they both knew that. But still. Whatever it was, she was excited about it.

She forced herself to work all morning, but by noon, her mind was wandering to where they'd go tonight, how he would look, and oh shit, what she should wear. The last time he'd seen her it was after she'd raced out of her house when Courtney had called her in a panic, and she had not at all been prepared to see anyone, let alone him. She needed to show that she could look good if she tried.

Something casual, chill, and cool. Something she would look incredibly sexy in, but still looked like a normal outfit to wear to a taqueria on the Friday night of a holiday weekend. All of that should be no problem at all for her, the person who had worn her holey Stanford T-shirt and threadbare yoga pants almost every day this week.

She dug into the back of her closet, the place she put stuff that she bought whenever she got a big rejection and let her online shopping fingers roam free.

Oooh, that leather jacket. She'd bought it last month when the *New Yorker* had rejected a piece she was sure they'd love. It had arrived in the middle of one of L.A.'s spring heat waves, so she hadn't even tried it on and had stuck the box in her closet.

She opened it and winced at the number on the receipt. What had she been thinking? Was it too late to return this?

Then she put it on. Holy shit, this thing made even her old yoga pants look hot. She adjusted the zippers and grinned at herself in the mirror. If she wore that, plus her one sexy pair of jeans that gave her an ass like one of those rap guys' girlfriends, she could wear any shirt and she would look great.

She sat back down at her desk and looked at her to-do list, full of crap she had no desire to do. After fifteen minutes of trying to make phone calls and just getting voice mail boxes—some of them full—she gave up. It was Friday afternoon; everyone on the East Coast had already cut out of work by now, and everyone on the West Coast was pretending they had. She might as well join them.

After an hour and a half of yoga, an hour of yoga recovery flat on her back on her couch, a shower, and an hour of trying on shoes and makeup to go with her outfit, she was ready for Carlos, only two minutes after he was supposed to pick her up. Luckily, he was five minutes late.

"Hey! I'm outside. Sorry I'm late," he said when he called. "Should I come up, or . . ."

"No, I'll come down," she said. She felt ridiculously high school. She rolled her eyes at herself. This wasn't a date, remember?

Carlos was standing at the door when Nik walked outside. She'd kind of expected him to be waiting for her in the car. That made her feel even more high school, but in a good way.

"Hi," she said to him.

He grinned at her.

"Holy shit, you look great."

She tried to keep her smile from stretching across her entire face but may have failed.

"Thanks! So do you." She reached up to hug him and he leaned down to kiss her. She hadn't quite expected them to be at the kiss hello stage yet, but she liked kissing him so much she'd take any excuse to kiss him.

"Hungry?" he asked, when they finally pulled away.

She wiped her lip gloss off his mouth with her thumb and walked with him to his car.

"Starving. I only had a salad for lunch in preparation for this meal." In retrospect, she should have at least had a snack after yoga. Oh well, at least she knew there would be plenty of food where they were going.

He opened the passenger door for her.

"That is one of the biggest compliments anyone has ever given me," he said.

She smiled at him as he started the car.

"You said you were the food expert. I'm trusting you here."

"You were right to trust me, and I'm very grateful, especially after I insulted you so gravely by questioning your allegiance to Mexican food."

She shook her head sadly.

"I'm still not over that. You're going to have to give me a little time."

He squeezed her thigh before moving his hand back to the gearshift.

"Take all the time you need."

He accelerated as he got onto the freeway.

"You know, I never learned how to drive a stick." She traced the outline of his fingers with her fingertips. "But boy, do I like watching other people do it."

He glanced down at her hand, then looked back up at the road.

"My dad made both me and my sister learn to drive stick before we could learn an automatic. He said if you learned an automatic first, you got too lazy to really learn how to drive, but if you learned how to drive on a stick, you'd be a better driver for life." He frowned at her, but still with a smile in his eyes. "I still can't believe you had the gall to say I drive too fast. Me, of all people."

She lifted her hand from his and pointed at the speedometer.

"You're currently going fifteen miles over the speed limit, Mr. Safety First."

He shrugged.

"I can't help it if everyone else on the road is so timid, can I?"

She laughed and shook her head and settled back into her seat.

"I hope you have passenger-side airbags and good insurance."

Fifteen minutes later, after a drive through some of the less gentrified parts of the Eastside, they pulled up in the parking lot at his new favorite taqueria.

"Here we go," he said. "Taqueria de los Campos. Before we go in, really, is there anything you don't won't eat? I mean, other than blue cheese and olives."

"Oh, there are plenty of things I won't eat other than blue

cheese and olives, but I don't think those things are going to be at a taqueria."

He narrowed his eyes at her.

"What do you mean? Have you never been to a real taqueria? There are lots of things there that plenty of people don't eat." He paused. "Wait. Do you go to . . . Chipotle?"

She laughed and opened the car door.

"Okay, yes, I have been to Chipotle in my time, but I've also been to a lot of real taquerias. I've lived in California most of my life, I told you!"

He got out of the car and came around to her.

"Hmm, okay. Where in California?"

He still sounded very suspicious.

"I grew up in Sacramento. My parents still live there and are very confused about why I live in L.A. now without what they see as a stable job, instead of moving back home. They're very supportive of my career, even though they don't understand it."

Carlos grinned at her.

"I've seen how that goes with some of my cousins who have jobs their parents have never heard of. Sacramento is respectable, but I'm still reserving judgment on your taqueria cred. What are the other things you don't eat?"

They walked the short way up to the entrance, and he opened the door for her.

"Jell-O in all forms, custard in all forms, but especially when it's inside of a doughnut, chicken breast, carrot cake, raw peaches—cooked ones are fine—and shredded coconut. There, are any of those things going to be inside of a taco?"

He sighed in relief.

"Chicken breast could potentially be inside of a taco, but don't worry, I would never order it here. And I promise, this place does not have any Jell-O or carrot cake tacos."

When they got up to the front of the line, Carlos ordered in Spanish without consulting her. She regretted her inability to speak the language. Sure, she spoke a little Spanish, just from living in California, and the bits that she'd learned from listening hard when she did interviews of Spanish-speaking sources with the assistance of interpreters. She'd taken French in high school and college, a decision she'd lamented for years once she realized how useful even semi-fluency in Spanish would have been to her life.

"What do you want to drink?" he asked her.

"Pineapple agua fresca, por favor," she said to him, in her not terrible but also not good accent, which Carlos and the counter guy both laughed at.

He paid, and they slid into an empty booth with their drinks and their order number on a stick.

"Did you grow up speaking Spanish?" she asked him.

He shook his head.

"No. My parents emigrated when they were both young—my mom was three; my dad was eight. They both grew up only speaking Spanish at home and English at school, and they got teased a lot for their accents and not speaking English well enough. They didn't speak Spanish to me or Angela when we were kids because they didn't want the same things to happen to us. I wish . . ." He sighed, and she resisted the impulse to grab his hand. "That's a long way of saying that no, I didn't, and I wish I had. Especially growing up in L.A., everyone would look at me and hear my name and speak to me in Spanish, and I couldn't respond. I didn't really learn until college. I took it in high school, but I always felt self-conscious about it there, I guess."

She took a sip of her agua fresca. She'd had other friends who grew up with Spanish-speaking parents who had the same thing happen, and they'd both hated and understood the choice that their parents had made.

"Sixty-three?" A man picked up their number and put two huge trays of food in their place.

"Oh my God."

There were so many tacos in front of her. Thank God she was hungry. She counted at least six different kinds, but there were at least two of each kind. And there were chips, and guacamole, and a big dish of refried beans and rice. It was a good thing her jeans were stretchy.

He laughed at the look on her face.

"I can't decide if you're excited or horrified."

She shook her head and kept her eyes on the food.

"I can't, either."

He picked up the squirt bottles of salsa at the corner of the booth. She reached for another, but he took it out of her hand.

"Wait. Only certain salsas go with certain tacos." She started to object, to say that she could select her own salsa, thank you very much, but she reconsidered.

"Okay, food guru, tell me what to do here."

He touched her hand and flashed a smile at her. She'd last seen that smile on Wednesday night, right before he pulled off her underwear. She was not in the habit of asking men to tell her what to do, but apparently, they liked it.

She wasn't planning to *get* in that habit, but it was always good to know these things.

"Well, when you put it that way . . ." He lined up the plates of tacos in front of her and added the salsa of his choosing to each one. "Now. Rank them. I'll tell you what everything is afterward."

She rubbed her hands together and took off her leather jacket. This date was already more fun than her usual "drinks at a hipster bar, dinner at the upscale pizza place next door afterward" L.A.-style dates.

She took bites of each taco in succession, and then second bites of all six.

"Okay." She looked down at all of her tacos, and then across the table at his; while she'd been tasting each one carefully, he'd decimated his.

"First, I have to say, ranking these from number six to number one doesn't give number six enough credit. I would eat this taco every day if I could, let's be clear." He motioned for her to get on with it. She picked up a plate and set it at the far end of the table against the window. "Six."

"Carne asada, but I'm sure you already knew that." She nodded and tried not to smile like her favorite teacher had just complimented her in front of the whole class. She put another plate next to the first one.

"That's tripas. Are you sure that wasn't too weird for you?"

Tripe. Huh. Okay, that was a little weird. She hadn't really expected tripe to be one of the things she'd eat tonight. Or that she'd rank it over steak.

"If it had been too weird, would I have kept eating it?" She hoped he didn't notice that she didn't quite answer the question.

She hesitated for a few seconds with the next selection, then moved a third plate over.

"Carnitas!" He pulled the basket of chips toward him and

squirted salsa on one of his empty plates. "Only fourth place for carnitas, wow."

She couldn't tell if that was a good wow or bad wow.

"I loved the carnitas! I've always thought carnitas was my favorite before, and it hurt me to put it in fourth place, but . . ."

He dipped a chip into his salsa with a huge grin on his face. "This is fun. Keep going."

None of the guys she'd dated in the past five years would have even imagined ordering this much food for two people. Not even for four people. Thank God she wasn't here with any of them.

She moved a fourth plate into line.

"Cabeza in third place!" Carlos said.

And she'd never dated anyone who would have ordered her a cow head taco. A delicious cow head taco, to be clear.

He rolled his sleeves up to his elbows, and she couldn't hold back a sigh at the sight of his forearms. Did men have any idea how sexy it was when they did that?

She moved the next plate in line.

"Lengua." He dug into the bowl of guacamole with a chip. "Well, you should have ranked that one the first, but you can't get everything right."

Why was she not surprised that his favorite was the tongue?

"As much as I love that one . . ."

"Mmmm, you sure do. I know that now." He smirked at her, and she tried hard not to laugh.

"As I was saying, as much as I love that one . . ." She pushed the last plate into line. "This is my favorite."

He held out his hand, and she slapped it.

"Respect. Al pastor is an excellent taco favorite to have, especially here."

She finished the al pastor taco and raised an eyebrow at him. "So did I pass?"

He stopped, a guacamole-laden chip halfway to his mouth. "What do you mean pass?"

She rolled her eyes at him.

"This test. I know it was a test, don't even try to pretend it wasn't."

At first he shrugged and didn't meet her eyes. Then he gave her a puppy dog smile.

"Okay, yes, you definitely passed, but I didn't really intend it to be a test. It was just that . . ."

Nik spooned some rice and beans onto a plate. She was already so full that putting more food on her plate seemed ridiculous, but she couldn't not try the rice and beans, could she? When she had a little bit of both on her plate, she sat up straight and looked Carlos in the eye.

"It was just that what? I'm going to make you finish that sentence now."

* * * * * * * *

Carlos sighed and put his fork down.

"It was just that you kind of seemed like a girl who stayed in the safe parts of L.A. and who moved in bougie kinds of circles, and who . . . who . . . I wasn't sure how you would react to a place like this and food like that."

She didn't break eye contact. He'd thought that maybe she'd get distracted by the food on her plate, but she'd clearly listened to every word he'd said.

"And who . . . dates the whitest of white guys? Is that what you were going to say?"

Well, yeah, but he'd caught himself at the last second.

"I was, but I thought the better of it!" Shit, she was going to get mad at him for this, wasn't she? She had every right to.

She laughed and reached for another chip.

"Don't judge me by Fisher, come on now. I'm not going to claim that he's the only white guy that I've dated, but he's definitely one of the worst."

He'd take her word for it. She seemed more relaxed about the Fisher thing than she had the last time they'd talked about it. Maybe it was her self-defense class making the difference.

"How's your self-defense class going? Are you kicking some ass?"

She put up her fists.

"I sure as hell am," she said, before putting her fists down. "I didn't really expect to enjoy the class; I think I expected it to be some empowerment bullshit, but I feel like I'm learning a lot, and it's actually really fun. The instructor is the owner of the gym, and she's pretty fantastic."

He'd kind of expected her class to be some empowerment bullshit, too. His dad had made Angela take a self-defense class when she went off to college, and Angie had complained about it the whole time. She'd said it was just talking about your feelings and beating up a dude covered in padding, but that she hadn't really learned how to defend herself. He'd had to take her into the backyard and show her how to throw a punch to feel comfortable with her leaving.

"Oh man, I'd love to hear more about that. That's the kind of place I'd love to silently pass their brochure to some of my patients. And their moms, though I bet it's outside their price range."

She shook her head.

"Probably not—that's one of the interesting things about it. She has a sliding scale for membership and all of the classes. Pretty great."

"Wow." As he well knew, it was hard for low- or even moderate-income people in L.A. to access a lot of the stuff that hipster L.A. took for granted. "Are you planning to write about it? I read that Anna Gardiner thing you told me you wrote for *Vogue*; it was great."

"You read it?" If he had known she would look so flattered when he told her that, he would have told her days ago. "Thanks, I'm glad you liked it. I actually hadn't even thought about writing about Natalie's Gym, but that's an idea." She shrugged. "We'll see."

"What other kinds of writing do you do? Is it all freelance, or are you on staff somewhere?"

"All freelance. After college, I got a job at the *New York Times*, which was overwhelming and amazing. I learned a ton about writing and researching there, especially about investigative reporting, just from listening to some of the reporters there and asking them a lot of questions." She made a face. "And asking for feedback on my own work, which was horrible at the time but ultimately very valuable."

He grinned at the look on her face.

"They were very blunt, huh?"

She dropped her head into her hands.

"You have no idea. God, I still get humiliated sometimes when I think about the draft of a story I gave one guy. Oh, it was so bad, and he told me, in lots of detail, why it was so bad. But you know, that one terrible conversation was probably worth at least an entire class of journalism school." She took a sip of her water. "Then I came back here to be an editor for the *L.A. Times* entertainment section. It was such a different job, but I learned a ton about the ins and outs of the industry here in L.A."

Hers was a very different part of L.A. than the one he'd grown up in. The part with the movie stars and the rich people that he'd always known existed, but it seemed so foreign compared to his life that it could have very well been across the country.

"This was a long way to answer your question about what kind of writing I do. I left the *L.A. Times* about a year and a half ago. There was a big buyout, but I was ready to go. I was getting tired of only doing celebrity stuff, as entertaining as it can be. Now I do a good combination of writing: some celebrity profiles, especially women of color. But also some investigative journalism, and other short fun pieces when I have time for them. It's been a little scary, but also fun to craft my career in this way."

He nodded. He'd known some of that from when he'd Googled her to find that Anna Gardiner story, but not all of it.

"What kind of investigative journalism? Who pays for stuff like that these days, other than like, the *New Yorker*?"

She grinned.

"I had a piece in the *New Yorker* last week, actually. My second piece there."

He'd walked right into that one, hadn't he?

"Holy shit, that's awesome! What was the story about?"

"Thanks. This one was a celebrity piece; it was a profile of a screenwriter who has two movies coming out this summer. I was really glad to get to write about her." Her grin lost a little of its sparkle. "I was really excited to see it in print, but I just realized I didn't even open the magazine. It came the same day as the Dodgers game, see."

He suddenly hated that Fisher guy. What a way to ruin the joy of her accomplishment.

He looked at their table: plates of half-eaten tacos lined up neatly, the beans and rice basically untouched on both of their plates, their drinks all empty.

"Do you want to get dessert?" he asked.

She laughed, and the sad look disappeared from her face.

"Oh my God, no, are you kidding me? I'm way too full to even think about dessert. I can't remember the last time I said that."

They waved good-bye to the staff as they walked out and got in his car. A few blocks down the road, she cleared her throat.

"I might be accused of being bougie by asking this, but I'm going to do it anyway: do you ever worry about your car, parking it in neighborhoods like this?"

He nodded.

"Nah, that's just common sense. At first I barely drove it anywhere but to work and home. I was so paranoid about break-ins, or accidents, or other cars parking too close to me. I *never* did valet, which in L.A., as you know, made everything more difficult."

He flicked his blinker on to turn onto the freeway, and thought about those first months after. A lot of it he barely even remembered. He only knew certain things had happened because friends had mentioned them later. Sometimes he'd searched through his emails for something unrelated and come across emails he'd sent friends, thanking them for their card or the food they'd sent or for coming to the funeral, and he had no memory not only of sending the emails but of receiving their card or food or seeing them at the funeral. It had been such a terrible time; he was glad that there was a fog over his memory of a lot of it. The car probably wasn't the only reason he'd barely gone anywhere but to work and his mom's house for months.

"What made you change?" she asked.

He shrugged and started to give her a bullshit answer. But the only answer he could think of was the truth.

"My friends, really. Especially my friend Drew. Some of it . . . a lot of it, probably, wasn't about the car at all, but was about my dad." He'd tried not to let anyone figure out what a hard time he was having with his dad's death. He especially didn't want his family to know. He knew he had to be there for his mom and for Angie, to be the rock they needed.

"One day at work, we were talking about a new case that had come in the day before. It was a middle-aged man who died suddenly of a heart attack, the same as my dad. When they described what happened and started asking questions for us to answer, I had to leave the room. I didn't think anyone noticed me leave. But that night, Drew asked if I wanted to get a beer when we both got off. We didn't talk about it, at all, but . . . it helped. And then the following week, he convinced me to join a basketball rec league. I knew he was doing it to force me out of the house for something other than work, but I did it anyway. And it helped."

He didn't look at her, but he could feel her watching him, listening to every word he said. She didn't touch him, but the softness in her voice felt like a caress.

"A sudden heart attack. That's terrible. I'm so sorry."

He nodded, very glad that they were in a car in the dark and she couldn't see the tears in his eyes.

"Thanks. Anyway, the car. I think I mostly realized I couldn't live in fear anymore. I mean, sure it could get broken into outside the taqueria, or I could have an accident any day to or from work.

Plus, I bought the car in honor of my dad—how did it honor him for me to be afraid to go anywhere in it? Good God, I can't imagine how ashamed he would have been if I didn't want to go to a taqueria because I was scared of what might happen to my car, you know?"

Why the hell was he talking to her about his dad? He never talked about him, not even to Angela or his mom. He'd decided to stop talking—or even thinking, for the most part—about his dad almost six months after he'd died. It had been too hard for him to deal with otherwise.

Fucking journalists, they knew just the questions to get you going.

"I'm glad you had good friends." She put her hand on his, and he thought she was going to say something else warm and sympathetic, which might be more than he could take right now. "I'm also glad you discovered that taqueria, because oh my God was that food good."

He laughed, relieved she'd changed the subject.

"So am I. I love that place. I try not to go there too often. I always eat too much when I'm there."

They talked about tacos the rest of the way to her apartment.

"I know this is insanely bougie of me, but so be it," she said as she opened her apartment door. "Do you want some sparkling water? It always makes me feel better after I eat an enormous meal. I have like four different flavors, minimum."

She kicked her shoes off by the door, so he followed suit.

"Hmmm, that depends. What flavors?"

She threw off her leather jacket, walked into the kitchen and opened the fridge, while he sat on the couch.

"Grapefruit, lemon, berry, and mango."

He sighed dramatically.

"Lime is my favorite, but I guess I can settle for grapefruit."

She grabbed the water out of the fridge and brought it over to the couch.

He drank some water, put his glass down on the coffee table, and put his arm around her.

"Sparkling water is good at settling your stomach after a big meal, but do you want to know something else that works for that?"

She rose her eyebrows.

"Hmmm, what?"

He ran his hand up and down her bare arm.

"Some good, healthy physical activity."

She took another sip of her water and set it down.

"Oh wow. I'm so glad you told me that. I'd always read the opposite, that you shouldn't eat before any strenuous activity."

He shook his head vigorously.

"Oh no, no, that's outdated advice. I'm a doctor, see, so I know all of the new and up-to-date research on this." He reached up and tugged on one of her curls, released it, tugged on another one.

"Mmmm. I'm so grateful that I have you, a fancy doctor, to tell little old me about this." She pulled him against her.

"I'm so glad you appreciate me." He kissed her neck and then trailed kisses down to the hollow between her breasts.

"I definitely do." His thumbs were on her nipples, hard peaks beneath the thin fabric of her shirt. She closed her eyes.

"The more strenuous, the better for your digestion, really." He pushed her back against the couch and lifted her shirt.

"Wow, that's so good to know. What . . ." She sucked in her breath and paused before she could continue. "What should we do? We could go for a nice walk."

He pulled her shirt off and tossed it to the side. Her breasts were full and luscious inside her sheer black bra. He couldn't stop looking at her. And touching her.

"A walk is a good idea. From what I remember from last time, the walk to your bedroom is really long. It took us a long time to get there. That seems like the perfect length for a walk to me."

She smiled up at him.

"Whatever you say, doctor."

He stood and took her hands to pull her up off the couch.

Chapter Twelve

"You should be honored. My friends were very nice to you tonight," Nik said.

Carlos and Nik were walking to his car the following Friday night. He'd texted her before leaving the hospital to see if she wanted to go out, and she'd texted him back that she was out with her friends, and he should come join them. He'd really wanted to see her, so he went. But that had made him nervous that this was more than a casual hookup thing to her.

Maybe he should talk to her about it, even though he hated bringing up stuff like that. But they'd been seeing kind of a lot of each other, and he didn't want her to get the wrong idea. After the taqueria last Friday night, he'd hung out at her house well into Saturday afternoon. And then they'd met up for burgers on Tuesday night and gone back to her place for some healthy adult exercise. And they'd been texting a lot this week. Were they spending too much time together?

Granted, she didn't act like the women he'd gone out with in the past who had wanted to be his girlfriend: she hadn't insisted on weekend plans far in advance or pushed him to invite her over to his house or told him he was the kind of guy who would be a great father. But making him spend an hour with her and her friends when she knew all he wanted was to be taking her clothes off was getting close.

"That was them being *nice*?" he asked. He was sort of kidding, but . . . only sort of.

She laughed.

"They only quizzed you for like five minutes."

It had felt like far longer.

Sure, he'd met her friends right after the baseball game, but that was before they'd started sleeping together. Did this whole "come meet me and my friends" thing mean she was getting the wrong idea about what he wanted here?

If he had to end things with her, he was going to be so mad. He hadn't had sex this good, with someone he actually enjoyed spending time with in . . . shit, since he could remember.

"Courtney gave you more than one compliment. That's basically a declaration of lifelong devotion coming from her."

When he'd told her how much he'd liked her spicy cupcake, she had told him that said something good about his character.

"Well, I'm glad, I guess, but please don't kill me if I say I'm glad they both had to get up early tomorrow morning so I could get you alone."

She looked at him out of the corner of her eye and smiled.

"That sounds promising. What did you have in mind?"

He grinned as they approached his car.

"Well, you know me. Before I do anything strenuous, I need a good dinner. What are you in the mood for?"

"Do you want to go out? Or get takeout?"

He put his arm around her.

"I can do either, but the idea of takeout on your couch sounds pretty great right now. It's been a long week."

She put her arms around his waist, and he pulled her close.

"How's your cousin doing? Everything okay there?"

He nodded.

"Thanks for asking. She's hanging in there, but I'm always on edge about it. Every time I get a call from anyone in my family, I jump. I would say that I can't wait for this to be over, except that the best outcome is for it to be like this for another nine or ten weeks, which seems unbearable right now."

He sighed and opened the passenger door for her.

"Thanks for listening to me ramble about my family, I appreciate it. I can't really talk to them about it, because then they all flip out."

She leaned over to kiss him when he got in the car. The kiss lasted for a long time.

"Ramble all you want," she said. "You just held up very well under cross-examination from my two best friends, so I owe you a night of lots of listening, something fun on the TV, and . . ."

He cocked his head to the side.

"*And?*"

"And whatever else you ask for," she said.

He grinned. He would worry about the other stuff later.

* * * * * * *

Nik woke up early the next morning, with Carlos sound asleep against her. Good God, this guy was fun. He had certainly taken her "whatever else you ask for" to heart, with very good results.

She turned back toward him and he nuzzled against her neck.

"Mmm, so you are awake," she said.

"I'm not awake. I'm having the most fantastic dream."

He had such a scratchy voice first thing in the morning. Just hearing it gave her goose bumps.

"What kind of dream?"

He ran his hand from her knee up her leg to her hip and rested his whole palm against her butt.

"I'm in bed with this incredibly sexy woman, for starters."

God, she liked it when he touched her.

"Mmm, tell me about her."

His hands kept moving up and down her body. They stopped to linger at her breasts, and she closed her eyes and sighed.

"Oh, she's something else. She's smart, she's funny, she surprises me at every turn, and her body . . . I just can't get enough of it."

That was definitely an excellent thing to hear from a man who woke up in your bed.

"She sounds incredible. Tell me more about the dream."

He pushed her onto her back and knelt above her.

"In my dream, we had amazing sex last night . . . multiple times, actually. God, what a great dream this has already been. And now . . ." He leaned down to kiss her mouth. "And now, if I'm lucky, we might get to do it again. Oh wow, I hope I don't wake up."

She played with his hair and relaxed at his touch.

"I hope you don't, either."

Now his mouth was on her breasts, and she sighed.

"Mmmmm. This is a great way to not wake up; I've got to say."

"Mmmmm?" He lifted his head. "Oh, you like that? I think there's an even better way to not wake up. Let me see if you agree."

He threw the covers to the foot of the bed and pushed her legs apart. She looked down at his head between her legs and grinned.

"Oh, I think I like this dream of yours a whole lot. Do you think you'll—OH MY GOD."

Those were the last discernable words she said for a long time.

When they both finally caught their breath, he kissed her cheek.

"Okay, you're going to think I'm crazy saying this after all of that food we ate last night, but . . . I'm starving."

She laughed into his chest.

"Well, you did have lots of good, healthy physical activity. It makes sense that that would make you hungry."

He rolled on top of her and tickled her.

"Oh, you're making fun of me now? Just for that, I'm going to make you breakfast." He sat up. "That is, if you have anything I can cook?"

She nodded.

"I went to the store the other day. There should be stuff in there. I'll make the coffee."

He pulled on boxers and went to investigate her kitchen. She grabbed a robe out of her closet and went to the bathroom before joining him. By the time she got there, he had a pile of food on her counter.

"Are you going to make *all* of that?" She opened the coffee maker and pulled out yesterday's filter and tossed it in the garbage.

"I'm deciding what to cook. A true artist takes time at his work."

She turned on her coffee grinder and scooped grounds into the fresh filter.

"Okay, Picasso. I make coffee strong; that okay with you?"

He laughed while he pulled bowls out of her cabinet.

"That's fine, but if I had said no, what were you going to do? I already know you wouldn't have made weaker coffee for me."

She poured water in the machine and turned it on.

"No, I would have just made sure you didn't use all the milk in whatever you're cooking in case you needed a lot of it for your cup."

He opened another cabinet.

"Good point, because I was thinking about making pancakes since I see you have syrup here. Any objections? Also, where's your flour?"

She reached for two mugs from the cabinet above the coffee maker and took the opportunity while his back was to her to admire his ass in his gray boxer briefs.

"No objections at all to pancakes, as long as you make bacon, too. And the dry goods are all under there."

He added a lot of sugar to his coffee, but she tried not to judge him for that. Some of her best friends added a lot of sugar to their coffee.

Once he was all set with ingredients and pans, she sat at the kitchen counter with her mug of coffee and watched him cook. Just as he flipped the first pancake with a flourish, she heard Courtney's voice in her head: *serious couples don't go to brunch; they stay home and cook for each other.*

Oh shit. Was this a sign that he wanted to be serious? She'd assumed it was clear that that wasn't what she was looking for right now, given the whole "dramatic breakup that he and thousands of other people witnessed just three weeks ago" thing, but maybe her state of mind wasn't clear to him?

Did she need to have an actual conversation about this with him? She hated having conversations like that.

But then . . . she'd avoided having an actual define-the-relationship talk with Fisher, and that didn't work out all that well.

Come to think about it, Carlos did seem like a serious relationship kind of guy. He was kind and considerate; he was close to his family; he'd just bought a *house*, for the love of God. Men don't buy houses if they don't want to get married soon after that. Damn it.

Carlos set a plate of golden brown pancakes and crisp bacon in front of her with a smile. She tried to smile back at him.

"Wow. What service."

He half bowed.

"I try. Syrup?"

She took a bite just as he sat down next to her. Oh, this was terrible. Not the pancakes—the pancakes were fantastic, that was the terrible part. If she never had these pancakes again because she'd accidentally found the one man in Los Angeles who wanted a serious relationship, she was going to be so mad.

"So, uh. The only problem is that . . ." She took a sip of coffee and tried the beginning of that sentence again. "I just wanted to . . . right now, I'm not sure if I'm . . ."

He looked at her like she had three heads.

"Nik. What are you trying to say?"

She shook her head out of frustration with herself.

"I'm sorry, I'm not making any sense. It's just that after the whole Fisher thing, and with work being so busy right now, I'm not in a good place for any sort of relationship. But like, this whole thing . . ." She gestured toward him, the kitchen, the couch, the bedroom. "This whole thing is great. And I like spending time with you a lot. I feel like we're becoming good friends. Just with"—she waved her hand in the direction of the bedroom—"that stuff going on, too. So I just wanted to see where you were with everything."

No one would believe she made her entire living by putting words together. Did any of the words she'd just said make sense in that order? She had no idea.

"OH." His shoulders relaxed, and he grinned at her. "Well, thank God for that, because I think this whole thing," he mimicked her gesture with his fork, "is great, too. And to be honest with you, between work and everything going on with my family, I don't have the energy for anything even approaching a relationship. So if you're cool with keeping *this* casual, so am I."

She let out a deep sigh and picked up a piece of bacon with her fingers.

"Excellent." She bit into the bacon, and the salty sweetness of the bacon and syrup combined exploded in her mouth. What a great morning.

He stood up, walked around the counter to get the rest of the bacon, and tossed a strip onto her plate.

"I promise we can hang out and eat pancakes and drink rosé and I won't propose to you on a JumboTron."

She clinked her coffee mug against his. Oh thank God. They wanted the exact same thing. This was perfect.

"That sounds pretty ideal."

Chapter Thirteen

Carlos was just driving out of the grocery store parking lot a week and a half later when Drew called. It had been a brutal day at work, so he'd decided to cook something elaborate for dinner to help himself relax.

"Hey, man, what's up?"

"Hey!" Drew's voice boomed through the speakers in his car. "How's the assistant director doing on this fine Wednesday?"

Drew had been the whole reason he'd even applied for the job in the first place. He hadn't actually seen the opening, but Drew—all the way up in Berkeley now—had and had emailed it to him immediately. Carlos had jumped at the opportunity to move back to the Eastside, but he hadn't been sure if they were looking for someone with his background for the job. When he got it, Drew maintained that he'd known he would all along.

"I'm still alive; that's the best thing I can say after today at work."

"Ahh, one of those days, huh?"

Carlos sighed.

"One of the worst kinds of days. You know the kind."

"Well, maybe this will make it better: you around this weekend to hang out with your best friend and his fiancée?"

Carlos downshifted as the light changed.

"Oh, you mean Jake and Melissa? Yeah, I'm probably going to see them this weekend, why do you ask?"

"I ask because you can go fuck yourself, that's why I ask," Drew said, and both of them cracked up.

"Okay, but seriously, you and Alexa are coming to town? You need a place to stay? You know I live on the Eastside now, right? I don't know if you know how to get to this side of town."

"You are such an asshole. Yes, I know you live on the Eastside now. But we don't need a place to stay. Alexa's got to go down there with her boss for a conference, so I'm tagging along."

"Awesome. Everything was so crazy at the engagement party I barely got to talk to you." He hadn't seen Drew since Christmastime and Alexa since before that. "I'll get to congratulate you two in person."

"And we'll get to see the new house, I hope?" Drew asked.

"Of course, but I haven't put in the basketball hoop yet."

"And meet whatshername?"

He never should have told Drew he was sleeping with Nik; he knew he'd get the wrong idea. But Drew had texted him the day after they'd first slept together and had asked if he'd seen her again, and it was impossible to not say he'd seen a hell of a lot of her the night before.

"Her name is Nik. I can check to see if she's free, but I told you, this thing with her is very casual."

It was a *frequent* casual thing—they'd only started sleeping together three weeks ago, and they'd already seen each other six times. But after Nik had been the one to bring up that she didn't want a relationship, he wasn't worried about how often they saw each other anymore.

How had he gotten so lucky? It was so rare for him to find women who didn't want a relationship, especially women who were interesting and funny. Not to mention hot. Thank God Nik had dropped into his life.

"Yeah, yeah, you told me. But, you know, check to see if she's free Saturday night. We'll even come to your precious Eastside."

He thought Drew and Alexa would both like her a lot, though. Alexa had always laughed at his jokes, so she'd like Nik's sense of humor.

"All it takes to get you to the Eastside is for you to move to the other end of the state."

"Yeah, yeah, yeah. I'll text you our flight info and details, okay?"

Carlos pulled into his driveway and grabbed the groceries from the back seat.

"Sounds good."

"Hey, how's Jessie?"

Carlos had just checked in with her before leaving work. He knew she was getting sick of him checking in on her every day, but that didn't mean he was going to stop doing it.

"Going stir-crazy, but otherwise hanging in there."

"Okay, I gotta go. Go make your risotto or enchiladas or whatever."

Carlos laughed as he set his groceries down in the kitchen and took the risotto rice out of the bag. It was good to have friends who knew you better than you knew yourself.

He turned on the basketball game to keep him company while

he cooked. One of the only things he'd made the time and effort for after moving into this house was to put his TV on a pivot, so he could watch it in the kitchen while he cooked, and then turn it so he could watch it from the couch while he ate. The ideal set up, really.

He chopped an onion, sliced the fresh mushrooms and soaked the dried ones, and peeled the asparagus. The rote movements gave him the feeling of zen that this kind of cooking always did for him. He couldn't think about the stuff that had happened at work that day or worry about what would happen tomorrow when he was busy carefully dicing an onion so that all of the pieces were the exact same size. Just as he turned the heat on underneath his big sauté pan, he heard his phone buzz and grabbed it out of his pocket. Nik.

I just finished a huge story and I'm starving, want to get dinner?

He texted her back without stopping to think.

I'm in the middle of making dinner. Want to come over? How do you feel about mushrooms?

Holy shit, what was he thinking? He never invited women over to his place; it was kind of a thing of his. After a few way too fast relationships in his mid-twenties, he'd learned to keep the women he was dating away from his space. If women came to your place, they always wanted to change things to how they liked them, probably in preparation to move in all too soon.

I feel great about mushrooms. What's your address? I'll leave here in about fifteen minutes. Does that work?

Okay, but wait. This was Nik. She'd made it very clear to him that this was a rebound for her, just quite not in those words. And unlike a few of the conversations he'd instigated with women about keeping a relationship casual where they'd *said* that was fine with them but had made it clear shortly afterward that that was absolutely not fine with them, he knew that Nik hadn't been bullshitting him.

4242 Sequoia Street. See you soon.

Plus, Nik was fun to cook for. She'd gone crazy over those pancakes he'd made her. And it seemed like they'd both had busy days. Some stress release with her in his big bed sounded like an excellent way to end this day.

* * * * * * *

As Nik walked up the front steps of Carlos's little gray cottage, she suddenly felt shy about basically inviting herself over to his house. Had he really wanted her to come over, or did he just ask because she'd texted him out of the blue and he didn't know what else to do? She wished she'd called him instead, even though the two of them never talked on the phone—it was always easier to tell from a voice how someone really felt than from a text message. Well, it was too late now. He opened the bright red front door before she reached it.

"Hey." Okay, he looked normal. "Come on in."

The house was as masculine and put together as Carlos always was. The living room had a big fat leather couch, a huge TV on one wall, and a fireplace against the other. She dropped her stuff by the door and followed him into the big open kitchen that looked like something out of the Williams Sonoma catalog.

He moved back to the pan on the stove and started stirring. He was wearing a soft blue cotton T-shirt, the gray pants that he'd clearly worn to work, and patterned socks that made her hold back a smile.

"This kitchen is incredible. You told me you were a good cook, but I didn't know you were, like, copper-pots-hanging-from-the-ceiling good."

He glanced up at the pots and shrugged. Was that a blush she saw? He wouldn't meet her eyes.

"The copper pots were definitely an extravagance. To be fair, the first one was a housewarming gift from Angie. But when I bought a house with a beautiful rack to hang pots, what was I supposed to do?"

She thought about her collection of high heels that she almost never wore but kept buying because of the built-in shoe shelves in her walk-in closet that displayed them so beautifully. She nodded.

"Obviously you had to buy pots to fill it; I get it."

He handed her a glass of wine.

She took a sip of the wine as she looked around the kitchen and big open living room. She liked it. Even without anything but the TV on the wall, it felt like a home.

"I didn't even ask what you wanted to drink. Sorry, I didn't have any rosé," he winked at her, "but that should go well with dinner."

Wait. This seemed way too cozy, didn't it? His nice little house, his big warm kitchen, Carlos at the stove, stirring together things that smelled delicious . . . maybe Courtney had a point after all.

No. They'd talked about this, remember? Carlos had looked *very* relieved when she'd said she wasn't in the place for a relationship. This wasn't that, this was just one friend making dinner for another friend. She and her friends did this all the time. This time, she and her friend would just happen to have sex afterward, that's all.

"I wouldn't dare to question you on wine. You told me to always trust you with food and drink recommendations, and I took that to heart."

She took another sip of wine and tried to let herself relax. She'd spent days wrestling with a big story that she still didn't know if she was good enough to write. While she'd had moments of thinking she'd nailed it, the rest of the time she worried it was a complete failure.

"Everything okay?" he asked.

She nodded.

"Yeah. I've just been holed up in my apartment for the past three days finishing that story, and now that it's done, I feel like I'm coming out of a coma." She took her sweater off and tossed it on a stool. "It's great to relax here with some wine and have you cooking a delicious-smelling dinner for me." He looked back down at the food with a smile. Was he blushing? Maybe.

"Thanks for inviting me to share your dinner, by the way. What are we having?"

He looked back up at her.

"Risotto. I hope you like it."

Wow, he wasn't kidding about being able to cook.

"I don't know anyone who knows how to make risotto. I'm pretty sure I've only had it in a restaurant."

He laughed as his big wooden spoon made rhythmic circles in the pan.

"Oh, I love making it." He poured some liquid from the smaller pot on the stove into the big one and stirred some more. "It's funny; I don't even really like eating it that much. I mean, I like it, but I would never choose to order it in a restaurant. But I love to make it."

She took another sip of her wine and looked around at his kitchen. He had four bowls lined up next to him, two with mushrooms in them, one with bacon, one with cheese. And then there were the two pots on the stove. But most amazingly, other than a cutting board with a knife sitting on top of it, there were no dirty dishes anywhere. The rest of the kitchen looked spotless.

"It seems like a lot of work for a Wednesday night," she said.

He nodded.

"It is—that's why I love it. When I've had a really long or difficult day, it relaxes me to cook. It gives me a break in the day to concentrate on something else. And risotto is especially great, because after you do a whole bunch of chopping, then you just have to stand there, preferably with a glass of wine, and slowly stir the rice until it's just right. Every so often, you add some liquid, and you stir some more. You can't rush it; you can't turn up the heat or add the liquid all at once to make it go faster. It's ready when it's ready. And so you just stand there and keep stirring, and everything settles down by the time the food is ready."

She'd never heard anyone be so eloquent about risotto before.

"Wow. I feel more relaxed just hearing you talk about making it."

He looked up and met her eyes, and she could feel his smile all the way down to her toes.

"What a nice compliment from the person who wrote that heartbreaking story about foster children in the *Times* Sunday magazine."

Now it was her turn to blush and look away. She didn't expect him to have read that story. She couldn't remember the last guy she'd dated who had read any of her work. Well, Justin had, but only ever to tell her how bad it was.

"Oh, you read that? I didn't . . ." She looked up at him and smiled back. "Thank you. I was proud of that story."

He poured more liquid in the risotto and kept stirring.

"Good. You should be. It was excellent. It's such a hard topic—I know from dealing with it with my patients who are foster kids—and you handled it so thoughtfully."

She sipped her wine so he wouldn't be able to see the sudden tears in her eyes. She cleared her throat.

"Thanks for saying that. It means a lot. I was feeling pretty down about my work today, so it was really good timing to hear that."

He reached out and touched her shoulder.

"I can't believe that someone as good as you ever feels down about your writing, but I'm happy I could help you realize how amazing you are."

She laughed. If he only knew.

"I think all writers feel down about their work sometimes . . . or most of the time. At least, I hope they do and I'm not the weird one here." She swallowed and looked down into her glass. "But also, I had an ex who was pretty insulting about my writing, and despite everything I've accomplished since then, sometimes it's still hard to get him out of my head."

Good Lord, a few sips of wine on a hard day and she started spilling everything.

Carlos touched her hair, then her cheek.

"Well, he was obviously an asshole who doesn't know anything about good writing or good people, and I'm glad for more than one reason that he's an ex."

She smiled at him.

"Me too." God, was she ever glad. "It feels stupid to still dwell on something a jerk said years ago, but for some reason I remember some of the negative stuff people have said about my writing like it's imprinted on the inside of my eyelids, and it's much harder to remember—or believe—the compliments."

He poured more wine into her glass.

"Well, now that you've told me that, I'll just have to repeat my compliments a few times, maybe in different words so they'll stick. Hey, Nik, I really loved that piece you wrote, especially how you managed to make it hopeful while acknowledging the pain."

Oh shit, now he really was going to make her cry.

"I wasn't fishing for a compliment there, but thank you."

Why was she so emotional tonight?

It was probably just because she was about to get her period and was feeling sensitive about everything. Plus, even though she couldn't remember the last time a guy she dated had given her a compliment on her writing, her friends did all the time.

See? She and Carlos *were* friends. They had actually been friends first, pretty much from the moment he'd pushed that cameraman out of the way at the stadium. They'd gotten to know each other pretty well before they started sleeping together and had had some pretty deep conversations about their lives long before they'd even thought about getting naked.

How refreshing, to actually be friends with a guy you were sleeping with.

"Um, can I help with anything?" she asked.

He shook his head and poured more liquid into the pan.

"Nope. But it's going to be about twenty more minutes until dinner is ready; do you want a snack?"

Oh thank God. After his wonderful speech about how you couldn't rush risotto, she'd felt like she couldn't mention that she could eat a horse right now. Maybe two.

"Sure," she said. "What do you have?"

He handed her his wooden spoon.

"Here, stir this."

She stood barefoot on the warm tile floor of the kitchen and tried to mimic the way she'd seen him stir the risotto. She heard him behind her open a door, then she heard plastic crinkle. After a minute or so, he came up behind her and took the spoon from her. She leaned back against his body and felt his warmth surround her.

"Here. I only gave us enough to stave off hunger, but not enough to spoil our dinners." He set a bowl down on the counter next to the stove. When she looked in the bowl, she started laughing.

"Are those Flamin' Hot Cheetos?"

He grinned.

"They are indeed. The best snack food ever invented, and I will hear no argument."

"No argument here. I love that a pediatrician had Flamin' Hot Cheetos tucked in the back of his pantry. Makes me feel a lot less guilty about my secret snack drawer."

They demolished the Cheetos in about three minutes flat and spent the rest of the risotto cooking time talking about their favorite snack foods.

"Okay, I think we're ready." He took bowls down from the cabinet and nodded over to the living room. "Sorry, I don't have a dinner table yet. I got rid of my old one when I moved because it didn't work in this space, but I haven't had time to get a new one yet. I just mostly eat at the coffee table."

"Oh no." She set her wineglass down and shook her head sadly.

"I wish you'd told me that before I came over. I can't eat a meal at a coffee table! Don't you know who I am?"

He grated cheese on top of a bowl of risotto and handed it to her.

"Oh, I'm sorry, your royal highness, please forgive me?"

She took the bowl and picked up her wineglass.

"I'll make an exception in this case, but I don't want you to think this is going to be a common occurrence."

He waved toward the living room.

"Go sit down, and I'll bring everything else over."

She padded into the living room and sank down into the couch.

"What is *in* this couch?" she asked him, when he came back into the living room, his bowl in one hand and forks for both of them in the other. "Angel wings? Unicorn feathers? Actual clouds from heaven?"

He set the food down onto the coffee table and handed her a fork before he went back into the kitchen.

"That couch is super comfortable, right? I got it at a furniture store's going-out-of-business sale—I always think those sales are fake because, I swear, some of those furniture companies go out of business like twice a year—but I don't even care if this one was fake because I love this couch and will defend it against all enemies."

He came back to the couch with his wineglass, the wine bottle, and a pile of napkins.

She topped off both of their wineglasses.

"Does . . . does your couch have a lot of enemies? Forgive me, I don't have a leather couch made of pillows sewn by a goddess, so I don't know these things."

He picked up his glass, his face serious.

"Oh yes. It's one of the hardest things about owning a couch like this. People try to storm your home all the time to destroy it because they think anything this magical must be a sin. They warn you about this at the furniture store before you buy it. They had to put a guard on it in the showroom. It was crazy." He looked at her with a straight face until her laughter finally made him crack a smile.

She stuck her fork into the risotto and took a bite.

"Oh my God."

He looked up, his fork halfway to his mouth.

"What? 'Oh my God' what?"

She was too busy eating to answer at first.

"Oh my God, this risotto, that's what 'Oh my God!' I had no idea it was going to be this good!"

His most smug smile spread over his face, but she didn't even care.

"Tell me more. What's so 'Oh my God' about it? I want details, please."

She waved her finger in his face and retreated to the far corner of the couch.

"Stop talking to me. I need to concentrate when I eat this."

When she was almost done with her bowl, one of the things he'd said about why he liked making risotto came back into her head.

"So what happened at work today that made you need to make risotto?" she asked.

He sighed and put his own fork down.

"It was just a really shitty day, with some of my least favorite parts of this job."

She took a sip of her wine and looked at him. He seemed like he wanted to talk, but she wanted to tread lightly. She still didn't know him that well.

"Least favorite as a doctor, or least favorite as a person? Not to say that doctors aren't people, but . . . you know what I mean."

He took her bowl without asking and went over to the kitchen to get them both seconds.

"Yeah, I know what you mean," he said when he came back. "No wonder you're such a good writer. You ask good questions. Least favorite as a person. Or rather, least favorite as a person who is also a doctor, and therefore has to be professional when I really just wanted to punch that man in the face. Calling CPS isn't nearly as satisfying."

Child Protective Services.

"Abuse?" she asked.

He nodded.

"Yeah. Stepdad. The girl was getting the cast off of her broken arm; I wasn't there when she came in for the arm, so I don't know what happened then, but a few things she said when I was taking it off worried me, so I managed to get him out of the room and got the details out of her." He stared down at his knees and sighed. "It's not new to me. I've seen it before, but it's a stomach punch every time."

She moved closer to him and took his hand. He held on tight but didn't say anything. She didn't ask any more questions; she figured now was the time to just be silent and let him talk or not talk as much as he wanted.

After a few minutes, he looked up at her and shrugged.

"On top of everything else, it makes me think of my dad. Which sucks, because between Father's Day this coming weekend and the anniversary of his death next Friday, I try to avoid thinking about my dad as much as possible in June."

She squeezed his hand. She hadn't realized that the anniversary of his father's death was right around Father's Day.

"Why does this make you think of your dad? Because he was so much better than that guy?"

He laughed and let go of her hand, but only so he could put his arm around her.

"Well that, too. But also because I remember when something similar happened to one of his students. This was when Angela and I were younger; I think I was around twelve and she was ten, something like that. And he sat us down at the kitchen table and told us that his student had come to him, and how if anyone tried to do anything like that to us, we could come to him, and if any of our friends were dealing with something like that, we could always come to him. My mom tried to stop him at one point, told us we were too young to hear all of that, but he said 'Susana, they need to know this, it's important!'" She ran her fingers through his hair, and he leaned his head on her shoulder. "He was right. It was important."

After a few minutes, he sat up and looked down at their almost empty dishes.

"Hey, do you want some ice cream? I went a little wild at the grocery store tonight. I have three flavors."

Wine, risotto, and three kinds of ice cream. It's like the man knew she was coming over.

"Bring them all out."

He stood and picked up her dishes.

"Will do. I'm sorry if this was too heavy. We can talk about something else."

She shook her head.

"I wouldn't have asked if I didn't want to talk about it. It's not too heavy."

He came back a few minutes later and set a bowl with three scoops of ice cream in it in front of her.

"What do we have here?" she asked.

"Dark chocolate brownie, vanilla, rum raisin," he said.

She took the spoon he handed her.

"I like all of those things." They sat together, eating ice cream and not talking for the next few minutes.

"Does Angela remember that? About your dad?" she asked him.

He shook his head.

"I have no idea. Angie and I don't really talk about my dad. Sometimes she brings him up, but it's too . . . I don't really want to talk to her about him. Partly it's because she's always bugging me to go to the doctor, probably because she's scared something will happen to me, too, but I'm too busy to deal with all of that right now. But also, it makes me too sad, I guess, which is stupid. It'll be five years next Friday. I shouldn't be sad about this anymore, but I guess I am."

There were so many things that she wanted to say to him, but who the hell was she to tell him how to deal with his grief over his dad's death? She'd never experienced that before. But one thing she knew for sure.

"It's not stupid," she said. "He was your dad. Of course you're still sad."

He wrapped his arms around her.

"Yeah. He was my dad," he said. "And he was a pretty great dad."

She took a deep breath.

"I bet Angela is still sad, too. It might make you feel better to talk to her about it. She's the only one who knows how it feels to have lost your dad."

He nodded slowly.

"That's true. She is."

She rubbed her hand against his stubbly cheek. Would he get mad at her for this?

"I know you're busy and I'm sure you're fine, but maybe think about going to the doctor? Just to make Angela feel better?"

He stiffened up.

"I'll think about it."

She maybe shouldn't have said anything.

"I'm sorry, it's probably not my business."

He shook his head.

"No, it's okay. One of the things I like about you is that you always say what you mean."

Huh. That was a thing that most people *didn't* like about her. She leaned up and kissed him on the cheek. He turned and kissed her on the lips.

"Thanks for listening. I'm sorry if I—"

She held her finger up to his lips to stop him.

"No apologies. We all need a shoulder to lean on sometimes. I wouldn't have offered mine if I didn't want to."

• • • • • • •

Carlos knew Nik well enough at this point to know that she didn't do anything she didn't want to. But he was used to being the one offering his shoulder for people to lean on. He wasn't sure how he felt about it being the other way around.

He couldn't believe he'd talked to her about his dad. He didn't talk to anyone about his dad. It had been kind of nice, actually, especially since Nik hadn't pounced on the topic and asked him a million questions. She'd just mostly listened.

"Oh, hey, Angie is at Jessie's house tonight for dinner. I should check to see if there have been any updates."

She took a spoonful of rum raisin ice cream.

"No problem. How's Jessie doing?"

"Bored, but okay. We just need to keep her there."

He pulled his phone out of his pocket to see four texts from Angie. His heart rate sped up, but when he clicked on them, they were four different selfies of her and Jessie together. At least, he thought the fourth one was of the two of them.

"What the hell is this picture?" He showed Nik the last one, with two faces covered in some white material with holes cut out for eyes and lips.

She shook her head at him, a disappointed look on her face.

"For someone with a sister and a cousin who's like a sister, you should know what a sheet mask is. The best kind of girlfriend activity. You pop them on, relax for ten to twenty minutes, usually take a few selfies, and take them off. You should try them; I bet it would help after a long day at work."

He laughed and put his arm around her.

"That's what a big-screen TV and basketball were invented for."

She handed him the remote from the coffee table and leaned her head on his chest.

"Speaking of, I'm impressed at your restraint. I know the playoffs are on."

So he turned on the game, and they spent the next hour curled up on the couch watching the second half of a pretty exciting game between two teams he couldn't care less about. His ideal post-work wind down kind of game—he got all the fun of the lead changes and the great shots, but none of the up and down emotions of a true fan of either of those teams.

"Ahhh, that was excellent," he said when the buzzer blew. Nik didn't respond. He pushed her hair back from her face. She was fast asleep, her head still on his chest. He bent down and kissed her forehead.

"Hey," he said in a low voice. "Time for bed."

Her eyes fluttered open, and she looked confused for a few seconds before she realized where she was. She sat up straight.

"I fell asleep, didn't I? I'm sorry."

He stood up and held out a hand to her.

"You missed an amazing game. I bet that breaks your heart. Let's go to bed."

He led her into his bedroom and she looked around.

"This is nice," she said. "Very peaceful."

He was just glad his clothes were no longer all over the floor and were in the hamper in the closet.

"Thanks. It is peaceful, but maybe too peaceful? I had no time to paint before I moved in here, and I keep thinking of painting this room, because it feels kind of depressing with all of the gray. Maybe some weekend I'll try to tackle it, once I figure out what I want instead."

She put her arms around him.

"As long as it isn't Dodger blue, any color works for me."

He leaned down to kiss her.

"I'll keep that in mind, though you know, I *am* a Dodger fan."

She ran her fingers through his hair and kissed his stubbly cheek.

"I know, don't remind me. I keep trying to forget that," she said as she unbuckled his belt.

"And here I was, about to say that if you were too tired for sex tonight, it was okay." He unbuttoned her jeans and pushed them to the floor. She kicked them to the side.

"Why did you think I took a little nap? I had to rest up."

She wrapped one leg around his waist, and he put his hands under her butt and lifted her. She laughed and wrapped her other leg around him.

"Well then, we need to make good use of that nap of yours, don't we?" He dropped her down on his bed. He liked the way she looked there, unsmiling, with her eyes roaming over his body. "You look good in my bed. I can't believe it's taken me this long to get you in it."

She stretched her arms above her body in a way that accentuated her breasts, almost, but not quite visible in her thin tank top.

"I can't believe it, either," she said. "I think it was because you didn't want to share this incredible bed with me. First your couch, then your bed—you are incredible at selecting furniture. I could stay here forever."

He pulled his clothes off before crawling above her onto the bed.

"Well then, you're in luck, because I'm going to keep you here for a damn long time. We have . . ." He glanced at the clock as he pulled her tank top over her head. "Eleven hours until I have to get up in the morning. Eleven and a half, if I push it. You're going to be very familiar with this bed."

She propped herself up so she could unhook her bra and tossed it to the side. Thank God she did—he was agile, but unhooking a woman's bra from behind her back while he was kneeling over her in bed might have been too much for even him.

And now those breasts of hers were bare for him. He cupped them with his hands, enjoying their fullness, their hard nipples in the middle of his palms. She stared up at him, her eyes heavy lidded, a smile hovering around the corners of her mouth.

"Do with me what you will, Dr. Ibarra. Your bed, your rules."

Holy shit, did that get him hot. He took a deep breath, and her smile got bigger.

"Oh, you like that, do you?" She glanced down. "Mmm, I can tell you like that."

He bent down to kiss her.

"If I had known it would be this fun to get you in my bed, I would have managed it weeks ago." He looked her naked body over and grinned. "Okay. Here's what we're going to do first . . ."

Chapter Fourteen

When Nik woke up the next morning, she was alone in Carlos's big pillowlike bed. She wondered briefly where he was, decided it was either in the bathroom or on a phone call, and abandoned thought to luxuriate in his fluffy blankets against her bare skin.

That was until she heard him coming back into the room. She stayed right where she was, ready for him to get back under the covers with her.

Instead, he leaned down and kissed her cheek, the only part of her body that wasn't covered by his blankets. She pulled down the covers and smiled up at him.

"Good morning," she said.

"Good morning," he said. "How do you feel about coffee?"

She smiled and turned over to face him. He had on gray sweatpants and nothing else.

"I feel great about coffee, but you know that. I always feel great about coffee."

He smiled back at her. Her hair probably looked insane right now. She usually tried to at least put it in a ponytail after they'd gone to bed, but last night . . . well, there hadn't been time.

"Excellent." He put a mug of coffee on the bedside table next to her. "Here you go."

She looked over at the mug, and then back up at him.

"Really? You made me coffee?" He nodded at her like the answer was obvious, which she guessed it was. She still couldn't believe it.

She sat up in glee. He'd actually made her coffee? He brought it to her in bed? No one had brought her coffee in bed since . . . wait, actually, no one had *ever* brought her coffee in bed. Other than the room-service waiters at hotels.

She picked up the mug and breathed in the hot, warm, earthy coffee smell.

"Now. How do you feel about breakfast?"

She looked up from her mug. Was this a trick question?

"I have very strong, positive feelings about breakfast at any given moment. Why . . . why do you ask?"

He walked toward the bedroom door.

"Wait here."

Seconds later, he was back with a tray in his hands. Okay, no, it wasn't a tray, it was a cookie sheet, but did she care about that? Not in the slightest. He set the cookie sheet/tray on her knees, and on it was a plate with a pile of golden scrambled eggs, three pieces of bacon, and two slices of generously buttered toast. Oh, and a knife and fork, and a little pot of jam. A little pot of jam? Now she knew this must be a dream.

"This looks amazing," she said, because that's what you say in dreams to people who bring you freshly made breakfast. "Did you make all of this?"

He smiled that same proud smile from when she'd complimented his risotto the night before. Apparently, no matter how good of a cook you were, you liked it when people told you your food was good. Now that she knew that, she'd tell him constantly.

"I did. I hope you like scrambled eggs. I wasn't sure. I know you like pancakes, but . . ."

Luckily, she was a fan of all breakfast foods.

"I love scrambled eggs. I love all of this."

She could never let Courtney know he'd made her breakfast *twice.* Oh shit, and he'd made her dinner last night, too. Courtney had such inane ways of judging relationships, but convincing her that it was just that Carlos loved to cook would be a losing battle.

He got back in the bed next to her, his own plate in his hands.

"You haven't even tried it yet. How do you know you love it?"

She picked up her fork and took a bite of eggs. Delicate and creamy, they were everything she wanted scrambled eggs to be.

"Now I've tried it and I know I love it. Satisfied?"

He nodded.

"Very much so."

Far too quickly, she'd finished all of her food and lay back down in bed.

"Oh my God, I'm so full I'm going to die."

He was still chewing on his last piece of bacon.

"Maybe you shouldn't have eaten so fast, hmmm?"

She pulled the blankets over her head.

"I worked up an appetite. I was hungry!" she said to the underside of his comforter.

He pushed his plate down to the foot of the bed and put his head under the blankets to join her.

"What did you say?"

They were almost nose to nose, tucked underneath his warm heavy blankets. It felt like they were in a cocoon together. She could happily stay like this with him all day.

"I said I worked up an appetite for all that food."

He put his hand on her knee and ran it up and down the side of her body. She'd kept the sheet wrapped around herself as she ate, but now her whole body was available to him again.

"You sure did. Why do you think I woke up early to make you breakfast? I thought you might be hungry."

"Mmmm, thank you for that." His hand kept moving up her body. She turned over onto her back, and he pushed her legs open. "What time is it? When do you have to be at work?"

He kissed her neck.

"Um. I think about seven thirty? I know how you feel about waking up early, but I thought the coffee and breakfast would help?"

Her eyes popped open and she pulled the covers down.

"Seven thirty in the *morning*?" She looked around the room, not seeing a clock anywhere that would confirm his statement. But then, why would he lie about that? "You woke me up at seven a.m.?"

He dropped kisses along her shoulder.

"I know, I know, I'm so sorry. But I was awake. And hungry. And I thought you might want some eggs . . ." he kissed her cheek, "and bacon . . ." he kissed her other cheek, "and strawberry jam . . ." he kissed her mouth. He made kissing into an art form. Never rushed, never impatient, no matter how fast and eager and forceful he was.

"Hmmmm. I guess you're going to have to find a way to make my hour of lost sleep up to me. Do you have any idea of how you're going to do that?"

She could feel him smile against her skin.

"Oh, I have some ideas."

Later, when he was frantically getting dressed to go to work, he stopped just as he'd buckled his belt.

"Oh, hey, are you free Saturday night?"

She picked up her jeans from the floor and pulled her phone out of the pocket.

"Let me check. Why, what's up?"

She scrolled through her calendar—birthday party Friday night, and ugh, a wedding shower with Dana on Saturday afternoon, but nothing Saturday night.

"Yeah, I'm free. Are you sure you don't mean Saturday afternoon? If you can give me a good excuse to get out of this wedding shower I have to go to, I'll love you forever."

Ooops. She turned to pull her jeans on and decided to pretend she'd never said that. Luckily, it didn't seem like Carlos had heard anything past "free."

"It's no big deal, but my buddy Drew and his fiancée, Alexa, will be in town, and I'm going to have dinner with them that night, if you want to join us."

Wait, what? He wanted her to meet his friend and his friend's fiancée? Part of the whole reason she had wanted to stay away from relationships was so she wouldn't have to hang out with people's annoying friends when she didn't want to. The last time she'd done that, she was with Fisher and his friends at Dodger Stadium, and the whole world knew how that one had ended.

Why hadn't she waited to see what he'd had in mind *before* saying she was free? She could have used the wedding shower to get out of this. It would have been the only good thing a wedding shower had ever done for the world!

"If you have work to do or whatever, it's cool." Carlos was digging through his sock drawer. "But Drew and Alexa are fun, and I think you'd like them."

He didn't seem to really care whether she went or not. That made her feel better. Maybe he was just inviting her so he'd have some company around his smug couple friends when they started talking about countertops or wedding flowers or the adorable bed-and-breakfast they'd stayed in on their last romantic getaway.

"Okay, sure," she said. "Just let me know when and where."

He had met *her* friends, after all.

"Will do!" he said as he put his watch on. They walked out of his house together, and he kissed her at the bottom of the steps. "I might just make it to work on time. See you Saturday."

She kissed him back.

"See you Saturday!"

What had she gotten herself in to?

• • • • • • •

"So *this* is the new house!" Drew said, standing at Carlos's front door on Saturday afternoon. "I can't believe you bought a house without consulting me."

Carlos waved Drew into the house.

"Please, you would have been useless during the entire process. The only reason I managed to actually find a house to buy was because I didn't have you around trying to convince me that I needed an in-house sauna or man cave or granite countertops or whatever thing it is they sell you on those house shows you like to watch."

Drew walked in the house and nodded as he looked around.

"You know, I've gotten Alexa hooked on those things, too? Sometimes on Saturdays she's all ready to go to the farmers' market and brunch and yoga and whatever else and, like, four hours later we're still on the couch deep into a house-shopping marathon. It's fantastic."

Carlos rolled his eyes. Then he looked at Drew's face. Damn it, the guy looked so fucking happy he could barely even make fun of him.

"I'll give you the grand tour as long as you don't tell me anything more about those shows. The house is pretty small, and I haven't done half the things I've wanted to do with it, but if you tell me that I need a double sink or recessed lighting or any of that bullshit, I'm kicking you out."

Drew accepted the beer Carlos handed him and took a long swig.

"I'm already a fan of this TV. Does it swivel so you can watch it both in the kitchen and from the couch?"

Carlos nodded and patted the top of the TV.

"It sure does. It makes me happy every day."

After a walk around the house, where Drew asked a surprising amount of questions about the heated floors in the bathroom and the kitchen, they ended up on the couch in the living room with the game on.

"Oh, hey, how's Jessie doing?"

Carlos automatically reached for his phone to check to see if anyone from the family had called him. Nothing.

"She's hanging in there. Her blood pressure is still high, and I'm still constantly worried about it, but her doctor doesn't seem to be. She's still only thirty-three weeks. I think my mom and aunt are saying rosaries every day about it. Hell, I should, too."

Drew patted him on the shoulder.

"She'll be okay, man. I'm sure her doctor is doing everything she should be."

She probably was, but that didn't make him any less terrified.

"Yeah. It's just that this time of year. I think everyone in my family gets pretty paranoid about health stuff. Me included."

Ever since Nik had brought it up, he'd been thinking about talking to Angela about their dad. Nik was probably right that Angie was the only person who knew what it was like to lose their dad. Maybe sharing that grief with her would help them both.

But he wasn't sure he was ready to do that. He'd spent almost five years trying to beat back his grief; the idea of welcoming it in felt obscene.

Carlos got up to get them chips and salsa and more beer. Drew immediately grabbed a chip, but hesitated before dipping it into the salsa. Carlos rolled his eyes.

"Oh my God, you haven't even been gone a year. I didn't forget you're scared of spicy food."

"I was just checking! I wasn't sure you stocked Drew-style salsa anymore."

Carlos leaned back against the couch cushions. Nik was right about this couch; it was pretty magical.

"I don't. I bought this just for you. Be honored. I wouldn't buy this bullshit for just anyone."

Drew put his hand over his heart.

"I am, man. I am."

At the next commercial break, Drew cleared his throat.

"Um, actually. Speaking of. There was something I wanted to ask you."

Speaking of what? Carlos raised his eyebrows at him.

"I'm flattered, but I don't think I'm ready to get married any time soon."

Drew threw a chip at him.

"Fuck you. I'm taken, remember?"

"Yeah, yeah, I remember," Carlos said.

"Anyway. I was going to say that if it wasn't for you, I probably never would have figured my shit out, and well, will you be my best man?"

Damn it. Carlos hadn't planned on getting emotional today, but he was surprisingly touched by this.

"Oh shit, man, of course I will."

"Thanks." Drew let out a deep breath. "I was going to ask when you were up in Berkeley for the engagement party, but you'd just found out about Jessie at that point and there was a lot going on. Just make sure your speech isn't too wild—my grandma is going to be there."

Carlos grinned.

"Oh, my speech is going to be fantastic." Carlos rubbed his hands together and reached for the good salsa. "This is going to be fun. Do you guys have a wedding date yet?"

Drew shook his head.

"Not yet—we're working on it. Probably sometime next summer. Hell, I'd do it tomorrow if I could. But you'll be the first to know as soon as we have a date. You better lock down that entire week for me."

Carlos laughed.

"You got it. I'm just trying to imagine what I would have thought if someone told me at this time last year that you'd be telling me a year later you'd be ready to get married 'tomorrow.' I would probably fall over in shock."

Drew picked up the empty salsa bowl and walked into the kitchen to refill it.

"You probably would have. Hell, I definitely would have. What can I say, sometimes when it hits, it hits."

At the next commercial break, Drew said—oh so casually—"Hey, so what's going on with this Dodgers-game girl? What's she like? We are going to get to meet her tonight, aren't we?"

Carlos rolled his eyes. Drew was doing that "we" thing that couples always did. Had he turned into one of those people already?

"Yes, 'we' are. Lucky for you, she was dying for an excuse to get out of some wedding shower she was supposed to go to, so you're it." Well, that was sort of true. Maybe that would stop Drew from trying to turn tonight's dinner into a whole couples' thing. "Don't make this into a big thing. I'm not ready to get married to her tomorrow."

"Okay, okay, it's not a big thing, I heard you the first time."

The smirk on Drew's face made Carlos pretty sure he hadn't heard him at all.

* * * * * * *

Dinner with Carlos, his friend, and his friend's probably perfect fiancée was the last thing Nik wanted to do. The one good thing about Fisher had been that all of his friends were so annoying that she'd made fun of them to their faces constantly without them even realizing it. She probably couldn't pull that off with Carlos's friends.

Also, she had no fucking idea what she should wear. Everyone at the shower was in cute little floral dresses, and she hadn't worn a cute little floral dress since she was seven years old. Her concession had been not wearing black to the shower in the first place. But tonight she wanted to not fit in a little less aggressively.

She stared into her closet for a full five minutes before she gave up and called Dana.

"Okay, I went to that boring shower with you; now you have to pay me back by getting me out of this dinner tonight."

"Why don't you want to go?" Dana asked. Nik could tell by her regular breathing that she was running. It was good that she liked Dana so much—otherwise she'd hate her for being able to have a regular conversation during exercise.

"He's not even my boyfriend. Why do I need to meet his friends? Plus, what if they hate me?"

They probably would hate her. They would think she was too mean or sarcastic or abrasive for Carlos.

"Why'd you tell him you would go, then?" Dana asked. "You usually don't say yes to things you don't want to do."

Maybe she should wear that leather motorcycle jacket again? She liked that jacket. It made her feel like a badass.

It would make her feel like a very sweaty badass tonight; it was well over eighty degrees outside. She put the jacket back in her closet with a sigh.

"That's not true. I do things I don't want to do all the time. I went to that stupid shower today with you, didn't I?"

Dana's loud huff from a normal person running would have just meant they were out of breath, but not from Dana.

"Courtney and I don't count. No really, why did you say yes?"

Nik sighed.

"He asked if I was free for dinner—was I supposed to lie? And he'd just . . ." No, she shouldn't tell Dana about Carlos making her breakfast. She wasn't Courtney, but she'd still react to that. "Plus, you guys have met him. It felt churlish to say no to meeting his friends."

"Okay, then you have to go. But they'll like you! We liked Carlos, didn't we? And Courtney and I are a pretty tough crowd when it comes to men. Wear that navy blue striped dress you wore to my birthday party. And do not wear those booties I know you're already thinking about wearing. They look like clown shoes."

She put the booties back into her closet.

"I hate you. You're the worst. I'll wear some sandals or something."

"I hate you, too," Dana said. "Now I've got to go. I'm about to meet my running partner."

Nik stopped halfway through picking up her silver sandals. They made her legs look great.

"Haven't you been running this whole time?"

"Just a mile, running to meet her." Nik had never said "just" and "a mile" about running in her life. "Okay, talk later! Let me know how it goes!"

Dinner was at Café Stella, one of her favorite restaurants in Silver Lake and one that had the advantage of being so close to her apartment she could walk there, even in her hot silver sandals. She told people she loved it despite how trendy and Instagrammable it was, but she had been known to post a few Instagrams from it herself. She saw Carlos when she walked in, but he was too busy talking to the two people on the other side of the table to notice her walking toward them.

Ugh, why was she so nervous about this?

"Hi," she said, when she was standing right next to the table.

"Hey!" Carlos jumped out of his chair and kissed her on the cheek. "I didn't even see you come in." They sat down, and she did a double take when she saw the woman across the table from her.

"Nik, these are my friends Drew and Alexa. Drew and Alexa, meet Nik."

Carlos had *not* told her that Alexa was black. From everything that he'd told her about Drew, mild salsa and all, it would never have occurred to her that he'd be engaged to a black woman.

And . . . judging by the quickly masked look of surprise on Alexa's face, Alexa hadn't known *she* was black. She hadn't thought to have the "did you tell your friends I'm black?" conversation with Carlos—she assumed that because he was Latino she didn't have to. Which was probably partly true; she hadn't been worried that his friends were racist. But if Alexa had been the white woman that she'd expected her to be, that look of surprise on her face would have been a hell of a lot more stressful. Instead, she felt some of her anxiety about this evening drain away.

"It's so nice to meet you both. I've heard a lot about you," she said. *Except that Alexa is black.*

"Same here," Drew said. "I, um, saw your claim to fame on SportsCenter before I even knew Carlos was there."

Alexa nudged him, none too subtly.

"What Drew meant to say right there was that—"

Nik laughed.

"I appreciate that, but it's okay. Three weeks ago, bringing that up would have made me 'accidentally' spill my drink on anyone who did it, but I'm not as sensitive about it anymore."

"So, Nik," Alexa said, "Carlos tells us you're a writer? What kind of stuff do you write?"

She wasn't as sensitive about the proposal anymore, but she was still glad Alexa changed the subject.

"A combination of investigative journalism and celebrity profiles. Getting to do a profile of Ivy Robinson in the middle of working on a story about foster kids was a real pick-me-up, let me tell you."

"The profile in *Vanity Fair*? You wrote that story?" Nik nodded and Alexa's eyes lit up. "That was such a fun read! My girlfriends and I kept texting each other quotes from it."

There was nothing like a pure spontaneous compliment to make you like someone.

"Thanks so much. I had a lot of fun writing it. I'm glad it came through for the reader. And . . . I think Carlos said you work for the mayor of Berkeley?"

Alexa nodded.

"Chief of staff."

"Wow, big job. How do you like it?"

Her wide smile said it all.

"I love it. Sometimes I hate it, obviously, and sometimes it drives me up a wall. But even in some of those times, I love it."

They talked about both of their jobs for a while, while the guys talked about doctor stuff, until the waitress interrupted.

"Have you guys had a chance to look at the drink menu?" she asked.

Both Nik and Alexa shook their heads; they had been too busy talking.

While Alexa looked at the drink menu, Nik looked around and smiled despite herself. The sunset through the glass roof of the restaurant tinted the sky a soft pink. There were plants growing everywhere and lights hanging from ropes overhead. Even she had to admit that it was stupidly romantic. Carlos reached over and took her hand under the table. The restaurant must be getting to him, too. She smiled at him.

"I'll have a glass of the sparkling rosé," Alexa said.

Carlos squeezed her hand. Nik looked down at her menu so she wouldn't giggle.

"Um, I'll have one of those, too, please," she said. He squeezed her hand harder and she squeezed back.

They switched their conversation to the food menu and the four of them hotly debated whether to get fries or mashed potatoes with their steaks (they decided on both).

After they ordered food, Alexa brought the conversation back to Nik's job.

"I loved all the stuff about Ivy's stylist in that piece. My best friend is a stylist in the Bay Area, and obviously that isn't as high profile a job as it is around here, but it was still such a great read for her, especially since Ivy's stylist is another black woman."

She still could not believe Carlos hadn't told her that Alexa was black.

"That's so interesting that your friend is a stylist. I hadn't really realized there were stylists outside of the celebrity centers of New York and L.A. But of course there are plenty of people who live elsewhere who need to get dressed, too. I guess I'm so stuck in this world I've gotten myopic about it."

Carlos tapped her on the hand that was just reaching for her wine.

"Excuse me. I hate to interrupt. But what the hell is a stylist?"

The rest of the table burst out laughing, even Drew. Carlos immediately turned on him.

"Oh, so this is something *you* know? You leave L.A. and now you're an expert?"

Nik was still laughing, more at the look on his face than anything else.

"I don't know why Drew knows it, but honestly, this isn't the kind of thing most people know unless you pay a lot of attention to celebrities, which, for good or bad, I do. A stylist is basically someone to help you get dressed, which sounds stupid, but for celebrities, it's totally necessary. And honestly, whenever I talk to one, I wish I had one myself."

Alexa nodded.

"Yeah, that's exactly what Maddie does. She has some local minor celebrities in her client list, but more of her clients are just really busy women who have to look polished, but don't have the time or inclination to figure out how to do it themselves. Using people like her has become more common, especially for women who aren't sample size, whether they're petite or plus-size or tall or anything else where shopping for clothes is a lot more of a pain. I'm just grateful she's my best friend and she helps me for free. I wouldn't be able to afford her on my salary. And I'll tell you how Drew knows what a stylist is—because Maddie told him he was no longer allowed to go out in public with me if he kept wearing those busted old canvas sneakers he loved so much, that's how."

Carlos's laugh boomed across the restaurant.

"You mean someone actually managed to get him to get rid of those things? I'd been trying for years! I'm convinced of the utility of stylists now—no need to say anything else."

While they were still waiting for their food, Nik got up to go to the bathroom and Alexa joined her. When they were washing their hands afterward, Nik looked at Alexa in the mirror, and the two glasses of sparkling wine on an almost empty stomach eliminated her filter.

"Okay, I just have to say. Carlos did *not* tell me that you were black."

Alexa dropped her hands on the counter.

"Neither of them told me you were black! What is wrong with them? I know Drew saw you on that video, so he definitely knew. I never saw it, though—I don't pay attention when he's watching most things on ESPN, except when Serena is playing. When you sat down, I almost killed them both."

Nik handed her a paper towel.

"I thought you looked surprised when I sat down."

Someone else walked into the bathroom, and Alexa lowered her voice.

"Pleasantly surprised, obviously, but I mean come on." She held open the door for Nik on the way out of the bathroom. "But hey, Carlos is great, so now I'm even happier for him."

Nik decided to ignore that comment. She knew that she and Carlos were on the same page, and if his friends wanted to do some kind of "we want everyone to find the happiness that we've found!!!" thing that newly engaged couples did, he would have to be the one to burst their bubble, not her.

After dinner, dessert, and a few after-dinner drinks, the four of them hugged good-bye.

"Well, that was a lot better than I thought it would be," Nik said when she got into Carlos's car.

Oops. She hadn't meant to say that out loud.

"What do you mean? You didn't think you were going to like my friends?"

She dodged that question.

"You didn't tell me Alexa is black!"

He froze, halfway through backing out of his parking spot.

"Seriously? I didn't?" He laughed. "I was just going to say that I'm sure I told you that, but then, I'm sure that's the kind of thing you'd remember."

She looked at him sideways, her eyebrows sky-high.

"You're absolutely right; I would have."

He shook his head as he drove the short distance to her apartment.

"I can't believe that. I'm sorry." He put his hand on her knee and smiled at her. "I guess I'm going to have to find a way to make that up to you, aren't I?"

She smiled back at him.

"Well, I did have plenty of rosé this evening."

Chapter Fifteen

Wednesday night after work, Carlos drove straight to Angela's apartment. The last time he was there he'd noticed that her cheap IKEA bookshelf was falling apart, so he'd bought her a new good one. He called when he was outside of her house.

"Hey!" she said when she answered the phone. "Did those million messages in the family group text drive you as crazy as it did me?"

He laughed and got out of the car.

"Oh my God, Angie—I checked my phone after a few hours of seeing patients and panicked because I had thirty-five new messages, but they were just Mom, Tia Eva, and Jessie all talking about Popsicles? What was even happening there?"

Angela sighed.

"I know! I'm sure Jessie's going stir-crazy, but that made even me want to yell at her."

Carlos popped open his trunk.

"Please tell her not to do that again. I know you'll get mad at me if I say it. But also, come open the door. I'm here."

He hung up the phone and lifted the box with her new bookshelf in it out of his trunk. He was at the front door of her building just as she opened it.

"What are you doing here? You didn't tell me you were coming over tonight."

He walked past her to the elevator.

"Do you have a hot date? I hope so."

She rolled her eyes as they got in the elevator.

"No, but good try. Just making dinner and getting some work done tonight. What's in that box?"

He followed her out of the elevator to her apartment.

"A new bookshelf. That old one of yours has got to go, and I knew if you bought yourself one you'd just make me put it together anyway, so I figured I'd do it on my own schedule."

"You bought me a bookshelf?" She opened the door for him. The smell of garlic wafted toward him. "And you're putting it together for me tonight? What did I do to deserve this?"

He set the box down on her living room floor and pulled it open.

"Probably very little. Where's that toolbox I bought you?"

She went to her hall closet and took the toolbox off of a shelf there. When he opened it, he was thrilled to see that things were all in the wrong places. She must have actually used it since the last time he was here.

"Do you want a beer? I have wine, but you always get all fussy about my wine, so I'm not even going to offer it to you this time."

He definitely couldn't have rosé around his sister.

"Yes, please." He slid all of the shelves out of the box and glanced at the instruction manual. This shouldn't take too long.

"Here." She handed him a beer and looked over the pile of wood and wood-like materials on her living room floor. "This looks like it'll be bigger and less flimsy than the one I had. Thanks, Carlos."

"No problem." He opened the little bag of screws and reached for a screwdriver. He should have bought Angie an electric screwdriver along with this tool kit. Oh well, now he knew what he'd get her for Christmas. "Are you still in the middle of cooking, or can you hang out and talk to me while I do this?"

She sat down on her easy chair and set a glass of wine on the table next to her.

"I put a roast chicken in the oven like thirty minutes ago, so I have plenty of time. If you want dinner to reward you after you're done, I'll have plenty of food once it's done cooking."

He screwed the side of the bookshelf to the bottom and grinned at her.

"Oooh, are you making those crispy potatoes to go along with it? I love those things. I could eat a million of them."

She shook her head and sighed. "Unfortunately, I am. I guess I won't have any potatoes left over for lunch tomorrow."

He picked up the other side and fitted a screw into the bottom of the bookcase.

"You definitely won't. You'll barely have enough for yourself."

She took a sip of her wine and watched him for a few minutes.

"Come on, you can tell me about your new girlfriend. I know you have one; I can sense it. I promise I won't tell Mama if you tell me!"

Of course. He should have known that as soon as she got him alone she would quiz him about that.

"God, no. Don't worry, if there's ever anything to tell you about in that category—which there won't be for a long time—I'll tell you first."

She moved to join him on the floor and picked up the bag of screws.

"You've just seemed much more relaxed over the past few weeks. It's nice."

"Mmmhmmm." He had been more relaxed over the past few weeks, come to think about it. But that was just because he'd been settling in at work.

He reached his palm out for another screw, and she handed it to him.

"You don't have any snacks or anything? I'm getting hungry, smelling that chicken cooking and knowing we won't get to eat for, like, thirty more minutes."

She shook her head and closed her eyes.

"You storm into my house without warning, take over my living room, claim all of my potatoes, and now you're demanding a snack?" She stood up. "Next time I'm not answering my phone when you call."

The emptiest of empty threats. He kept screwing the back of the bookshelf in while she rummaged around the kitchen.

"I was wondering," he said, his eyes focused on the bookshelf pieces. "What did you do with the money from Dad's life insurance?"

From the corner of his eye, he saw her walk back into the room, but he didn't look up.

"That trip," she said after a long pause. She sat down on the couch in front of him. "Remember that trip I took with Jessie to Italy a year later? That's what I spent it on."

He stopped pretending he was still occupied with the bookshelf and looked up at her, but she was looking down at her lap.

"I felt like I should spend it on my student loans or a down payment or something, but after you bought that car, I kind of felt free to do what I really wanted to do with it."

He hadn't told anyone in his family that was how he'd bought his car.

"Wait," he said. "How did you know that I used mine to buy the car?"

She rolled her eyes at him.

"Carlos. I'm not an idiot. And I know you better than anyone. Do you think I thought you got a sudden raise or something?"

She had a good point.

"Anyway, your trip," he said.

She nodded.

"I'd always wanted to go to Italy, ever since he bought me *A Room with a View* when I was a kid. Dad always made fun of me for how obsessed I was with that book and with the idea of going to Italy someday. 'Mexico isn't good enough for you?' he would say. But he took me to see the movie when there was a showing of it on the big screen at the ArcLight that time and out to Italian food afterward. And at Christmas he would always slip me little things about Italy, like cookbooks or Italian language books, stuff like that."

Her voice caught, and she stopped for a second.

"Anyway, I did use some of the money to pay off my credit card debt. But the rest paid for tickets for me and Jessie to fly to Rome and train tickets to Florence and Venice." She laughed. "Jessie got so mad at me for insisting on paying for her, but I told her that Dad would flip out if I went alone, and he would want her to go with me—all of which she knew was totally true."

He shook his head.

"I thought you guys went because Jessie got that promotion."

She looked at the framed picture on the wall of her and Jessie on a balcony with Italy in the background.

"That's what we told Mama and Tia Eva. We knew I would get lectures from them if we told them the truth. Jessie did get that promotion. But it came well after I'd already booked our tickets. Our excuse before it happened was going to be that one of us had had a terrible breakup, but we hadn't decided who yet."

He shook his head.

"I'm not sure if that would have worked as well with them."

She leaned back against the couch and laughed.

"It definitely wouldn't have."

He reached for the bookshelf pieces again.

"So um," he said as he lined up the little wooden dowels. "About Friday."

She slowly straightened up.

"What about Friday?" Her voice was soft, gentle. It made him concentrate hard on inserting the dowels into the sides of the bookshelf, so he wouldn't have to look at her as he talked.

"I don't know if you have any plans. But I thought it might be nice if we could do something together that day. And maybe . . ." For some terrible reason, his voice caught. "Maybe talk about Dad."

She sat down next to him and put both arms around him. He abandoned the bookshelf and hugged his little sister close.

"I would love that," she said. "I would love that a lot."

He wiped his eyes and hoped she didn't notice.

"So would I."

* * * * * * *

Nik got a text from Carlos on her way into Natalie's Gym on Thursday night.

What're you up to on Saturday? Want to help me make enchiladas? I'm making a huge batch so Jessie can have some for her freezer, but I promise we'll get to eat some of our labor.

She had no idea how to make enchiladas, but she had no doubt Carlos would tell her exactly what to do. And she knew the result would be delicious, if he was in charge.

What time and what should I bring?

She asked the person at the front desk where she could find Natalie, and was directed to an office in the back.

4ish. Bring some beer, no offense to rosé.

"Hi." Nik poked her head into Natalie's office. "Do you have a second?"

She'd thought for the past few weeks about Carlos's suggestion to write a piece about Natalie's Gym and had decided he might be right. A gym in L.A. that had a sliding scale was unusual in the first place, and one that was as positive about all kinds of bodies as Natalie's was like a unicorn. A ton of women's magazines would jump at a story about a woman-owned gym in L.A., especially with someone as perky and photogenic as Natalie at the heart of it.

Natalie looked up and smiled at her.

"Nik! Of course. Hi!" How was Natalie's hair always so perfect? This woman worked out for a living, and yet she had a perfect swinging blond ponytail.

"Hi. I wanted to ask you if you were open to me writing a story about you and your gym."

Natalie's smile faded. She stared blankly at her and didn't say anything. So Nik kept talking.

"I've written for the *L.A.* and *New York Times*, *Variety*, *GQ*, the *New Yorker*, and a lot more. You can look me up to check out my work to make sure I'm legit. This isn't why I started coming to your gym—I started for very different reasons—but it's pretty rare to find a place that promotes feminism, actually practices being inclusive, and is accessible to women of so many different backgrounds and socioeconomic classes. So I want to write about it."

Natalie still didn't say anything. Uh-oh. Nik didn't really want to write this story without Natalie's cooperation and permission.

"Yes." Natalie nodded, but still wasn't smiling. "Okay. Email me and we can schedule a time to talk in the next few weeks. Does that work for you?"

Nik took the card Natalie handed to her and gave her one of her own.

"Absolutely. Thanks so much, and I'll be in touch. See you in there."

Natalie nodded and turned back to her computer.

Nik left Natalie's office and walked into the locker room to change for class. Natalie hadn't seemed happy about the idea of Nik writing about the gym, even though this was only a good thing for her business. This piece was either going to be a disaster or more interesting than she thought.

At the bar after class, as soon as they got their drinks, Courtney zeroed in on Dana.

"Okay, spill it."

Dana's eyes widened.

"Spill what? What are you talking about?"

Nik was equally confused.

"Yeah, spill what?" she asked Courtney.

Courtney glared at Nik.

"Not you too. Are you too busy with your new man to see what's right in front of your face?"

She gestured at Dana.

"This one is over here smiling like there's no tomorrow, beaming at her phone when she thinks we don't see her, AND when I stopped by her house the other day to drop off cupcakes, she had a huge vase of gorgeous peonies in her bedroom and she said she had to go for a run as soon as I looked at them."

Oooh. Nik looked at Dana, who had a very happy, and very guilty, look on her face.

Courtney banged her hand on the table.

"Who." BANG. "Is." BANG. "The New Woman?" BANG. BANG. BANG.

By this time the whole bar was looking at them, and Dana, shaking with laughter, had her face in her hands. Finally she sat up.

"Okay. Courtney's right. I didn't tell you guys because . . ." She sighed. "I didn't tell you guys because The New Woman is Natalie. And since we're still all in the class with her for another week, I thought—"

Nik was glad her glass wasn't in her hand, or she would have dropped it.

"Natalie, our Natalie? Natalie from the gym? Tall? Blond? HOT? That Natalie?" she asked.

Courtney was still staring dumbfounded at Dana.

"That Natalie," Dana said. "Anyway, it's still pretty new—I asked her a question after class a few weeks ago, and one thing led to another and we became running partners."

That's not how "one thing led to another" was supposed to end.

"And then?" Nik asked.

"And one day, we got back to my place after a run, and I invited her inside for some vitamin water, and then . . ."

Courtney leapt across the table to throw her arms around Dana.

"I'm so mad at you for keeping this a secret from us," she said, while hugging her tightly.

Nik shook her head. "Now I'm going to have to put a long disclaimer on my story about the gym—I can't even believe this." She tried to frown, but Dana was grinning so hard it was impossible not to grin back at her.

"Don't get too excited, you guys," Dana said. "Again, it's only been a few weeks, but things are good so far."

Nik sat back and smiled.

"Now who's mad at me for signing all of us up for self-defense classes, huh? You two will never be able to argue with me ever again."

They both threw ice at her.

Chapter Sixteen

Nik pulled up to Carlos's house late Saturday afternoon, with a six-pack of beer in her hand and her old Stanford T-shirt on. She had a feeling that enchilada making was a messy endeavor.

"Hey! Come on in." Carlos wrapped his arms around her and held on tight.

"Everything okay?" she asked.

He nodded and kissed her hair.

"It's been a kind of emotional week, that's all. Glad you're here."

She pulled his head down to her and kissed him.

"I'm glad to be here."

They stood like that for a while, until he kissed the top of her head and pulled away.

"Okay. Let's get cooking."

They walked together into the kitchen, which looked prepared for battle. There were packs of tortillas stacked in one corner, bags of dried chilies in another, aluminum baking pans all over the kitchen table, and many other ingredients that she didn't recognize lined up on the counter. Her eyes widened.

"You ready for this?" Carlos surveyed the kitchen and rubbed his hands together.

She wasn't totally sure, but she nodded anyway.

"The first thing we have to do is to make the sauces," he said.

Sauces, plural. This dude didn't play around. She handed him the six-pack, and he took two beers out of it and put the rest in the fridge.

"Excellent. Let me get you started and I can pull out some snacks for us."

Soon, she was standing over the sink, pulling the papery skins off what seemed like hundreds of tomatillos. He was standing next to her, quartering onions, and lining them up on a big cookie sheet with garlic and a variety of green peppers.

It felt peaceful, standing there and cooking with him. Some game was on the TV, but on low, so it was perfect background noise. They weren't talking, but the silence between them felt easy. She could feel him smiling next to her.

When she was done, she washed and dried the weirdly shaped little fruits and lined them up in even rows on the cookie sheet.

"Perfect." He'd moved on to shredding the pot full of beef. It smelled amazing. She opened her mouth and he slid a piece between her lips.

"Oh my God, that's good," she said.

"Now I know that you are sincere when you say that in bed, because you say it just like that."

She smirked at him.

"Or I could be lying both times."

He shook his head.

"Impossible. I know how good that meat is. If I'm cocky about anything, it's my enchiladas."

She shook her head as she washed her hands.

"'If he's cocky about anything,' he says."

He laughed and picked up the two cookie sheets full of vegetables.

"Open the oven so I can get these inside?"

Once the vegetables were broiling, she turned to him.

"What's next?"

He nodded at the other side of the stove.

"We need to get the chilies stemmed and seeded, and then soak them long enough so they soften. Put those on, and pull the chilies apart over the garbage can so the seeds come out, pull the stems off, then drop the pieces in that big pot."

She opened the bags of chilies as he carefully transferred all of the shredded beef from the cutting board to a big bowl. Once the bags were all open, she ripped each dried chili open with her fingers, and let the dry seeds rain out into the garbage can. Some of the seeds kind of stuck to the inside of the chilies, so she scraped them out with a fingernail before tossing the chili pieces into the pot on the stove.

"Beef enchiladas and chicken enchiladas . . . there are no vegetarians in your family, I take it?"

Carlos opened the oven again and took the sheet pans of vegetables out.

"God, no. They would probably all flip out if I brought over vegetarian enchiladas. Which is a shame, because I make some really good ones with cheese and onions in the same kind of red chile sauce we're making now. I just save those for parties with my friends instead of my family; even my carnivore friends happily eat them."

She rubbed her fingernail against a stubborn seed to loosen it from the pepper.

"That sounds delicious. I'd eat those in a second."

Carlos tipped all of the vegetables into a big pitcher.

"Excellent, you might just get the opportunity some time."

He stuck a bunch of cilantro leaves and a handheld blender inside the pitcher, and in about thirty seconds the roasted vegetables had become a fragrant olive-green sauce.

"See?" He turned to her for the first time in a while. "Now the tomatillo sauce is all . . . oh my God, what are you doing?"

She stopped, just as she'd pulled the stem off another dried chili.

"What? Isn't this what you told me to do?"

She had no idea why he was looking at her with that appalled look on his face.

He crossed the kitchen and picked up a box that had been sitting next to the bags of chilies.

"Gloves! Nik! Holy shit, you've been touching all of those chilies with your bare hands. Did I forget to tell you to put gloves on? Oh no."

She had no idea what he was talking about.

"What do gloves have to do with anything?"

He took her by the waist and pulled her over to the sink.

"You were touching dried hot chilies—and their seeds—with your bare hands. Your fingers are going to be on fire soon." He turned on the water and handed her the bottle of dish soap.

Oh.

Oooooh.

She poured the soap over her hands and scrubbed them with his sponge.

"I'm going to say something I don't normally say out loud, and especially not to men. I am an idiot."

He laughed but still looked concerned.

"I refuse to agree with that statement on the grounds that it may cause you to murder me."

She laughed.

"No, it's not your fault." She felt really stupid. "The box was sitting right there. I should have paid attention." She wiggled her nose. "It's okay. You don't have to stand over me and supervise my hand washing. Move on to your next task."

He picked up the box of surgical gloves and pulled a pair on.

"Okay, just keep washing your hands for a few more minutes while I work on these chilies."

She nodded. She reached up to scratch her nose, but caught herself just in time.

For the next few minutes he pulled the chilies open—taking a lot less care to remove all of the seeds than she had—while she scrubbed her hands. Finally, she turned off the water and turned to him.

"I think my hands are all right. But the thing is that my nose . . ."

He dropped a dried chili into the pot, with his latex-encased hands, and picked up another.

"Okay great, we must have caught it in time. Pull some gloves on and let's go."

She couldn't stand it anymore.

"I will in one second, but the thing is that my nose is on fire."

He dropped the chili and turned to her.

"What did you say?"

She grabbed his hand. It was getting worse by the second.

"My nose is on fire! My face! My face is on fire!"

He slowly looked up at her. Her face felt like it was bright red. How had it gotten so hot so fast? She wanted to submerge her head in a cold bathtub. Or a lake. Or maybe the ocean would help. No, too much salt.

"Your face. Oh shit. You touched your face, didn't you?"

She threw her hands in the air.

"Who cares, what does it matter? I mean, I guess I did, but I don't remember doing it, but also it's kind of moot right now because my face is on fire! What do we do to make this stop?"

She knew she wasn't being rational, but she didn't care. Because her face was on fire and getting hotter by the second.

Carlos opened the fridge and muttered to himself as he looked through it.

"Milk is good for capsaicin burns, but it's not like you can sit there with your nose in a bowl of milk, hmmmm."

He was being altogether too calm about this. What the fuck was he talking about, "capsaicin." This was not the time for fancy medical words. Had he not noticed that her FACE WAS ON FIRE?

"Carlos!"

"Sorry, sorry. What about this?" He took a tub of sour cream out of the fridge.

She took it from him.

"What do you mean 'what about this?' What's this going to do?" Why the hell was she even asking questions? She would literally do anything right now to make this stop.

He took the lid off of the tub of sour cream.

"Put it all over your face."

She narrowed her eyes at him, but scooped a big dollop out of the tub with her fingers anyway.

"Are you sure about this?"

He nodded.

"Of course I'm sure; I'm a doctor, aren't I? Smear a big layer of sour cream everywhere it hurts."

How the hell had she gotten herself here? This morning, she was waking up in her nice, normal bed in her nice, normal apartment in Silver Lake, and just a few hours later, a man was standing in front of her ordering her to smear sour cream all over her face. And the worst part was, she was going to do it.

"Fine, but if this doesn't work, I'm going to kill you and bury your body far, far away."

He nodded.

"You have my permission."

She patted the sour cream all over her nostrils, cheeks, and upper lip. It felt so soothing that she immediately applied more.

"There," he said. "Does that feel better?"

She dug her fingers back into the tub for more.

"God, yes. I'm not sure if it feels better because it's cold or if there's more to it, but I don't care right now—all that matters is that it feels better. Put the rest back in the fridge so that if it's the cold, I can put more on when this stuff warms up." She took a deep breath as the heat finally started to recede. "Please. I meant to say please, right there."

He grinned and put the tub back in the fridge. She turned to the sink and washed her hands to get the sour cream off, and then immediately took two surgical gloves from the box and put them on. After this experience, she wanted to wear them everywhere. She could be like one of those never nudes, except just for her hands. Who knew when hot chilies could attack you? Better to be prepared. People might think she was a lunatic, but those would just be uninformed people who had never experienced what she'd just experienced.

Carlos put his arm around her.

"Are you feeling better?" he asked. "It seems like the sour cream is helping?"

She turned to face him.

"Yeah, I think so. I feel like I'm cooling—"

Carlos burst out laughing.

"You . . . oh my god . . . the . . . your face!"

He was laughing so hard he bent over. She put her gloved hands on her hips while she waited for him to calm down from laughing at, not with, her. It wasn't her fault that his fucking chilies set her face on fire.

"It's just . . . you just . . ." He was laughing too hard to talk. Finally, he grabbed her by the hand and pulled her out of the kitchen and into the hallway that led to his bedroom.

"Where are you taking me? Are you trying to take me to bed?" She gestured to her face, which she knew from experience was set in a death glare. "Does this look like my 'I want to have sex' face?"

He stopped in the hallway and doubled over again, before he pulled himself together and dragged her into the bathroom.

"That! Look at that!" He pushed her in front of the mirror.

She'd been so distracted by gratitude for her face feeling better, that she'd sort of forgotten that she had *smeared sour cream all over her face.*

"Oh my God."

Carlos was shaking with laughter behind her.

"I know!"

"I look . . . I look like a drunken clown."

Carlos pointed at her. "You said it! I didn't! I did not say that! Remember, I did not say that!"

"Oh my God." She turned to Carlos, who started laughing

again as soon as she turned around. She grinned, felt the drying sour cream crack as her face moved, and giggled at the ridiculous sensation. Soon, she was laughing so hard she could barely breathe.

She held up her gloved hands and laughed even harder.

"I'm sorry for laughing at you!" Carlos said, while still laughing at her. But she couldn't really blame him. "Does it still hurt? Do you need more sour cream?"

She shook her head, unable to talk. Eventually, she took a deep breath to answer him.

"More sour cream for my face, you mean? What do you think I am, a baked potato? Are you going to give me some butter and salt next?"

That destroyed both of them. Soon, they were both sitting on his bathroom floor, shaking with laughter and holding each other upright. Tears were streaming down her face, driving paths through the tacky sour cream, and that made her laugh even harder.

Finally, her laughter subsided.

"I'm sorry I yelled at you for laughing at me. And, you know, just in general."

He rested his arm around her shoulders.

"That's okay. Your face was on fire. I feel like you're allowed to yell when your face is on fire."

She took a deep breath.

"Oh my God, I feel like I've been exercising; my abs hurt from laughing that much."

He ran his hands through her hair.

"God, the last time I laughed that much was . . ." He paused for a while. "I can't even remember the last time I laughed that much. That felt pretty good."

She smiled up at him.

"Well, that makes it almost worth setting my face on fire, then." He opened his mouth, and she lifted her index finger and shook it at him. "I said *almost* worth it. Don't get any funny ideas."

He laughed.

"Okay, I have a confession to make."

Oh no. It was never good news when a man said that to you.

"What is it?"

He took a deep breath.

"I had no idea if the sour cream would work. When I said I was sure, what I meant was that I seriously couldn't think of anything else."

She punched him on the arm, and he fell back against the bathroom floor with a grin on his face.

"You asshole. I thought this was going to be a real confession. I'm very angry at you for making me smear sour cream on my face on a lark, but it worked so I can't really be mad at you, which makes me even madder."

He stood and offered her his hand to pull her up off of the floor.

"I know, it's a real conundrum, isn't it? Ready to attack these enchiladas again? This time with gloves on?"

She nodded.

"You know what they say. No glove, no love."

He groaned and pushed her ahead of him back into the kitchen.

• • • • • • •

An hour later, Carlos looked around his kitchen, satisfied. Nik was covering the last of the six trays of enchiladas with aluminum foil; soon they'd all go in the oven. She'd offered to wash the dishes, but he'd thought it would be cruel to let her wash the pot that the enchilada sauce had cooked in—those were the chilies that had attacked her, after all. So instead he was standing at the stove, elbow deep in soap bubbles, as he scrubbed all of his pans clean.

"Don't you have a dishwasher?" she asked him.

He nodded.

"Yeah, why?"

She looked at him like he'd lost his mind.

"Because you're scouring your pots like that by hand—why don't you just put them in the dishwasher?"

He rinsed the second to last pot and put it in his dish drainer.

"No child of Susana Ibarra would put pots in a dishwasher. Look, it took me until after med school to not completely wash my dishes before putting them in the dishwasher, okay? I have heard people say that they put pots in the dishwasher, in the same way I've heard people say they didn't have student loans or they drove to the Westside without traffic or they got a dirt-cheap plane ticket to Europe. All of those things seem imaginary to me, just in the same way putting my pots in the dishwasher would be."

She wet a paper towel and wiped down his counters.

"I get it. Some things, we just can't fight."

When the pots were done, he slid the first two trays into the oven and looked over at Nik.

"While we wait, why don't we . . ." Oh no. She still had sour cream on her face, but now it was dry and crusty. "Why don't we . . ." He couldn't laugh at her again; she'd kill him this time.

"Why don't we what?" She moved over to him and put her hand on his. Just then, a big flake of sour cream fell off of her face and onto the floor.

That did it. He leaned against the sink, laughing so hard he couldn't stand up straight.

"It's still . . ." He took a deep breath so he could talk. "It's still there! The sour cream! It's just all white and flaky now! You look like you have a skin disease!"

She didn't laugh. She just stared at him, until he got spooked and quieted down. Shit, he'd really pissed her off this time.

Finally, she moved closer to him.

"Carlos?" she asked.

"Yeah?" Oh no.

"Do you think I'm sexy?" And with that, she took the edge of the sheet of sour cream on her face and peeled it off in a big strip.

They laughed even harder this time than last time. Every time they would quiet down for a second, she would rub at her face and more disgusting white sour cream flakes would come off, and they'd both start back up again.

While they were still gasping with laughter, he heard the jingle of his ringtone. He pulled his phone out of his pocket. Jessie, probably calling to check on the status of her enchiladas.

"Hey, Jess!" he said, with laughter still in his voice. "Don't worry, they're in the oven. I'll bring them over for your nice big freezer tom—"

"Carlos, I'm at the hospital. They're saying I have to have the baby now. I'm scared."

"What?" He'd never heard this panicked tone in Jessie's voice before. "Back up, tell me what's going on."

He moved out of the kitchen into the living room.

"I took my blood pressure today, and it was high, so Jon and I came to the hospital. But I thought it would be okay, because that's happened a few times in the last few weeks and they just gave me a few more tests and sent me home." He could hear the tears in her voice. "But this time, after the other tests, they all looked really worried. Right now they're deciding if they're going to induce me or if I need to have an emergency C-section."

At that she broke down.

"I didn't want to have a C-section. I really wanted to . . . I had my birth plan ready so early. I knew just what I wanted to do . . . and I'm only thirty-four weeks; it's too early. What if there's something wrong with my baby?"

It broke his heart to hear Jessie cry like this. He wanted to cry just listening to her. Nik had come over to him, and without thinking, he reached for her hand. She wrapped her other arm around his waist.

"Jessie, where's Jon? Where's your mom? I'm coming. I'll be there as fast as I can get there, okay?"

Nik squeezed his hand and tried to pull away, but he wouldn't let her.

"Jon's here. He's calling his parents. I haven't called Mom yet; I wanted to call you first."

He nodded. The tension that had left his shoulders in the past two hours all fell back on them.

"Okay. Call your mom now. I'm on my way, okay? You or Jon call me if anything happens before I get there. I love you."

She sniffed and took a breath.

"I love you, too. See you soon."

When he hung up the phone, Nik put her arms around him. He sat down and pulled her onto his lap. He buried his head in her chest. Neither of them spoke.

Finally, he lifted his head.

"She sounded so scared. I've never heard Jessie sound scared before about anything." He pulled Nik closer. "I have to go now."

She nodded.

"I know."

But he sat there with his arms around her for a minute, her head in his chest, his nose in her hair. It was so hard to let go, but he did.

"Go, they need you," she said.

He walked into his bedroom to throw on a clean shirt and grab a hoodie. He came back out and sat at the table while he put his shoes on. Nik stood next to him and stroked his hair while he tied his shoes.

When he stood up and saw the kitchen, he put his head in his hands.

"Oh shit. What am I going to do about the enchiladas?"

She shook her head.

"Don't worry about that. I'll stay here and deal with them. Just give me whatever instructions you need to."

He hugged her.

"Oh, thank you so much." He checked the timer. "Okay, those are done in thirty minutes. When you take those out, the chicken ones cook for only twenty, with five minutes with the aluminum foil off at the end." He stepped back. "Are you sure? You don't have to do this, I can just . . ." She put her finger on his mouth to stop him from talking anymore.

"I'm sure. Go to the hospital. Keep me posted about Jessie?"

He kissed her hard on the mouth as an answer.

Chapter Seventeen

On his way up to the maternity floor, Carlos wondered if anyone else in his family had gotten to the hospital yet. Probably not, but Tia Eva and his mom must be right behind him. He'd talked to Angela in the car on the way there, but she was on her way from Santa Monica, so it could take her God only knew how long to get there.

He quickened his pace as he got closer to Jessie's room. What if she wasn't there? What if she was already in surgery and hadn't had time to tell him? The room door was closed, and he knocked only once before opening it.

"Jessie!" She was on the bed, Jon sitting next to her and holding her hand.

"Thought you might be done with me already, huh?" she said. But she said it with a crack in her voice.

He made it to her bed in three steps so he could hug her.

"No, asshole, I thought you might already be in surgery, that's all." He stood back. "What's the plan? How are you?"

She took a deep breath and closed her eyes.

"The doctor said they're going to do a C-section. Soon," Jon said. He squeezed Jessie's hand. "It's going to be okay. They do these all the time here."

Carlos took her other hand.

"They do, I promise. I work here, remember? Would I work at a place where I'd worry about my cousin having surgery? Hell no. You and the baby will be great. I promise."

She nodded without opening her eyes.

"Thirty-four weeks is a pretty scary time to do this. My poor little girl. I thought I could hold on at least another month for her."

Carlos put his finger under Jessie's chin until she opened her eyes and looked at him.

"Jess. Jessica. Do not blame yourself. This isn't your fault. You have done everything right. *Everything.* You came to the hospital today because you just wanted to double-check, even though you thought it was fine—that was you making all of the right decisions to keep your little girl as healthy as she can possibly be. Doing this C-section, even though it's something you never wanted, is you making another choice for your little girl, okay? This hospital has a great NICU, and you're in really good hands. I promise."

She nodded as tears slid down her face.

"You'll stay? Until she's out? Until it's all done?"

He gripped her hand.

"You're going to have to send me away—that's how long I'm going to stay."

The door banged open, and his mother and aunt stormed into the room.

"Jessica!" He stood back to allow his aunt to throw her arms around Jessie. "Mommy will take care of everything."

He and Jon locked eyes. He barely managed to not laugh out loud. Leave it to Tia Eva to give them some levity.

It was only about ten minutes later when the doctors came into the room to prep Jessie for the surgery and kicked everyone but Jon out. They all filed into the nearest waiting room. Thank God his mom was here to calm Tia Eva down. He put his arms around his mom for a minute. She hated hospitals.

"Anyone want anything while we wait?" he asked them. "I can go to the cafeteria to get us something to eat or drink."

"Oh, I couldn't eat anything!" Tia Eva said.

His mom smiled at him. They both knew she'd want something as soon as he left.

"I'm sure Tia won't be able to eat anything, but why don't you bring us back some coffee and maybe some cookies or something like that? We might be here for a while. Coffee might be good. Don't you think, Carlos?"

"Great idea, Mama," he said, and walked out of the waiting room before Tia Eva thought of something she might want.

On his way down in the elevator, he pulled his phone out of his pocket. Shit, he'd forgotten to charge it last night, and now he was down to three percent battery. Did he still have that charger in his office? He hoped so, or else this was going to be a very long night.

He had texts from many of his family members, but he ignored them all and clicked on the text from Nik.

How's Jessie? How are you?

He sighed. He wished he was back at his house with her, laughing and eating enchiladas. He could really use one of her hugs right now.

She's about to have an emergency c-section. I got to talk to her for a little bit. She's anxious and scared but powering through. I'm in the waiting room with my mom and aunt for the foreseeable future, just escaped to the cafeteria for drinks and snacks.

The elevator doors opened, and he walked into the cafeteria. All hospital cafeterias were terrible in their own ways. His, like many newer hospitals, had been trying to do a healthy food push, which meant that the food was no longer terrible junk food, but terrible healthy food.

Is Angie there yet? That'll help, right?

He filled up three coffee cups, one with a ton of milk and sugar for his aunt and two others with decreasing amounts of both for his mom and himself. He found a stack of oatmeal raisin cookies and grabbed as many as he could carry. He texted Nik when he was in line to pay.

Not yet, she's on her way from a meeting on the westside so it could be a while.

Oh shit, he needed to let Angie know about the C-section as soon as possible. But his battery was almost gone, and he did not want to tell her with his mom and aunt right there. He could run to his office right now, but Tia Eva was probably upstairs even more worried than he was. He needed to get back there. And he couldn't text Angie about this from his almost dead phone—she'd freak out when she couldn't get in touch with him.

Nik already knew what was going on. Could she call Angela?

No, he didn't want that. He liked to keep his personal life and his family strictly separate. And plus, Angela would go crazy with the whole "girlfriend" thing then.

But this was an emergency, and he didn't seem to have a better option.

Can I ask you a huge favor? Can you call my sister and let her know Jessie's in surgery now for a c-section? Long story but she doesn't know yet and my battery is almost out. I might have a charger somewhere, but I should let her know asap.

He stared at his phone until she texted him back. Luckily, there were a number of people ahead of him in line. Saturday early evenings were busy times in hospital cafeterias.

Of course, just text me her number.

He sent Angie's number to Nik and walked back to the elevator balancing all of his beverages and food.

• • • • • • •

Nik checked the timer on her phone. Five more minutes before she needed to take the enchiladas out of the oven. She had a minute to call Angela before the timer went off.

The problem was that the thought of calling Angela freaked her out. Would his sister be mad about her having this news when actual family didn't? Nik wouldn't blame her if she did. Also, she had no idea what Carlos had told Angela about her, if anything. She knew that Carlos and his sister were really close, but she didn't know if they talked about stuff like this. At the bar after the baseball game, Angela had seemed relaxed and funny, just like Carlos . . . but it could be a different story if she knew Nik was sleeping with her brother.

"Oh my God, just call her already," she said out loud to Carlos's sliding glass window. The window didn't respond.

She cold-called people all the time—it was literally part of her job—and yet she was frozen with her finger over the phone.

She sighed and hit call. Maybe Angela wouldn't pick up? Most people didn't pick up calls from numbers they didn't know. Maybe she could just leave Angela a message. She obviously wouldn't call back, and then—

"Hello? Hello, this is Angela, who's this? Is it the hospital?"

Nik cleared her throat.

"Hi, Angela. Um, no, not the hospital. This is Nik. We met at Dodger Stadium?"

Oh Lord, she was doing that uptalk thing that she always instructed younger women against doing. Come on, Nikole. Get it together.

"Oh. Hi, Nik. Uh . . ."

Right, she should get on with it.

"Carlos asked me to call you. He's at the hospital and his battery is almost dead, but he knew you'd want an update."

"Oh." That was a weird "Oh," right? Maybe. It sounded more like an "ooooh." But she'd only met Angela once—that might just be how she talked. "Thanks for calling. What's going on with Jessie?"

"Carlos said they just brought Jessie in to get an emergency C-section, and that your mom and your aunt are both there at the hospital with him."

Angela let out a deep breath.

"Oh no. I know she was trying so hard to avoid a C-section. She must be so scared."

Nik nodded as she stared through the window. One of Carlos's neighbors, an older man with big glasses and a cane whom she'd seen a few times before, walked by and waved at her. She waved back.

"She talked to Carlos when they first told her it was a possibility, and I think she was pretty worried. I know Carlos got to the hospital in time to see her before the surgery, and I'm sure that helped."

Nik's timer went off, and she pushed buttons on her phone madly to make it stop making noise.

"What was that?" Angela asked.

"Oh, I'm at Carlos's house. We were making enchiladas for Jessie when he got the call, so I stayed here to let them finish in the oven. That was just my timer."

Why was she babbling? She could have just said that was her phone timer and let it alone.

"Oh." *That* "Oh" had definitely been more . . . smug? Hmmm. "Okay. Is there anything else he said to tell me?"

Nik wedged the phone between her shoulder and ear and put oven mitts on. She didn't need to burn her hands, too.

"That's everything I know. I hope you get there soon, and I hope all goes well with your cousin."

Nik opened the oven and carefully took out the trays of enchiladas.

"Thanks, Nik. And thanks for calling."

"Bye, Angie."

Oh shit. She'd slipped and called his sister Angie. That's what Carlos always called her, and so that's how Nik thought of her, but she'd very clearly introduced herself as Angela when they'd met.

Well, now his sister probably hated her.

Or maybe his sister barely gave her a second thought, since her mind was kind of occupied with her cousin undergoing emergency surgery at that exact moment? Yes, that was more likely. Way to make everything about yourself, Nikole.

She slid the remaining two trays of enchiladas into the oven. Cooking and agonizing over whether people were mad at her. This was definitely not how she usually spent Saturday nights.

She picked up her bag from where she'd dropped it by the door and brought it over to Carlos's couch. Thank goodness she'd brought her laptop with her; at least she could get some work done while she waited to hear what was going on with Jessie and her baby.

She set her laptop on the coffee table, opened it, and instead of getting work done, mindlessly scrolled through her various social media news feeds for way too long. No, this wasn't helpful. She stood up and walked back into the kitchen. Maybe she needed a snack. Oh God, yes, a snack sounded like a great idea. And Carlos had tortilla chips, how perfect. Something she could stress-eat for hours as she got more and more tense, just what she needed.

Shit, the enchiladas. She'd put the second round in the oven right after getting off the phone with Angela, but she hadn't set her timer. Carlos had said twenty minutes, but she had no idea how long they'd already been in there. Five minutes, ten? She could check them, but she didn't have a clue what enchiladas would look like after five minutes versus after ten versus after fifteen, so that would be no help. She set her timer for fifteen minutes and crossed her fingers.

You guys, I'm freaking out—I'm at Carlos's house and he left in a rush because his cousin is going to have an emergency c-section, and I stayed here to babysit the enchiladas we were making her, and I may have ruined them. That was a slight overstatement, but that's how it felt to her, okay? Now I'm sitting here waiting to hear any news and stress eating chips.

That reminded her. She got up and went to the fridge and got the jar of salsa.

It must have been an emergency, who the fuck would leave you in charge of food in the oven?

Thanks, Courtney. Always there with a kind word.

No, but seriously, of course you're freaking out, that's stressful. Do you know what's going on? Do they need cupcakes? I'm just packing up the shop—we were open late tonight, I have some left over.

Ooh, cupcakes were a great idea. Not for Carlos, for herself.

I desperately want all of your cupcakes, but I feel like they strike the wrong note when no one knows what's going to happen. Like, "here's some cupcakes to celebrate this stressful emergency!" you know? He texted me after he got to the hospital and said they were bringing her in for surgery, but that's all I know.

She wanted to text him again, but she had no idea if his phone had power yet. And even if it did, he was probably busy with his family; he probably didn't want to hear from her. She reached for another chip just as Dana texted.

Oh no, Nik! Poor Carlos and his poor cousin. Do you need anything?

Did she need anything? Yes, lots of things: Carlos to be on the couch next to her; his cousin—who she'd never met, but felt a kinship to because of their shared love for serial killer books—to be okay; his cousin's baby to be okay; his sister to not hate her for calling her Angie; to know what to do right now; cupcakes. Dana couldn't get her any of those things, though.

No, I'm okay. I have my laptop here, I'll be fine. Just worried, that's all.

Both of her friends texted back in quick succession.

Okay, keep us posted. We're here if you need anything!

Let me know if you need bourbon, or change your mind about cupcakes, or if you need anything else.

She spent the next thirty minutes trying to find something to occupy her mind: she finished cleaning the kitchen; she tried and failed to edit the story she'd been working on that day; she took the enchiladas out of the oven; she thought about snooping in his medicine cabinet—it was really the perfect opportunity to do some snooping when he wasn't around to catch her—but she didn't have the heart to do it. Everywhere she went, she kept her phone in her pocket, but he never texted.

She felt so helpless. She kept remembering that look on his face when he'd answered the phone and heard his cousin crying, and how when he'd gotten off the phone, he hadn't said a word but had held on to her so tightly. She wanted to do something, anything, to fix this, to make him feel better, but there was nothing she could do.

Finally, she texted him out of sheer anxiety.

Any news? How are you doing?

He texted back right away. He must have found a charger.

Starving. Wish I had some of those enchiladas we made. No news yet but it should be soon—c-sections don't take all that long. I might start freaking out if we don't hear something soon, actually.

"Might" start freaking out—she was pretty sure he was already freaked out and just trying to keep it together.

Keep me posted, okay? If you have time.

She opened a cabinet door in the kitchen to grab the aluminum foil to cover the enchilada pans, and next to it, she saw a stack of paper plates and plastic cutlery.

Should she . . . ?

No, that was ridiculous.

But Carlos and his whole family were all at the hospital. And they were starving. And all the food was right there. And the hospital was only about fifteen minutes away. And this was the one thing she could do to help.

She wrapped a pan in aluminum foil and put it in a grocery bag, stacked the paper plates and plastic forks in another, and was in her car three minutes later.

The entire way to the hospital, she kept thinking about turning around. He probably didn't want her there. If they were really hungry, they could probably get food from the cafeteria or something, couldn't they? But she kept thinking about his last text and the look on his face when he'd hung up the phone and the sound of his cousin crying on the phone to him, so she kept going.

She parked in the hospital parking garage and carefully lifted the bag full of still warm enchiladas out of the back seat of her car. Then she stopped, put everything down, and put lipstick on before she picked it all back up again. She carried everything into the hospital and asked the way to the maternity ward.

"Are you family?" the woman at the front desk asked her.

"No . . . but a family friend," she said. That was only sort of a lie, right? She lifted the bags she was carrying. "I'm bringing food to the family. She's in an emergency C-section now, and the family is all in the waiting room."

She really hoped the woman didn't ask her Jessie's last name, because she'd just realized she didn't know it.

"Oh, that's great. It's the seventh floor. Go on up. Turn left. You won't be able to miss the waiting room."

She was right; she couldn't miss it. She could hear them talking as she approached the waiting room. That must be a good sign. If anything bad had happened, they'd all be pretty quiet.

This was a terrible idea. Why hadn't she texted Courtney and Dana when she'd thought of it? They would have told her it was a terrible idea. This is what happens when you don't ask your friends for advice—you make stupid decisions.

She could still turn around and go back. Maybe she should still turn around and go back?

She straightened her shoulders and walked in.

• • • • • • •

"Nik!" Carlos stood up when he saw Nik walk through the door. What the hell was she doing there?

She had two big grocery bags in her hand and a very tentative smile on her face. He didn't meet her eyes.

"I thought you guys might be hungry, so I brought some enchiladas over."

Did she think that's what he was asking for when he texted her that he wished he'd had some of the enchiladas? Because, wow, that had not been what he meant.

He tried to smile and took the bags from her. Now he had to introduce her to his mother. He hadn't introduced a woman to his mother since he was in his early twenties.

"Mama, Tia Eva, this is my friend Nik. She was helping me make enchiladas for Jessie when I got Jessie's call, so, um . . ." He looked down at the bags. "I hope you're as hungry as I am."

He opened the bags and set out the food, all without looking at Nik. His stomach rumbled when he unwrapped the tight aluminum foil from the baking pans.

"Nikole, did you say? It's nice to meet you," his mother said. Nik handed him the paper plates, and he dished up enchiladas for his mom.

"It's nice to meet you, too," Nik said.

"How do you and Carlos know each other?" Tia Eva asked her.

Oh shit. How were they supposed to answer this?

"Through me," Angela said from behind them. "Thanks for bringing over the food, Nik!"

Thank God for Angela. And this had the benefit of even being sort of true. As Angie hugged Nik, she stared right at him. Her smile was very smug. Damn it.

"It was no problem at all," Nik said. "But um, I should go, I don't want to intrude, I know this is family time. I'll just talk to you later and you can let me know how everything goes, okay?"

"Oh no, you can't go now!" His mom picked up a paper plate. "You have to stay and eat enchiladas with us after making all that effort." She scooped two enchiladas onto Nik's plate and handed it to her without waiting for a response.

Nik glanced at Carlos and shrugged. He turned away to dish up his own plate. Maybe her feelings were hurt that he hadn't been thrilled when she walked in, but it was her own fault for showing up without checking with him first. She went to sit on the other side of the room with her food.

Angela looked at him, at Nik sitting alone, and back at him with a glare. *Fine.* He made a plate for himself and sat down next to Nik. He wasn't sure what to say to her, not with his mom and aunt right across the room and his sister . . . oh wow, his sister sat down right next to him.

"They could have been a little spicier, you know, Carlos," his mom said. "What kinds of chilies did you use? You should have added hotter ones in there. You're too used to cooking for," she glanced in Nik's direction, "your friends, not your family."

He and Nik looked at each other for a split second with laughter in their eyes, and both immediately looked away. He could only imagine how long she'd have had to keep the sour cream on her face if he'd used hotter chilies.

"No, Mama—I usually make it spicier, but I toned down the spice in these because I was making them for Jessie for after the baby, and I know a lot of breastfeeding mothers like to avoid food that's too spicy. It can upset the baby's stomach."

His aunt made a hand motion like she was batting the whole idea of what he'd said out of the room.

"*Our* babies don't get their stomachs upset by spicy food. You're listening to too many of those other doctors. I'm sure Jessie isn't worried about that."

Carlos knew there was no point in responding to that one.

"Where did you get the meat?" his aunt asked. "It's good, but you probably paid too much for it, in one of those fancy grocery stories you go to over there."

"I got it at El Rancho market, Tia Eva."

Tia Eva took another bite and changed the subject. Carlos tried not to smile.

Soon, his mom and aunt were in a deep discussion about the woman who used to live across the street from them with her children.

"I'm sorry," Nik said under her breath to him. "I wasn't thinking. I was just worried about everything, but I shouldn't have just shown up here. I'll go as soon as I finish my food."

He shrugged.

"Now that you're here, you might as well stay for a little while."

She scooped some enchilada onto her fork.

"Well, I don't know what your mom and aunt were complaining about: these are the best enchiladas I've ever had."

He grinned at her. It always thrilled him when she complimented his cooking; he couldn't help it.

"I'm glad you liked them, especially after what they did to you. And I feel better, now that I got some food in me. I was so stressed before you got here—*my* blood pressure was probably sky-high."

She looked at him sideways.

"Hmm, you know one way to find out how high your blood pressure is? Going to the doctor."

Did she really need to bring that up right now? With his sister right there? He looked away.

She nudged him with her knee.

"I'm sorry. You left me such a perfect opening there, but I should have resisted. This isn't the time for that. Forget I said anything and have another enchilada."

He shook his head and smiled, despite himself. He nudged her with his knee back.

"I can't stand you. Did you know that?"

She grinned at him. "I know."

He touched her hand for a second. He couldn't help it. Even though he hated that she'd come, he felt better with her here next to him. He sighed.

"Sorry if I seem on edge, I'm just so worried. I'm five minutes away from charging in there and waving my badge around and demanding answers." He paused. "That *might* get me fired, but I'd probably get the answers first."

She laughed.

"Yeah, maybe don't do that. At least, not just yet."

She took his empty plate and Angela's and got up to toss them away. While she was gone, Angie leaned over to him.

"I knew it," she said.

He didn't have time to respond before Nik sat back down.

She sat closer to him this time, so close that her shoulder was touching his. Every part of him wanted to put his arm around her, but instead he moved his legs so he was touching hers. She smiled but didn't look at him.

They sat like that in silence for a few minutes, until Angela leaned over.

"Carlos, I'm going crazy here. Is it supposed to take this long? Do you think something is wrong?"

He opened his mouth to answer, when Jon burst into the room.

"Everyone is okay!" he said, with a huge smile on his face.

The whole room was on their feet. Nik put her hand on his arm.

"Jessica? The baby?" Tia Eva asked, her voice wavering.

"Jessie is fine and the baby is, too!" he said. Tears started running down his face.

Oh thank God.

"When can we see them?" he asked Jon. "Everything's fine? Really?"

Tia Eva was sobbing into Jon's arms. He looked up from her and nodded at Carlos.

"Really. They're both hooked up to a few machines, and the baby's going to have to stay in the hospital for a week or so, they think, but the doctors say she'll be all right. I'm not sure when you can see them, but sometime tonight. I've got to get back to them right away, but I wanted to tell you all the good news."

Carlos's hand somehow made its way into Nik's. She squeezed hard, and he squeezed back.

"What's her name?" His mom asked, just as Jon was about to leave the room. "Jessie said you hadn't decided yet."

He smiled.

"I think she wanted to be the one to tell you guys. I don't want to spoil that for her. Just a little while longer."

And before anyone else could ask him a question, he raced back down the hall.

Carlos pulled Nik and Angela together into a hug and buried his head in Nik's shoulder.

"They're going to be all right!" That was all he could say, over and over.

When he finally let them go, he realized his face was wet.

"I don't even know why I'm crying," Nik said. "I don't even like babies."

He and Angela both laughed as the tears streamed from their eyes.

Carlos wiped his eyes with his sleeve, and then went over to hug his mom and his aunt.

After a few minutes, he came back to Nik. She'd found a box of tissues. She took a few and handed the box to Angela, who brought them over to their mom and aunt.

"Oh thank God," he said. "I'm so relieved. I'm so happy."

He gave her another enormous hug.

"I don't even know Jessie," she said. "I don't know why I'm crying."

He grinned.

"You probably got some chili in your eye; don't worry about it."

She laughed between her tears.

"That must be it." She pulled away and wiped her eyes again. "I should go now, though. I don't want to be in the way. This is a family thing."

Carlos shook his head.

"Oh no you don't. You can't leave now. Wait at least until we find out if we can see Jessie."

Carlos sat back down and threw his arms around both Angela and Nik. Luckily, he was pretty sure his mom and aunt were too distracted by their discussion of what the baby name could be to notice.

Finally, Jon bounced back into the room.

"You can all see Jessie, but only for a few minutes, okay? The baby is in the NICU. I'm going back to her, but I'll take you to Jessie first."

"Jessica!" Tia Eva raced into the room and threw her arms around Jessie. "I was so worried. I love you so much."

Well, that did it. The whole room was crying again. Including both him and Jon.

When it was his turn to give Jessie a hug, he pulled Nik along with him.

"This is Nik. She's the one who recommended all of those creepy books I bought you that you loved. She dropped by to bring food for all of us while we were waiting, and I made her stay so she could meet you."

Jessie was glowing, despite the tears still streaming down her face. She reached out to grab Nik's hand.

"Nik, it's so nice to meet you. Those books kept me from going crazy over the past five weeks, I can't thank you enough."

Nik smiled back at her.

"I was happy to help. And I'm so happy that everything went well today."

Jessie beamed at her.

"Me too. We still have a bumpy road ahead. She'll be in the NICU for a while, and I'm"—more tears spilled from her eyes, and Carlos put his hand on her shoulder—"worried, but the doctors seem very optimistic, so I'm going to be optimistic, too."

"What is her NAME?" his mom said from the other side of the room.

Jessie smiled. He and Nik stepped back so everyone could see her.

"Her name." Jessie looked at her mom and smiled. "Her name is Eva Jane. After her two grandmothers."

Tia Eva charged the bed and would have tackled Jessie with her hug if Carlos hadn't intervened.

Chapter Eighteen

As soon as Carlos walked inside his house, he fell down onto his couch and tugged Nik down with him.

"I am so damn tired," he said.

He buried his head in the curve of her neck and finally let his face relax.

"I could not be happier right now to be here on the couch with you. I managed to keep it together around my family for most of the night, and now I need to let myself fall apart for, like, thirty seconds."

She wrapped her arms around him. He breathed in her smell, her warmth, her presence. They lay there in silence for a long time.

She kissed him on the cheek.

"Hey. I'm really sorry that I showed up at the hospital without checking with you. I think I made something already stressful for you harder. I feel really bad about that."

He'd already forgotten that he'd been irritated when Nik walked in. So much had happened tonight.

"No, it's okay," he said. "I was surprised when you showed up, but I think having you—and the enchiladas—there made it easier on everyone. Plus, my mom hates hospitals and getting to criticize my cooking helped take her mind off of things."

She ran her fingers slowly through his hair and he closed his eyes. He wished he could stay like this forever.

"When my dad died . . . my mom was at the hospital with him by herself. She'd called both me and Angie, but neither of us got there in time. It was pretty hard on her. I don't think she's set foot in a hospital since. I could tell she was having a tough time there tonight, especially since we were all so worried." He bent down and kissed her hand. "The enchiladas helped. Thank you."

She squeezed his hand.

"Did you . . . how was yesterday?"

He pushed her hair back from her face and smiled at her. Of course she'd remembered.

"I spent the evening with Angie. She said Mama likes to spend the day at church. Angie usually spends it with friends or Jessie. The first year Angie asked me if I wanted to meet up with her, but I told her I had to work. Which was true, but I'd switched with someone to make sure I was working all day that day." He ran his finger down her cheek. "But yesterday the two of us ate a lot of tacos and drank some of Dad's favorite beer, and just . . . talked." He never would have spent the anniversary of his dad's death with Angela if it hadn't been for Nik. He was so glad he had. "Thanks for . . . well, thanks."

She smiled up at him.

"You're welcome."

He leaned forward the few inches between them and kissed her. It had been so hard to not kiss her in the hospital. She kissed him back hard. They dove into each other like they were parched, like it had been just weeks and not hours since they'd last kissed, like she'd wanted to kiss him in these last few hours as much as he'd wanted to kiss her.

He started to pull off her shirt, then stopped and sat up.

"Come to bed. Please?"

She stood up and reached her hand out to him.

Once in his bedroom, he wasted no time in undressing her. She stood there and let him unbutton her shirt, pull off her tank top, unzip her jeans and pull them down to the floor, until she was in only a matching set of a hot pink bra and underwear.

"Where did this come from?" he asked her, as he ran his finger over the lace on the bra.

She smiled and reached for him, but he stepped away. He wanted to concentrate on her first.

"I bought it last week," she said. "I thought you might like it."

He touched the lace at her hip and ran his finger underneath it. He kept going until she gasped. He liked it when she made that noise.

"Lie down," he said. She obeyed him at once.

"Open your legs." He knelt on the bed in between her legs and stroked her underwear again, first on the outside, and then on the inside.

"You were right. I do like these. I like them a lot. But it's time for them to go." He grabbed them from each side and pulled them off her body. She looked down at him. She was already breathing hard. So was he.

He bent his head down to where the underwear had been.

"Let's see how much you like something now."

By her gasps and screams and fingernails in his back, she liked that a lot, too.

"You have *got* to get those clothes off," she said afterward, as he crawled over her body.

"I had to wait! You would have drawn blood otherwise. Take pity on a poor man."

She inspected her fingernails and laughed.

"I'll cut them before next time." She lay there and watched him as he jumped off the bed, threw his clothes off, and rolled a condom on.

He climbed back on top of her and paused.

"We need to get this off, as much as I love it." He unsnapped her bra and threw it aside. "Ahhh, that's better." He caressed her breasts, and she moaned and closed her eyes. He slid inside of her while her eyes were still closed, and she smiled and clenched around him as their bodies came together.

Afterward, he collapsed on top of her, his head nestled in the hollow between her breasts.

"Mmmm. You know what?" he asked her.

"What?"

"You taste like chilies."

They both laughed until they cried. He fell asleep, still with a smile on his face.

Carlos woke up the next morning, Nik's head on his chest, her curls tickling his nose. He looked down at her and smiled. He was so happy to have her with him. He wished she could be with him all the time. His life was so much better with her in it.

"Holy shit." He sat bolt upright, and she groaned and rolled onto his pillow.

"What? Do you have to be at the hospital?"

He shook his head and stared at her.

"I'm in love with you! I love you!"

He hadn't meant for this to happen. He'd just thought they were going along, having great sex and hanging out a lot, too, sure, but that it was all just fun. But along the way, he'd fallen in love with this smart, abrasive, caring, hilarious woman.

Now she sat up.

"What? You what?"

He turned to face her. How had he not realized this was happening? She was still half asleep, her hair was standing up straight, and she had that scowl on her face that she always had first thing in the morning. He loved her so much.

"I was just lying here awake and thinking about yesterday, and how happy I was that you were at the hospital, and how happy I was to wake up in bed with you, and how happy I always am with you. And I realized I love you."

Sure, he hadn't meant for this to happen, but he was so glad it had. They would be perfect together. They were *already* perfect together. They got along so well; they laughed together so much; they'd understood each other from the very beginning. Her friends liked him; his friends like her. Hell, his family even liked her after last night. The timing was all wrong, but that didn't matter. This was going to be so great.

She rubbed her eyes and wrapped the sheet tighter around her body.

"Are you sure you're awake? You had a pretty stressful day yesterday. If this is you talking in your sleep or the end of a dream or something, it's okay, I won't be mad. Go back to sleep and we can pretend this never happened."

That was the weirdest reaction to an "I love you" that he'd ever heard of.

"I don't want to pretend this never happened! I'm in love with you!"

"Oh my God, will you stop saying that?" She looked terrified. Why did she look like that?

"Really? That's your reaction?" he asked her.

She shook her head.

"I'm sorry. I didn't mean it like that; it's just you woke me up with this and I'm so confused."

He got out of bed.

"Okay. Let me go make us some coffee. I'll be back."

He pulled sweatpants on and went into the kitchen. Had he been dreaming? Was this just him being emotional after last night and making some big declaration for no reason?

No. This wasn't that. He loved her. If the emotions of last night had made him realize it earlier, fine, but it would have come out at some point anyway.

Had he measured the right amount of coffee into the filter? He'd been so busy thinking about Nik that he couldn't tell. He dumped it all out into a bowl and measured it again and put all of it, plus two more scoops, back into the machine.

When he went back into the bedroom Nik had put on yoga pants and his old UCLA T-shirt. She was sitting on the edge of the bed. He handed her coffee and sat down next to her.

"I thought about this when I was making the coffee, and the thing is, I love you."

She wrapped her hands around her coffee cup and let out a deep breath.

"Okay. What do you mean you love me? That doesn't make

sense. We haven't even known each other for that long. You told me you didn't want a relationship!"

He took a gulp of his way too hot coffee and winced.

"That's all true. Well, except that it does make sense, it makes perfect sense to me. Also, we've known each other long enough to know how we feel about each other. We've seen each other in some serious ups and some pretty bad downs. When I'm having a hard time, you're the perfect person to have around, because you're warm and comforting, but you're also honest with me, even when you're saying something I don't necessarily want to hear. And you know exactly when and how to make me laugh."

He took another sip of coffee. It was still too hot.

"And, I did say I didn't want a relationship. But you know what?" He made a wide gesture around the two of them. "This is a relationship! We see each other at least twice a week. You wake up here in my bed and you stay here and hang out with me instead of racing home. We text all the time. You helped me make food for my cousin. I met your friends; you met my friends. You met my family!"

She blew on the top of the coffee but didn't take a sip.

"I know, but that all doesn't mean we're in a relationship. It just means that we're good friends. Good friends, who also sometimes have sex."

He raised his eyebrows.

"Sometimes?"

She rolled her eyes.

"More than sometimes, but you know what I mean!" She finally took a sip of her coffee. He watched her face while she drank it. He loved that way she always closed her eyes and smiled at the first sip of coffee every morning. How had it taken him this long to realize that he loved her? Sure, it had only been six weeks, but now that he realized it, he knew he'd felt this way for a while.

"I do know what you mean, but I have plenty of good friends—even good female friends—and I don't feel about them the way I feel about you, sex or no sex."

She raised her mug to her mouth again but lowered it without drinking any.

"I just . . . I thought we were both clear about what we wanted here. I was having a great time—I *am* having a great time with you. I just didn't expect this today. Or ever."

He set his mug down on his bedside table and took her hand.

"Look. I didn't intend for this to happen, but it did. Can we talk about what happens next?"

She didn't let go of his hand, but she didn't exactly hold on to it, either.

"I don't really know what you want me to say. I was happy going along the way we had been going."

He nodded.

"So was I. I'm happy to keep going along the way we've been going, too."

She narrowed her eyes at him.

"I think there's a 'but' at the end of that sentence."

He couldn't help but laugh at the skeptical look on her face. She always read him so well. That was another reason he loved her.

"Fine, you're right. I'm happy to keep going along the way we've been going, *but* I'm in love with you. I get if you're not ready to say it back right now, but I can't pretend that's not how I feel."

She let go of his hand. Fuck.

"Carlos." She started with his name. That was never a good sign. "I like you so much, and we've had a great time together, but this isn't what I want." He tried to break in, but she stopped him. "That you say you love me . . . it changes things. It changes everything."

Why was she acting like this? What was wrong with her?

"Why do you say that it changes everything? It doesn't have to! And if it changes things, can't it change them for the better?"

She shook her head.

"No. No, it can't change things for the better. It never does. It'll mean you'll want more from me, things I'm not prepared to give you, and it'll ruin everything good about what we had." She put her coffee cup down. "Don't you think this was just an endorphin high or something from last night? You can say yes. I won't get mad. I'm pretty sure you'll be relieved in a day or so that I didn't take you seriously about this."

He stood up. He couldn't believe what he was hearing.

"No, I won't. I won't be glad you didn't take me seriously. This isn't an endorphin high, and I don't want to keep fucking doing what we had been doing. I'm in love with you, Nik! We have something special here, and I know you know it, too. In the short time you and I have known each other, we've been there for each other in all the ways that count. I've told you things about my life and my work and my family that I've never told anyone else."

He looked at her, sitting at the end of his bed staring down into her coffee cup instead of looking at him. He was suddenly furious.

"Does that even matter to you? Or is it just that you're good at asking questions, so you used me as journalism practice, to get me to spill all of my secrets? Did you think you'd won something when you got me to talk to you about my dad's death? 'Stupid Carlos, he doesn't realize I don't give a fuck about him. I'm just taking notes on what technique worked this time.' Was that it?"

She stood up to face him. At least now she was looking at him.

"Or is it just that you get off on getting men to fall in love with you and then rejecting them? Five months for Fisher, what's it been, six, seven weeks for me? Was I your new record? I bet you're thrilled now. Are you going to go celebrate tonight? Another guy that the great Nik Paterson couldn't care less about fell in love with her; where's the confetti?"

"No, Carlos, what a shitty thing to say. You know that wasn't it. You know I really do care about you."

He turned his back on her and grabbed a shirt out of his dresser.

"That's bullshit. I tell you I love you, and you tell me you *care* about me."

He pulled the shirt on as he walked out of his bedroom. He grabbed his keys off of his coffee table.

"Are you seriously going to leave right now while we're still in the middle of this?" she said from the hallway.

He didn't look at her as he slid on the shoes next to his front door.

"We're not in the middle of this anymore. We're done with this. Isn't that what you've been telling me? I can't believe you met my family. I wish you hadn't bothered to come to the hospital last night. If you really cared about me, you wouldn't have wasted my time. Fuck caring about me."

He saw her flinch right before he slammed the door.

Chapter Nineteen

Nik stood in Carlos's living room and stared at the front door. What the hell had just happened?

Her bag was on the floor by the couch. She dug through it for her phone.

Where are you guys? I think Carlos and I just broke up?

As she waited for Courtney or Dana to text back, she collected her stuff from throughout his house: her oversized Stanford hoodie that she'd left here a few weeks ago in his closet, her bobby pins on the nightstand, a travel-sized bottle of her conditioner in his shower. As she walked around and tossed her things in her bag, she got more and more angry. What the fuck was wrong with him, springing "I love you" on her like that and then getting mad at her for not falling all over herself being thrilled about it?

Trust her to get involved with the kind of guy who was so full of himself he imagined his love was God's gift to any woman.

Oh shit. At the shop and I can't leave. Come here? I have bourbon in the back.

Nik put her shoes on and grabbed her keys out of her bag.

Be there in 15 min.

She'd known from the beginning that he was arrogant and thought he knew everything, but she'd let herself ignore that because he was so much fun. She never should have dated him in the first place.

It took more like thirty minutes to get to Cupcake Park, given the vicissitudes of L.A. traffic and parking. Thirty minutes of listening to her most angry music on repeat and fantasizing about hitting cars with baseball bats. So when she walked up to the shop and was faced with a line out the door, she almost pushed herself through the crowd of chattering, happy people like a battering ram.

Luckily, she came to her senses before she ruined her friend's business. She turned around and went through the alley and in the back door. She couldn't help but think about when Carlos had rescued them when Courtney had her cupcake crisis . . . and about everything that happened later that night. Damn him.

She went through the kitchen and into the shop.

"Hey," she said to Courtney, as she popped up behind her. Courtney jumped and spun around.

"Holy shit, you scared me to death. I was wondering if you were stuck in this line."

Nik shook her head.

"I saw it and came through the back door. But this is amazing, look at all of the people here, and it's only nine a.m."

Courtney nodded and loaded half a dozen confetti cupcakes into a box.

"I know, it was like this yesterday, too. The *L.A. Times* did a piece on the shop this week, *and* someone on the Food Network came by this week and Instagrammed all the cupcakes she bought, so people are going wild."

How had she missed all of this? She'd known everything that had happened with Courtney's shop for the past year, and she'd missed an article in the *Times*?

"This is so awesome, Courtney!" she said, and hugged her friend. "You're a hit!"

Courtney hugged her back, but quickly turned back to her cupcakes.

"It's great for business. I just hope we don't screw it up. I made triple the cupcakes this morning, with more flavors than we usually have most days because I thought it would be like this today and I wanted to make sure to capitalize on this. Keep your fingers crossed."

Nik held up her crossed fingers as they walked into the back room.

"Dana texted that she's on her way," Courtney said. "Tell her to come through the back. I'm going to take some more cupcakes out front, and I'll shoot back in here as soon as I can take a break, okay? Don't say *anything* until I get here."

Nik sat down on one of the chairs at Courtney's worktable. She glared at the tray of spicy chocolate cupcakes and took a lime coconut off of the tray next to it.

Suddenly all of her anger left her, and she just felt sad. Another depressing end to a relationship. And this one felt worse than any ending had since Justin. She had really *liked* Carlos. Damn it.

Dana walked in five minutes later, still wearing her running clothes.

"Hey, there you are. It's a mob scene out there."

"Hey!" Nik stood up to hug her, sweaty running clothes and all. "How are things with Natalie?"

Dana beamed.

"Great. I was just finishing a workout with her at the gym when I got your text." Dana looked at her. "We can talk about that later, though. Are you okay?"

Nik shook her head.

"I'm not great."

Dana pulled her in close.

"Oh, honey, what happened?"

Nik let herself be comforted by Dana's tight hug for a few moments.

"I can't tell you anything until Courtney gets back here, because she'll—"

"Destroy both of you, yes." Courtney walked back into the kitchen with three cups of coffee on a tray and set them on the table. She opened a cabinet, reached into the back, and pulled out a bottle of bourbon, and poured a tot into each of their cups.

"Okay. My staff can hold down the fort for a little while. What did he do, and how painful will it be when I kill him?"

Nik took a swig of coffee and winced. That was a lot more bourbon than she'd expected.

"He told me he loved me. And when I didn't say it back, he was furious, said I used him up and discarded him like I do every man I date, and stormed out of his house. You know, garden-variety Nik breakup." She sighed and reached for her drink again.

Courtney shook her head and poured more bourbon into Nik's cup.

"Okay, obviously we hate him now, but I'm going to need you

to back up here. He told you he loved you? Did you see this coming? Did you . . . were you glad that he said it? How did he make you feel like shit? What happened in between the 'I love you' and the storming out of the house part? I feel like we're missing a lot here."

Nik glanced down at herself and realized she was still wearing Carlos's old UCLA T-shirt. She reached for another cupcake.

"No, I didn't see it coming! It came out of nowhere first thing this morning. And no, of course I wasn't glad he said it! You guys know how I feel about 'I love you's! I don't get this. I was so happy with the way things were, and he had to fuck it all up."

"Did you . . . tell him that?" Dana asked.

She shrugged. So fucking what if she had?

"More or less. We had a deal! We talked about this! He said he didn't want anything serious. I relied on that! And then he springs this 'I love you' bullshit on me this morning."

Dana narrowed her eyes.

"When you say 'more or less,' what exactly do you mean? What did you say to him?"

Oh God. Now Dana, the romantic, was going to get all upset on Carlos's behalf, she just knew it.

"I told him that he was probably just feeling emotional because of last night. Oh!" She just realized she'd texted them about Jessie but had never given them the update. "The baby was born last night. She and Jessie are both okay."

"Oh, that's so great!" Dana said. "But wait. You told him that he was just being emotional? Didn't you think that would upset him?"

Well, yes, *now* she did.

"I didn't think about that before I said it! Look, I was kind of flustered when he sprang this on me, okay? It was first thing in the morning—everyone *knows* I'm not at my best first thing in the morning anyway. I was exhausted because we were at the hospital for hours last night, we got back to his house super late, and then—"

Courtney broke in.

"Wait a second. You were at the hospital with him? When did that happen? How?"

So much had happened in the past twenty-four hours.

"It's a long story, but like I texted you guys, I'd been at his house helping him make enchiladas for his cousin, and . . ." She saw Dana and Courtney exchange a glance and stopped. "What? What does that look mean?"

"Nothing," Courtney said. "Go on. You were helping him cook enchiladas for his pregnant cousin, and?"

She knew it didn't mean "nothing," but she went on anyway.

"And we had just put the first batch in the oven when he got the call from his cousin in the hospital. So he raced there, and I stayed back to finish baking them."

Why were they making her go through this whole timeline? They knew this part already; she'd texted them last night. She'd also told them the important part, which was that Carlos had ruined everything.

"But how did you get from there to the hospital?" Courtney asked.

"I texted him to check in and see how he and his family were doing, and he said they were all stressed and hungry, so I packed up one of the pans of enchiladas with some paper plates and took them over there, which meant that I was there when they found out that Jessie and the baby were both okay. We were all so relieved."

She'd been so happy just last night, of course it all had to come crashing down this morning.

Courtney and Dana exchanged those annoying looks again. Why were they looking at her—and each other—like that?

"You brought them food to the hospital. Did he ask you to bring it, or . . ." Dana raised her eyebrows.

She shook her head.

"No, and that's the other thing! When I walked into the waiting room, he didn't seem happy that I was there at ALL. He barely looked at me, and his sister had to jump in to answer the 'How do you two know each other?' question from his mom." She'd thought he'd gotten over that. She'd thought in the end he was happy to have her there. And she'd been so happy to be there, to share that experience with Carlos and his family. That's why what he'd said this morning had felt like such a slap in the face. "I tried to leave after dropping off the food, because it didn't seem like he wanted me there, but his mom insisted that I stay and eat. But obviously I shouldn't have gone: this morning, one of his comebacks to me saying that I thought this was just a casual thing was 'You met my family!' like that automatically made us married or something." She refused to let herself cry. "And he said he wished I hadn't come.

"Anyway," she said, before either of them could say anything comforting. That would just put her over the edge. "Why is it so weird that I brought them food to the hospital?"

Dana put her hand on her arm.

"It just . . . that doesn't seem like you, that's all."

Nik shook Dana's hand off and took a huge bite of her cupcake. She tried to calm down as she chewed. It didn't work.

"That's a pretty mean thing for one of my best friends to say about me. You don't think I'd bring food for you in the hospital if you were sitting there waiting for a family member?"

Dana reached for her arm again.

"Of course you would. That's my point. You would for me, you would for Courtney, you would for probably a handful of other people, but that's it. I love you with my whole heart, Nik, but you don't do favors for people you don't care about. I can't picture you doing something like that for any of the guys you've dated in the last five years. The rest, you'd absolutely contribute to flowers or food or whatever, if someone else organized it, but a hospital visit? No, come on."

Nik sat and thought about that. Okay, she had a point there.

"Even if that's true, what does it matter? I'm not saying I don't care about him. I *told* him I cared about him! But when I told him that, he acted like I'd told him his food was just as good as the food from Taco Bell or something. I said I was happy to keep going the way we'd been going, and we could just pretend he'd never said 'I love you.'"

"What did he say when you said that?" Courtney asked.

Nik put her head in her hands.

"He got really mad. Why do people think 'I love you' is the only meaningful thing you can say to a person? Why did he have to say he loved me?"

"Nik." Courtney's voice was gentle, which meant she was about to say something bad. "Why does it scare you so much for someone to say they love you?"

She shook her head.

"It doesn't scare me! I just know from experience that that's when everything gets bad, that's all."

Dana sighed.

"Justin really did a number on you, didn't he? Just because he was an asshole doesn't mean they're all going to be like that."

She leaned her head on Dana's shoulder and thought about denying that this had anything to do with Justin, but what was the point? Courtney got up and fetched the bourbon bottle and poured more into all of their coffee cups. Nik took a sip and sighed.

"I don't think about him that much anymore, except for that time I profiled the quarterback of his favorite team for *GQ* and pictured his face when he'd see my byline. Well, and those times when I have low moments and I hear his voice in my head. But Justin, in his terrible way, did me a favor. First, he made me feel like there was something wrong with my writing, then he made me feel like there was something wrong with me for loving writing and my career. But the end result of all of that was that he made me sure that I don't ever want to let anyone make me feel that bad ever again."

Courtney pushed her chair around the table so the three of them were all shoulder to shoulder.

"I know, honey," Dana said. "But that doesn't mean you have to close yourself off to everyone forever. You are great at being strong, and there's no one else that either of us would have on our side in a fight. But it's okay to be vulnerable with more people than just the two of us, you know? Letting yourself have feelings for people is scary, I know it is, but you can't go through life with most people at arm's length. Not everyone is going to be like Justin."

Nik buried her head in Dana's shoulder.

"I know," she said. "But—counterpoint: what if I don't *want* to be vulnerable with people other than you guys?"

Dana and Courtney didn't even respond to that.

Nik sighed.

"I hate this. This is all Fisher's fault. If he hadn't done that stupid proposal in the first place, none of this would have ever happened, and I never would have even met Carlos."

"Would you really want that?" Courtney asked.

"Yes! Okay, fine, no. I just wish Carlos had listened to me!" Nik said. "Okay, maybe telling him he was being emotional was a shitty thing to say, but I didn't know how to react and I didn't want this to ruin everything, but everything is ruined anyway."

She put her head down on the table. Dana and Courtney immediately put their arms around her.

"I'm so mad at him for how mean he was to me this morning, but I hate that I hurt his feelings. See, this is another reason why I never should have dated him in the first place. I should have stuck to my streak of dating guys I couldn't care less about. When I do that and we break up, I feel fine! Look at Fisher—did I care if I hurt his feelings? Not really! I need to find another Fisher."

"No you don't," Dana and Courtney said in unison.

She shook her head.

"There must be something wrong with me. Here I have this great, smart, kind, hot man telling me he loves me, and I recoil. Everything was so great, and now it's over, and he thinks I'm an unfeeling asshole. Maybe I am."

Courtney got up and grabbed a box of tissues out of a cabinet and brought them over to her. She sat up and took a handful.

"Okay, first of all, if he thinks that, Carlos doesn't know you at all. You are loving and kind and funny and the best damn cheerleader anyone has ever had."

Damn it, now Courtney was going to make her cry even more.

"Second, there's nothing wrong with you. I'm not saying that you're perfect, but who is? It's okay to not react perfectly all the time; it's okay to say no to people; it's okay even to not love someone back."

Nik wiped her eyes and nodded.

"What if I want to be perfect though?"

Dana laughed.

"As my mother would say, it's nice to want things."

All three of them laughed.

"Your mom *would* say that," Nik said. "Have you told her about Natalie yet?"

Dana shook her head. "It's only been a little while. I just told you guys! But . . ." she smiled. "Hopefully soon."

Nik reached for her now cold bourbon and coffee drink and drained the cup.

"I've got to try to make a bourbon and coffee cupcake," Courtney said. "Oh fuck. Speaking of cupcakes, I have to get back out there."

Nik stood up.

"Give me an apron, I'll help. You don't want people complaining on Yelp about your long, slow line."

Courtney tossed an apron to her from the closet.

"Good, you owe me for all the cupcakes you just ate."

* * * * * * *

Carlos forced himself to turn off the shower. Usually when he took a shower it helped him figure out the answer to whatever he was stressed about, but this shower had just made everything worse. As soon as he stepped inside, he saw the empty space where Nik's bottle of conditioner used to be. She really had made sure to take every reminder of her existence out of his house, hadn't she? Not that he could forget her.

Nor could he forget how ashamed of himself he was. He was thirty-four, not fourteen; he was a little too old to storm out of his house full of righteous anger. Granted, he was still furious at Nik for the way she'd reacted this morning, but he was probably just as mad at himself for blowing up at her.

Maybe he'd been naive, but he hadn't expected her reaction this morning at all. It wasn't that he was so arrogant he thought any woman who was lucky enough for him to fall in love with her should be overjoyed . . . okay, fine, a *little* part of him may have thought that. He'd always just figured that when he got ready to seriously date someone, finding the someone would be the easy part.

Maybe she was right. Maybe he wasn't in love with her after all. Maybe this was just a momentary feeling, because of all of the emotion from last night and then all of the sex they'd had afterward. Maybe he could just . . .

He put his jeans on and sighed. Bullshit. He knew he loved her; he knew it to his core. He loved her for her kindness, her ability to laugh both at him and at herself, and her intelligence. But most of all, he loved her for that feeling he had when he sat next to her on his couch in silence or woke up next to her in bed, that feeling of peace and happiness. That he was with someone who understood him and everything about him. That everything was right with the world.

He sat down on his bed to put his shoes on. He had to pick up Angela, go to the hospital with her to check in on Jessie and the baby, and potentially throw his weight around if anything wasn't perfect. What he wanted to do was to go for a long run or play basketball all afternoon with people he didn't like or drive his car really fast along winding roads for three hours. Anything to not have to think or talk to people.

"Hey!" Angela hugged him when she got in his car, and he hugged her back. Great, now he felt like an asshole for being so grumpy about this visit.

"Hey. Have you talked to Jessie today? I texted her this morning, but she hadn't seen the doctor yet."

"Yeah." Angela settled back into the car. "That's what she told me, too. She sounded anxious about the baby. I think it's killing her that she can't be there with her the whole time."

One of Angie's feet tapped against the passenger-side door. It was a nervous habit she'd had since she was little. It drove him crazy, but he forced himself not to yell at her to stop.

"Of course it is. It'll be easier once she can move around more."

"The baby is going to be okay, right? They weren't just saying that last night?"

He nodded. There were no guarantees, but everything he'd heard last night had satisfied him.

"Nothing is certain, but let's put it this way: if I'd been really worried, I would have been at the hospital and inside that NICU by dawn."

Angie stopped tapping her foot.

"Okay, that does make me feel better." She turned and looked behind her. "No Nik? Where is she?"

Damn it. Of course Angie would do this today.

"No, she had work to do." He sped up as he got onto the freeway. Maybe she would be distracted by him driving too fast and would abandon this line of questioning.

"I'm happy for you, you know," she said. "So happy that I'm not even going to gloat about how I've known for weeks there was something going on there."

He should have known that nothing could distract Angie when she got going.

"Nothing's going on there. She was just at my house when I got Jessie's call and the enchiladas were still in the oven, so she said she'd stay to finish them. And then when she checked in to see how things were going, I said we were all hungry, so she brought them over, that's all." He shrugged. "No big deal."

Angela had a big grin on her face. It made him want to throw things.

"Mmmmhmm. Any girl you're dating who I get to meet is a big deal."

He cut around another car in the fast lane and gritted his teeth. Did Angie really have to do this right now?

"You'd already met Nik. You met her at the exact same time I did." Thank God the hospital exit was in only three miles.

"You know that doesn't count. You don't bring girls around the family; we both know that. And Nik met everyone who matters last night, so I'm just saying, it sounds serious."

He shook his head.

"It's not serious. Last night was an emergency; don't think too much of it." Oh God, this was going to be a disaster. Everyone was going to keep asking him about Nik for months, and he would have to be reminded about how he'd felt this morning over and over again.

"Oh, please with that 'it's not serious' bullshit. I was sitting right there when she brought up you going to the doctor, and if that doesn't say serious, I don't know what does. Don't worry, I won't say anything to Mama. She already called me this morning to ask what I knew about her, but I didn't say much. Mama was so happy that you'd found a nice girl who takes care of you. She said she'd be happier if she were a Mexican girl, but at this point she'd take anything, and I told her that—"

He couldn't take this anymore.

"We broke up, okay? We broke up this morning. I told her I loved her; she didn't feel the same way; we broke up. She's the first person in years that I've talked to about Dad, which probably should have been my sign that I was falling in love with her, but I didn't realize it until this morning. But it doesn't matter, because we broke up."

He didn't look in Angie's direction. He didn't want to see the look of sympathy he knew was on her face.

"Oh, Carlos. I'm so sorry."

He shrugged.

"It's probably for the best. I can't date anyone seriously now. You guys need me. I should have never gotten involved so closely with her as it was."

Angie turned her whole body toward him.

"What are you talking about? Who needs you?"

He glanced at her. Why was she playing dumb?

"The family. You, Mama, Tia Eva, even Jessie sometimes, though she has Jon for most things. Who would put together your bookshelf or change your light bulbs on those high ceilings of yours or go shopping with Mama or answer all of your phone calls? I don't have time to do all of those things and get involved with someone. I shouldn't have let myself get so close to Nik in the first place."

He looked at Angela, expecting her to be nodding at all of this. Instead, she was looking at him like he had two heads.

"Carlos. Are you really trying to tell me that you think you can't date someone seriously because you have to be free to put together bookshelves for me on a moment's notice?"

He shook his head.

"Not just that, it's a lot of things—you know that. Dad's gone, so I need to—"

She cut him off.

"That's the stupidest thing I've ever heard. I know I'm your little sister, but I'm a grown woman. I can put together my own bookshelves or pay someone else to do it. Mama is not a little old lady. She doesn't need someone to go to the grocery store with her. She goes with you because she likes to spend time with you. We don't need you to put your life on hold to take care of us. We can take care of ourselves. I'm pretty sure I speak for Mama—and Jessie and Tia Eva—when I say that we want you to be happy, not spending all of your leisure time doing errands for us."

Angie clearly didn't understand.

"I know you can take care of yourselves. That's not the point. What if I fell in love with some woman, and I was with her when there was an emergency? I would never forgive myself if I wasn't there for someone in the family when they needed me."

Angie put her hand over his.

"But there would be nothing to forgive. You and I both weren't there when Dad died, and I hate that, too. But it was no one's fault, and you can't spend your life trying to make sure something like that doesn't happen again."

He pulled off the freeway and made the turn toward the hospital.

"This isn't about Dad! It's just that I'm a doctor, and—"

Angie talked over him.

"Plus, you *did* fall in love with a woman, and you *were* with her last night when there was an emergency, and what happened? She sent you off to the hospital to take care of your family, and then she showed up a few hours later because she thought you needed her. Which you did. You don't always have to be the hero, Carlos, and you definitely don't need to be my dad. It's okay to just be my brother."

Finally, he exploded.

"Angela, can we please stop talking about this? You've made your point: you don't need me, I'm wasting my life, et cetera, et cetera. I get it—enough. Can we please just concentrate on Jessie and little Eva today?"

Angie nodded. She was silent until they got out of the car in the hospital parking garage.

"I'm sorry if I made things worse. That's not what I meant to do."

He pulled her hair.

"No, I'm sorry for getting mad."

She gave him a one-armed hug.

"You know I'm here if you ever want to talk, right?"

He nodded as they got in the elevator.

"I know. Thanks. Now, let's go see our new little cousin."

Chapter Twenty

The sparkly sign in front of Natalie's Gym was the first thing to make Nik smile in days.

She never should have gone out with Carlos in the first place. After everything with Fisher, she should have kept her distance from Carlos and all other men for at least several months, if not years. And now she'd spent the last three days inside her apartment with too many pints of ice cream, trying and failing to concentrate on her work instead of how much she missed Carlos.

She was even doing that thing where she caught herself checking her phone every time it buzzed, hoping it was him. She hated doing that thing. She'd always felt scornful toward the kind of woman who would do that thing. Why was she such a bitch? Now she felt sympathy for those women and even shittier about herself right now.

And the buzz from her phone was never him. She hadn't heard

a single thing from Carlos since he'd slammed that door on Sunday morning.

Enough wallowing. She'd finally pinned Natalie down for an interview time for her story about the gym, thank goodness. She was looking forward to talking to Natalie, if only to get her mind off of herself for once this week.

She still felt lucky that Natalie had even agreed to the interview. Between her hesitation when Nik had brought it up and her slow response to Nik's emails about scheduling a time, it was clear that she was reluctant about this story for some reason.

She walked into the gym and knocked on Natalie's open door.

"Hi!" Natalie said. "Come on in." She was smiling, but Nik could see her hands trembling. She couldn't tell if it was because Natalie was just nervous about being interviewed in general—lots of people were like that—or if there was something specific that she was anxious about. Either way, Nik knew she had to have a gentle approach in this interview.

"Hi!" Nik echoed her. "Does this time still work?"

Natalie nodded and waved her inside.

"Yes, sure, of course. Close the door so we can talk. I told Jamila I'll be busy for the next hour and to only interrupt if it's an emergency."

"Great." Nik sat down, took out her phone and recorder, and flicked them both to record. She always had a duplicate now, just in case. "Before we start, I want to make sure that it's okay that I record our conversation so that I can make sure to be accurate when I write about this."

Natalie glanced down at the recording devices and swallowed hard.

"Sure, yes, of course."

Nik took her notebook out of her bag but didn't open it yet.

"You know, Natalie," she said, "you don't know me that well. So it makes sense that you wouldn't really trust me yet." Natalie tried to cut in, but she kept talking. "It's okay, it doesn't hurt my feelings that you don't trust me. A lot of people have reasons not to trust writers or strangers or anyone at all. I can tell that you're nervous about this interview. Lots of people don't like being interviewed—it's normal to be anxious. But please know I'm not trying to trick you or do some gotcha piece about your gym or anything like that. I'm not that kind of person, and I'm not that kind of writer."

Natalie looked straight at Nik the whole time she was talking. When she stopped, Natalie slowly lowered her hands onto the table.

"I know," she said. "I mean, I knew all of that, about you. Mostly because of Dana, but it still helps to have you say it."

"Good." Nik smiled back at her. "Speaking of Dana, if there's anything you say to me today that you want to be off the record, please know that I wouldn't tell her about it."

Natalie's smile was faint, but it was there.

"Thank you for saying that."

Nik opened her notebook to her list of questions.

"Why don't we get started? I stumbled upon your gym kind of accidentally—I was searching for a self-defense class to take with my girlfriends, and your Punch Like a Girl series happened to start just a few days later, so I booked it on an impulse. I'd never even heard of your gym before, but it already has a very loyal clientele. Where did you get the idea to start this gym? How long have you been around?"

Natalie's smile was stronger now.

"Just over a year. I know it's pretty young for a gym, but I feel like I managed to tap into a need that was out there—a place for women of all kinds to feel supported and comfortable within their own skin, but more than just that, a place that could make all of us feel stronger, both inside and outside, and allow us to face our fears. A lot of people are afraid of the gym, and I hate that. I wanted this to be a place that people would look forward to going to, where people could be excited about working out and exercising, without the fear and shame and ridicule."

She'd gotten more animated and comfortable as she talked, and Nik hoped she stayed like that.

"Well, at least from my point of view, as someone who has always hated gyms, you've succeeded," Nik said. "Why don't we back up a little—how long had you wanted to open a gym? Have you worked at gyms in the past?"

"Oh God, I feel like I've spent my life in gyms," Natalie said. "I was a cheerleader in college, which meant I worked out a ton."

Nik laughed.

"Of course you were a cheerleader in college. I should have known." She paused. "That's a compliment of your teaching style, by the way. I've never had someone cheer me on so well for anything."

Natalie's cheeks got bright red, but she looked pleased. She was more relaxed now. Maybe it had been just nerves about being interviewed.

"That's so good to hear. Thank you. And then I graduated from college during a time when it was impossible to find a job. I was a math major." Nik managed to keep her face from looking surprised, but barely. And then she wanted to smack herself. Why was she still underestimating this woman, just because of what she looked like? "And I was looking for jobs in business or consulting or even teaching, and there was nothing. So to pay my rent, I got a job working at the front desk of the gym near me. After a while, I got curious about what the personal trainers did, so I started asking one of them a bunch of questions about her job: how she got it, what the certification was like, all that stuff. And eventually, I took the plunge."

As Natalie told her all about her personal training certification she seemed to be getting more relaxed.

"I was one of the top trainers by the time I left. My parents kept asking me if I was going to get a different job, go corporate, maybe go to business school. But I really loved my job. And I was good at it."

Nik nodded.

"I bet you were. I've had trainers before, and none of them were even half as good as one of your classes." It helped to flatter sources during interviews, but this had the benefit of being true. "Why did you leave the gym?"

Natalie turned to her glass of green juice again, but not before Nik saw that her eyes had filled with tears.

"I got married. One of my clients." She shrugged. She still looked down at her juice. "Such a cliché, I know."

Nik shrugged along with her.

"Clichés wouldn't be clichés if they didn't happen all the time." Of course the whole problem was the husband. "So . . . why did you leave the gym after getting married? Did you decide to go to grad school after all?"

She shook her head. She still had tears in her eyes, but she was looking straight ahead now.

"No. My husband didn't think it was appropriate for me to

keep working as a trainer after we were married. He said there would be too much touching other people; he knew I was bi, and he said he didn't have a problem with it, but it meant that working with women was a problem for him, too. So I quit." Nik raised her eyebrows but didn't ask a question. Natalie answered it anyway. "I know what you're going to say. Before I met him, I would have said the same thing. I didn't . . . by the time we were married, he'd convinced me of a lot of things. He said my job now was to take care of our house and him and that he'd take care of supporting me. I thought that was so sweet."

Sweet was one word for that.

"When did you stop thinking it was sweet?" she asked.

Natalie put her hand over her eyes for a second. She put it down and sat up straighter.

"I'm sorry. I don't usually talk about this."

Nik reached across the table and touched her hand.

"No need to apologize. You're doing great, so great."

Natalie smiled faintly.

"You sound like me when you say that."

Nik squeezed her hand, then let go.

"What can I say? I learned from the best."

Natalie's smile got a little bigger and then faded.

"What did you ask? When did I stop thinking it was sweet? It took a while." She shook her head. "That's not true. I don't think I ever thought it was sweet. But somehow I'd stopped trusting myself and my feelings."

Nik let out a deep breath. That sounded all too familiar.

"When I told him I missed the gym, he yelled at me for being ungrateful, and I thought he was right. But I really hated not having my own money. We had a joint bank account, and whenever I bought anything, he asked me a million questions about it, so eventually I just stopped buying things other than groceries. Sometimes I would get cash back and hide the cash."

Natalie picked up a piece of paper from her desk, crumpled it into a ball, and straightened it out.

"But I thought all of that was normal and showed how much he loved me. There are all of those commercials and things in women's magazines about hiding things you buy from your husband. They always make it seem like a thing all women do, that it's a joke we're all in together. So I didn't think having to sneak around to buy new sports bras was a big deal."

She sighed and took a deep breath. Nik thought about all of the articles and ads she'd seen that had made that exact joke. Good God, sometimes it felt like all of society was complicit in trying to make life harder for women.

"Even when he made it harder and harder for me to see my friends, I thought it was normal. People didn't see their friends that much after they got married, right? He said people who loved each other shouldn't have anything to hide from each other, so he should be able to read all of my emails and texts. So I stopped texting my friends very much. I didn't really see them much, either. Sometimes I would sneak out and get coffee with my best friend, Kiki. But I just thought he was acting like that because he loved me so much."

How could anyone ever trust someone again after someone they loved had made them feel so isolated and doubt their own instincts?

She certainly never had. Well, she'd started to trust Carlos, but that had been a mistake.

"I've had a lot of therapy since that time, and now I know there is such a thing as 'emotional abuse.' But I'd never heard that term then. So when my friends and family told me there was something wrong, it would just make me frustrated and mad at them. He never hit me; everything was fine! How could they think I was one of those poor, beaten-down, abused women? That wasn't me. Didn't they know me?"

Tears poured down Natalie's face.

Nik pulled a packet of tissues out of her bag—she always came prepared with them for interviews, just in case—and handed a stack to Natalie. Natalie took a deep breath and started again.

"I wasn't abused. It was just that my husband loved me more than anyone had ever loved me, and he wanted all of me. And if he got mad at me sometimes because he wanted fish for dinner and I'd made chicken, or if I went to the wrong gas station to fill up gas for his car, or when I miscarried but didn't lose the pregnancy weight right away, it was only because he wanted me to be perfect. He wanted me to be the best I could be; that was all."

Now Nik wasn't sure if she wanted to cry or if she wanted to take her new punching skills on the road and knock this man into oblivion. Maybe both.

"How did you realize what was going on? How did you decide to get out?"

Natalie looked down at her desk for a long moment.

"I wish I could say it was one thing, but it wasn't. The first time I remember consciously thinking 'This is not the life I want' was when I went running one day soon after he'd told me to lose weight after the miscarriage. All I wanted was to stay home under the covers, but I knew he would know if I didn't exercise—we both had those fitness bracelet things, and he could see my activity all day. It made me feel like I was constantly being spied on." She looked down at her bare wrist. "I guess I was. So I went running because I had to, and I hated every second. I hadn't talked to my family or any of my friends in months, so I didn't know where to turn."

Nik hated Natalie's husband, all men, and all of society for making Natalie feel like a relationship like the one she'd been in was normal.

"About a month after the miscarriage, I went to my doctor. The whole point of the visit was to see when I could start trying to get pregnant again. But when I was sitting there waiting for her, I realized that the idea of getting pregnant and having his baby and that baby tying me to him and that life forever made me feel panicky. I got up and left, and I told him the doctor said we shouldn't try for a few more months. A few days later, I logged in to an old email account that I'd had from before I got married, one that he didn't know I had. And that day I emailed Kiki and my mom. I didn't say anything, really, just hi, and asked how they were doing, stuff like that. They both responded right away, and I started emailing them more and more. And one day, I went for a run with Kiki. I didn't quite tell her everything, but I told her a lot."

God bless Kiki. She had to remember to give Courtney and Dana extra-big hugs the next time she saw them.

"How did you get out?"

Natalie pulled another tissue out of the packet.

"After weeks of emails, Mom ended one of hers with something like 'What do you think about coming home to visit? I have to drive down that way for work next week, and I can pick you up?' I said yes right away, and I told her that I'd meet her at Kiki's office. I spent the next six days terrified he'd see that email somehow or suspect something, but he didn't. That morning, I left my phone at home under the couch cushions and I took a taxi to Kiki's office. I took that fucking fitness bracelet off in the taxi and left it deep in the back seat, and I've never worn one since. When I got there and saw Kiki and my mom, that's when I really broke down for the first time."

Nik wished Kiki and Natalie's mom were there so she could hug them, too.

Natalie opened a drawer and pulled out two bottles of water.

"Want one? I'm thirsty after all of this crying." Nik took one and took a long sip. After that story, she would have even taken green juice.

"I guess that got kind of far away from why I started this gym. Except that I can't really tell one part of it without telling the whole of it. I lived with my parents for a while afterward—working at a local gym, getting more comfortable with myself, and going to lots of therapy. I let all of the money from my divorce settlement sit in the bank. Luckily for me, my mom is a lawyer and called in a favor with one of her divorce lawyer friends who took my case."

Nik smiled.

"Good job, Mom. Okay, let's go back to my initial question: where did you get the idea to start this gym?"

Natalie grinned at her.

"One day, I had an appointment with a client, and she came in spitting mad. She'd been on the treadmill before meeting me, and the guy next to her started lecturing her about her form. She was a marathon runner, mind you. And I thought of how great it could be if we had a gym for women of all shapes and sizes, where we could learn about our bodies and how strong we are without having to be on display to men while we did it. A place for all women: black and white; gay and straight; Latina and Asian; cis and trans; athletes and couch potatoes; and everything in between. And then

I thought about the money I had in the bank. And after about a year of research and planning, Natalie's Gym was born."

This story was going to be so good. Her editor at *O* magazine was going to love it.

"What about the boxing classes? Did you teach those before? Did you always know you wanted them when you decided to start the gym?"

Natalie nodded.

"I never taught them before coming here, but I took them at a few different gyms after the breakup and really loved them. They were one of the first things I knew I wanted at this place."

"What was your goal in teaching these classes? Why were they important to you?"

Natalie made a fist, flexed her hand, and made a fist again.

"Women who know how to fight hold themselves differently. I've seen that in the women who've taught me, in the women who've taken my classes, and especially in myself. You walk into any situation with an attitude that you've got this, you can defend yourself, you are strong. My marriage sapped me of a lot of my strength, and what made it worse were the constant messages I got from society that women are weak, women should be afraid, women should settle for whatever they can get. And I want the women who walk into this gym to know that women have power and agency and deserve great things in life."

"Amen," Nik said.

Natalie high-fived her.

"And it starts so young!" she said. "I really want to do a program for teenage girls. They need more things to counteract the messages that they get that there's something wrong with being a girl, that they should hide the things about themselves that make them unique and fun and strong." She grinned. "That's why I called the class 'Punch Like a Girl'—there's this constant message that to do anything like a girl is weak. I wanted to turn that on its head."

Carlos's teen clinic would probably be really into the idea of partnering with Natalie's Gym on a program like that, especially after things he'd told her about some of his patients and the abuse that they'd suffered.

She tried to shake off thoughts of him, but it was impossible. She had to ask Natalie the question she'd been wondering the entire time they'd been talking.

"This is a personal question, and I understand if you don't want to answer, especially since Dana is my friend. But how did you learn to trust people again after what happened to you?"

Natalie shook her head slowly.

"It was really hard. I beat myself up for a while after my marriage ended. I blamed myself for trusting my ex, for letting him control me, for giving in to everything. I didn't trust my own judgment for a long time. The whole time I was researching the idea for this gym, I kept second-guessing myself, thinking it was a terrible idea. But I was right; I did have a good idea, and even just doing all of that research was me learning to trust myself. Once I learned to trust myself, my instincts, and my emotions, trusting other people was a lot easier."

Nik drove home a few hours later, after lots of time hanging around the gym, and even taking one of those cycling classes that she always mocked Dana for loving. She couldn't stop thinking about everything that Natalie had said, but especially that last part. Did she trust herself? With her work, definitely. With anything else? She had no idea.

Chapter Twenty-one

When Carlos's phone rang on the way home from the hospital on Saturday night, he grabbed for it.

Drew. Not Nik. Why did he keep doing this to himself? She wasn't going to call him. Not after what he'd said to her.

He sighed and answered the phone.

"Hey, man, what's up?"

"Hey," Drew said. "How's the baby?"

He'd texted Drew right before he had left the hospital on the night the baby was born but hadn't talked to him since. He hadn't really been in the mood to hear stories of relationship bliss. And he really hadn't wanted to deal with telling him about Nik. But he couldn't avoid his best friend forever.

"Still in the NICU, but doing pretty well. I'm on the way home from the hospital right now, just spent a few hours hanging out with her and Jessie." Jessie had been released on Wednesday. Her blood pressure wasn't quite normal, but it was getting lower every day. But little Eva still had at least another few days in the hospital so her tiny lungs could improve and she could gain weight.

"I'm on my way *to* the hospital. I'm on call and just got called back in. How's Jessie?"

"She got released on Wednesday, but she's only left the hospital to sleep. She's at Eva's side all day. But all of the signs are good. Such a relief."

"Great. I bet Jessie won't relax until Eva's at home, though."

He thought of Jessie's anxious face and how Jon kept trying to force her to eat.

"Not one bit."

Drew coughed.

"So I have some news."

Uh-oh. That could be anything.

"Okay . . ."

Drew laughed.

"You sound so suspicious. We have a wedding date! Mark it on your calendar in bright red, et cetera."

A wedding date, of course. He should have expected that.

"Great, when is it?"

Drew laughed.

"Here's the thing: it's in October."

He counted the months in his head.

"This October? Four months from now October?" He grinned. "Wait. Do you have *other* news to tell me?"

"What do you . . . oh God, no, Alexa isn't pregnant! We're moving fast, but not that fast. Our favorite venue had a cancellation, and after Alexa had pulled some strings to get us to the top of the waiting list, we couldn't say no. Alexa's already been frantically looking for wedding dresses with her friend Maddie. And apparently, I need to start frantically doing something—I'm just not sure what that something is. So I figured I'd call you, because you're really good at telling me what to do."

Carlos laughed. He was indeed really good at telling Drew what to do.

"You finally acknowledge this now. You spent years complaining about it."

"Look, I always did what you said . . . eventually. Anyway, I think we need to find tuxes or something? You want to come up again some weekend soon and we can sort that out?"

Carlos got off the freeway exit for his house. A trip up to the Bay Area sounded like the break from his life that he needed.

"As soon as the baby's at home with Jessie and Jon, I'll drive up there. I was just thinking that I needed a long solo drive."

"Perfect. Tux shopping sounds basically terrible, but at least we'll get a fun weekend out of it. Oh, and please text me how to spell Nik's name so we don't get it wrong on the invite."

Shit. He couldn't dodge this one.

"Actually . . . you don't need to know how to spell her name. We broke up."

He heard a horn honk at the other end of the line.

"What? I almost ran a red light. When? What happened?"

It felt so depressing to say it out loud, but he had no real choice.

"Last weekend. Sunday morning, the day after Jessie had the baby. We were at the hospital together . . . long story, it's not important. Anyway, I told her I was in love with her and . . . it didn't go well."

"Catch me up here: you're in love with her? I thought you gave me some bullshit about how it wasn't serious."

He sighed.

"I guess you realized that was bullshit sooner than I did. But it doesn't matter; she doesn't feel the same way."

He'd only told this terrible story twice and he was already sick of it.

"Oof. She was at the hospital when Jessie had the baby? So she met your family?"

Thanks, Drew, for narrowing in on one of his sore spots.

"Unfortunately. Get this—she sent cupcakes to Jessie at the hospital on Monday."

He had been both touched and furious when he'd walked into Jessie's hospital room on Monday to see that Cupcake Park box. He knew, even before Jessie had told him, that they'd come from Nik.

"That was so nice of her," Drew said. "I bet you wanted to smash every single one of those cupcakes with the bottom of your foot."

"I wanted to throw them out the fucking window."

He heard the noises from the other end of the phone that signaled that Drew had driven into the parking garage.

"Do you have to go?"

"Nah, I have at least three or four more minutes," Drew said. "The staff parking is way on the top floors. It'll take a while to get up there. What do you mean it didn't go well? I'm guessing she didn't say it back?"

Carlos pulled up in front of his house and turned off his car, but he didn't bother to go inside yet.

"Not only did she not say it back, she said it would be better if we could pretend I'd never said it, which wasn't exactly the reaction I'd hoped for. So I got mad, said some not great stuff to her, left the house, and drove away." He sighed. "You don't have to tell me that I didn't handle it well. I already know that."

He looked out the window while he was talking. Damn, he really needed to mow his lawn.

"Have you talked to her since?" Drew asked.

Carlos sighed again.

"No. I want to, but I don't know what to say. I don't know if there's anything I can say."

He'd thought about texting her, especially after Jessie got those cupcakes. He'd wanted to say thank you and to apologize for being such an ass. Mostly the latter. But after he'd seen all of those texts from Fisher after *their* dramatic breakup, he sort of felt like he should avoid texting her anything. He didn't want to be that guy.

"Hmmmm," Drew said. Carlos heard him get out of his car. "I can think of a few things. I seem to remember a certain conversation last year right around this time . . ."

"That was different—you hadn't told Alexa how you felt," Carlos said. He should have known Drew would throw his own advice back in his face.

He'd be lying, though, if he tried to pretend that the only reason that he hadn't texted Nik was because of Fisher's crazy texts. The real reason was: what if it didn't make any difference?

He'd obviously sprung the whole thing on her too fast, which had been a big part of the reason everything escalated like it did. He should have done it all so differently. He's already thought of at least five or six better ways he should have told her. He wanted another chance to talk to her about everything. About them. But it all still felt so tender. He wasn't ready for her to reject him again.

"I know, I know. Sorry, forget my advice. What I should have said was, that fucking sucks; do you want to come up here this weekend and get really drunk with me? We can pick out some incredibly ugly tuxes for the wedding if you want."

Carlos laughed.

"Alexa would skin me alive. And really, man, thanks. I would, if the baby wasn't still in the hospital. But as soon as she's home, I'm on my way. I'll keep you posted."

A weekend getting drunk with Drew sounded like exactly what he needed.

"Awesome, I'm looking forward to it. Okay, now I really do have to go."

"Tell Alexa I said hi."

He hung up the phone and got out of his car. Talking to Drew had helped in some ways and made it worse in others. He was so happy about marrying Alexa in just a few months that it made the breakup feel even worse.

Oh well. He walked up his front steps and unlocked his door. Drew couldn't sit around in his underwear on his couch and eat pizza and drink beer all night like he could. Who had it better, huh?

He tried not to answer that.

* * * * * * *

Nik jumped at the noise outside on Monday afternoon. Did people *really* need to set fireworks off in the middle of the afternoon? The Fourth of July wasn't even for a few days. The amateur fireworks got earlier every damn year. She stood up to get some water and realized she couldn't remember the last time she'd left the house. Oh right, for her last self-defense class. Four days ago. She'd been buried in work all week—or as her friends claimed when they tried to get her to go out to brunch that weekend and she'd refused, she had buried herself in work.

At least she'd been able to concentrate on work again. It was a relief to dive headfirst into a story and not let herself think about Carlos, and what he was probably doing right now, and how much she missed him, and why she hadn't heard a single thing from him in the eight days since he'd slammed his front door. The thing was, as soon as she stopped working, those things were all she could think about.

She looked down at herself and winced. She was wearing the same leggings she'd been wearing for days and a threadbare tank top. And she desperately needed a shower.

Twenty minutes later, she left her house, showered; in a mostly clean pair of jeans, a gray T-shirt, and her biggest pair of sunglasses; and with her hair in a topknot. See, she could act like a human being. Sort of.

She walked the mile to the coffee shop while she listened to the audiobook of her latest true crime book. She wished she could tell Carlos to get it for Jessie.

She still wasn't sure if she'd done the right thing when she'd sent Jessie cupcakes. But she'd been a few hospital rooms away when Jessie had had her baby. She'd cried along with Carlos's whole family when Eva was born, and she'd seen the tiny baby just hours later. It still hurt, more than she wanted to acknowledge, that Carlos had said it was a waste for her to meet his family, after everything they'd shared that night. But it felt wrong to pretend none of that had happened, that she didn't care, just because she and Carlos were over. So she'd sent the cupcakes, the ones that Carlos had told her that Jessie and her husband had particularly liked. None of the spicy chocolate ones.

She thought about sitting down to drink her large iced coffee at the coffee shop, but she hadn't brought a book or her laptop, and she didn't feel like staring at the tiny bright screen of her phone. She wandered down the street and half-heartedly glanced into boutiques, but she wasn't really in the mood for shopping. After a few blocks, she turned around and walked home.

She was still in the world of the murderous cult as she approached her building. It wasn't until she was halfway up the steps that she saw someone standing by the front door.

Fisher. Fisher was standing by the front door.

"What the fuck are you doing here?" she said to him. She backed away to stand on the sidewalk. She didn't want to talk to him in the shadows of her building. He followed her.

"Hi, Nik." He put his hand on her waist. She immediately stepped away. "I've missed you."

Was he fucking kidding her?

"I haven't missed you. What are you doing here?"

He tossed his hair back and smiled.

"I should have expected that from you. You're always making little jokes, aren't you? I hoped I'd get a warmer greeting, though, after everything we were to each other."

"You hoped you'd get a warmer greeting?" She had actually dated this guy. For months, even. What in God's name had she been thinking? "After those texts you sent me? You can go straight to hell."

He smiled his gleaming white smile at her and tried to put his arm around her. She stepped away again, but he followed.

"Look, I know we both got a little heated after the Dodgers game, and I'm sorry if I said anything to upset you, but—"

"*If*? Was that supposed to be an apology?"

The smile was still plastered on his face. How had she ever found him attractive?

"Look, can we go somewhere a little more private and talk?" He looked around at the people driving and walking by them and grimaced. "Upstairs, maybe?"

She tossed the rest of her iced coffee into the trash can at the curb.

"No. Say what you have to say to me here. You seem to like having important conversations in public. Why stop now?"

He sighed.

"Just keep your voice down, okay? I got a lot of bad publicity last time. I don't want to have to deal with that again."

Well, now she'd have to turn up the volume.

"Bad publicity last time . . . I can't even believe you. Spit it out, Fisher. What are you doing here? I thought you got the message that I didn't want to see or talk to you anymore."

Finally his smile dropped away, and he moved closer to her. She backed away again.

"Look, Nik. Haven't you realized by now what a mistake you made? We had a good thing going. Mutually beneficial, isn't that what they call it? Good for you for many reasons, and quite frankly, it was good for me to be seen with you. People had this impression of me that I was shallow and only good for the dumb-guy parts, and no one would even send me the good scripts."

For good reason. The dude had a great body but couldn't act his way out of a paper bag.

"But more than once," he continued, "directors would talk to you at parties, and then they would see me with you and they would be a lot nicer to me. And my agent told me people said they thought there must be more to me if I was dating someone smart and interesting and urban like you."

Urban. She wondered if Fisher's agent had really said that or if that was Fisher's translation from "black." At least now she knew where the out-of-the-blue proposal had come from.

"So you proposed to me, in public, without talking to me about it first, because you thought it would help you get ahead in your career?"

He nodded eagerly.

"It would have! I still don't understand why you said no. It would have been great for you, too." He waved his arm up and down her body. "I mean, look at you. People who look like you don't usually get to go to the places I would take you. You had so many more opportunities, dating a person like me." He smacked her butt.

Without even thinking about it, she took a step back, shifted her weight onto her back heel, pulled her fist back, and punched Fisher right in the face.

"Oh wow. It really does hurt your hand," she said as Fisher writhed on the ground at her feet.

A woman walking with a baby stroller stopped next to them.

"That was amazing!" she said. "How did you learn to punch like that?"

Nik shook out her fingers. The pain was worth it. She grinned at the woman.

"Natalie's Gym, over on Larchmont. It's fantastic; you should take one of her classes!"

The woman rocked the stroller back and forth with her foot while she took out her phone and made a note.

"Natalie's Gym. Thank you! Great job." She started to walk away with the baby, and then turned back and looked down at Fisher, who was still on the ground. "I bet you've had that coming to you for years!" She waved good-bye to Nik as she walked off.

Nik looked down at Fisher.

"Stop moaning. You're fine; you're not even bleeding."

He struggled to his feet and glared at her.

"My face is my most precious commodity, next to my body. I can't believe this." He turned his back on her and walked to his car. "I should call the police on you."

"What, and tell them you got punched by a girl?"

Nik laughed all the way up to her apartment. She kept replaying the scene in her mind where she'd punched Fisher, and it made her happier every time.

She unlocked her front door and dug around in her freezer until she found a bag of frozen vegetables for her knuckles. Just think, less than two months ago she'd been so freaked out by Fisher's texts that she'd had to have Carlos search her apartment, and now, she'd knocked him to the ground all by herself. Carlos would love this story so much.

Shit. She couldn't tell Carlos.

She sank down on the couch and put her head in her hands.

She had plenty of people to tell who would be excited for her. Courtney and Dana would crack up. Natalie would be thrilled. So why did it hurt so much that she couldn't tell Carlos?

Because Carlos would have been so proud. He was the only one who knew how far she'd come. He'd seen her that night; he'd been worried about her; he'd cheered her decision to go to Natalie's class. Courtney and Dana had guessed, and Natalie had helped, but Carlos *knew.* He'd been so ready to protect her, but she'd protected herself.

He would have loved that. He would have been so happy for her and impressed that she'd stood up for herself. That's what was so great about Carlos, damn it. Why did he have to go and ruin everything?

Courtney and Dana had said that she needed to learn how to be vulnerable, but she'd been vulnerable with Carlos in a way she hadn't been with any guy in years. She'd let him know how scared she was that first night they'd gone out, when she'd let him search her apartment. She'd told him what Justin had said about her writing and how it still made her insecure sometimes. She'd cried with him when the baby was born. Maybe none of those things would be a big deal for someone else, but they were for her.

Ugh, why was she back to thinking about Carlos? She went to the kitchen to pour herself a drink. She deserved one for her triumph.

Maybe not rosé—she wasn't going to let Carlos's jokes about it ruin her favorite wine forever, but why push herself right now? She made a gin and tonic and brought it back over to the couch.

"Cheers!" She lifted the glass with her unbruised hand. It had been so great to watch Fisher fall to the ground. She took a sip of her drink, thought of the bruise that was probably already marring his perfect face, and smiled. God bless that woman in the stroller.

She took out her phone to text her girlfriends.

Fisher was waiting in front of my building when I got home today, and long story short, I punched him in the face.

Mere seconds later, Dana texted back.

!!!!!!!!!!!!!!

And then like twenty of the fist-in-the-air and fireworks emojis.

Courtney screeched in.

WHAT

OMG

TELL US EVERYTHING

Nik grinned and relaxed into her couch cushions. Who needed Carlos when you had girlfriends?

She texted them the whole story—one-handed—and then, halfway through her gin and tonic, she fell asleep on the couch. She woke up two hours later from a dream about Carlos high-fiving her. When she realized it was just a dream, she started to cry.

Should she text him and tell him what happened? God knows she wanted to. But he was probably still pretty mad at her.

And if he wasn't? Texting him wasn't fair to him. He deserved more than she could give him—than she knew how to give him.

Instead, she texted a picture of her raw knuckles to her friends. Their responses made her smile through her tears.

Chapter Twenty-two

Carlos sat at his desk and stared at his phone. His meeting had been canceled at the last minute. That unfortunately gave him time to make that phone call he'd been avoiding all week.

All week? He'd avoided making that call for the past five years.

He picked up the phone.

"Yes, hi. I'd like to schedule an appointment with Dr. Guerriero? Just a physical. Yes, Carlos Ibarra." He swallowed hard, as the person on the other end took his insurance information. "I totally understand if you can't get me in for a while—oh, you have a cancellation tomorrow? I don't know if . . ." He took a deep breath. "What time tomorrow?"

He hung up the phone and stared out the window. Tomorrow. Damn it.

No, tomorrow was too soon. He should call back to reschedule. He picked up the phone.

"Dr. Ibarra?" One of the nurses poked her head into his office, and he put the phone down again. "There's someone at the front desk to see you. She says she's your cousin?"

He stood up. If Jessie had left the NICU to come over to his office to see him, it was either really good or really bad news.

"I'll be right there."

He almost ran down the hall.

"Jessie?" He poked his head into the waiting room. The huge smile on her face answered his question. She ran over to him, and he threw open the door so she could follow him back to his office. But the door was barely shut before she threw her arms around him.

"We get to take her home today! Yesterday they said maybe, but I was too scared to tell anyone. Last night I couldn't sleep, partly because of the fireworks going on all night, but mostly because I was just praying that I would have my baby at home with me by tonight. And my prayers were answered. Just a few hours for them to do all of the paperwork and to give us all of her instructions. Oh, Carlos! I get to take my baby home!"

He hugged her tight and pulled her down the hall to his office. Once the door was closed, he hugged her again.

"I didn't think she'd be able to go home this early. You've got a fighter on your hands. When they told me you were here to see me, I . . ." He wiped his eyes. "Anyway, this is wonderful. I'm so happy for you and for Eva, who won the mom lottery." He took a step back and handed her the tissue box on his desk. "Where's Jon? Do you need help getting Eva home?"

Jessie took a handful of tissues and shook her head.

"He's upstairs with Eva. I've barely stopped crying since the doctors told us she could go home today."

Carlos gently pushed her down in one of the chairs in front of his desk and sat next to her.

"And you, you're okay?" He shook his head. "No, you don't have to tell me. I'm your cousin, not your doctor."

She leaned over to hug him.

"Just for that, I'll tell you that my blood pressure is almost normal. And I can even fit into some of my pre-pregnancy shoes now. Not clothes, let's not be ambitious, but I was getting very nervous I'd never be able to wear those Tory Burch flats again, so that was a tiny relief."

His office phone rang and he ignored it.

"I don't know who Tory is, but if that's a relief to you, it is to me, too. Do you need anything? Food, diapers, a crib, bottles, anything?"

She laughed, even though tears were still trickling down her face.

"Don't forget, you already brought me those enchiladas. We've already defrosted one pan and have been eating them all week. And I think my mom has spent all day every day since Eva was born cooking for her little namesake; my freezer is going to be filled to bursting soon. I don't even know what else we need. I'm mad at myself for not letting my friends push the date of my shower up. I thought it was tempting fate, if you can believe that. Thank God someone already bought us the bassinet so she has somewhere to sleep."

He made a mental note to buy whatever was the most expensive thing on the registry. Okay, okay, maybe Angela was right; he could pull back a little. The second most expensive thing.

She stood up.

"I should go. I probably have to sign a bunch of stuff, and I can't wait to get our little girl out of this hospital, even though I'm sort of terrified to pull her away from the people taking care of her."

Carlos put his hand on her shoulder.

"You and Jon, *you* are the people taking care of her. And you'll do a wonderful job, I promise."

She punched his arm.

"Damn you, Carlos. I *just* stopped crying, and now you've got to get me started again?"

She leaned in for a hug, and he kissed her on the forehead.

"I'm so happy for you, Jessie. And I can't wait to spoil little Eva rotten."

She opened his office door.

"I can't wait for that, either. Oh, and you thanked your friend Nik for me for the cupcakes, right? Tell her I said that was so thoughtful. I want to send her a thank-you card, but this week has just been . . ."

He had not thanked Nik on Jessie's behalf, no.

"Don't worry about it. You've been kind of preoccupied this week; she understands." He was sure Nik *did* understand, so that wasn't exactly a lie. "Go back upstairs to your baby. Call me if you have any questions at all, okay?"

Right, right, she was his cousin, not his patient. This shit was hard.

"Actually, you should probably call the NICU and not me, they know this stuff better than I do. But let me know if you need anything at all, okay?"

She nodded.

"I will. Have I ever told you how glad I am that you're my cousin?"

He grinned.

"I'm not sure, refresh my memory about why? You had at least ten or fifteen reasons, correct? Can you list them for me?"

She walked into the hallway.

"Never, you're cocky enough as it is."

She disappeared toward the elevators with another wave over her shoulder, and he went laughing back to his desk.

Maybe he *should* text Nik to thank her for the cupcakes. He couldn't keep pretending to Jessie that he'd done that without actually doing it, right?

And wouldn't Nik want to know that Eva was okay and was getting to go home from the hospital? She'd been there the night Eva was born; she'd cried along with everyone else. Shouldn't he let her know?

He laughed at himself. That was a pretext, and he knew it. He didn't need to thank Nik; he needed to apologize to Nik. He hated what he'd said to her that awful morning, he hated the memory of the hurt look on her face when he'd walked out of his house, and he hated that she'd remember him like that. Even if she didn't love him back, he didn't want her to hate him.

An email was probably the way to do this, not a text. A text felt too immediate. Like he'd be expecting a response.

He scrolled back through his work emails until he found her email address.

To: Nikole@NikoleDPaterson.com
From: Carlos_Ibarra@eastsidemedicalcenter.com
Subject: cupcakes

Jessie wanted me to make sure to thank you for the cupcakes. They made her so happy. She appreciated it a lot. So did I. She's doing a lot better and Eva is, too—they're taking her home from the hospital today.

I'm sorry for what I said that morning and how I acted. I can't apologize enough.

You don't have to respond to this.

Carlos

That seemed so blunt and inarticulate, but at least it was all true.

He pressed send.

· · · · · · ·

Nik pulled into the grocery store parking lot at ten on Friday night. It was her favorite time to go to the grocery store, and she hadn't been able to go on a Friday night in a while. The place was almost empty, the employees were in party moods, and the other people who were there on Friday nights were always buying huge bags of chips and cartons of cheap beer, which always made Nik so happy she wasn't going to their terrible parties.

As she walked inside, a bleary-eyed man carrying a huge bag of diapers almost knocked into her on his way out.

"Sorry!" he shouted. Then he walked into the parking lot right into the path of a car that braked just in time. Poor guy probably hadn't slept in a week.

That made her think of Jessie and Jon, and baby Eva. And Carlos.

She'd barely been able to think about anything else since she'd gotten Carlos's email the day before. She'd written and deleted about five responses until she'd finally given up.

She walked through the store, still thinking about the email.

She stopped in the baked goods aisle and stared at four shelves full of different gluten-free flours without really seeing them. She wanted so much to respond, but she had no idea what to say.

She shook her head to try to clear her mind. Thinking like this was not going to help. And for God's sake, especially not in the grocery store. She had a list, remember? And—she finally realized what she was staring at—sorghum flour was not on it. She pushed her cart until she found olive oil and checked it off her list.

She sped through the store, grabbing bananas, granola, bread, tomatoes, bacon. Oh good, she could make herself a BLT when she got home tonight. People always said it was a bad idea to go to the grocery store while hungry, but she always made herself delicious meals when she got home from the grocery store on those Friday nights.

She made her way to the dairy aisle to stock up on yogurt. When she saw the big tubs of sour cream, she laughed out loud, startling the employee stocking the dairy case. She didn't think she would ever be able to see sour cream without remembering when she'd spackled her face with it after she'd set herself on fire with chilies. And when she laughed so hard with Carlos about it that they'd ended up sitting on the bathroom floor in tears. She grabbed six containers of yogurt, still with a smile on her face.

Would she always think about Carlos whenever she saw sour cream? She hoped so, despite everything. Seeing that sour cream made her think of how happy she'd been around him, at every moment. It made her think of how proud he was of all of her accomplishments, from writing for the *New Yorker* to signing up for boxing class. It made her think of how he'd dropped everything to help her, more than once, and how happy she was to be able to help him the night Eva was born. She never wanted to stop thinking about him.

Wait.

Holy shit.

Oh no.

WAS THIS WHAT LOVE WAS?

Being happy when you thought about someone; wanting to never stop thinking about them, even when you were fighting; having every damn thing in the grocery store remind you of them, from diapers to sour cream; wanting to be a better writer and friend and person because of how they were and how they made you feel; wanting to be with them, all the time, even though you kept fighting it.

Motherfucker.

She was in love with him.

Now what?

She walked to the register like she was in a dream. She didn't know how to do this. How did a person even handle this sort of thing?

She didn't like this; she didn't like it at all. She felt gooey and vulnerable and helpless. She didn't like feeling any of those things. If this was what Natalie had meant by trusting herself and her emotions, she wasn't a fan of it at all.

When she'd been with Justin, she'd felt anxious and needy and constantly on edge, like she had to prove herself all the time. Thinking about him had never made her feel happy like thinking about Carlos did. She knew Carlos loved her—as difficult and prickly and loud as she was—just for being her. And she loved him for being the funny, kind, warm person he was. She loved him so much.

Oh no, this was awful.

She preferred her comfortable, easy, safe flings with guys she didn't care about to all of these terrible feelings. Her first instinct was to get in her car, get on the freeway going east, and just keep driving.

Yes, that was a good idea. She should drive until she hit the desert and then stay there. That way, she would never have to deal with this and maybe eventually it would go away.

She stuck her credit card in the stupid card reader that beeped at her like she'd done something wrong and thought hard about that plan. She could go right now. These bananas and that granola, plus the bottled water that she'd bought weeks ago and had been too lazy to take out of her trunk, all of that could last her a few weeks, right? Not that she would have any way of knowing. She hadn't driven to the desert or slept outside since . . . okay, it was definitely within the last ten years—she'd be fine.

She pushed her cart to her car and loaded her groceries into the trunk. What all did she need, anyway? Food, water, a bucket of some sort? There must be an REI that was open late nearby somewhere where she could buy one and a flashlight and an emergency sleeping bag that would become an actual cocoon for her so she didn't have to deal with how she'd fucked everything up.

She sat in her car but didn't turn it on.

She put her head down on her steering wheel. And, oops, she honked the horn with her nose. She sat up with a jerk and waved an apology to the dog in the car facing hers. It still barked at her.

Maybe driving to the desert in the middle of the night in July wasn't the best idea she'd ever had, but the alternative was to actually think about this, and how she didn't know how to do this, and what if his email had meant he was apologizing for saying he loved her because he hadn't actually meant it, and how she didn't know what she would do if she never saw him again, and the desert sounded better than all of that.

The Vons parking lot was no place to figure this out. Maybe . . . maybe Carlos would be waiting on her doorstep this time. Yes, she would go home, and he'd be waiting for her there. She would leap into his arms and say she loved him and that she was sorry for everything, and he would say he'd never stopped loving her, and they'd go upstairs and have lots of sex, and everything would be perfect.

She started her car and raced home, convinced more and more every moment that that was what was going to happen. It made perfect sense. He had sent that email so she would be ready to leap into his arms when he showed up! Which she would!

She pulled into the parking lot behind her building and walked around to the front with her groceries, ready to pretend to be surprised as soon as she saw him.

But no one was there.

Fuck.

Did this mean she was going to have to figure out how to fix this herself?

She walked into her apartment and put her entire grocery bag in her refrigerator, too tired and confused to unload it.

She pulled out her phone to text Courtney and Dana. But what was she going to say to them? "I just realized I'm in love with Carlos and don't know what to do"? She already knew what they would tell her to do.

TELL HIM—that's what they would say. Courtney would use all caps; Dana wouldn't but would use exclamation points, but the message would remain the same.

But didn't they know how hard it would be to tell him something like that?

Yeah, they'd been her friends for fifteen years. She was pretty sure they knew. But they would tell her to do it anyway. The assholes.

When she realized that she was cursing at her friends because of their imaginary conversation with her, she knew she'd gone fully around the bend. Okay, tonight she was going to make no impulsive decisions, neither driving to the desert nor texting anyone would happen. She turned off her phone and went straight to bed. Maybe in the morning she would be over this love nonsense.

She woke up the next morning after ten full hours of sleep and stumbled to the kitchen to make coffee. She opened the refrigerator to get milk and did a double take at the full grocery bag stuffed onto the middle shelf of her refrigerator.

"Why the fuck did I do that? Was I drunk last night?"

Oh. It all came back to her now. Way worse than drunk.

The coffee pot beeped at her, and she poured herself a cup and drank about half of it like a very hot tequila shot.

She sat down and stared into her coffee mug for five full minutes. Then she took out her phone to text her friends.

I realized I'm in love with Carlos and I don't know what to do.

She sat there, staring at her phone, waiting for their responses.

OMG. This is so exciting! I knew it! You've got to tell him!

That was Dana, of course. Wait a minute, what did she mean, she knew it?

FINALLY. But why are you telling us, tell HIM.

"Finally" was not the response she had expected to get.

Why are you guys acting like this is old news? I just realized it last night and I almost had a breakdown in the Vons parking lot!

She poured another mug full of coffee. What had she been thinking last night, granola? All she wanted right now was a doughnut.

Oh, honey, we've known this for weeks, but it doesn't matter that you're late to the party. All that matters is that you got here at all. Right, Dana?

Right! Go get him!

She hated them so much.

"Go get him!" they said. Like that was easy. Like she knew how to do something like that. Like she wasn't terrified to do it.

She finished her cup of coffee and poured another one. Then she picked up her phone and scrolled back through her call log until she found the number. She took a deep breath.

"Hi, Angela? Hi, this is Nik. We, um. We met at the Dodgers game, and . . . yeah, that Nik. I need a favor."

Chapter Twenty-three

Carlos didn't think he'd ever get Angela to leave Jessie's side. They'd been there for the past four hours, and the way Angie looked at Eva, it seemed like they'd be there for another four hours, minimum. The original plan had been for Angie to go today and for him to go tomorrow, but Angie had called him that morning and said Jessie wanted to see them both today, since her mom was coming over tomorrow. He didn't quite understand the logic there, but he chalked it up to hormones and went along with it.

Plus, it wasn't like he had anything better to do.

"Hey, man," he said to Jon when Jessie and Angie were giggling about something in the corner, Eva sound asleep on Jon's chest. "I'm sorry we've been here for so long. I'm sure you two wanted to be alone with your baby more in these first few weeks."

Jon laughed.

"Thanks, but I've known my wife's family long enough to know that there isn't going to be a day in the next month, minimum, when we'll be alone with our baby. And you know what, that's fine with me. These past few months have been so stressful, and now we have this tiny baby who we are responsible for, and I'm grateful for every bit of help from everyone in your family, because I sure as hell don't know what I'm doing." He looked down at his daughter on his chest and then back up at Carlos. "I'm glad she has you guys. Come over anytime."

Carlos patted him on the shoulder, realizing just in time to do it softly enough so he wouldn't wake the baby.

"We're going to be over so often that you're going to get sick of us. I already adore my new little cousin."

Jon stroked Eva's mass of dark hair.

"Anytime you want to come entertain her late at night so we can sleep, just let us know."

Angela stood up and interrupted their laughter.

"Hey, Carlos, you ready to go? We should probably give Jessie and Jon some time alone with their baby."

He stood up too.

"I was just saying that to Jon." He rubbed Eva's little head as a good-bye and hugged Jessie.

"I thought you were trying to get us to move in," he said to Angie once they'd gotten in the car.

"Oh." She looked out the passenger window. "I just thought Jessie needed some company, that's all." She turned to look at him. "Was that all right? You didn't have plans tonight, did you?"

On a Saturday night? Of course he didn't have plans. The person that he'd had plans with for most of the Saturday nights this summer clearly never wanted to see him again. She hadn't even replied to his email.

Sure, he'd said she didn't have to, but he'd still really wanted her to reply.

"No," was all he said. He didn't want to sound too bitter. "I was happy to stay there as long as they needed us."

Angie let out a relieved sigh.

"Oh good, that's okay then."

He dropped her off at her apartment, then drove the short distance to his house. His only plan on this Saturday night was to watch the Dodgers game from the couch. Whatever snack he ate along with it would have to be low in cholesterol, after what his doctor had said on Friday, but he could handle that.

He unlocked his front door and stepped inside.

What the hell?

There were blue and white streamers, Dodger pennants, and boxes of Cracker Jack everywhere. And standing directly across from him, wearing a blue and white baseball T-shirt and jeans, was Nik.

"Hi," she said.

"Nik." My God, it was so good to see her. He wanted to cross the room in one leap and embrace her. He wanted to tell her how much he'd missed her. He wanted to tell her how much he loved her, still. Wait, no, that's what started all the problems in the first place. He dropped his keys on the table by the door and didn't move. "Hi."

"Hi," she said again and smiled. "I, um. I got your email. I know you said I didn't have to respond, but I have something to . . . I want to . . ." She shook her head. "Hold on."

She pulled aside the blue tarp that had been covering his TV, and he looked at the brightly lit screen.

CARLOS

I LOVE YOU
NIK

"I wanted an actual JumboTron," she said, "But it would have been really hard to get one of those inside your house, so I decided to work with what I had: a laptop hooked up to a TV and terrible graphic design skills."

He took a step toward her. He kept looking from her to the screen and back to her.

"Is this for real?" he said.

She rolled her eyes at him.

"You know me too well to ask me that, come on. Would I, Nikole Paterson, do something like this as a joke?"

He shook his head and took another step toward her.

"You wouldn't, but I had to make sure. And I wanted you to say it out loud."

She looked straight into his eyes.

"Carlos. I love you. I'm in love with you. I realized it in the sour cream aisle at Vons last night. Isn't that a ridiculous place to realize you're in love with someone? Well, that's how it happened to me. I saw the sour cream, and I laughed, and I thought about you, and I thought about how happy you make me and how much I missed you, and then I realized what all of those feelings meant, and then I felt like a fool for letting you go." Tears were streaming down her face by that point. He wiped them away with his thumb. "So I thought I should tell you, and I'm sorry—I'm so sorry—that I didn't realize it earlier, and that I was so skittish and scared when you said you loved me."

He pulled her into his arms. He couldn't remember the last time he'd been this happy.

"Oh, Nik."

She pulled back.

"Wait, wait, let me finish. I've spent so long being afraid of love, because the last time I was in love, the man I loved only loved one part of me, but not all of me, and I thought love meant having to sacrifice a part of yourself. But then I was with you, and you loved every part of me, even the parts I don't like. And that scared me more, because I thought there must be some trick and that I couldn't let myself believe it or I'd fall into the trap. But finally I realized it wasn't a trap."

He held her face in his hands and kissed her.

She kissed him back with so much joy and sincerity and love that he almost started crying. He pulled her down onto his couch and kept his arms around her.

"I missed you so much," he said. "I kept wanting to call you, to say you were right and to just pretend I didn't love you, just so I would have you in my life again, but I couldn't bring myself to do it."

She wiped her eyes.

"If you had, it probably would have crushed me. I would have pretended it hadn't, gone along with it, and we would have done this same stupid thing for like another year or two before I finally admitted to myself how much I loved you. So it's a good thing you didn't."

She kissed him again.

"How's Eva?" she asked.

"Tiny. Beautiful. Perfect," he said. "Jessie and Jon are exhausted but so happy and totally in love with their daughter. Thanks again for the cupcakes. Jessie really did tell me to say that; it wasn't just an excuse to email you."

She smiled.

"I wondered. And sort of hoped." She took a deep breath. "Carlos, I'm still not sure if I know how to love someone, and I really don't know if I know how to let myself be loved, so I hope you'll be patient with me as I figure out how to do this. But I really love you so I hope you will be."

"I will be as patient as you need me to, but I think you know how to love someone a lot better than you think," he said.

She smiled at him and kissed him again.

"I really hope so," she said. "I missed you so much, too. I kept trying to deny to myself how much I missed you, and how much a part of my life you'd become, and how important you were to me. And then when I realized it, it terrified me. I was so scared to feel this way. If we're being honest, which I hope . . . " she paused and closed her eyes for a moment. "Sorry, I just . . . " He ran his fingers through her curls and waited for her to collect herself. She leaned her head on his shoulder for a second, sat up straight and started again. "If we're being honest, which I hope we can always be to each other, I'm still scared to feel this way." She laughed. "As if you hadn't already noticed that."

He kissed her cheek. He'd noticed. But he'd also noticed that, despite her fear, she was still here. Sitting next to him.

"And then I was scared that you wouldn't still feel the same way. That I'd been right the first time, that it was all because of emotion and adrenaline and you'd realized you were better off without me."

"You weren't right the first time," he said. "Even though I tried to convince myself you were."

"Thank God for that," she said.

"Thank God for that sour cream," he said. "I can't believe I'm going to have to be in debt to sour cream for the rest of my life. We can't tell anyone that part of the story, it isn't romantic at all. It couldn't have been something sexier?"

"Like what? Eggplant? Hot dogs? Bananas?"

He laughed and pulled her against him.

"I was thinking, I don't know, chilies, or bacon, or even your favorite rosé. But for this"—he gestured to the TV, the decorations, to Nik—"for you? I'd take anything."

"See? That was so . . . " She beamed at him, as tears ran down her face. "You're much better at this romance stuff than I am."

He wiped the tears away with his thumb and kissed her again.

"You're doing great," he said.

He looked around his house with a grin.

"I can't believe this," he said. "I'm so happy you're here."

"Good," she said. "Because I can't believe I pulled this all together at the last minute today, so you'd better appreciate it."

And then he realized something.

"ANGELA."

She leaned back against the couch cushions and laughed.

"Angela, indeed. She gave me the key and kept you away until I was all ready for you. I had to make my case to her first, though. Let me tell you, she was very suspicious when I called her this morning."

That's why they'd stayed at Jessie's for so long.

"I bet she was. But she always liked you. Plus, she knew you were the reason I finally went to the doctor."

She sat up with a jerk.

"You went to the doctor? Really?"

He gave her a tentative smile.

"I went yesterday."

She threw her arms around him.

"Oh, Carlos, I know how hard that must have been for you. I'm so proud of you!"

He buried his nose in her hair. That coconut smell made him so happy.

"It was really hard. But I did it. And I'm okay. My cholesterol is a little high, but not anything my doctor is super worried about, so I'll cut back the red meat and add more leafy greens and I should be able to manage it."

She ran her hands through his hair.

"I am so glad to hear that. Oh! I have some news, too."

He pulled back and looked at her, and she smiled.

"I punched Fisher in the face."

He jumped up from the couch.

"You what? Oh my God." He picked her up and swung her in a circle. "You are a superhero. What the fuck did that bastard do this time? I can't wait to hear everything."

She held up her hand and wiggled her fingers.

"He went down like a ton of bricks, it was amazing. My knuckles are still a little raw. I'm so sad you weren't there to see it, but luckily, plenty of people walking and driving down my street did. He was so mad about that. It was so great."

He sat back on the couch and pulled her down next to him.

"I love you so much."

She beamed at him.

"I know."

The Proposal

. . . .

Jasmine Guillory

READING GROUP DISCUSSION QUESTIONS

1. In this day and age, social media is inescapable. How would you react if you went viral for a mishap?

2. Communication plays a huge role in any relationship, and in both of Nik's romantic relationships with Fisher and Carlos, neither of them are on the same page. How could this have been solved? Have you ever had communication issues in a relationship that spiraled out of control?

3. Nik and Carlos both think they can have a physical relationship without getting their feelings involved. Do you think it's possible to have a successful friends-with-benefits relationship? What are the first clues that Nik and Carlos start to feel something more for each other?

4. Carlos woos Nik with his amazing cooking skills. Have you ever had a date cook you a meal that impressed you? What was it?

5. Grief is never easy to get through. Discuss how the death of Carlos's father impacts his life and relationships.

6. Even though he's a doctor, Carlos refuses to get a wellness physical. Discuss why Carlos won't see a doctor. Do you have any similar contradictions in your life?

7. After Nik's encounter with Fisher, she signs up for self-defense classes with friends. Have you ever taken a self-defense class? Was there ever a time you wish you had, or were thankful you had?

8. Have you ever had a relationship, romantic or nonromantic, that you thought would be casual but ended up being very meaningful to your life?

A CONVERSATION WITH JASMINE GUILLORY

1. Nik is completely caught off guard by Fisher's proposal, which could have been prevented if they had better communication. What do you think is most important for a proposal?

The two most important things in any proposal are: 1) both parties have discussed marriage before the question is popped, and 2) it's done in a way that makes both parties happy. Private or public, a proposal should be one that both the person asking and the person being asked would want. One of my favorite ways I was involved in a proposal was for a good friend of mine: she and her now husband had discussed marriage, she knew he wanted to propose with a ring, but they also both wanted the ring to be a surprise to her. Enter me! I went ring shopping with her to a number of different jewelry stores, and we figured out what she liked, what she didn't like, and what looked good on her finger. Then I sent her fiancé an email with all the key information he needed, and he sent me some pictures of possibilities for my critique. In the end, she got a ring that she loved, he was confident in his choices, and they were both thrilled to start a life together.

2. Was any of *The Proposal* inspired by real life?

As a matter of fact, a key scene was! A number of years ago, I was making enchiladas with my mom and sister, and I was peeling the skin from dried chilies without wearing the gloves my mom had told me to wear (I don't even have the excuse that I was young at the time—I think I was in my thirties). I accidentally touched my face, and my skin was on fire, just as Nik's was when she did the same thing. My sister frantically googled solutions, and she's the one who told me to put sour cream on my face. I looked just as ridiculous as you can imagine, but I promise you: if you're ever in this kind of situation, sour cream works!

3. How did you get the idea for Natalie's Gym?

A good friend was taking a boxing class for women, and the idea intrigued me. And I talked to more women who have taken and taught classes like that who loved everything about them. Women are so often taught to swallow their anger, but at the same time, the world tells us to be afraid of what can happen to us. Boxing teaches women that we can be powerful and that our anger can be a gift, as well as how to use our strength. I named Natalie's Gym after a friend of mine who battled cancer for five years. She was the strongest person I've ever known.

4. What's your go-to taco recipe?

I make and eat tacos a LOT, and often they're from whatever I have in the house, put on top of a warm tortilla with some salsa and avocado. But when I want to get fancy, I make carnitas:

• *Carnitas* •

4 pounds pork shoulder
1 orange (peel and reserve the zest in big strips, juice the orange and reserve the juice)
5 cups water
6 garlic cloves, minced
2 onions, diced
2 jalapeños, diced
1 cinnamon stick
2 bay leaves
1 teaspoon dried oregano
1 ½ teaspoons kosher salt

Cut the meat into 1-inch-thick cubes (or ask your butcher to do this for you). Put the pork in a large pot, and add the rest of the ingredients. Bring to a boil, then reduce to a simmer. Simmer for about 1 ½–2 hours, and add more water if you need to in order to keep the pork submerged. Once the meat is tender, turn the heat back up to a boil, and boil until all the water is gone from the pot (about 20–30 minutes). Keep cooking, stirring frequently (and carefully!) to get the carnitas crispy.

Shred the meat and place on top of warmed tortillas with salsa verde* or your favorite salsa, some chopped cilantro, and cubes of avocado. Enjoy!

*I'll send out a newsletter with my favorite recipe for salsa verde soon. Sign up on my website, jasmineguillory.com.

Don't miss THE WEDDING PARTY,
the next book from Jasmine Guillory,
coming soon from Berkley.

Keep reading to see where it all began with an
excerpt from THE WEDDING DATE,
available now!

Alexa Monroe walked into the Fairmont hotel in San Francisco that Thursday night wearing her favorite red heels, feeling jittery from coffee, and carrying a bottle of Veuve Clicquot champagne in her purse. She took out her phone to text her sister, Olivia, upstairs in one of the guest rooms.

Getting on the elevator!!!

It was always good to give Olivia a little more advance warning than most people. It didn't matter that Olivia had just made partner at her New York law firm; some things didn't change.

Oh no, was just about to get in the shower.

Alexa got Olivia's text just as she stepped into the elevator. She laughed out loud as she pushed the number of her sister's floor, the laughter calming her nerves. Alexa couldn't wait to celebrate with her older sister, despite . . . no, maybe because their relationship was still tricky after all these years.

The elevator glided in the air, in that smooth, noiseless way elevators in expensive hotels do, while Alexa checked her purse for the third time to make sure she'd tossed the fancy crackers and Brie in there. They would need a pre-dinner snack to soak up all of that champagne, after all. She wished she'd found the time to make brownies the night before. Olivia loved her brownies.

She spied the cheese and crackers in the corner of her purse, tucked away from the heavy champagne bottle. Just then, the elevator stopped with a jerk. A second later, the lights went out.

"What's going on?" she said out loud to herself.

A few seconds later, a dim light came on, but the elevator stayed motionless. She looked up and around, and jumped to see a man with a suitcase in the opposite corner of the elevator.

"Were you here this whole time?" she asked.

"What am I, a genie?" He grinned back at her.

"I guess you don't really look like a genie." He was a tall white guy, with tanned skin, rumpled dark brown hair, and about a day's worth of scruff where a beard would be. She had a sudden urge to rub her hand on his cheek to see how prickly it was. How exactly had she missed seeing *this* man get on the elevator with her?

"Thank you, I think. But isn't that what a genie would say?" he asked. "You're not claustrophobic, are you?"

"Um, I don't think so. Why, were you going to bust us out of here with your genie powers if I said I was?"

He laughed.

"I guess you'll never know if I'm a genie now," he said.

"Well, there was that time I got an MRI," she said. "Being inside that tiny machine wasn't much fun. Maybe I am claustrophobic."

"Sorry, you already lost your chance to see my powers." He moved to the front of the elevator and picked up the emergency phone.

"Let's see if they can give us an ETA on getting out of here."

She tried not to stare at him in the dim lighting, but she couldn't miss the opportunity to check out his butt in his perfectly fitted jeans. It was as good as the rest of him. She tried to wipe the grin off her face in case he turned around.

Stuff like this never happened to her. Not the stuck-in-the-elevator thing—her life was full of minor crises like that. No, it was being stuck in an elevator with a hot guy that was the unusual part. She was always the one sitting on an airplane next to a chatty toddler, or a knitting grandma, or a bored college student; never a hot guy to be found.

After about a minute of him saying, "Okay . . . okay," in progressively tenser tones, he hung up the phone.

"Well . . ." He paused and smiled at her. "Wait, I don't even know your name, my new elevator friend."

"Alexa, and you, Genie?"

"Drew. Nice to meet you, Alexa."

"Drew, it's a pleasure, but . . ."

"Right, these circumstances are not ideal. So, the bad news is that there's a power outage in the whole hotel."

Her phone lit up just then with a text from Olivia.

My power went out. Where are you??

"Ahhh, yes, I was just alerted to that." Alexa held her phone up before she texted Olivia back.

Whole hotel, I'm stuck in the elevator.

"At least that means they were telling the truth," Drew said. "The good news, or so they tell me, is that they have generators, so the elevators should start moving shortly."

She slid down to the floor, placing her purse gently beside her. It would be a tragedy to break that champagne bottle.

"We might as well wait in comfort," she said. Her favorite red heels were relatively comfortable for the first five hours, but she'd been wearing them for nine plus.

He shrugged off his leather jacket, gifting her a glimpse of his stomach muscles as his gray T-shirt shifted. Mmmm. Hot, funny guy who occasionally flashed his abs. Was it her birthday?

"So, are you a guest here, Drew? Where are you coming from?" she asked him so she wouldn't stare.

"Just flew in from L.A. And you?" He sat down next to her.

"Oh, I live here. Well, over in Berkeley, anyway. I'm just in the hotel visiting someone."

He glanced at her phone, her shoes, and back up at her.

"A pretty special someone, with those shoes on, and all of that smiling you were doing when you didn't even notice someone else got on the elevator with you."

"A very special someone," she said, and his grin got wider. "Wait, no, not *that* kind of special someone! My older sister! She's in town from New York for work."

Yep, this was how she usually acted around hot guys. Scared to make eye contact, stared at his abs, said something awkward.

"Ahhhh." He laughed. "Okay, yes, I did think it was *that* kind of special someone. Do you two have a hot night in the city planned?"

She crossed her legs and adjusted her black wrap dress so she didn't accidentally flash her underwear at this dude on top of everything else.

"Sort of. We're celebrating. She just made partner at her law firm!" Alexa smiled down at her purse full of treats before looking back up at him. Not even cheese could compete with this dude.

He narrowed his eyes at her. Light brown eyes, with a really dark rim around them. His eyes were so pretty that she looked away again. Thank God her brown skin meant her cheeks couldn't get too pink, otherwise he'd be able to see them glow in the dark.

"Okay, I'm happy for your sister, but what is in that bag? You keep looking at it like it holds the Holy Grail."

She laughed.

"Just champagne and a few snacks. The plan is to drink the champagne here and then go out to dinner . . . Well, that was the plan, but we'll see how long we're stuck in this elevator."

Drew scooted closer to her and looked in her purse. Alexa pushed it toward him, so he could see better in the dim light. She never let people poke around in her purse, but hey, this was a cute guy and a weird situation.

"Okay good, we have sustenance if we're stuck here for hours. Champagne is so convenient because no corkscrew is needed, and then we've got . . . Oh, look at that, cheese and crackers, the perfect stuck-in-an-elevator snack."

She leaned back against the wood-paneled wall.

"Have you been stuck in an elevator before with a variety of snacks and been able to determine which ones are best for this situation?" she asked.

"No, but come on, cheese and crackers are obviously the best possible option here. First of all, you had the foresight to bring a soft cheese, so we won't need a knife to cut it; we can just use the crackers to pull off bits and spread it with our fingers. And second, have you ever not enjoyed cheese and crackers? Ever not thought, 'Oh boy, these cheese and crackers are exactly what I need right now'?"

She considered for a moment.

"Stop, no, stop even thinking about it," he said. "You know the answer is no. Cheese and crackers are objectively the perfect snack."

She laughed and pried his fingers away from the box of crackers.

"Okay, fine, you're right. But you didn't manage to talk me into sharing Olivia's you-made-partner cheese and crackers with you, you know."

He stretched his legs out along the floor and took another glance into her purse.

"I was afraid of that. Well, I can only hope we'll be here so long that you'll take pity on me."

She slipped her shoes halfway off, just enough to relieve the pressure on her toes.

"No offense, Drew, but my goal is not to be stuck in this elevator with you all night." Although those abs . . . No, remember Olivia? Her sister? Right, Olivia, okay, yes, Olivia. Time to ask him another question so she'd stop staring. "Don't *you* have plans tonight? What are you doing here in San Francisco for the weekend anyway?"

He made a face.

"Wedding."

She made a face back at him.

"Don't say it like it's a prison sentence."

He slumped against the wall.

"If prison sentences lasted for a weekend, this one would qualify. Okay, fine, a prison in a cushy hotel, but still."

She looked around at the dim, still elevator.

"Not so cushy right now. What's so terrible about this wedding?"

He threw his hands in the air.

"Let me count the ways." He held up one finger. "One: it's my ex-girlfriend's wedding."

Alexa winced. She'd been there. Exes' weddings were always a trial, even in the best circumstances.

Second finger. "Two: she's marrying one of my best friends from med school."

Alexa covered her eyes. Okay, he maybe had a point.

"Were they . . ."

"No, she wasn't cheating on me with him, but . . . let's just say I wasn't particularly pleased about how it all happened, shall we?"

"Ouch. Well, I understand why you—"

He held up a third finger. "THREE."

She sat up straight.

"There's another one? A third finger?"

"Oh yes." He waved his middle finger in the air. "As a matter of fact, this is the worst of the fingers. Three: I am a groomsman."

She swung around and faced him, mouth wide open.

"Are you kidding me? A groomsman? What? Why? How?"

"Yes, you are asking the important questions. The ones that Josh, Molly, and I all should have asked before this nightmare of a wedding weekend started. What and why indeed. *What* could have possibly inspired him to ask me to be a groomsman? *Why* would he do that? *Why* would she allow it? *WHY* would I say yes? *How* did this happen? All of those questions should have been asked, and yet, here we all are."

"Oh my God, Drew. That's almost enough for me to give you some cheese."

He patted her shoulder. Cheese? Hell, if he'd let his hand linger there for a few more seconds, she would have given him a lot more than cheese.

"Alexa, I'm touched. I truly am. And then"—he waved another finger in the air—"there's four."

"Oh good Lord, what could four possibly be? Are your divorced parents coming to the wedding with their spouses, too, or something?"

He laughed.

"No, but good guess. What a nightmare that would be. No, four is that I am not only a groomsman in the wedding of my ex-girlfriend and former best friend, but I am a dateless groomsman in the wedding of my ex-girlfriend and former best friend. My date bailed on me at the last minute, so I'm going to look pathetic, and I'll probably get drunk and hit on a bridesmaid—the whole thing is going to be a nightmare."

She brushed that off with a wave of her hand.

"Oh please, you'll be fine. Weddings are great places to meet people. It's better that you're without a date. As my friend Colleen always says, 'Don't bring a sandwich to a buffet.'"

He let out a bark of laughter.

"I'm definitely going to steal that saying. And while in most situations I would say that your friend Colleen is totally right, this is that five percent of situations where a sandwich would save me from all of the food poisoning in the buffet. I'm going to get so many pitying looks, you have no idea. And the worst part is that I RSVP'd with a plus-one, so there's going to be an empty seat at the head table. And lots of 'What happened to your girlfriend, Drew, couldn't make it?' And I'm going to have to smile and take it, but there's like a thirty percent possibility I'm going to have one too many glasses of bourbon and go rogue."

She touched his hand and tried not to linger there.

"Okay, yes, sometimes a sandwich is a necessary security blanket. I'm sorry that yours bailed on you."

He looked down into her purse again.

"Alexa, I'm going to need you to stop talking about sandwiches if you don't want me to steal that cheese."

She grabbed her purse and moved it to her other side.

"Now temptation is farther away. Isn't that better?"

He looked at her, at the purse, back at her. She smiled and kept her hand on the strap.

"So, Drew. What happened to your girlfriend?"

He narrowed his eyes at her, and she laughed again.

"Okay, first of all, Emma wasn't my girlfriend. We were just hanging out, that's all."

Alexa frowned at him. This guy had to be in his thirties like her. Hadn't people stopped "just hanging out" with people by their thirties?

"Don't look at me like that! I'm not a girlfriend kind of guy! And when I could tell that she might want something more serious, I ended it. I was nice about it! I don't do girlfriends. I haven't had a girlfriend since . . ." He sighed. "Molly. Anyway. Except I forgot that I needed a date for this damn wedding."

Alexa pointed to the fourth finger that he'd raised in the air.

"Wait," she said. "How, exactly, is that your date 'bailing' on you?"

He shook the finger at her.

"Don't do that! Don't blame this on me. It's not my fault. It's not her fault, either—she was going to come to the wedding with me anyway, but her dad's having surgery tomorrow, so she couldn't come." Those ab muscles moved in a lovely way when he sighed. "And, of course, I'm sorry about her dad. I don't blame her for that at all. I do, however, think this is just more evidence that I've been cursed when it comes to this wedding."

Alexa laughed and relaxed against the wall. If she happened to move closer to Drew while doing so, that was just an extra benefit. Hey, it's not like she was in danger of becoming this guy's not-girlfriend. She could at least get a few accidental touches of his arm in before this elevator started back up again.

"You probably did something to deserve it."

Drew reached around her and grabbed her purse.

"Oh, really? I pour out my heart to you about this nightmare of a wedding and how now I won't have a date and all of the terrible things that will happen to me because of that, and when you hear my tale of woe, you tell me that I did something to deserve it? Just for that, I'm taking some cheese."

He reached into her purse but hesitated for a second and raised his eyebrows at her. She sighed and nodded.

"Okay, fine, you can have a little cheese, but you'd better save some for Olivia. And no tearing it off with your fingers. What kind of a Neanderthal do you think I am? There's a knife in there."

He beamed at her. Good Lord, that was a dangerous smile. She looked away and found the butter knife so she wouldn't throw herself at him.

He'd just bitten into his third cheese-laden cracker when the overhead lights came on and the elevator started with a jerk.

In fall I worked in the beet fields topping the beets, cutting off the leafy part. It was easier for me but dirtier, because the ground and the beets were often wet. The next year, 1941, I again spent some time with the sugar beets, but after that we moved to Winnipeg and my working days on the farms were over.

There is one experience that has remained in my memory because of its nasty character. It was during haymaking time in July that I worked for a farmer about six miles away. I hitched a team to the hayrack and drove off into the field to load up with hay. I had already noticed the mosquitoes were bad but when I got into the field they were worse. They were swarming around me and the horses like bees. The horses had to stand still at the row of hay so I could load but the mosquitoes tormented them so much they could not stand still. After about half an hour I gave up and drove back with an empty hayrack and asked the farmer for help. He just gave up for the day. The next day he put blankets on the horses to protect them. We bought mosquito netting which I hung over my straw hat and my shoulders. Then I put on a windbreaker to hold the netting and keep the mosquitoes off my shirt. It was suffocating, working like that in July, but it was the only way to cope with the mosquitoes.

ANIMALS, BIRDS AND INSECTS

At our lovely home in Bobcaygeon the dining table was located in front of a wide window, looking out at the front lawn and at Pigeon Lake just beyond the lawn. The lawn had trees around it, which just opened up so we could see the lake. Here Norah and I used to eat our meals and observe the world of nature all around us—an ideal way of life. The front door was close by and when it was open we could hear a variety of birds singing, varying with the time of day and with the seasons. The front lawn produced a profusion of worms and insects, to the great delight of the robins. If we got tired of the robins, we could look out onto the lake and watch the ducks with their young ducklings, or sometimes a loon, a beaver, or a fish jumping.

When we saw the birds eating worms and insects on the lawn we did not regard them as vicious carnivores; we had no sympathy for worms and insects. However, we were not always happy with the birds. One spring while we were absent, a number of a rare kind of woodpecker visited our place and caused serious damage to a number of our trees. They were champion "woodpeckers". They had made large holes in a number of our good trees, not in the hollow ones. The holes were big enough for me to push my fist into them. I filled the holes up with concrete and the trees survived. Because I love trees, I was left with bad feelings and some fear for these woodpeckers.

Bats aren't birds, but because they fly like birds we usually think of them as birds. Most people, as far as I know, don't like to think of them at all, period. They are a detestable part of creation, usually associated in people's minds with ghosts, witches and hobgoblins. When one of our visitors complained about a bat in her bedroom, I searched through the room carefully and, finding no bat, concluded she must have had a bad dream.

A few years later we had two experiences with bats that proved to be more than just dreams. We woke up one night because something was flying across our bed from one side of the room to the other. It's difficult to get up in the middle of the night, especially if you suspect it's all just part of a bad dream. The question was, why does the bat keep on flying across our bed? Why does it want to wake us up? Why isn't it afraid of people? Is it trying to communicate with us? It was scary to have this creature zooming across a few inches above our heads. Maybe it was trying to scare us. We finally got tired of the disturbance and got out of bed, with only negative feelings in our mind. We chased it around for a considerable time and finally it flew into a small washroom. We knew it couldn't get out of there so we went back to bed in peace. Next morning I carefully searched the washroom but the bat had vanished. However, there was no way it could have gotten out of the room. I could not understand it, but had to admit that maybe some of the stories told about bats might be true.

About a month later we had another experience, but this time it was two bats zooming across our bed. Animals have a curious fascination with and attraction to human beings. We have a large house, but they cruised around as close to us as they could get. We did not appreciate their attention and got up in an ugly mood. We chased them around the house for an hour or two, and they finally gave up and hid. In the morning I found both of them sleeping, hidden in the curtains. I picked them off and disposed of them properly.

Our house in Bobcaygeon is built on limestone bedrock. The lot has only from three to eight inches of soil on top of this rock. The limestone rock consists of flat layers, with the top layer being about 12 inches thick. This layer has separated from the rock below. As this layer dries out it splits into blocks measuring about four square feet and larger. The result is a large network of tunnels in the top layer of rock. The soil keeps on filtering down between the cracks, and I had to keep on adding topsoil to the lawn by the truckload. You can imagine the wonderful maze of tunnels available to moles and rats for underground travel. There was a good population of them taking advantage of this underground system. They did a lot of damage to us, eating the roots of peonies, rhubarb and other plants.

One summer evening when we were sitting in the living room we heard a gnawing sound in the kitchen. It sounded like a rat or a mole. I knew there was a part of the wall underneath the sink that had not been properly sealed off; that is where we heard the gnawing sound. I made noises to scare the animal away, but they had no effect on the gnawing. We resigned ourselves to having an unwanted visitor in the house. However, we were not prepared for what happened.

In the middle of the night we were wakened by noises close to the bed. It sounded like articles being dropped or pushed over. We got up and put on the lights to make sure it wasn't a burglar, but found no burglar. We couldn't even see any articles that had been pushed over. We went back to bed but it did not take long until the noises started again. This time I had my flashlight ready. We finally spotted a small animal scurrying around in the room. If a rat had gotten into the house, why did he spend his time around us? Why was he attracted to us? I had always understood that rats try to keep their presence a secret. This experience was new to me.

We did not sleep much that night. We chased the rat all over the house but could not get him. The next day I got a bag of concrete mix and plugged up the hole in the wall, solidly, to prevent any more rats from entering. The second night the battle started all over again. The rat would not let us sleep. Once the rat ran up a vase filled with dried ornamental plants and I thought I had him, but I fumbled it. Finally we managed to chase him into the cabinet under the kitchen sink, where he had entered, but where the escape now was sealed. We firmly closed the doors of the cabinet and slept the rest of the night. In the morning I found the rat in the plastic garbage bag under the sink. I disposed of him without any feelings of sympathy.

We had always had swallows in the loft of the garage and accepted them as part of the establishment. But one year our relations with them were seriously strained. To get to my tool shop I had to walk through the garage, and I used my tools a lot. This year I noticed the birds objected to my presence in the garage. At first I paid no attention to them and tried not to annoy them when I entered. Before long they became threatening, flying at me and just missing my face by inches. It wasn't even safe for me to get the car out of the garage, so I let the car stand on the driveway. Even there they flew at me when I went to the car. Our driveway was built in a large circle, so that when we came in we could drive around and leave again. The two birds would fly continuously in a circle around the driveway whenever anyone was on the driveway. It was nerve-wracking to face these birds, so we put the car in our side driveway.

Something had to be done; we were fugitives on our own property. I found a wide board and, as the birds came whistling past me, I would suddenly swing up the board. The intention was for the bird to smash into the board if I timed it right. After some hours of practice, finally one of the birds hit the board and was killed. But the battle continued. The lone bird brought in reinforcements, and now there were three birds. The odds against me were increasing. I decided to take down the nest in the garage. I dressed heavily and put a large parka over my head. I put up a large ladder and climbed up and pulled down the nest with the young ones. The birds were furious but I was desperate. I disposed of the nest and its contents. Now I had three mad birds whistling around the driveway. I went back to work with my wide board. After some time another bird smashed into the board and dropped dead. Then I took a good rest. When I returned the birds were gone. The battle was over and peace returned at last. I had no objection to the birds in the first case, but when they declared war on us we had little choice but to protect ourselves. I have had a few reservations about birds ever since.

The next episode takes us to France, to my first year in Paris, when I lived in the Cuban university residence. It had been a first-class building at one time, but it was beginning to age and little maintenance had been done on it. This time the battle was with the lowly cockroach, and a great battle it turned out to be, carefully planned and executed.

When I moved in I found a can of insect spray on the balcony, so I was aware that insects were present. I also noticed the wall behind the bathtub was crumbling to pieces and would doubtless be the entry site for the cockroaches. However, I did not notice any insects around so I did not worry about the situation.

A month or so later I was sitting at the table, ready to begin my supper. The bathroom door was behind me. Something made me look around. There on the floor was a lone cockroach, a huge one, slowly advancing out from the bathroom. Somehow he had made me aware that he was approaching. He stopped, then advanced, slowly nearing my chair. Then with one jump he flew up onto the table and regarded me. Was he trying to conclude a peace treaty, or was he making a declaration of war? I looked back on the floor and saw three more, lined up and waiting. This was ominous. Slowly the cockroach advanced toward my food. I hesitated for some seconds. Could I negotiate with him? How? I made my decision. I hit him and snuffed out his life. This was the signal for battle. The guards on the floor knew what I had done and they signaled for the forces to enter and fight. I saw the floor going into the bathroom covered with cockroaches, advancing steadily. I grabbed some papers and started slugging them, on the left and on the right side. They tried to get around me and pressed me back in the centre. For a while I was struggling with all my might. Then in a slight lull of the battle I managed to get a hold of the spray can. This gave me an advantage and my blows became more lethal. They had to retreat into the bathroom, leaving the floor littered with their dead corpses. In the bathroom they put up a good rear guard action, coming at me from all sides, but slowly they retreated behind the bathtub and vanished into the wall, leaving their dead behind. I sprayed the critical part of the wall behind the bathtub thoroughly, then I swept up the dead cockroaches. We had a few more skirmishes some days later but on a smaller scale. After that I kept them out by keeping their entrance points well sprayed. My experience with cockroaches is that they can be controlled easily by keeping the kitchen spotlessly clean and by spraying their entry points.

My battle with the cockroaches had puzzling overtones. They obviously sent an ambassador ahead to deal with me. But how could we negotiate? I doubt if his demands would have been acceptable to me if I could have understood him. He was backed up by guards in control of a formidable army that fought bravely. I could only see insects, but I was impressed with the fact that the enemies that faced me were not "mere insects". I don't know what they were.

I loved to go and sit on the dock at Bobcaygeon to take a short rest, especially on warm summer days when I had a lot of work to do and was getting tired. It's very pleasant to sit on the dock and watch the ducks swimming by, the sailboats cruising on the lake, and listen to the birds in the trees behind me. But there was someone in the water watching me. Before long I would see the fish jump out of the water and take a look at me, from a fair distance. He would then make a large circle and jump out to look at me again, about ten feet closer. He would keep this up, slowly coming closer to me. Sometimes he would come close enough that I could see his body in the water. He weighed at least ten pounds. As a rule he was usually there when I sat on the dock in the afternoon. Sometimes there was a school of fish, maybe ten of them, and they would circle around close to the dock. They liked to observe me. I have tried my fishing rod on them, but the rule is that jumping fish don't bite. Evidently the fish themselves made the rule.

My experiences with animal life have always puzzled me, but my understanding of them has failed to come up with any explanations of their mysterious ways.

A CHRISTIAN AT POSTAL STATION D

During my work at the Post Office I was transferred on short notice from Station C in Fort Rouge to Station D on Portage Avenue, located just east of Harman's Drug Store. (This Postal Station no longer exists.) I replaced a letter carrier who had been taken off his route on false charges of serious misdemeanors. It was here that my Christian faith was subjected to severe testing.

I don't think my supervisor at Station C had any intention of causing me harm when he phoned his counterpart at Station D to introduce me and inform him that I was coming in the next morning, but that is what happened. To introduce me he said I was a fine Christian, and to be easy on me. That was all it took. In many social groups the word "Christian" is a synonym for "sissy", and the request to go easy on me only underlined that connotation. Before I continue I must add that the staff at Station D was not at all mean or cruel, even if they enjoyed a period of poking cruel fun at me.

When I arrived the first morning the supervisor was already at work sorting the mail on my worktable. A new route, with a new sorting case to learn, is always a real challenge; it takes a few confused days to settle in. He managed to help me get sorted and tied up, the mail, that is, and also accompanied me on the street for a while. I think he really believed I was a sissy, but I got along fine with him once I was established.

After lunch we were back to work at 1:00 p.m. and had an hour to get our mail ready so we could get out on the street by 2:00 p.m. During this hour we were all sitting at our cases, sorting our mail, and that is when the action started. One person would pretend to inadvertently say a swear word, and then a number of others would pipe up:

"Oh, no! You can't swear now! Daniel is here. He's a Christian! He can't listen to words like that."

Then the whole crowd would whistle and make derogatory remarks about me.

I was completely floored. Someone would come and put his arm around my shoulder with a false pretence at sympathy and tell me not to listen to the awful language. While I was desperately trying to cope with my work, the group was maliciously enjoying themselves at my expense. It seriously tested my spiritual stamina but I did not fail, even if I felt shattered at times. I could do little but keep quiet and suffer.

The second morning my supervisor again helped me get the mail ready, but I was beginning to learn the case and the route. My route was heavy, it received a lot of mail, and I realized I needed to get in earlier so I could get my mail sorted myself. I found out that the mail truck brought in the mail just after 6:00 a.m. and that two other carriers came at that time to get into the building when the truck driver put the mail in. Transit buses only started going at 6:00 a.m. but I found that they sent out a special bus to pick up transit drivers at 5:00 a.m. On the third morning I took that early bus and got to Station D by 6:00 a.m. so I could get into the building with the mail delivery. Once in, I started sorting my mail immediately and was almost sorted up by the time my supervisor arrived at 6:45 a.m. From then on I was on my own and needed no help.

The mocking continued but it was slowly becoming evident I was no sissy. I took a good look at the staff and concluded that, in fact, they were a "grandmotherly" group of men. Not all of them, though. There was one man, the most uncouth person in the group, who worked hard and was always the first one to get out on the street in the morning. The supervisory letter carrier who did holiday relief was also a fast worker. It was my aim to be able to get out with the first man; let's call him Mac. He sort of looked down on the others as being sissies and it would give me standing to walk out with him. The time came when I achieved my goal and walked out with Mac.

I remember only too well one of the first mornings that I walked out with Mac, leaving the slower group behind inside. The sun was shining peacefully and I felt I was beginning to cope with my situation. I enjoyed my work and it gave me a good feeling of satisfaction. However, Mac was preparing an even severer test of my Christian stamina than I had faced so far.

We walked onto Portage Avenue at about 8:45 a.m., just when office staff are hurrying to get to work before the boss checks in. A lovely young lady was walking towards us.

"Look at those beautiful legs, Daniel," Mac remarked as he looked at me. "What do you think of that?"

He knew it wasn't my kind of talk and I just turned my eyes down. Another pretty woman walked past a few seconds later.

"Look, Daniel," he said. "How would you like to go to bed with those legs?"

He was becoming more difficult but we had reached the corner and parted, each to his own route. I soon forgot all about it but Mac didn't. His plan was well made.

We were sorting our mail after lunch time when Mac suddenly raised his voice.

"You wouldn't believe it! This fellow Daniel was supposed to be such a good Christian, but you should have heard him this morning."

By now everyone is looking at me, whistling in anticipation.

Mac continued, "'See that lovely girl there,' he said, 'Boy, has she got lovely legs!' And then, when another woman came past, can you imagine? He says to me, 'Man! Would I love to go to bed with her.'"

The group went wild. The hooting and the mocking must have lasted at least five minutes. I was utterly shocked. I couldn't say a word. Fortunately I said nothing, and it was the best course I could have taken. At least a few of them must have felt a bit of shame at what they were doing to me. Because I had not reacted to what he had done, Mac eased off somewhat in his abuse of me. I still went out together with him on most mornings.

But my trials were not over. The supervisory letter carrier, let's call him Jack, started going out with Mac and myself, we three being the fastest carriers and thus the first to get out on the street. Having had breakfast around 5:00 a.m. we were decidedly hungry by this time. The practice was to stop off at Harman's Drug Store for a quick coffee and donut before starting on our delivery.

This morning, when Jack was with us, Mac called to the waitress as soon as we sat down, "Coffee and donuts for us, and Daniel is paying." I was sitting between them and was much smaller than they were, and felt even smaller this morning. I wondered what they were planning to perpetrate on me now. I also realized I was lost if I tried to avoid them. I could not get away from them because we were working in the same office.

They repeated the same process the next morning and I felt even smaller. I knew I had to face up to these two characters and the only technique that might work was in the realm of psychology. I was ready for them the third morning. Before we were seated I already called the waitress, "We'll have coffee and donuts, all three, and I'm paying." They had not expected this technique. It made both of them thoroughly ashamed. They had expected me to fight back, but I had turned the other cheek. This can be very effective. I had won the battle. We had coffee and donuts many a morning after that and they treated me many a time, a lot more than they owed me.

The Postal Station was manned by the Letter Carrier category, but we also had one or two Postal Clerks working inside sorting mail. Postal Clerks were rated one step higher than Letter Carriers, they were paid more and had other privileges. They also liked to make us feel they were superior. Our group of letter carriers accepted that situation as being quite proper. This subservience to the class system was characteristic to persons of British origin. Later on, when more persons of non-British origin entered the Postal Service this sense of inferiority vanished. I helped to make it vanish.

One lunch hour we discussed what we hoped our children would become when they grew up. I said I wanted my children to go to university. They told me that was impossible; our supervisor's children could attend university but the children of a common letter carrier couldn't, a typically British statement. Well, my children all did attend university.

We had a smart young clerk working in our office sorting out the mail that we threw back. He had become a bit almighty with me at times, so I was very careful to be correct with all mail that I turned back. One day he picked on me. He just sorted back to me the letters I had returned. When he did it the second time I decided it was enough. He did this sort of thing at times to remind the carriers that he was above them. I threw the letters down in front of him and told him sharply,

"These letters don't belong to me, and you know it. Don't sort them back to me again!"

He looked at the letters and knew that he was wrong, but none of our letter carriers had ever talked to him like that before. You could see it in his face. I walked back to my desk and never had any more trouble with him. In fact, we became good friends. He respected me for not being falsely subservient.

I had fought my battles as a Christian and I had won, without any verbal battles, except the last one. Basically, I had turned the other cheek as Jesus had told us to do. A few problems continued but they were minor. My reputation as a worker was enough to put me a notch above most of the staff, and they knew that I was no "sissy".

My supreme reward came on my last day at Station D. I only stayed there for half a year and then I returned to Station C. On my last day I had to come back to the office after I finished my route to clean out my desk. There was Mac waiting for me. He came up to me with tears in his eyes and apologized for the way they had treated me. Even now, in my old age, I can still see him and my heart chokes up as I hear his voice. The sufferings I had gone through seemed as nothing after that. I said at the beginning that he was the rudest man in the group, but he was also the only one who came and told me he was sorry.

When persons mock us as Christians, it means they are searching; they are trying us out to see if our faith is real. They are not satisfied with oral professions; they want to see what the Christian faith does to our everyday behaviour.

MANITOU LODGE

Manitou Lodge is located in Pine Falls, a paper-mill town owned by the Abitibi Company. The hotel was built to accommodate Abitibi officials, single employees, short-term employees, guests, etc. Pine Falls is a well-planned company town, in a scenic location, built on land acquired from the Fort Alexander Indian Reserve.

Before I tell about my life in Manitou Lodge, I must relate how I came to live there. It was not in my plans originally. When I was transferred to Fort Alexander I took over a separate school building, situated about three miles east of the main school building. This building had one classroom plus attached living quarters. It meant that I was living alone on the Reserve, not a good situation. I had the choice of having a phone installed in my building, or I could do without. The Principal advised me to be without a phone. Because there were few telephones on the Reserve, the Principal said my neighbours would be bothering me to use the phone at any time of the day or night. The previous year a teacher had been shot at by an Indian because the teacher had refused to let him use the phone. I wanted a phone but realized it would not be wise, so I didn't get a phone.

My first month at the school passed peacefully. On the weekends, as a rule, I drove in to Winnipeg. Then one Sunday when I returned I noticed that some objects in my suite had been moved. There was no damage and no evidence of how anyone could have entered the building. The next Sunday there were more signs that someone had been in my living quarters because some food had been eaten, but no damage had been done.

On the third Sunday I returned late in the afternoon. It was a warm day and the sun was still high. I had an ominous feeling of foreboding when I entered the yard, so I stopped in front of the school instead of driving around to the back, as I usually did. Instead of entering my suite I went into the classroom. My fears were justified. There were books scattered all over the classroom. I walked to my desk and saw my keys lying there, which I had left in my suite. Also, I heard voices in my living quarters. I walked right out, got in my car, and drove off to see the Principal. I met him on the road and told him the story. He told me to go back to the caretaker's place while he went to call the police. The caretaker went to the school to see that no one escaped. In about ten minutes the police arrived and took over. They picked up three punks in the basement where they had gone to hide. If I had entered the suite alone, doubtless I would have been beaten up.

My living quarters were a mess. The food was eaten, my clothes and bed were dirtied, and the rest was broken up. I saw there was no way I could continue to live there. The Principal suggested that I stay in the hotel at Pine Falls. I salvaged what I could and moved into Manitou Lodge. That is where I lived for almost six years, and that is where this chapter starts.

In the chapter "My Decline?" I discussed some of the problems I had during my first year at Fort Alexander. The religious contentions, which I managed to survive, overshadowed much of what I experienced the first year at Fort Alexander. Once I had escaped the machinations of the evangelicals, I settled down and was able to rebuild my life.

The next few years were a unique period in the history of Manitou Lodge, an outstanding time which developed a special culture, such as happens from time to time, although rarely. There was an influx of new teachers at this time into the area, which comprised three school districts: Pine Falls, Fort Alexander, and Powerview. Some of the things I relate may seem strange to you, and maybe they are strange; however, they were very much part of our way of life.

The second year the hotel was filled to capacity, mostly with young people of both sexes. The outsider who walks past a hotel and knows a few things about the inhabitants loves to imagine all kinds of possible activities and behaviour going on in there. Oddly enough, the female residents of the hotel were only too happy to gratify the pleasures of the gossipers with as much suggestive evidence as needed. Gossipers generally need very little evidence to substantiate the wildest dreams of the outsiders. I must admit that the female residents did very little to satisfy any wild dreams the male insiders might have.

A few unwritten laws were clearly established. If a male was visiting a female in her room or vice versa, the door was always left open at least six inches, so anyone walking past could see what was going on inside. This rule was strict; anyone breaking it was shunned by the rest of the crowd. Everything that went on in the hotel was common knowledge, and usually by the time breakfast was over we all knew of any unusual events that had happened the previous evening or night. There were people who were outside of our crowd. A girl from town took a room in the hotel next to the entrance, so she could have her boyfriends in whenever she so wished. None of our crowd ever talked to her.

Some girls love to be gossiped about, often to the sheer embarrassment of the males involved. Five-pin bowling was a popular sport in town. I was captain of a team, comprised of four girls from the hotel and one young fellow from in town. The bowling alley was only a block away from the hotel. I'd get the girls rounded up and we'd head for the alley. As soon as we got out of the door the young women would burst into singing and giggling, hollering and hooting so they could be heard all over town.

"If that's how they behave outside, you can just imagine what goes on in the hotel, when they are finished with the bowling." You may recognize this typical remark of a good gossiper.

A few remarks about the bowling alley are appropriate at this point. The bowling alley was in the basement of the theatre. The men's washroom served both parts, being situated between the two levels and having an entrance at each level. When the women discovered this they consistently used it as a shortcut to go from the theatre to the bowling alley, instead of going outside to get from one part to the other. Seeing how handy it was they also decided to use it as a suitable place for dressing the kids in wintertime, leaving the floor stacked with children's winter clothing. When the men wanted to use their washroom, well, it was more suitable to go outside behind the theatre, if they had "to go".

One other event was quite typical of what so often happens. Our Indian Affairs Teachers' group had a bowling evening, getting in as many teachers from other schools as possible. Included in our group was an elderly Anglican minister who had never bowled before. We assured him it was a fun evening and not to worry about his score. We showed him how to hold the ball and how to let it go, and then wished him well. Well, you can guess what happened. He scored higher than most of us did, including myself.

My social contact with the feminine sex during my stay at the hotel was an experience that was altogether new to me. I believe it was basically the feminine element that created clear rules for moral behaviour in the hotel, but the feminine presence also had a strong influence on our everyday life, sometimes rather exasperating.

Let me relate a few examples. Occasionally I would have outside men come to visit me. That was what the girls were waiting for. Walking up and down the hotel halls it was easy to hear men talking in the room. By 9:00 p.m. some of the girls would have changed into their dressing gowns, obviously getting ready for the night. Then they would scout the halls to see if anyone had a visitor. Then they would pair up and gaily walk up and down the hall singing love songs and giggling. When the visitor heard this he could easily conclude they were just waiting for him to leave. At another occasion the young teacher knocked and asked if she could borrow my typewriter for a while. She promised to return it later, coming into the room just far enough for the visitor to see the state of dress she was in. My friend did not have much to leave to his imagination; for him it was evident what was going on. Another time, a young lady just knocked on the door and then looked in. "Oh," she said, "I thought you were alone." As if she couldn't hear us talking. "I'll see you later then," and off she went. What could I say? My friends were convinced by what they saw. They did not gossip about me, to my knowledge; they just "knew" what was going on and they were *jealous*. Little did they know the truth, but if it made them happy, so what! Of course, this behaviour was not confined to me—it was general.

The dining room in which we took our meals was also a public restaurant. To us it was home, and often our behaviour was more private than public. I remember one incident. One of the young male teachers had suffered a cut on his thumb and his hand was bandaged up. At supper time this was discussed and one of the young women knelt down in front of him, making a great fuss about his poor thumb. The dear fellow felt so enthralled by this loving attention that his sore thumb didn't matter at all. But what did the outsiders think while they were dining at the next tables and watching this motherly scene?

Later, to make the restaurant more popular, they started to play music during the dinner hour to provide a romantic atmosphere for dining. I remember one time when a young woman and I danced to a popular waltz selection, circling around among the tables. We provided live entertainment, but who knows what else? The result of all this was that we became blasé about gossipers. Living together the way we did in a hotel, outside people will imagine all kinds of stories, and we might as well ignore them, realizing that they are happy with their gossip.

It was a distinctly family atmosphere in which we lived, but family situations have troubles as well as happiness. One of the male teachers came down for breakfast one morning after a booze party the night before, only to find the hotel manager waiting for him, who promptly ushered him into his office. What had he done? Everyone else already knew except he. One modest young lady teacher had been soundly asleep when suddenly, in the middle of the night, she heard someone open her locked door and come into her room. Then he wanted to get into bed with her. She objected, but he seemed to be too drunk to listen to her. It was only in desperation that she got him out. His story was different. True, he had been drinking, but he had returned to his room, using his key, and there he found a woman in his bed who would not let him get into his own bed. Well, his story did not wash. They took his key and tried it on the lady's room and sure enough, it unlocked her door. They tried it further and it unlocked some of the other doors as well. He could have had his choice. He had been too drunk to know what he was doing or even to remember what he had done. The result was that all the locks in the hotel had to be changed because most of the keys unlocked more than one room.

My second year at Manitou Lodge began with a bang, figuratively speaking. Terry, who was rated as my best friend, was young and enthusiastic, but overly so. He arrived in Pine Falls before I did and arranged for us to have rooms next to each other on the main floor. The two rooms shared a bathroom located between the rooms, which made the rent more reasonable. Plans were being made for an exciting year ahead. However, I had previously reserved a room with private bath on the second floor. Terry was disappointed, but I stuck to my arrangement. I was fully involved with the social affairs of our teachers, but I avoided the shenanigans of the younger, irresponsible crowd most of the time. One detestable custom that developed at the hotel was the liquor parties. Somebody's room was cleared as much as possible and the centre was piled up with beer, wine and liquor. The gang that assembled would then drink until the centre had been cleared and that usually took all night, and frequently more than 24 hours. Teachers did not take part except on weekends. I have never been to such a party; I kept to a high standard of behaviour.

One night, when I had a room in the basement, there was a liquor party going on in the room next to me. It was impossible for me to get to sleep, so I knocked on the wall between us to remind them they were keeping me awake. The result was that my neighbour came to my door and started banging on it. Every room had a button to call the front office. I was afraid he would knock my door down so I called the office, and when the bouncer appeared the noise quieted down somewhat.

Now an anecdote about this neighbour which I find interesting for the insight it provides into the interaction between male and female personalities. He was a man who liked to present himself with a show of bravado, although he had little to boast about. He started dating one of the young waitresses in the hotel about half his age. I was surprised at her because I knew her well and saw her to be a fine young woman. He pretended to be rich and important, so she took him up on it. He started buying her gifts and they became more expensive with each gift. Finally they left together to live in B.C. It didn't take many months until she was back again, alone. He had kept on bragging about his money and she had spent every dollar he had. Then she dumped him. The lesson is clear: if a man wants to brag about himself, he deserves to be taken up on it. The young woman would have been an altogether person with a man who deserved respect. I have never yet met a woman who has tried to take advantage of me. Women want to be respected.

Just as important in the social life at the hotel, as was the female element, were the R.C.M.P. The area needed a lot of police to keep it under control, and many of them lodged at the hotel. Our relations with them were interesting, but we found it advisable to show them proper respect and not make too many mistakes with them. They could always get even with us.

One evening Gordon was visiting me. His brother was supposed to pick him up, but when midnight came and no brother, I decided to take him home. We went out to the parking lot, and as we were walking to the car Gordon saw a beer bottle lying on the ground and picked it up. He held it up to see if it was empty, and just then lights went on and a police car pulled up to see what we were doing. To them it appeared that we were drinking. As I walked to my car one officer stopped me, figuring I was trying to break into the car. I explained that it was my car and the door key worked in the lock, so he let me alone. Gordon had more trouble explaining what he was doing with the beer bottle. For a while I was afraid we might end up in the clink, but they finally let us go. The next day when I drove to Gordon's place a police was following me. Gordon was sitting in the living room and saw it, but I didn't see the blinking lights because my rear window was too low and it cut off the lights on top of the police car from my view. When I turned into Gordon's place the police car followed me. He searched my car and examined my papers, but everything was right so he let me go.

Another time, the R.C.M.P. stopped me on the highway three days in a row to search my car and examine my papers, but always let me go. One of my friends got a ticket for not stopping at a stop sign. He claimed he had stopped but the policeman told him he had stopped ten feet from the stop sign, and that didn't count. Too bad! Actually, we realized how important the police presence was for our safety and we did not mind having a few problems with them ourselves.

R.C.M.P. officers are always very supportive of each other in various events, especially in the case of weddings. It was a cold winter weekend when one of our police officers was getting married and the police had congregated from far and wide to take part in the celebrations. There were police roaming around all over in the hotel. There was also a surplus of young men around the place that cold Saturday with nothing to do but look for trouble. We knew that when the wedding ceremony took place every police officer would be present at the wedding. What a perfect opportunity for us. The wedding car was standing in the parking lot, appropriately decorated. There was a lot of snow that winter and the snowplow had pushed up a five-foot wall of snow at the back of the parking lot. A perfect situation. Sentries were posted to make sure no police were observing what we were about to do. Then we grabbed the wedding car, a row of guys on each side, lifted it over the five-foot wall of snow, and carried it into the bush. Then we disappeared, fast. We didn't come back for supper either. We never heard any more about it, but we sure missed seeing what happened after the ceremony.

The police had a lot of work to do around the place. My room overlooked the hotel parking lot and I could see what went on night after night. Around midnight, shortly before closing time, the natives would come to the vendor's door to stock up with beer for the night. Once they had the beer they couldn't wait till they got home, so they started drinking in the parking lot. It was against the law to be drinking outside publicly and it only created disturbances. The police had a difficult time getting the parking lot cleared of Indians after midnight. However, that was not the end of their problems. After the Indians were cleared away the white punks would appear and cause trouble. They were hard to deal with and often hung around all night. On several occasions the hotel night-watchman got beat up by them.

One summery Sunday on the highway to Winnipeg I met about six police cars; obviously there had been an accident. The police were motioning us on, but I slowed down enough to take a good look. It involved a police cruiser; that is why they were pushing us, they didn't want us to see what had happened. The police car had struck an agricultural machine being pulled by a tractor. The machine was a field sprayer with a pipe about 25 feet long. To move it on the road the pipe had been rotated 90 degrees, so it was parallel with the road. The police car had hit this long pipe so that it went through the radiator and under the hood. It looked so funny I laughed all the way home and woke up during the night laughing. How could a policeman do that?

On Monday morning I was down early for breakfast. An R.C.M.P. was already at the table so I sat down opposite him.

"You should have seen what I saw yesterday on the highway," I said with a chuckle in my throat. "It was the funniest accident I have seen."

He didn't respond to my story at all; in fact, he seemed to slouch down in his chair. "What is wrong?" I asked. "It wasn't you, was it?"

"Yes, it was me," he said.

"How could you do it?" I asked, still a bit mystified.

"It wasn't difficult," he said. "It was a rough weekend and I had been driving for 36 hours without a rest. I just couldn't stay awake."

Then I felt ashamed for my attitude. It's easy to laugh when you don't know the reasons, but certainly I should have been more sympathetic to begin with. I had been very rude and I did my best to apologize.

Now I take you to a lighter episode. On pleasant evenings we often gathered into a group and went for a walk. The paper mill was an interesting area to roam around. This evening we walked as far as the forestry fire lookout-tower. It was tempting to see how far up the tower we dared to climb. We had a brave 18-year-old fellow with us, let's call him Bill, who had a flair for showing off. He came from a broken family and showed the results, but he was really a fine young man. Bill started to climb, talking as he went, which showed that he was scared. When he was halfway up he felt he had convinced us of his bravery, so he came back down to safety. Then two young girls started to climb. They climbed up right to the top without any bravado at all. Our brave Bill had been put to shame thoroughly. He looked like a drenched dog, coming in from a thunderstorm.

There was a young waitress working at the hotel who was truly a remarkable woman. Mary, not her real name, became pregnant at the age of 14 so she married the guy, not much older than she was, hoping to raise a family. Before long she had a miscarriage and the marriage seemed unnecessary. However, she wanted children and tried for more, but without success. Finally they adopted one Indian boy and then another, so they had two children. Then she became pregnant and they had another boy of their own. This was too much for her husband, who was still a teenager, so he deserted her. That is when I got to know her, a young woman of 18 working as a waitress to support her three children. She was always cheerful, with never a complaint. This is why I remember her; she was remarkable. Then the Indian father of one of her boys went to court to try and get his son back. To some people this might seem a good opportunity for her to ease her responsibilities, but this 18-year-old woman thought otherwise. She fought back and kept her Indian children.

Some time later when I talked to her she told me she had a boyfriend. He was an engineering student at the University of Manitoba. He visited her on weekends. What about the three children? She told me he was spending more time with the boys than he was spending with her. "I'm not sure if he is going after me to get the boys, or if he is really interested in me," she told me. I have often wondered what happened with this couple, but I have never heard. One thing I know; a woman with her strength of character is bound to come out on top.

During my stay at Manitou Lodge I was undergoing severe personal trials which were not connected with life at the Lodge. At times it seemed I was becoming insane. In the middle of the night one time I woke up in horror. There was a soft object close to my face; it didn't touch me but I could feel its presence. I woke up with a shriek and then looked at the object. It was a human head floating in space. The room had a window that faced the parking lot which was well lit, and thus had enough light for me to see, but not distinctly. I stared at the head in fear, and it bobbed up and down, floating around the room. I was wide awake and clear in my mind, but frightened. It tried to avoid my gaze and moved further away. In about ten minutes it disappeared. Then I got up, put on the lights, and searched the room thoroughly. Why, I don't know, I didn't expect to find that head hiding someplace, but I had to calm my fears. Then I went back to bed, but I left the lights on.

The following night the same thing happened. The head didn't touch me but I could feel it close to me, and it scared me enough that I woke up yelling for help. I did not try to identify the face because I was afraid to do so, for fear of who it might be. Maybe it was a composite face. I could always make it go away by staring at it. From then on I left the bathroom light on during the night. It always felt as if there was more than a head present, but with more light I could immediately see there was only a head, and not a person. Slowly it came less frequently, but for about a year it had me scared to the extent I was almost crazy. Sometimes I wondered if I was mentally deranged. The thought of the episode still makes me jittery.

Another experience hit me one morning, but this was very different. When I woke up I felt something was wrong with my thumb. I went into the bathroom to clean up and realized it might be serious. It would be necessary for me to be very careful with my thumb. But as I was going to wash myself, I jabbed the thumb on the sink and the pain was excruciating. I realized I would faint so I made a dash for my bed, but I didn't make it. I collapsed on the floor. When I came to again I looked at my watch and it showed 45 minutes since my alarm clock had gone off. Could I really have been unconscious that long? I phoned in sick that morning and took three days off before I went back to school. The doctor said I had a pinched nerve in my thumb. This has happened several times in my life. It appears without warning and is dangerous because I easily become unconscious if I hurt the afflicted spot. It takes several weeks to heal completely.

Now for a happier story. I had always been underweight until I got to Pine Falls where I finally came up to normal. However, a number of my friends were overweight and needed to reduce. Weight Watchers was active in town so my friends joined up. Weight Watchers has very strict rules and enforces them as severely as possible. Every Thursday evening they had a meeting which included a tough sermon against cheating, among other items, and a weigh-in. Anyone that hadn't lost weight was severely interrogated, and heaven help the person who had gained. However, weight watchers are sinners like the rest of us, and Thursday evening after the meeting was the safest time to indulge in forbidden foods. You had a whole week to try and lose what you had gained the evening after the sermon. They had been preparing food the last couple of days to feast late Thursday evening. I always made sure I knew where the party was and used the claims of friendship to introduce my presence. After all, no one had forbidden me to eat what I wanted. They did make the most delicious things to eat for that evening, but I was the only one who went home with a clear conscience.

The lady in charge of Weight Watchers always kept her eyes open wherever she went to see if she could catch any of her flock eating foods they shouldn't have, or even buying it. At the junction of highways 59 and 11 there was a small service station and store. The store carried a lot of junk food; that is, forbidden food. One day a group of us stopped off there, two cars filled with passengers, most of whom were weight watchers. We were just coming out of the store, loaded with forbidden food, when who should come driving up, yes, the Weight Watchers lady. They were caught in the act. Their reactions could not have been more agonizing if they had been caught red-handed in the act of adultery. There were a lot of guilty consciences that left the scene and dreaded the thought of what they had to face the next Thursday. To me it was a lot of fun; I wasn't guilty.

The distance from Manitou Lodge to the school on the North shore where I taught was about seven miles by road. In the winter-time we could take a shortcut on the ice over the river and it was only three miles, so we often crossed on the frozen river. It was safe but we had to be careful. We could see open water on the river from the road we used. The ice road was actually reinforced to make it safe for travel. In the beginning of winter the route was marked out and then they drilled holes in the ice so the water would come up and flood the ice, and then freeze. That way the crust of the ice was thickened and made strong enough to carry trucks loaded with pulpwood. The pulpwood was dumped on the ice for use by the mill in spring. In the parts of the river that had rapids the ice would never freeze. One of these spots was not far from the road we used to cross the river. These open spots were good for ice fishing. This was done during the night. The fishermen would put a shining lantern on the ice close to the water. This attracted the fish and they would take them by spearing the fish. Some of our schoolboys were very good at this. I have watched them at night fishing in this manner. When the boys fell asleep in class during the day we knew they had been fishing all night. We did not worry about them sleeping in class; at least they had been working. The fish were mostly marias and not good for eating, but they sold them to the fox farms who took all the fish they could get.

It was the year that Prime Minister Trudeau invoked the War Measures Act and called out the military to restore order in Quebec, that we had a charming young lady teacher from Quebec in our midst. It was immediately obvious that she was an exceptional woman and had great abilities to attract and manipulate the opposite sex. Her brother was one of the group of young men who were charged in the kidnapping and assassination of a high statesman in Quebec. Perhaps she was involved in the insurgency as well and had thought it wise to escape from the scene. These factors aside, she made it clear that the reason for her presence was to look over the men and see if she could find someone worthy of her attention. She picked them carefully and dated them one by one, usually on the weekend. Her exploits became part of the regular discussions among the hotel residents. She set high standards for the men and their success rate was zero. We started teasing Terry (his real name), whom I have mentioned earlier, that he would most likely be on her list in the near future. Terry objected that no way would he let her make a fool of him, which was what she was doing with the men.

However, Terry's day came. It was a beautiful, crisp, romantic morning with fresh snow on the ground, and hoar-frost covering the evergreen trees. It was a lovely day for pictures, so she asked Terry if he would drive her around and help her take pictures, as she had no car. It was a very innocent request, typical of her technique, and it caught Terry off guard. He suspected nothing; her charm was enough to befuddle any man's brain. She kept Terry busy all morning. When we saw him at lunch time we warned him that he was in for it. He objected, "What's wrong with taking pictures?" It was no use talking to him. She kept him going all afternoon as well, and then asked him to take her to the community dance that evening. When Terry came in for supper that evening he was up in the clouds. He had made it! He was taking her dancing that night. We told him this was the way she had worked other guys, but Terry wouldn't listen. You can't reason with a man when he's got a woman in his blood.

Terry did take her to the dance that evening but they had barely entered the dance hall when she realized that she had had as much of Terry as she could stand. She picked up another guy and left Terry standing cold. It was all over! Terry was crushed.

Early in the evening someone told me Terry was back in his room. It seemed impossible, this was to be the evening of his life! I went to see him and found him in tears, lying on his bed. "I want to die, I can't live without her!" he kept moaning over and over. Slowly I got the details of what had happened out of him. I told him we had been reminding him all day what would happen. He needed to realize he had made a fool of himself and to straighten up. It was no use, he kept on moaning that he could not live without her. A few hours later I went to see him again. He was still lying there sobbing, but his voice was becoming weaker. I didn't know what to do. Before I went to bed I checked in to see Terry again. By now he was almost unconscious, just barely mumbling words out of his mouth. I was afraid he was going to die during the night but didn't know what to do. If I took him to the hospital to be treated for "acute lovesickness" I might get laughed out of town. Fortunately, Terry was still alive the next morning but his recuperation was slow. His senses had been seriously deranged. Also, I am not sure if the mocking and jokes he had to put up with helped or hindered his recovery, but he was subjected to a lot of it. He had made a thorough fool of himself.

I should add a few words about this woman from Quebec. I have sat and talked with her in the coffee shop a number of times. I found her a reasonable and intelligent woman to converse with. There was no way that she would have thought of an old man like me as being in her trial book and so we had a normal, person-to-person relationship. I still believe that in most cases, if not all, it is the man who determines by his actions how a woman is going to behave towards him.

UNEXPECTED HONOUR IN KAMLOOPS

Little did we know what lay ahead of us as Bob and I motored into the small city of Kamloops one sunny summer day, although we had some reasons to fear that we might not be welcome. Also, because we had been camping and hiking for some time, we had not heard any news reports for a week.

Bob was a school teacher whom I had met at Manitou Lodge in Pine Falls, and we had decided to spend the summer in the Rockies. Bob had become a good Canadian, but his past was rather unsavory, from a Canadian viewpoint. He had been a card-carrying member of the International Communist Party in Europe, and had been sent to Canada to do undercover work, specifically at the University of Toronto. Anyone who has read university student newspapers is well aware of the communist influence in this news media. He told me frankly that university students are the most gullible and the most easily led group of people in Canada. He never had to take any personal risks in protest marches and other activities because the students were only too eager to step up and take all the risks while he kept safely in the background. However, his parents and family members also moved to Canada. They had no Communist connections but they were under continual R.C.M.P. surveillance on account of him. That is why he decided to drop the Communist Party and become a true Canadian. However, it is not easy to get rid of one's past. This worry was in the back of his mind that summer forenoon when we walked into the R.C.M.P. office.

Why were we stopping at the R.C.M.P. office? The reason was that Bob's younger brother "Jack" had aspired to be an R.C.M.P. officer and he had succeeded, by going west, in removing himself from his older brother's connection with the Communist Party. There had been little communication between the two brothers just to make sure that Jack did not come under any suspicions. However, Bob wanted to know how he was doing, and as we were passing through Kamloops, this was his opportunity. All Bob knew was that his brother was stationed in Kamloops. He did not know his address and the only way to find him was to go to the R.C.M.P. office.

We walked up to the desk clerk and Bob inquired about Jack. Instead of answering, the clerk immediately called for the police chief to come. This was unusual and our hearts tensed up. What could be the reason for this? The Chief entered, a large man, but his face was beaming with smiles. He shook our hands and congratulated us. What was happening? We were stupefied. The Chief seemed perplexed as well at our queer reaction. “Haven’t you heard?” he asked. “No,” we replied. “We’ve been camping in the Rockies for weeks now.”

Then he explained what had happened. Only two days ago the largest drug bust ever had been pulled off in British Columbia by the R.C.M.P. and Bob’s brother was the key figure in the whole operation. He was honoured on the front pages of all the newspapers across Canada. The police were so jubilant about the affair that the appearance of a brother was enough to make heroes of us as well. Jack was on duty that day, so we had to wait until evening to see him. However, the Chief took us to his lovely home and his wife entertained us during the afternoon. Then Bob’s brother joined us and the Chief and his wife gave us a grand dinner and entertained us all evening. It was an eventful day, happening as it did without any premonition of what was ahead of us. It just dropped down on us as a gift from heaven.

Undercover police work is risky, and questionable as well, on account of the procedures that may need to be taken. The story took place during the years when the hippies were an important feature of our social structure. Jack entered the scene in Kamloops as just another hippie. He was well supplied with money by the R.C.M.P., but no one knew where it came from. He got a job in a used clothing store; this was where the hippies congregated because they only wore used clothing. When a hippie has lots of money, it immediately tells the others that he must be involved with the drug trade. Thus his connections started and grew until he had infiltrated the whole drug system in B.C. He was very fond of girls as well, and the girls who circulated among the drug dealers were a valuable source of information. His work continued until the day his information was complete, and then the R.C.M.P. closed in and took over. That happened two days before our arrival.

When we met Jack he still had to be very careful about his safety. Not everybody had been picked up by the police. Jack had already been assaulted and shot at after the plot broke open.

He got the next day off and we spent it together, driving in and around Kamloops. When we stopped to eat, Jack always parked his car in front of the restaurant, and inside we sat so he could see his car at all times. We made it safely through the day but realized that we were taking chances.

PEOPLE I KNEW IN PARIS

Takayuki

Takayuki was a quiet, unassuming young Japanese student, about 20 years old. He sat in the back of the classroom and we scarcely noticed him. That is, until one day when he raised his hand to ask a question. The professor had just mentioned a rare usage of a small French word and he wanted her to repeat what she had said; he did not think that what he had understood was correct. She was surprised; she wasn't sure whether her statement was correct or not. She promised to check the statement and report back the next day. The next day she admitted she had been wrong. She was slightly shaken up, realizing that a foreign student in a beginner class had corrected her on an item of grammar that seldom came up even in advanced classes. Nobody ever questioned anything Takayuki said after that occasion. He never spoke unless he was absolutely sure of himself.

Slowly we drifted together into a warm friendship, although we were very different in some ways. He was a strong Marxist and I was a converted Evangelical; supposedly the two should have little in common. I don't think he had acquired Marxism by studying Karl Marx, because he lived by strong ethical and moral principles. He was steadfast and sure of himself, kind and polite, and never showed signs of uncertainty or hesitation.

Takayuki, myself and a young French fellow often travelled together on excursions outside of Paris, as well as exploring the city itself. Takayuki was always the leader; he knew where we were going and what we wanted to see or do. He was not afraid to walk into any place and ask for the information that interested him.

We often travelled together on the underground subway system, or Metro. The underground stations in Paris are awesomely complex and confusing. They have a good sign system to direct people and I managed to find my way around, but when I emerged above ground I had no sense of direction whatever. Takayuki, however, always knew exactly which way to go when we came up; he was utterly amazing in this. He was a very useful person to travel with.

Takayuki was studying for a post graduate degree and much of our activities involved his studies. He later became a Professor of French Studies in a university outside of Tokyo. He was interested in French literature in general, but the author he chose for his thesis was the dramatist Racine. This was a strange choice for a Marxist atheist to make. Racine is one of France's greatest poets, but he was also a faithful religious believer in God. I believe he is the only prominent French poet who testified to an actual conversion experience in his mature adult years. He was connected with the convent Port-Royal-des-Champs, at which the nuns experienced an evangelical awakening. The result was that the Catholic Church broke up the convent and closed it. This was where Racine spent his youth and was educated. As is common with youth, he rebelled against his religious upbringing, but returned to it later with a strong affirmation of faith. The convent was located about 25 miles from Paris, and Takayuki and I went out there several times to spend time where Racine spent his formative years. We walked the paths that Racine had walked and visited the ruins of the buildings he had known. Takayuki thoroughly prepared himself so he could write his thesis on Racine with a sense of authentic reality. Racine was one of my favourite poets as well. We also visited the convent Port-Royal in Paris, which was an abbey dependent on Port-Royal-des-Champs outside of Paris. Racine spent considerable time here too.

There was another incident where Takayuki seriously compromised his atheistic position. It involved my other Marxist friend WoLap, whom I mentioned in the first chapter. It was Christmas time and the three of us had decided to attend the traditional Midnight Mass at the famous Notre Dame Church in the centre of Paris. We knew there would be a large crowd and that the doors opened at 9:00 p.m. To be sure we would get in we arrived at the church about 8:30 p.m. Already there were two long line-ups stretching across the large open area in front of the church. We wondered if we would make it but the church has a vast interior and when the doors opened, the huge crowd almost vanished inside. We chose a suitable place up front and then settled in on the rickety chairs to wait for midnight.

We had been sitting for a while when, after a thoughtful interlude, one of my atheist friends spoke up. "Isn't it ridiculous for an atheist to be sitting in a church waiting for hours to hear something that is just nonsense to him?" I could see his point all right, and felt amused by his frankness. However, the authorities realized the crowd might get restless, so at 10:00 p.m. they put on a good concert of classical music which we thoroughly enjoyed. Midnight finally came and all three of us appreciated the deep religious emotion of the Christmas Mass that followed. There was another concert of traditional religious music that followed the mass, so we stayed for that as well. It was about 2:00 a.m. when we decided to leave, although there was another concert to follow. The deciding factor was we could still get transportation home at that hour. We had spent almost six hours in the church taking part in a religious service. I thought that was admirable on the part of my atheist friends; few of my saved friends are that dedicated to the worship of God.

It happens occasionally to people who are sure of themselves and who seldom make mistakes that they do slip up and make foolish errors, and it happened to Takayuki as well. It involved Chisako, the friendly Japanese student I mentioned earlier. Because all three of us were in several of the same classes, we often met together. Chisako came from the wealthy Toyota family and showed some signs of being a pampered wealthy young woman. Her intellectual abilities were limited, according to Takayuki. When she talked about her future and the great things she planned to achieve it made Takayuki disgusted because it was evident she was incapable of realizing her dreams. She was just a nice young woman, though well-to-do, as far as Takayuki was concerned.

Takayuki was having trouble with his camera; it did not advance properly. He had gone through several rolls of film and had only managed to get a few pictures on each roll. The three of us were together one time when he was complaining about the camera, not knowing what to do about it. Chisako picked up the camera and told Takayuki what he had been doing wrong. It was a very simple matter and he had failed to see it. To have Chisako correct him was a humiliation that hurt, as he remarked to me afterwards. He took it with a humble spirit, true to his polite character.

Takayuki had planned a trip to Spain and wanted me to come along but I couldn't, so he went alone. He wanted to take a look at the military establishment of the Enemy, the American military base in Spain. He had deep feelings of animosity towards the United States. When he returned he had a very confused story to tell about his experience at the Enemy base. He had ventured as close to it as he had dared to go, looking at the main entrance of the U.S. military base from the other side of the street. One of the military guards had seen the young Japanese man looking at them and had come over to his side of the street, with a smile on his face, to shake his hand and express friendly feelings to him, although neither could speak or understand the other's language. "Why would he do that?" Takayuki asked me. He understood that all Americans hated the Japanese as enemies as a result of the war. I tried to explain to him that most Americans don't harbour hatreds, that it is in their character to forgive, and that with the war over they no longer regarded the Japanese as enemies. What he had experienced told him that I was right, but it was not an easy matter for him to comprehend.

We did go on a two-week excursion to Italy together. We were spending a night in Switzerland and Takayuki had set his heart on buying a genuine Swiss watch. Japanese manufacturers were already taking over part of the Swiss watch market but for Takayuki they were only copying the Swiss product, and he wanted to get the real thing. When we arrived in Geneva the businesses had just closed for the day. Takayuki had to do some fast work to get someone to open up but he managed to get a real watch, a Swiss watch.

Europe is a crowded country and space for development is frequently a problem. A century ago it was trains; now it is roads. Highways often have to be built through crowded areas and are barely squeezed in. Sometimes they even go underground. Highways need rest-stops and we met with some ingenious solutions to the problem of space. When we stopped for lunch one day we found that the restaurant was situated on top of the highway, occupying only air space. This way it could be accessed from both sides of the highway and only car parking space was needed.

Takayuki and I were first to come off the bus and first in the line-up at the cafeteria-style restaurant. We were a few minutes early; the food was out but the price list had not yet been posted. We had missed breakfast that day and were hungry, so we helped ourselves generously. At the cashier we found that the prices were higher than we had expected, but it was our first meal so we could afford it. The people behind us watched us and acted accordingly, figuring it must be a good deal. Being surprised by the cost of the food they came back to us later and blamed us for misleading them. Of course, we hadn't known the prices either. The food itself was excellent. We had the best pasta casserole dish I have ever eaten.

On another occasion it was Takayuki and I who got stung. It happened at Florence or at Bologna, I don't remember which. A bus load of us made a special trip to the city to have dinner in a famous restaurant. Language is a problem but we managed to read what was on the menu. Our problem arose from the details that were not on the menu. We saw the price for steak was reasonable, so that is what we ordered. The steak was excellent, much like my mother used to make. When the bills for the meals were passed out neither of us received one, but Takayuki was summoned in to see the manager. The rest of the group headed for the bus and we were holding up their departure. It took a while, but Takayuki finally came out of the office with a queer smile on his face. My turn came next. The price for the steak on the menu meant per 100 grams, even though it did not say that. Italians would have understood that. That increased our bill by at least three times. There was no one who spoke French fluently so it took time for the manager to explain the situation. Oh well, the steak was delicious! The bus was already moving when I got out after paying, but I managed to get on.

There was another occasion where my escape from a critical situation was almost breathless. Five of us had made a side trip by train somewhere in Italy. We were having something to eat in the railway station when we realized that the train should be leaving in a matter of minutes. A problem we frequently had in Italy was that business people often could not make change when we wanted to pay for something. In a restaurant they would often add the bills together and make one person pay, who would then have to collect from the others. This time it fell on me. The warning bell for the train went and the others ran off while I was still trying to settle up for our food. Finally I ran after them, and then I remembered there were four tracks and I did not know which one to take. I could not follow the others as they were already gone. Fortunately, I chose the right track and made it on the train which was already moving. It was a close call. What would I have done if I had missed the train? Thank God that He remembered me that day!

I am telling this story as if Takayuki and I were always together. This is far from true. Even on the trip to Italy we often went our own ways, possibly because we were so excited about all the things we wanted to do that sometimes we forgot about each other. Of course I had other friends too. Takayuki was an excellent friend, despite the fact that he was a Marxist and I was a Christian.

A Lady from Iran

I was in the American residence for breakfast, I had picked up my food in the serving line and then looked for a place to sit down. Most of the tables were occupied, but I noticed one table with an empty chair, the other one occupied by a well-dressed young lady. As I have pointed out previously, in Paris you can take a vacant spot at a table although the other places are taken. So I sat down with this young lady. Of course, I asked her permission first.

Slowly we started talking and introduced ourselves. When she said she was from Iran I felt truly surprised. I told her so. Regarding her appearance, she could have come from London or New York; besides, she had come alone to Paris to study. She explained to me that I was thinking in the past, that the situation in Iran had changed greatly, and women were becoming increasingly liberated. Sitting in front of her I realized she was proof that what she said was true.

This incident happened before the time of Khomeini. The Shah was still the head of Iran and was steadily leading the nation into a process of westernization. Actually, at this time there was a lot of propaganda against the Shah being circulated in Paris, especially by the Communists. "En bas le Shah" (Down with the Shah) was scrawled all over. It was only a few years later when Khomeini took over in Iran and reversed the clock, putting the country back into darkness.

I have often wondered what happened to the fine young lady with whom I chatted that morning at the breakfast table.

A Girl from Russia

She was a young Communist from Russia, studying in Paris. Someone brought her into our circle of students, which is how I met her. She was a vivacious, exciting girl of about 18-20 years. It wasn't many weeks after she came before I noticed she was having nervous problems. I mentioned this to a German student who knew her better and she informed me the Russian girl's permit for foreign residence had expired and the Russian authorities wanted her to return. She wasn't quite ready to return yet. She told me herself she was going to visit London first before she returned home because she might never have another chance. However, the Russian authorities were applying strong pressure on her and they could always threaten to persecute her relatives back home in Russia, not an empty threat.

The last time I saw her was at an event in downtown Paris where she was with our group. As we were late leaving for home we took a taxi, about five of us. The taxi dropped us off one by one as we reached our destinations. The Russian girl lived the furthest out so she would be the last one on the taxi.

Because we were all worried about our Russian friend, we talked about her again the next day. The German student said she knew the Russian girl had no money in her purse the night before to pay for the taxi. No one knew how she managed with the taxi driver. No one saw her again. She just vanished.

I wouldn't be surprised if the Russian Secret Service was waiting for her when the taxi brought her back.

Cambodians

We had a dramatic experience one evening at our regular Thursday meeting of the APLI club. One of our members brought in five Cambodian students looking for help. This was just after the Khmer Rouge had overthrown the government of Cambodia and was beginning its horrendous slaughter of the other ethnic groups that had constituted the old regime. These students had been sent to Paris to study by the previous government; the new tribe in control would doubtless immediately cancel their travel permits and cut off their support, forcing them to return, which would mean certain death. They were hoping France would accept them as refugees, but so far they had no word. It gave me a weird feeling that these five students sitting in front of me would be facing a firing squad or worse in a couple of weeks unless France took them in.

I never heard what happened.

Association Protestante pour les Liaisons Inter-Universitaire

It is called APLI for short and means Protestant Association for Inter-University Liaisons. It was a small group in a large city. Fortunately I had picked up a folder inviting students to join and it was the best thing that happened to me in Paris.

It is very difficult to break into French society. The first two months in Europe I felt very lonely. I looked at every notice and picked up every folder I saw, hoping something would lead me to connections, but it seemed hopeless. Then one day as I was walking out of an office I noticed a small pile of folders on the desk. What's the use, I thought, but then as I was in the hall I reversed myself and said, what's the use of giving up? I walked back and picked up a copy and it opened up a new world to me.

The next step was to locate the address. I found it on the map without trouble, but when I walked around the block there was no such number and no such name on the buildings. I gave up that day but I told myself I had to try again. The next time I asked someone on the street for help. He told me it might be in the inner court and that I should look for the door that leads inside. I succeeded. I found the entrance to the inner court and also the name I was looking for on one of the buildings.

The lady in charge, Madame Bouteiller, was friendly. She told me their main work was to help foreign students find a place to live, but they also had meetings every Thursday evening. All I had to do was pay a membership fee and I was welcome to attend. This was the beginning of my French connection.

The work of the society was supported by the Protestant Church, especially by some well-to-do people who were interested in helping students in need. I met some of the leading people, but mainly I got to know the younger people who attended the Thursday socials. The evenings were always lively; they included an evening meal and some special speaker or activity. We had a wide variety of events. For instance, one of our people was a high official in the Foreign Affairs Department and could bring in senior statesmen from around the world.

One time we had a police officer from London, England, talking to us. He told us how the cops operated in London, walking the streets alone without a gun. This was unimaginable for a French person. In Paris the police patrolled the streets in a van carrying at least five armed cops. It was an interesting evening, watching the astonished expressions of the French people present.

Another evening we had a music professor explaining to us how classical music is created. She invited us to a series of lectures on music she was giving at a different location. Norah and I decided to attend the lectures, but the biggest adventure was just to find the location. The city block was easy to find, but then we had to find the entrance to the inner court, go through several other businesses, through the back entrance of one, and there we found her studio. Paris can be an adventurous place even in its dullest spots.

Frequently top diplomatic persons from other countries came to talk to us. This resulted from the fact that the society was helping many students from other countries. The club also planned sightseeing walks in Paris or tours into the countryside by car. One place we visited several times was the famous palace of Fontainebleau, about 25 miles from Paris. The forests in the area are famous for hiking and as a picnic area.

One two-day trip stands out in my memory. They expected a number of people but only four showed up that Saturday morning, on April 12, 1975. These included the young French leader with a car, a young Lebanese man, a Japanese girl and myself. It was an odd group, all strangers to each other, but off we went.

Our first destination was a vineyard and winery owned by someone who was known to APLI people. It must have been located almost in the centre of France. Our driver had a good map but had to stop repeatedly to ask for directions. Once you get off the main highways maps are of little help in France. We found the place around lunch time. They were busy but they gave us something to eat. Then we walked through the vineyards and inspected the buildings where wine-making was in progress. It was a large family affair which made it an interesting visit.

In the afternoon we continued on and visited the Chateau d'Angers, which is listed as 305 kilometres southwest of Paris. It is a ruin with an interesting history. The lord had been accused of treason by the King of France and ordered to tear down his fortifications. He had delayed the operation until the King prepared to use force against him. Then he started to take down the walls, a layer of stone at a time to show he was complying, but still delaying the process. His delaying plan worked because by the time the wall was down to half its height, the order to destroy it was lifted. The castle was converted into a museum and contains many interesting exhibits. The moat around the walls was beautifully landscaped with flowers and green lawns.

By the time night came we were tired and ready for a good rest. Our leader had connections with a Catholic church in a small town. They allowed us to sleep in their church the night of Saturday to Sunday. We had to get up early on Sunday on account of morning Mass. We had brought along sleeping bags and were ready for the situation. The Japanese girl we put up in the choir loft and we slept down in the main part of the church near the entrance to make sure our girl was safe from intruders.

Sunday morning we were off early, leaving breakfast for later. Breakfast has little importance in France. We visited a number of other palaces and forts that day. One was the Chateau de Saumur, a huge establishment. On our way home we dined at another restaurant located like a bridge over the highway. It was an eventful weekend; our small group got along very well.

The office and meeting place of the APLI were located in a church which was no longer recognizable from the street. Originally it was situated in the centre of a lot, with landscaping around it. As Paris expanded and space became scarce, the whole area around the church had been filled in with building construction such as shops and offices. The original church was still functioning but much of its space was used by other groups when there were no church services.

It so happened that on the evening we had our social gathering there was also a ladies' group of aerobic dancers meeting in another part of the church. However, there was only one entrance we all had to use. They had to undress and change into their gym clothing, and the only space for them to do it was in the entrance hall. As a result, when we came in, we had to squeeze through a group of half-dressed women. In Canada this might cause some excitement but Parisians have reached the point where naked women don't arouse much interest anymore. The clothing they left lying around the hall was more of a problem. When the series of classes was finished the ladies presented a concert to the public and invited us to attend, free of charge. This was to make up for the inconvenience they had caused us.

Women are everywhere and they have a tendency to lead to adventure. During my first year at Paris I met a young lady from India at our APLI meetings. I was always interested in meeting people from new countries and India was new to me then. She came from a wealthy family and often talked about her daddy, but never her mother. The second evening I met her she twisted my arm and got me to escort her home. She stayed at a Salvation Army hostel just outside of Paris and had to be back by 11:00 p.m. It meant we had to leave shortly after 10:00 p.m. We had to go to the train station and take the train to the first stop outside of Paris. From there she had about a ten-minute walk through a poorly lit area to get to the hostel; no wonder she wanted someone to come along with her. Going by train in France is easy and fast. We bought tickets from a machine and boarded the train; no one checked us as a rule. However, I always kept my ticket in case I might be checked. After I saw my friend throw her ticket out I warned her to hold onto it next time. On the next trip we were checked; we had to exit through a gate and hand in our tickets which, fortunately, we had both kept.

As soon as we reached the Salvation Army hostel I turned back because I had very little time left to catch the last train going back to Paris. I didn't mind doing this a few times but after that it became a burden. Besides that, we always had to rush to make it. Then it happened. We were a couple of minutes late and the Salvation Army door was closed for the night. We both had to go back to Paris. She decided she would stay in a hotel for the night. It was too late to go hunting for a hotel. I suggested it might be better if she came and stayed in my place for the night, but that was out of the question. We got off at a different railway station where I knew we would find hotels. Then she made me go in and inquire about a room for her. The first hotels were too expensive for her. The hotel clerks gave me a very suspicious look at my inquiries for a room, so I made her come in with me, but that didn't help the situation much. Finally we found a suitable place. I was well aware of hotel rules—no visitors allowed—but the clerk repeated them to me; he evidently didn't trust my motives. As soon as my friend had paid I noticed the other man in the hotel had moved over to the stairway to make sure I did not go up with the lady. Hotels are very strict about visitors in France. My only thought was about getting home.

I had good reason to be worried. We had wandered off in our search for a hotel and I didn't even know where I was. Looking at my watch I realized the subway was closed for the night. I knew there are special night buses going but could not locate them. The only solution was to find my directions and walk home across Paris. It only took a couple of hours. It's not the only time I have had to do it.

Visiting my Uncle Daniel's Grave

Uncle Daniel joined the Canadian forces as a youth during World War I. His unit was sent to England for training and then to France to face the German war machine. In those days human life was freely expendable and soldiers were slaughtered in great numbers. The morals of war have changed greatly since that time. My uncle was one of those who laid down their lives for their country. His body is buried in northern France, not far from Vimy Ridge.

It occurred to me while I was living in Paris that I should visit my uncle's grave. I wrote home to my parents to get information to identify him so I could locate his grave. Then I went to the French Legion and asked if they could find the location of his grave. At first this seemed hopeless but they finally found his name in the records.

I had already been consulting with a French friend, Joseph Luhan, about the matter and he offered to drive me out to find the grave. He had a high position in the French diplomatic corps. It was a nice spring morning when he, his wife and I set out for the northern part of France.

Mr. Luhan had a good road map but he still had to ask for further directions locally before we found the cemetery. It was located at Sains-en-Gabelle. The inscription on the tombstone said my uncle was killed in August, 1917, at the age of 21. It was not a military cemetery but a small local place which had a section for soldiers fallen in the war.

Besides this trip, my friends also invited me into their home a number of times, for dinner. They had a lovely apartment, but compact, as most French homes are. It was crowded with mementos and handicrafts from around the world, a very rich display.

An American Girl

The French people of Paris, and others as well, had a distinct stereotype of the American citizen. He/she was clearly identifiable and the description was not complimentary. We had a number of American students around, but strangely, none of them fit the stereotype. Well, there are always exceptions, my French friends would say, but there seemed to be no examples of the stereotype.

This American girl, I'll call her Sandy, was in one of my classes and I talked with her occasionally. Sandy was modest and quiet, but still open for a bit of adventure. She always carried a Study Bible with her books which was a testimony to her Christian faith. It was usually on top when she put her books down. That was all; it was silent evidence of her faith.

One day she approached me. "Would you like to come with me to a new place to eat?"

"Why not?" I replied. "But will I need tickets?"

"I have tickets," Sandy said. "It's a place for Jewish students in a Jewish building. They'll let us in."

Finding a place to eat was always a problem, so I was game for any new discovery. I also knew that a girl could get in where a guy wouldn't manage. All I had to do was stay with her. That's about the way it worked out, too. A Jewish place with kosher food wouldn't have many other people coming in, so maybe they didn't have any set rules about non-residents coming in.

We ate there several times, always with the feeling that we were barging in on them. The food was good and we enjoyed it. Then Sandy ran out of tickets and our adventure ended.

My Arab Friend

He was a fine young person and I liked him. He was a classmate and we talked together at times. Towards the end of the year there were a number of farewell parties and he gave one of them. He invited me to come and I was pleased to accept.

He gave me a clear address to come to, but it takes more than the address to find a place in Paris, and that was all the information I had. I should have asked him for more.

I found the street address without trouble. I climbed the stairs to the sixth floor and found the apartment number. So far, so good. I knocked on the door and asked for my Arab friend. The man who opened the door told me I had the wrong suite. The number was right, but that didn't matter. When I asked him further he told me there could be another suite in the block with the same number, but he didn't know where.

Back down again, I looked for another staircase. I opened the caretaker's room and it was completely dark, but it looked as if there were stairs in the corner.

In France they have a small red light, a little larger than a pinhead, close to the door. You press it and the regular lights come on for about 30 seconds, just enough to get you to the next red light. If you can't find that then you're lost in darkness. However, I couldn't find the first red light, and I wasn't going up in complete darkness.

Finally I decided to go to a store and buy some matches to use for a light. On the street I met another student who was also coming to the party. While we were talking we heard a call from higher up. Our friend looked down from a window and said he was coming down to bring us up.

He showed us where the little red light was in the caretaker's room. With another red light we reached the fifth floor. There we walked down a long hall, climbed through a window onto the roof, walked a stretch on the roof, climbed back through a window, and up two flights of stairs. It was a little complicated but we finally reached his place. The living room was already filled with a circle of friends sitting on the floor. They were preparing the food in the kitchen. We had a variety of food dishes to eat and enjoyed our evening.

But the highlight of the evening was just to find the place.

Marian's Friend in Paris

Her name has slipped from my memory, so let's call her Kathy. I had never heard of Kathy until one day a letter arrived from my daughter Marian, saying Kathy would arrive in Paris a few days later and would I show her around? A young girl of 20, certainly I would. I knew she was too young to have developed into the common tourist-type traveller, and my older age had never matured me either. During my two years in Paris I never once visited the regular tourist traps with their chorus-girl attractions. Instead, I loved the natural charm of the streets, the cafes, the small theatres and the parks, which the tourists barely touch. I was not mistaken about Kathy.

She had made reservations at a good hotel and that is where we met. I had several important classes to attend and she wanted to spend some time on her own, but we spent most of the time wandering through Paris, with its endless attractions and charm.

However, Kathy had some serious matters on her mind. She wanted a pair of French leather boots, a popular item at that period, and she wanted to buy them in Paris. She had gone into several shoe stores on her own and found none that fitted her; her legs were a bit too chubby. I assured her we would find boots that fitted, so off we went to the downtown shopping streets. Kathy was not fat, but her figure was typically American. Unbelievably, the boots she tried on were all too tight; she could not wear them. She had never had that problem in Canada. Why in Paris?

I tried to explain. Apartment blocks in Paris rise to about eight stories and seldom have elevators. Underground subway stations have some escalators, but you still have to walk many stairs and long corridors. That is why French women, without exception, have such beautiful slim legs. Kathy was disappointed that she got no boots, but above all she felt embarrassed and humiliated about her figure.

Then Kathy remembered she had another item on her "must get" list. It was a copper kettle, the kind that came from somewhere in northern Africa. They were the rage with collectors in many parts of the world at that time. Actually I believe they were a good usable kitchen utensil as well. I knew immediately where to go because I had already seen them. We headed for the Marche aux Puces, the largest flea market I have seen, at the Porte de Clignancourt, just on the north edge of Paris.

We were a little on the late side and the vendors were already starting to pack up. We spotted an Arab who was busy tying up about a dozen kettles, getting them ready so he could carry them off. Kathy immediately spotted the one she wanted. She could not speak French so I had to do the bargaining. The price he quoted was too high so I told Kathy we would have to look elsewhere. She didn't want to leave and the vendor noticed this. I suggested an offer, only about half the price he asked, and then the Arab wanted to leave. But there was hesitation on both sides. I knew the Arab would try to make a sale because it was the end of the day. I told Kathy to get the money out of her purse. Then I warned her not to let go of the money until she had a firm grip on the kettle. When the Arab had a grip on the money he let go of the kettle and the sale was finalized. Kathy got a good deal on the kettle.

Then we had to look around for a suitable basket to hold the kettle so it was easy to carry.

Kathy was accumulating more stuff than her two suitcases could hold. When the day came to go to the airport I went along and helped her carry her purchases. After handing in the suitcases she still had a large purse, three bulky shopping bags, and the basket with the kettle left. She also had to carry her travel documents in her hand. Only a woman can handle this kind of situation.

Later I heard that when she was in the waiting room she discovered she still had some French money left. She had gone into the duty-free store and bought two bottles of wine with it. That had been more than she could carry and she dropped one bottle, which broke. I'm sure I could never have managed with all the hand baggage she carried onto the plane.

Madame Bouteiller

We got to know her as the lady in charge of APLI, but she also invited us into her home. She and her husband lived just outside of Paris and they owned a free-standing house. In Paris itself I have never seen a single house surrounded by open space. Homes in Paris were all located in apartment blocks or squeezed into empty parts of buildings serving various purposes. Outside of Paris we saw many single houses.

At the Bouteiller home we experience a delightful French way of entertaining visitors. They sent us a card saying they would be "receiving on Sunday from 2:00 to 9:00 p.m." At first we did not understand what it meant, but we accepted. It meant that they were at home and visitors could come and go within those hours. They had ample food ready so people could eat as they wished. It was a pleasant custom, and we met and talked with many French people.

IMPRESSIONS OF CHINA, 1980

After several days in Hong Kong, Norah and I were finally in the train on our way to China. Our friends in Hong Kong had highlighted our stay there, taking us to many places often missed in regular tours. They also told us we would find life in China much slower and more primitive.

On the train, Chinese customs officials gave us forms to fill out to record everything we were bringing with us. We would have to account for these goods when leaving. That put some apprehension into our spirits. We knew China was a communist state and we feared we might have a real communist experience ahead of us. Norah had been in serious trouble during a trip to communist Poland a few years earlier.

Actually it never happened. Our suitcases were never searched, neither on entry nor on our departure from China. We had no problems with the customs or with security people and we never faced soldiers on duty, as Norah had in Poland.

Another regulation that faced us concerned money. The officials told us China had a special issue of money for tourists only, and that we were not allowed to possess the regular Chinese money. As well, we were only allowed to enter special tourist stores.

A common proverb says that rules are made to be broken, and our stay in China fully confirmed this. Already by the second day we found we could freely enter the local stores and the shopkeepers had no hesitation about taking our "funny money". Before long we had our wallets filled with regular Chinese money which we got as change when buying goods. Shopping posed no language problems because all the goods in the stores had the prices clearly marked. We found the prices very reasonable. There were no signs ever to indicate we were being watched and we soon felt free to roam wherever we pleased.

What appealed to us most was that there were no beggars on the streets, in contrast to the Philippines which we visited before coming to Hong Kong. The Chinese people were honest and courteous without exception. It helps the tourists to relax and enjoy their visit. From a moral viewpoint we found that communist China rated highly.

Our first stop was the city of Canton. It was in May and the climate was warm and humid, the atmosphere filled with a light fog. It filled us with a dreamy, romantic feeling, heightened as we visited the lovely tearooms set in a beautiful garden area, usually watered by a pool.

However, the tea they served was less romantic. It was a watery green tea, served in large mugs. It didn't agree with my expectations. The food likewise was not appetizing. It always smelled and tasted as if it had been fried or cooked in rancid grease. In the airport shops we could buy good salted peanuts and excellent dried fruit. We soon learned to keep them in our pockets and when we were in the restaurant we often ate more from our pockets than from the plates on the table.

We were also given the choice whether we wanted to take our meals from the Chinese or American menu. Once made, this choice stayed with a person for all the meals. Norah normally practiced a good spirit of pluralism, recognizing the equality of other cultures, so I was surprised when she chose the American menu. I took the Chinese menu because I wanted the full experience of the Chinese contact. However, I wasn't sure if I would make it to the end. In fact, there was not a great difference between the food from the two menus. By the time our visit was over we were both facing serious stomach problems and glad to get back to our usual food. This was the experience of most of the people in our group.

Our next visit was the city of Guilin, a most interesting place. There were jagged rocks or mountains sticking up all around but they were coming out of a flat terrain. It was just like the pictures I had seen back home. I have spent much time in mountainous country but never before had I seen mountains standing on a flat plain.

The drabness of everything began to sink in on us. No place did we see any use made of paint, inside or outside of buildings. Evidently paint was unknown in China. Looking out from our hotel window we saw that all the roofs of the houses were the same colour, made of the same material. The water in the rivers was always muddy with a yellowish tint. Life seemed to be slow, plain and uninteresting.

The countryside was hilly wherever we went. In the southern half of China all the agricultural land is terraced and naturally irrigated, with the water supply carefully controlled. It was the season when rice was being planted and we saw the various stages of the operation wherever we went. The fields all had standing water on them. Some were being plowed, by a man guiding a simple plow pulled by a water buffalo through the water-covered fields. Next we saw plowed fields with bundles of rice plants lying strewn around. In other fields we saw people standing in the water, carefully planting each rice plant in neat rows. If we had not witnessed these scenes with our own eyes we would not have believed that the whole rice crop of China is planted in this fashion. Will machines ever take over this work? Hardly; I can not imagine how these small terraced fields can ever be farmed by machines.

We saw an interesting sight one day as we were travelling on the bus. The road was partly blocked by a pile of rock. Sitting beside the rock was an old woman toiling away with a hammer, breaking the rock up into gravel and heaping it up into a separate pile. Gravel must be scarce in this country!

Then we moved on to Changsha, going further towards the north. This city prides itself on its connections with Chairman Mao Zedong. It was on Orange Island where many of the revolutionaries, including Mao, held secret meetings and planned their strategy to take full control of China. A large stone tablet has been erected on this island with a poem inscribed by Chairman Mao. At a smaller town we saw the birthplace of Mao. It is actually a large villa and obviously Mao came from a wealthy upper-class family.

In all of China we saw no private cars. The vehicle traffic consisted of buses, trucks and government cars. The common people used bicycles, by the millions. Trucks were in short supply and most freight was moved by carts pulled by human beings. At one railway yard we saw a stream of carts coming out loaded with coal, pulled by men. Others were more fortunate and pulled carts loaded with cabbage, baskets of eggs, or other produce. Another time we saw a long row of men beside the highway, each pulling a pig. Evidently the pigs were being taken to the slaughterhouse.

Then we moved north to Sian. Most of the old wall that had protected the city in the past was still standing. Outside of the city wall we visited the Wild Goose Pagoda and were allowed to climb to the top. Not far from here we visited the most spectacular archaeological site of all. It had been discovered only a few years previously when a farmer digging a well had struck a statue instead of water. The government took over and found an army of life-size statues, tens of thousands of soldiers in battle array. Pictures were not allowed and the area was enclosed with a wall and covered over to control the onslaught of the media while excavation was in progress, but the Japanese had already managed to take pictures secretly. It was an awesome panorama!

As we travelled further north we began to see carts pulled by horses instead of by people; the rice paddies were replaced by wheat fields which were large enough to be worked by machines. Life, however, continued to be simple. Apartment blocks did not have running water. People came out to get water from taps on the sidewalk. Streets were wide and it was common to see people doing their laundry on the sidewalk, and cooking and eating their meals outside as well.

Beijing was an impressive city with many old palaces set in large park areas. It seems the rich have always lived in grand style off the backs of the poor. The Forbidden City is the most grandiose of all. It must have been an ostentatious affair at the height of its glory. We visited Mao's tomb at the south end of Tiananmen Square and got a good look at the old revolutionary. On the west side of the large open square is the Great Hall of the People, which we were not allowed to enter. On the other side is a similar building transformed into a museum, and we were permitted to go in. The main street of Beijing is a vast road, with about eight traffic lanes on each side; however, there was hardly any traffic on it. Obviously it was built for the army, troop movements and special military parades.

Once we arrived as far north as Beijing our hearts were set on the Great Wall of China. Norah and I were both thrilled when the day came and our bus headed for the Great Wall. It was a long trip, with the road leading ever higher into the mountains. China does not have many good highways and thus they are crowded with traffic, buses and trucks. In many places in the mountains, the road was not wide enough for buses and trucks to pass and it meant much backing up and manoeuvring. In fact, the trip up the mountains was as breathtaking as the Great Wall itself. We arrived finally and walked on the Wall, built on top of a mountain range. They had rebuilt a good stretch of it, but when we got to the end of this part we could see that the original wall had deteriorated badly since it was first built. It was an impressive sight!

We noticed that the front seat on our tour bus was often empty, which is unusual because people usually compete for the front seat to get a better view. Norah and I decided to take advantage of this opportunity and moved up to the front seat. This happened while driving on city streets. We soon discovered why the seat had been left empty. Traffic was heavy with bicycles and hand-pulled carts. The bus was going at a good speed. The driver knew that a tourist bus had the right of way and did not worry about what was in front of him. However, the rest of the traffic dared him and did not get out of his way until the last split second before getting hit. This situation kept occurring constantly. They always managed to just barely escape getting hit and it did not take long until our nerves were on edge and we moved back in the bus. I imagine the bus driver enjoyed himself because he knew that if he did hit someone the victim would get the blame.

Our visit included a number of concerts but Chinese music did not appeal to us; it sounded too much like a circus. However, there was one session of entertainment that stands out in my memory. We had toured a large chinaware factory, seeing the production of cups and plates at close range. After a tour we always had a discussion with the manager who very humbly answered our questions, even though some of them were less than complimentary. Then they served us tea and dainties, and this time we had the privilege of listening to two young Chinese girls play the accordion. First they played Chinese music and then switched over to popular American songs. They asked us for requests and, to our surprise, they played all the songs we named. If they did not recognize the title they asked the person to sing a few lines to give them the tune. Amazingly, they played everything that was requested. I wonder how they had learned all the American songs, some of which even I had not heard.

We toured a number of factories where fancy artwork was being hand-produced. China is famous for its jade carvings. We went through one factory where they carved beautiful jade art objects. It takes a lot of cheap labor to put products on the market at prices that will sell. In another factory they were doing fine silk embroidery, making lovely art pictures on silk. It is a beautiful art form, but it requires fine eyesight and eyes don't last long with this work. The most complicated work we saw was where they made cloissoné dishes and bowls. It starts with a plain copper bowl; a design is made with fine, shaped pieces of copper wire glued to this bowl and the spaces are filled in with liquid enamel. The bowl is then baked in a kiln, and finally it is sanded and polished to a beautiful finish. This process gives an idea of the amount of hand labor involved in making just one bowl. Although these art products, mostly produced for the tourist trade, were made in a factory, they were still highly dependent on hand labor and the artistic skills of the people at work.

The use of language took a new twist in China. I have already mentioned "funny money". When we looked for the washrooms, we were advised to ask for the "happy place". The palaces and parks we visited had many names such as "Temple of Heaven Park", "Hall of Cultivating Happiness", "Garden of Harmonious Interest", "Hall of Supreme Harmony" and so on. The impression we got was that by ascribing these high-sounding names to important places they would then attain these high states of happiness and wisdom. We saw it as just another human attempt to gain the gifts only God can give. I believe these lovely expressions only masked the fact that these qualities were absent in the lives of the Chinese people. As we saw it, their lives were drab and colourless.

We were impressed with the vastness of China, especially the enormous amount of physical labor required to produce the food and the goods necessary to sustain the nation.

CHALLENGING CONFLICTS WITH INDIAN AFFAIRS

They were the difficult years in my life. I had lost my teaching position at Morris High School during the winter due to a nervous breakdown; I had gone back to the Post Office as a sorting clerk, a job too difficult for me; my marriage was slowly breaking up with no hope for reconciliation. This was my situation when on November 17, 1964, I took my first assignment as a teacher with Indian Affairs. I was located at Bloodvein, situated on the eastern side of Lake Winnipeg, and worked under the Mennonite Mission. It was the first year their school was recognized by Indian Affairs.

The school year went by slowly, leading me through many new adventures and giving me an initial insight into the workings of Indian Affairs. The Department had an attractive booklet they used to attract prospective teachers. It described conditions on the reserves and had pictures of the schools and housing accommodations for teachers. The pictures were all taken when the buildings were new and gave no indication of the shape they were in when the new teacher was assigned to them. Later, when I objected that the booklet was deceptive, they withdrew it.

When I was first hired the Superintendent told me that the following year he would transfer me to Hollow Water Reserve, which had road access, and after that he would take me to Fort Alexander, a good location. When I inquired about the move at the end of the year, I found out that it had been an empty promise; no one knew about it. However, I applied to be moved and got the transfer to Hollow Water. They also promised to look after my housing needs there, another promise they conveniently forgot.

At Hollow Water I had my first confrontation with the Department of Indian Affairs, as related in a previous chapter, "*Lover's Lane*". It was not a clean encounter, I admit, and I was beginning to realize that I would have to take my gloves off if I was going to stand up to Indian Affairs' superintendents, both in Winnipeg and Ottawa.

Why did I get involved in this type of activity? There were several reasons. I saw how they controlled the Indians by making glowing promises to them and forgetting them as soon as they were off the reserve. I saw how they were doing very much the same thing to the teachers. The teachers were being harassed on the reserve in many ways but Indian Affairs gave them very little support of any kind. It was out of concern and sympathy for my fellow men, natives and whites, that I took up the fight for more humane and honest treatment of them by the government. The travail of marriage breakdown under which I was suffering led me to take risks in life that I would not normally have taken.

My role as a leader covered a broad perspective of activities to enrich the teaching experiences of the teachers. Our union council developed many social events throughout the year to brighten the lives of the teachers. Personally I made a point of frequently visiting teachers that I knew were having problems, on other reserves as well as the one where I taught. As teachers, we always made a practice of sharing information with each other; how we dealt with our problems, and what teaching methods we felt were effective. This was of great help, especially for new teachers.

With respect to union activities, I received some excellent instructions from my Principal, John Zyzneiwski, on how to proceed. (He became a superintendent with Indian Affairs later.) I list them as follows:

1. Complaints have to be in writing. My Superintendent told me later that if a complaint is not serious enough for the teacher to put it down in writing, it is not worth his time to consider it. I agreed with him.

2. Letters have to be absolutely polite. The most severe criticism can be expressed in polite language so even your grandmother would not be offended.

3. Keep a carbon copy of each letter you write. If a reply is not forthcoming in a reasonable time, write another letter repeating the contents of the first letter plus the date when it was mailed, and ask for the matter to be dealt with. If the matter still does not get attention, you are now free to contact a higher level of authority, always using a polite procedure, and reviewing the steps you have already taken. I found this works marvellously well. After a few scuffles my letters always got careful attention.

4. Never take up personal complaints. You are there to help others; officials can only fight back when you are working for your own benefit.

I found that these principles were an excellent guide. As a union leader with the Public Service Alliance of Canada, I had an unfair advantage over my superintendent in Winnipeg. All my union correspondence went directly to the union office in Ottawa, and they took up complaints with the Indian Affairs office there. It meant that I was always going over the head of my superintendent in Winnipeg. Ottawa officials loved to keep a check on the lower superintendents in the provinces. It was an ideal set-up for me but my local superintendent detested it. As a rule, I kept up a polite relationship with him, but he would have liked to knife me in the back, if possible. He tried several times, figuratively speaking, but did not succeed.

How to teach the native children to speak and write English correctly was a crucial problem for the school curriculum. They had just brought in a new Oral English program when I started and it caused a lot of problems. It was a major university thesis that someone not acquainted with our native people had written and it was not at all set up for our situation. However, the Department demanded that we teach it just as it was and use it extensively. Most teachers didn't know how to work it. I realized it was important and did my best. Actually it became an important tool in the hands of our superintendents to criticize teachers they did not like, an easy complaint against teachers to force them to leave. Many teachers were so baffled and confused by it that they were relieved to go. It took many years until Indian Affairs realized there was no gain from a method that was too poorly written to be used in our schools.

During my second year when I was at Hollow Water, we had a special Teachers' In-Service dealing with the Oral English program, at the Fort Alexander School. A couple of days later the Superintendent arrived at my classroom just after classes had started. He told me he wanted to observe my teaching and sat down in the back. During lunch time he told me why he had come. At the In-Service I had made a statement which displeased him and he wanted to check on what I was doing with the Oral English. I think there had been one inappropriate word in my statement, made without thinking carefully. He told me he was pleased with what I was doing and encouraged me to continue. Mr. Rehaluk was a tough superintendent but he was fair and supportive as well. However, it was his last year in our district.

Accommodation for teachers living on the reserve always posed many problems. When I was transferred from Bloodvein to Hollow Water I was given a firm promise they would provide me with suitable accommodation. When the day came, nothing had been done.

A teacher with a family was moved to the school at Black River into a house without furniture in it. It was classed as furnished and the teacher was charged a monthly rental for the furniture, but it did not arrive until Christmas time. Imagine yourself in his situation. Many buildings for the teachers were ransacked by the natives over the summer period and not repaired before the new teacher moved in. The schools were often in a similar condition. Ordering school supplies was always slow. They were usually purchased on the tender system with the purchase going to the lowest tender. The supplier was well aware he could ship all his old leftover stock to Indian Affairs' schools and get away with it. Teachers' complaints were too slow in filtering through the system to have any final effect.

The new teacher had many problems. His accommodation might be without furniture, windows and doors. Buying food was often difficult. He couldn't understand the new Oral English program, but he had to teach it, or else. School supplies were in a mess, if he could find any. If he asked for help he was classed as a complainer. But his biggest problem was how to work with his classroom of native children, a challenge for which he was poorly prepared. Most new teachers came in with idealist aspirations, much like that of a missionary going out with the gospel to a foreign country. Idealism doesn't last on the reserve. It is much better to go for the reason of getting a pay cheque at the end of the month. The native people can understand that, but they don't like to be treated with a paternalistic attitude or as objects of charity.

There was little use in working with Indian Affairs to improve conditions for the teachers and upgrade the standard of education in the schools. Their attitude forced us to use "dirty techniques". By working with the PSAC office in Ottawa we went over the heads of our provincial superintendents. Often we took our complaints to the opposition party in Parliament, which was always cooperative. MP Herb Gray, who was in opposition at the time, gave us valuable support. We also got strong support from radio talk shows in Ontario. All in all, we were a thorny nuisance to the government and they tried to force us to use proper procedures, but without success. They advised us of regulations in the books that we were required to obey, but they were afraid to enforce them. I don't know why.

In 1969 the PSAC in Ottawa chose me to be the Manitoba representative for Indian Affairs' teachers. In April of that year I flew to Ottawa to work on the Bargaining Committee with delegates from across Canada. It was our duty to take the resolutions that had come in from all the union locals, organize and combine them in logical form, and prioritize them. We were expected to know what the members from our province meant with their resolutions and which ones they rated most important. The result of our work then went to the Bargaining Team to use when bargaining with the government actually began.

We found that our values as professional teachers often clashed with the priorities of our union chiefs in Ottawa, who tended to be union people first, while we put our professional obligations first. In other words, they put the demand for higher wages on top, while we asked for an improved education system. Most of the teachers who resigned from Indian Affairs left solely because they could not cope with the problems of teaching on an Indian Reserve. Those who stayed were concerned about the failure of our schools to prepare the native children for the new world they were entering.

Organizing teachers' conventions was another area in which I assisted. My memory is sketchy here and I can only refer to two Convention programs which I have been able to locate. In the announcement for the 1966 Convention, at the Royal Alexandra Hotel in Winnipeg, I am listed as a member of the Committee. In the 1967 Convention I am listed as a member of the Executive. A basic reason for putting me in a position of some authority was to keep me from being a troublemaker. It is a technique I have often used with people under me and it works well. Actually, at this point, Indian Affairs officials made most of the decisions for organizing the conventions.

There was another convention which I organized almost alone, but the documents I have on hand do not give specific details. It came later and was held at the Fort Alexander School. It started in what was almost a confrontational situation.

We were having an in-service seminar at the Fort Alexander School and at the end, making his farewell statements, the Superintendent remarked that they wanted the teachers to take over the organization of the conventions. I realized that this statement most likely was just an empty promise, but I decided to take it seriously. Before he could walk away from the podium I spoke up, saying,

"But how can we do this without any organization, seeing we won't meet again all together for a year?"

"Well," he said, "I guess you could get organized now." The tone of his voice showed he was taken aback.

"I nominate Mr. Heinrichs to organize the next convention," one of the teachers spoke up without hesitation. Another seconded the motion.

That put me on the spot. I looked at the Superintendent and saw he was caught and afraid to back out. I had inadvertently acquired a new responsibility which I had hardly bargained for. I had to manoeuvre quickly.

I stood up and agreed to take over on the condition that I could choose a committee from the teachers present who, similar to me, could not refuse. I picked about five teachers, from different schools, so we would be a representative committee.

The Superintendent and I both left the meeting with mixed feelings. The development had taken place very speedily and without premeditation. Words can bring swift reactions.

I knew I would have to be very careful not to get into trouble with my superiors. I had a year to work on the project; it takes at least that much time to organize a convention. First I contacted the schools involved to get the teachers' suggestions for the convention agenda. Then I met with the committee to draw up a program for the convention from the suggestions we had received. We then sent the suggested program to the schools for further feedback. At each step I made a report to the Superintendent of the procedure we were following. He never acknowledged any of our reports.

The next step was to assemble the speakers that the convention would feature. Prominent people are often booked up well in advance and half a year's notice sometimes is too late. I can only remember a few details. We had a speaker from the Catholic School at the Qu'Appelle Indian Reserve who was a prominent person in the field of education on Indian Reserves. Also, we had a group from the Manitoba Theatre Centre who demonstrated the use of dramatics in classroom teaching.

As a result of our teamwork the convention proceeded smoothly. We had assigned a key role to the Superintendent to make sure he would be pleased. We also gave a prominent place to the Oral English program which was of special importance to the Department. The topic of "Guidance and Counseling in Indian Schools" also got serious attention. It resulted in our Guidance teacher losing his position when he could not defend himself. Twice the Superintendent attacked me publicly, but both times I was able to defend myself effectively, and thus came through unscathed. It was the last large convention we held, as the move was to replace them with smaller, less costly in-service seminars.

The date has slipped my memory but one of the years at Fort Alexander stood out in importance. It was a boom year; we had a lot of new teachers come in, and most of them stayed at Manitou Lodge in Pine Falls, where I was living. Many fine people entered my life at that time and stayed with me.

It was also a year in which the Department made more than its usual quota of mistakes. They may have changed their office procedures that year, I don't know. Many of the new teachers failed to get their pay cheques, and the cheques that did come were often wrong. School starts in September but one of the teachers did not get his first cheque until well into December. He came from Windsor, Ontario, and had serious problems coping without money. Everyone found it difficult when their cheques did not come. The excuse of Treasury Office was that they could not pay the teachers until they had supplied all their documentation. Teachers were not plentiful at the time, and it seems that the hiring officers had accepted many new teachers and put them to work before they had been fully documented. Our argument was that if a person has been hired and is doing his work he should be paid.

Our union had a lot of strong correspondence with the Department of Indian Affairs that year, plus a considerable variation of not too polite publicity. It was effective. The government set up a special fund so new teachers would receive interim cheques as soon as they started working. The next year was much quieter.

For some years the Department had been taking steps to train the native people to run their own affairs. It took time because the native people lived in almost complete ignorance of the outside world, even in 1964 when I first had contact with Indian Reserves.

The first step in bringing the native people into the contemporary scene was the School Committee, made up of prominent native people on each reserve. It was supposed to involve the people in the day to day operation of the schools. After a few years they began to realize what it was all about and began to seek more authority in running their own affairs. Today this movement has accelerated. The leaders have been slow to develop a sense of responsibility to the people they are serving, and to account for the money they are handling. This is still true today on many reserves.

It was in connection with this movement that I had a head-on encounter with a top official from Ottawa, around 1970. It was a large teachers' meeting sponsored by Indian Affairs, and there were about half a dozen superintendents present. Everything went smoothly until the last and keynote speaker took the floor. He came from Ottawa with a special message to the teachers concerning the impending takeover of the schools by the native people.

The teachers were fearful about the new developments but generally took a positive attitude to the needs of the Indian people. It came as a shock to us when the speaker warned us of the problems we would have with the Indian leaders and the difficulties that lay ahead of us when they took over. His speech was completely negative; what we needed was positive encouragement to prepare us for the coming changes.

I sat in amazement, frankly bewildered. When he closed his speech he made the customary remark, asking if anyone had a question or comment to make, but quickly turned around so as to avoid any questions.

However, I was on my feet and speaking before he had finished his last word. I told him in no uncertain words that his speech was completely out of place and unacceptable. I directly accused him that we had had more problems with the Department of Indian Affairs than we expected to have with the Indians, who had come to our help many times in the past when the Department had failed us.

My attack was unheard of; the officials were aghast at my audacity and erupted in an uproar against me. I was afraid they would "tar and feather me". No one had ever dared to publicly insult a top official from Ottawa before. I made my exit as soon as possible, though with difficulty.

No action was taken against me as a result of my attack. I never heard anything further about it. I had only spoken the truth.

During the winter of 1973 at Fort Alexander the Indians were beginning to feel their power and first flexed their muscles. They realized they had to exercise their powers to establish the fact that they actually had them. The event involved only the South Shore School which left me out of it as I taught at the North Shore School, a separate unit.

The affair can properly be called a “Kangaroo Court”. There had been complaints about the white teachers for some time and the Indian Chief and Band decided that they would hold their own court to deal with the matters. The date was set for a Sunday and the accused teachers were ordered to attend on threat of dismissal. I phoned the Superintendent in Winnipeg to ask for his assistance but he refused to become involved. I was not allowed to attend myself but I kept in close touch. I sat at a telephone and had several teachers at the school call me at intervals to keep me informed.

The Indian Band members had been called in to the meeting but no one else was allowed. The accused teachers were brought in one at a time and charges were brought against them. They had no defense. Some of the charges were silly, like wearing improper gym clothing. Some were more serious. One of the most highly qualified and most capable of the teachers was a Chinese girl from Dauphin. The Band felt insulted that the Department would send a “Chink” to teach in their schools. It was a serious matter for them and they warned her to leave the Reserve. About four teachers were told they would not be rehired at the end of the year, and several were advised to leave sooner. A number of others were warned that they also might be forced out. However, order at the court was well maintained and no violence occurred.

It should be noted that at this time the Chief had already moved into the school and taken over the Principal’s office, who had been forced to find other quarters. To all appearances the Chief was already in charge of the school. The situation on the South Shore was very fluid that year. Several times the Chief had to take his family into Winnipeg for reasons of safety because he was being attacked on the Reserve by rebels against his authority.

The teachers accused at the “Kangaroo Court” all decided to stay but several were brought under such heavy verbal abuse in the school that they broke down under the strain. When they collapsed mentally they left the reserve and their teaching position. The Chinese teacher was one of them. It only took her a few weeks before she picked up a better teaching position in a large school in Edmonton.

I kept on warning teachers that our union contract with PSAC gave us little protection on the reserve, and the Department of Indian Affairs would do little to protect us. What we needed was to negotiate with the Indian people and make an agreement with them, preferably with the national alliance of Indian Bands. The teachers agreed, verbally, but I could not lead them to action.

Another event happened in the beginning of June that year. The Chief closed the school for Friday and called a general meeting for Friday and Saturday to deal with school problems. This time it included both schools on the Fort Alexander Reserve and involved about 30 teachers.

For some reason the Chief had to go to Winnipeg the first day and as a result our discussions were relatively peaceful. The Band had chosen about 30 to 50 prominent members from the reserve to work with us. The teachers themselves were well aware that the school system was failing the native children and were fully open to suggestions for changes in the system. There was little antagonism between the two groups. However, when the Chief returned home that evening and heard the results of the day's sessions he was not pleased.

The next day the Chief took over the proceedings. He told us straight that he was not satisfied with Friday's discussions. All we were doing was sweeping their complaints "under the rug" and the day for that was *past*, he warned us. He wanted action! I could see he was determined to start a fight.

The Chief became decidedly antagonistic. The teachers began to mumble—they felt they were not to blame for the situation; they had little choice but to do what the Department told them to do. Besides, they got very little support from the parents.

I realized it would take my utmost ability to prevent an all-out battle. I stood up and spoke with the strongest voice of authority I could muster. It was necessary for me to control the teachers. I told the teachers we could not defend ourselves, that we had to take the blame for what was happening in the schools. Then I told the Chief we had no recourse but to listen to him. We needed change in the schools to give the children a better education and we looked to him to bring it about.

The teachers quieted down and raised no further protests. The Chief was stunned. He had expected me to fight back. Probably he had never encountered a situation like this before. It took a while before anyone spoke again. Then slowly the Indian people started talking, realizing the teachers had a difficult job to perform and got little support from the parents. The people present showed a lot of wisdom and by lunch time the antagonism was over. Even the Chief softened up and put away his belligerence. He called a picnic for the afternoon and ordered refreshments for the teachers. Many differences were smoothed over in friendly personal discussions that afternoon and a number of teachers were rehired. The affair ended with a much better understanding between Indians and teachers.

For me it was an amazing victory. I had humbly turned the “other cheek” and won the battle. The school year ended with amicable relations between all. It was also my last year at Fort Alexander.

Sad to say, the peace did not last long.

The next year relations worsened again and conflict became the rule, more often than not. The Indians were pushing to establish their powers and the teachers were shortsighted and afraid of change. The Department of Indian Affairs sadly lacked leadership. They were firmly addicted to the old policy of “let sleeping dogs lie” but the “dogs” were no longer asleep.

Indian Affairs officials were of little help in dealing with the problems that Indians and teachers faced. Indeed, considering the meagre efforts they made to fulfil their responsibilities, it is difficult to see how their positions were justified.

For some years I had been making suggestions for changes in our school system, through written reports as well as verbal discussions. Only some pupils successfully finished Elementary School, very few finished High School. The school did little to prepare them for the complicated and strange world they faced in adulthood.

During my last year I worked with PSAC to make them realize we needed a new system of dealing with the Indian Bands. Our union agreement made no sense to the Indians. As a result of my efforts, PSAC appointed a special person to look into the problem. I had lengthy discussions with him and he even visited me in Winnipeg after I had already left Indian Affairs. However, after my departure I could no longer keep up the work, and without my efforts the move soon vanished.

The whole situation has shown little improvement to this day. Indian schools are still failing the children and officials are playing politics to protect their positions.

OXFORD HOUSE INDIAN RESERVE

Oxford House Indian Reserve is situated on Oxford Lake, about 100 miles northeast of Lake Winnipeg, far out in Manitoba's northern wilderness. It is mainly serviced by air, but in wintertime a road is opened over frozen lakes and land so truck traffic can come in.

The area is beautiful; my first impression was, this is where I would like to settle down. I thought of all the interesting things I could do here. With a motorboat I could travel all over the lake and probably some rivers as well. Fishing was excellent. With a skidoo the whole wilderness was open to explore. The reserve had a good road about five miles long and a number of vehicles had been brought in on the winter road. A motorcycle would be just wonderful for the summer; I could use it on the road and also on many of the trails. Sad to say, there were many problems attached to these attractive prospects.

The reserve itself could have been so beautiful, but the people had no pride at all in their surroundings. The whole reserve area was literally covered with garbage from one end to the other. I have heard many white people expound on the native people's attachment to their land but from all the evidence I saw it was certainly a lazy, dirty and careless attachment. Garbage is thrown out of the house through the windows and the wind and the dogs scatter it all over. I was overwhelmed! The concept that the land belongs to everyone in common means that no one person can clean up his own area because others will immediately mess it up. Everything works down to the lowest common denominator.

The teachers' housing was all new in 1975, the year I was posted to Oxford House, and we were its first occupants. The school was not quite completed but ready for us to start classes. It was an ideal situation for the teachers. A lot of money had been spent on the school, with a good gym and a well-stocked library. The teachers' units likewise were built to a good standard and were comfortable.

The first day of school was spent assigning the teachers to the various classes and to special duties, acquainting them with the new school and the reserve, and with special instructions. One special instruction was that one of the main school entrances would remain closed until the construction crew had left the reserve. The housing for the workmen was located at that end of the school yard. The principal explained that we had to keep the girls away from the workers' bedrooms or else we'd never get them back into the school again that day. At first the teachers hesitated to take this seriously but the principal explained they had had a lot of problems with the girls during the summer. He also warned us to keep the bedroom windows shut in our own units. The previous year a teacher had found a native girl in his bed when he retired for the night. She had come in through the window.

Most of the teachers were young, except the nuns and I. Most of the teachers were married couples, with both spouses teaching, except myself and a young lady teacher recently immigrated from the Philippines. The result was that in many activities Cata and I were put together to act as another couple. She was attractive enough but I could have wished for another partner. She was an active person but did not feel safe walking alone in the reserve, so she usually dragged me along wherever she wanted to go. Of course, I had to go to many of the same places, such as the stores and the Post Office, and it was better than sitting at home. It also led to gossip among the native people.

One week we had a number of servicemen doing a special job on the reserve. Several of them were married Filipino men. Naturally, Cata was happy to visit with persons of her own ethnic group, but she was a little too excited with them. Our motel units were fairly close together. At 10:00 p.m. that night she knocked at my door. She explained that the Filipino men were in her unit and they wouldn't leave, they wanted to go to bed with her. She wanted me to come and put them out. I said she should have expected this when she asked them in for a visit, but my advice was too late. She finally persuaded me to come over but, fortunately, we found the men had left on their own.

Another evening, about 10:00 p.m., Cata knocked on my door again. It wasn't men this time, it was the furniture. She couldn't stand it the way it was arranged and she needed help to push it around. So I went over and helped her move the furniture. The next evening she was back again but a little later. She couldn't sleep because the furniture was still in the wrong place. So we moved furniture again but it wasn't the end of the problem. She was back on the third night, more cranky than ever. We pushed the furniture back into the arrangement it had been before we started moving it. By this time I was getting crabby myself. I told her this was it and there would be no more furniture moving. It was experiences such as these that helped me lose my interest in women.

But we had more serious matters to cope with than women. Our motel unit was new and had not been through cold weather. When the temperature dropped we found the heating system could not raise our room temperature above 50 degrees Fahrenheit. The heating system was located in a crawl space below the motel building. I went down myself, with the caretaker, to try the adjustments but nothing worked. The furnace was set as high as possible. Servicemen were brought in from other places but no one could adjust the furnace. It looked as if we might have to find other lodging. Finally they brought in a proper serviceman from Winnipeg and he fixed it with a few simple adjustments. Indian Affairs does the right thing only after everything else has been tried.

"Native Power" was slowly becoming a reality on the reserves and Oxford House was no exception. The Indians can control who comes onto the reserve and have the right to expel anyone they don't like on 48 hours notice. It is a very effective tool. They had expelled one teacher the previous year and were itching to do it again. They were well aware of the principle that you have to use your powers to retain them and strengthen them.

The Band put a full time home-school coordinator into the school to witness personally what was going on in school and report back to the Indian Council. In plain words, a spy. She was a young married woman with a family. She was capable and intelligent and, as it turned out, fair and honest as well. In fact, instead of being a spy, she gave the teachers all the support she could. When a substitute teacher was needed she often took over the classroom and thus was fully aware of a teacher's problems. We seldom find persons of her quality and integrity among the white people. The Chief, who was also a woman, likewise was an excellent person whom I learned to respect.

Once a month the Band held a meeting with the teachers to allow reserve people to bring complaints against the teachers. Most complaints related to discipline problems in the school. Some of the meetings were rather loud but we managed to get through the year without any teachers being expelled. Personally, I never had any attack directed against me at these sessions.

Dogs were a problem on the reserve. I don't understand why the Indians kept dogs but it must be a matter of tradition. It was criminal the way they treated their dogs. In summer the dogs could manage by scavenging for garbage or by hunting wildlife. In winter things were tough and the dogs were kept tied up among the trees. We could hear them barking and howling all night. By spring they were starved to skin and bones, and then they were turned loose again so they could hunt. The problem was they would turn wild and form packs. This happened one day. They formed a long line of dogs and raced in large circles howling like wolves. That afternoon the pack came right through the settlement and hauled a baby out of a baby carriage as the mother was pushing the carriage. The mother and baby were visiting on the reserve. Norah (see below) was outside at the time and saw the incident. Fortunately there was a man with a gun not far away and he shot the dog. Otherwise the baby would have been killed. The Band Council met the next day and ordered that all dogs running loose should be shot. A lot of dogs were killed and it became safe to go outside again.

Due to some political wrangling the airstrip at Oxford House was closed the whole year I was there. That only meant there was no one in the office. The planes came in and out as usual but they just dumped their loads on the ground. The Postmistress would meet the plane with the outgoing mail and pick up the mail that was brought in. Usually there were other people around who would take the goods and bring them into the airstrip building. They would also spread the word around for people to come and get their parcels. It was messy but it worked. In the North you learn to survive and cope with whatever situation you face, while the politicians sit in their comfortable offices and argue.

During the school break at Easter time I travelled to Toronto, where Norah and I were married on April 1. She came back with me to Oxford House, well dressed for the "North", only to find it was warmer there than it had been in Toronto when we left. It was a very nice spring in the north that year and Norah enjoyed tramping through the reserve—an all-new experience for her, although she was frightened by the dog incident.

The teachers loved to socialize and we had many enjoyable times together. One time Norah, I and two young male teachers sat down for a card game of rummy. The two guys were ribbing each other all through the game, acting tough, as young fellows like to do. I thought nothing of it because I was used to it. Norah played quietly saying very little. Also, she was leading with her score almost to the finish, when I managed to top her. She sort of showed up the "tough guys".

The next day when I came home for lunch she asked me about the "big fight" that had happened. I hadn't heard anything about a fight, I told her, and we dropped the subject.

However, at supper time she brought up the subject again and I was curious about what had happened. I finally realized she was referring to what had happened at our rummy game last night. She was sure the two men had been seriously angry with each other. I assured her that the two fellows were only having a good time with their "tough talk". She couldn't understand it, and it was only as she watched them during the following days that she accepted my explanation, but it made no sense to her. She was experiencing a major cultural change coming from "proper Toronto" to the "Wild West". She had also stepped down from the upper middle class to the ordinary lower class. She tried to understand, but at times she found my "Wild West" manners not wholly to her satisfaction. However, she was always open to new experiences and I believe that on the whole she enjoyed her stay at Oxford House.

Oxford House could have been a wonderful place if it hadn't been for the people. Our principal was a very capable teacher and a fine person to work under. He had many years of experience in Indian schools. During those years he had made an enemy of another teacher. This teacher had become a superintendent, and during the year I was at Oxford House he was put in charge of the area which included our school. I had no problems with the new superintendent myself, but we soon all realized that the enmity between him and our principal had almost mortal dimensions. We realized that the new superintendent identified us with the principal and that the sooner we left the better. About half of the teachers quit at the end of the year. All the rest, except two nuns, were forced out the next year. The new superintendent "cleaned the slate". It is sad to think that such things still happen in a supposedly civilized country.

ITALIAN CITIES

Venice

The old part of Venice is a city that excites the imagination. It is not only old, it is ancient. It throbs with history, its buildings are adorned with the costliest of ornamentation, and the whole area is sinking into the sea. Indeed, in certain weather conditions the sea invades and covers the streets.

Takayuki, my Japanese friend, and I noticed an advertisement for a two-week tour to Italy for students over the Easter holidays. The price was right so we decided to go.

We were excited about Venice, the first city we visited. Venice was often referred to in the French and English literature I have studied and it has acquired a strong romantic character. The part it has played in history strengthens this romantic reputation. Our dreams became reality one afternoon when we arrived in Venice.

Our tour bus stopped at the hostel where we would be staying for several days. We took our suitcases off the bus and scrambled for suitable beds, wasting no time. The whole group was excited. Somebody pointed out which direction to go for city streetcars and off we went. We had a good distance to go from our hostel to the old part of Venice.

We had no sooner pushed our way onto the first streetcar when we realized we did not know what we were doing. We spoke very little Italian and the driver did not understand French. However, he made it clear that we were on the wrong streetcar. He also gave us the number of the car we wanted. When we got on the right tram, we found out the fare depended on the distance we wanted to travel. This, however, was easy because we were going to the end of the line.

Old Venice is located on an island and the streetcar had to cross a long causeway to reach it. It dropped us off in a large staging area, like a railway yard. (According to the map it is a railway yard. There is a harbour on the island and the train takes the freight to and from the ships.) We had to cross a bridge to get to Old Venice so off we went, on the run. Walking was too slow for us.

There is no car or truck traffic in Old Venice. The Grand Canal makes a large S-curve through the island, carrying sea water from one side to the other. The whole area is honeycombed with smaller canals so boats have access to most buildings. The streets are mainly for walking.

Some streets were so narrow that by stretching out my arms I could touch a building on each side. The bridges across the Grand Canal were arched to make it easy for boats to pass underneath. They also had roofs overhead. There were boats everywhere on the canals.

When evening approached it suddenly occurred to me that I had not taken note of the address of our hostel, nor did I know which streetcar to take to get there. In my excitement I had acted very foolishly. I looked around until I found Takayuki, and I stayed with him until we had to return for the night. He was never at a loss for the information we needed.

The next day we continued our explorations. The most popular place was a large open courtyard around the Palais des Doges. Beside the palace is a large tower and on the other side of the court is the Basilique San Marco. The church is not imposing from the outside but the inside is marvelous. It looks as if all the walls are covered with layers of gold. The sculptures and ornamentation are fantastic.

We had an exciting time at Old Venice and the time there passed quickly. We also visited Bologna and Florence, and then headed for Rome.

Rome

Rome is not only the capital of Italy but a city with a tremendous worldwide history. It was founded by Romulus who, with his twin brother Remus, had been nursed by a she-wolf about eight centuries before Christ, as tradition relates the story. When the city of Rome grew into a powerful nation it became the ruler of the known world. It has never ceased to be an important city, and it continues to have worldwide influence through the Catholic Church which is governed by the Vatican.

As our tour bus approached Rome it became clear that the driver was in strange territory and was very uncertain of himself. He probably didn't even have a decent map. Takayuki was sitting on needles; he had prepared himself fully for the trip and knew exactly what route we should be taking. He could have gone to the front and directed the driver, but he was afraid the driver would be insulted. After we had passed several highway exits leading to Rome the driver decided to exit and find his way into the city. He had exited too early and spent an extra hour making his way through narrow streets.

Our destination was a youth hostel on a main street and the driver had the number. However, he had to drive up and down the street several times because there was no such number nor hostel in sight. Finally he realized that it must be off the street behind a large building, and that's where we found it.

Excitement in the bus was running high as we found our destination. But you wouldn't guess what the excitement was all about. In Venice it had been the OLD CITY but here it was ICE CREAM. Parisians have heard about ice cream, but usually they travel to Holland to get it. In Paris it is made of highly flavoured, coloured water, and it tastes awful. Another product we were unable to buy in Paris was coffee cream.

No sooner had we put our suitcases into the dormitory than we were off to find an ice cream bar. Fortunately, there was a place close by and we thoroughly enjoyed the ice cream, a rare treat for Parisians. After that we returned to our senses and acted normal again.

This time I made certain I had our address written down before I ventured away from our domicile. I had learned my lesson in Venice.

Rome is truly a wonderful city. The old part of the city, Ancient Rome, is naturally the first and most important attraction. The Palatino is the oldest area but there are many other old buildings scattered throughout the city. The Palatino was still in a state of excavation, with rubble lying around all over. We were allowed to enter the area but the work was only half finished.

Not far away we could see the famous amphitheatre, or Colosseum, where the gladiators fought each other and the Christians were torn by the lions. To approach it we walked through the arch built by Constantine to glorify his victory parades. History acquired a graphic reality as we walked this parade route and into the buildings where so many glorious or cruel events had taken place.

One day as we were walking near the Colosseum we met some of our friends. They had found an interesting place to eat nearby and asked us to join them. We liked the idea. The place was just a large house among other houses. The host led us through their living room, through several bedrooms, and finally into a room with a large table surrounded by chairs. Here we ordered our meals and were served, spending a few happy hours together while eating an excellent home-cooked meal. It was the kind of experience I look back to with fond memories of Rome.

Another interesting area I visited several times was the Villa Borghese located in northern Rome. Evidently it had been a large estate with a palace in former times. Now it is a public park area, with pools and many intricate garden areas. I found it an intriguing place to walk and spend time.

One day I walked through Hadrian's Mausoleum, a huge circular tomb, which rates next to the Colisseum for its great size. It has walkways and chambers inside but has the feeling of being a large solid mass. During the centuries it was converted into a large fortress and was connected to the Vatican by underground tunnels. Its immensity is impressive.

The Vatican is indeed a magnificent set of buildings. Postcard pictures do not at all give a true concept of its great size. As I was in

Rome over Easter I went to the Vatican on Easter morning to listen to the Pope's annual Easter Day sermon. The crowd gathered outside in front of St. Peter's was immense; there must have been about 75,000 people in the square. It was an event to be remembered.

On another day Takayuki and I went to walk through St. Peter's Cathedral and to see the Vatican Art Gallery. The cathedral is unbelievably large and has retained its religious atmosphere, in contrast to Westminster Abbey in London. The art gallery is excellent and compares favourably with any other art gallery I have seen. The Sistine Chapel was in the process of having its paintings cleaned to restore them to their original lustre, but that did not keep us from enjoying the unsurpassed genius of its art. We came away with a deep reverence for the great achievements of Michelangelo.

All Christians must have heard of the persecution of the early Christians in Rome and how they hid in the catacombs to protect themselves. I wanted to see the catacombs, so I took a tour bus out of town to see them, a drive of about half an hour. It was weird, because the highway we took was flanked on both sides by high solid walls of stone; we couldn't see the countryside. It felt like we were driving in a tunnel. But it was even more weird when we went down into the earth and walked around in the dark, gloomy underground tunnels and realized this was where our early Christian brothers and sisters lived for years in danger, and often died there too. History often is unbelievable until you walk in the same paths, and then it has strange transforming powers. It felt much the same as walking around in the Colisseum.

Our tour was supposed to take us to Naples and Pompeii, but our bus broke down in Rome and by the time it was repaired we had to head back home.

THE CLASSROOM

"Are you having fun?"

They were the first words she asked me as I met one of the professors who had taught me a few years earlier at Teachers College. My answer was a little shaky; it took me a number of years before I learned how to work positively with children, but I carefully guarded her question in my mind as I sought to develop my teaching abilities.

There are several principles that have guided my philosophy of teaching. Children love to work; they are not lazy! If they slouch off, the reasons lie elsewhere. Secondly, the secret of good discipline is good teaching. Several of my principals have emphasized this, and I realized they could go into any classroom and demonstrate their claim. It's easier to blame the pupils when they fail but basically the teacher should look at himself.

Looking at teaching methods, I found that the most important factor for me was to be fully prepared to teach as soon as I walked into a classroom. On entering, I walked to the blackboard, wrote down the page number of the text we were using, and then turned to the class. They were just settling down in their seats but I immediately picked on the noisiest one. "Why haven't you got your book out?" If he didn't know what I meant I just pointed to the blackboard. As I circulated among the pupils it only took a minute until everyone was ready.

My Daily Plan Book was always written up, and I carried full lesson outlines with me so I could start teaching without any hesitation. However, even the best made plans don't always work out. In case this should happen I carried alternative lesson material with me which I could use at a moment's notice. It has happened that my regular lesson did not work out, so I just stopped and took out some material I had tested before and knew would work. The pupils appreciate it when the teacher realizes he has made a mistake. As a rule I also kept a good book handy so I could read an interesting story to the pupils to keep the classroom atmosphere from deteriorating.

During my time as a teacher the school classroom underwent a transformation from a rigidly structured place to a more open or freer area. The military atmosphere was replaced by a friendlier structure. The "open-area" school was the ultimate goal but it proved to be a mistake and did not last very long. Each teaching group needs to have its own classroom but that is where a more open structure is feasible.

Every teaching situation needs to be treated as unique and not be over-controlled by rules from above. Superintendents don't appreciate this but teachers insist they need to develop a system that will work for them and their classrooms. When a teacher's classroom functions successfully, supervisors usually are satisfied and don't argue about specific rules. That has been my experience.

In Indian schools generally it is useless to assign homework. The conditions in the home make it impossible for kids to do school work at home. I limited my teaching time and gave the pupils enough time to do all their work during class periods. While they were studying I went around and helped the pupils personally with their problems, and corrected their work at their desks. It worked out very well. The pupils who needed it got a lot of personal help and the others could spend their free time reading a book. It was a good system.

At the beginning of a class, during the teaching part, I insisted that pupils sit in proper orderly rows. That only took about ten minutes. Then I let them sit where they wanted. They could change seats, push them together, or sit at larger library tables in the back. I found that even if they sat side by side they would not copy from each other. Indian children avoided cheating and tried to do their own work.

At one school in a Grade 6 classroom, I had acquired a very special set of Readers which we kept on a separate shelf. They were extraordinary and could be used in many different ways. When school started to get boring I would take a class period to use these books. As soon as I announced my decision the kids knew what to do. The desks were moved together into a solid block and I had to scramble to get hold of a desk and get into the mob. The classroom was transformed in a minute and we had a full period of learning fun, which passed very quickly. I wonder what happened to those books? Probably I was the only one who ever used them.

Stimulations came from various directions with the result that I kept on trying different teaching methods. In Grade 6 Social Studies we took History of Canada and this presented some new opportunities for me. We did not have a specific textbook for the course but instead had a good assortment of books covering specific periods. I also brought in a stack of books from the library for the pupils to use. I divided the course into specific subject or time areas, such as: Explorers on the Oceans, Explorers on Land, The Indian Tribes, The Habitants, etc. Then I made an assignment booklet listing the persons and topics in a subject area. The pupil had to report on a minimum number of these questions but he could choose which ones. Each question required a write-up, a drawing to illustrate the answer, and a map if possible. I provided blank maps. The assignment booklet suggested books to study for different topics, and the pupil had to list which books he used. Some kids were good at writing, others did better with their drawings. They all did well with the project.

When they were finished with a question they brought their papers in to me to be checked. If satisfactory, they were put into a paper envelope; each pupil had a separate envelope. When a subject area was finished, all a pupil's papers were stapled into a booklet. At the end of the year, a pupil had finished about six booklets. The pupil had learned how to do research study on his own and had solid proof in his hands to show what he had accomplished. It also resulted in an orderly, quiet classroom.

At Oxford House I had a Grade 8 class for Social Studies. Our classroom was small, so we had three rows of desks close together from side to side. The first morning when the students came in I took a good look at them and realized they would require a supreme effort—all I could handle. Half of the boys were taller than I was, and they all occupied the front row of seats. They wanted to be right up front where the action was—an unusual situation. As a rule, the big boys always head for the back seats. There was little room left in front, so I shoved my desk into the corner and we were ready for action.

The course consisted of World History and World Geography. The texts were interesting but poorly written. My experience is that most authors of textbooks have flunked their English exams. However, the subject matter was interesting and I was determined that we would have fun in our class—the only way I could see to cope with this group. My aim was to keep these kids in school by entertaining them with Social Studies, even if they did not learn much from an academic point of view. A factor that helped me was that about every other week the R.C.M.P. took away about three to five of the worst boys on some criminal charges, which eased the tension for a week.

My usual procedure was to discuss the subject of the day and then put a bare outline on the blackboard to be filled in with notes. The students read the text and suggested what I should write on the blackboard. This led into further discussion on what the book actually said, and the arguments led the students to read carefully to support their suggestions. If we happened to find a section in the textbook that was well written, I asked the students to make notes on their own and hand their notebooks in to me for correction.

When I asked my students for written work I considered it an important task and I expected their best. In return I did my part—I personally read and corrected everything they wrote. My students knew that everything they wrote was important to me. Another policy was that I never marked mistakes. Instead I checked off in red ink the answers that were correct. This allowed a student to correct his mistakes and hand his notebook back to me to get more check marks. Periodically I added up how many correct checks a student had and this I used for his standing on his report card. With this system, in arithmetic I expected a student to have all his answers correct on every page.

To get back to my Social Studies class, we did enjoy our studies that year and I can report that I never once lost control of that group. Teachers rotated from room to room for different subjects and it happened fairly often the classroom would go out of control with other teachers. Then the Principal would have to come in to restore order.

The teaching of English was another area of instruction that required a lot of imagination. Grammar has gone out of fashion and the result is that the teaching of English is a subject with little substance. It has also become a boring subject for students. My experience is that if properly taught, grammar can be an interesting study.

We started our English lessons with simple exercises. First we chose a noun and wrote it on a circle of paper. Then we made petals to go around the noun, to make it look like a flower. Each petal had an adjective modifying the noun. It was a challenge to see how many adjectives we could find for different nouns. It was fun! Then we used the nouns in sentences and wrote them on the blackboard. Now we could work with verbs and adverbs as well. Slowly the sentences became more difficult as we worked with them together on the blackboard. Then we went into phrases and clauses. Working together, the pupils kept up a high level of enthusiasm. After this the pupils would write their own sentences and mark the various parts with a system we developed. Writing sentences becomes fun when you can do things with its parts.

Another method of teaching started by having pupils do some creative writing. From this I picked out a number of faulty sentences. These sentences I put into a new assignment and made copies for the pupils. Then they had to correct the sentences or rewrite them. We then put them on the blackboard to correct together. It became an exciting challenge.

Next we studied paragraphs. Rules for writing paragraphs are fairly simple, but when we looked for examples of good paragraphs in other textbooks we were in trouble. Even the English text had few good paragraphs. I was shocked at the discovery. What's wrong with textbook authors?

I seldom followed the text we had for teaching English, but in my Daily Plan Book I wrote up my lesson plans as if I was. The Superintendent might walk in at any time and examine my Plan Book and I needed to satisfy him. It was almost a crime for us to be teaching grammar. As far as actual teaching was concerned, I ascertained the needs and weaknesses of my students and taught them the English skills they lacked.

At Fort Alexander I had an excellent Grade 5 class one year that I will never forget. They had an exceptional teacher the year before and I reaped the benefits of her abilities. It seemed everything I tried with them turned out a success. I divided the class into groups of four or five pupils, letting them choose who they wanted to be with. They could then work together as a group on various activities. This included singing, choral reading or doing a short play. They could write the poem for the choral reading or choose it from books. The same thing held for the plays. If they finished their regular work early they could practice what they wanted. It provided some real incentive for them. When the class had time we would listen to a group perform. We also had a number of pupils who sang duets or solos without hesitation. We started devoting an hour, on Friday afternoons, to a special program when they could perform for the class. The pupils set up the program without me. By the end of the year this program took up most of the afternoon. This was a feature I carried over into succeeding years with other groups. The small groups did not work too well with later classes but I changed the format somewhat and we continued with the activities.

I usually taught a short course in music at the beginning of the school year before my voice deteriorated from too much talking. I had a simple procedure. First we learned how to clap a rhythm, choosing a song with a 3/4 rhythm. After the pupils had an idea of rhythm we went on to study the scale in the key of C. We wrote in the notes and memorized them. Then we sang the scale, taking the note from a tuning device I had. We put measures on the scale and wrote in the notes of our song. This meant we had to learn the value of notes to get three beats into each measure. Again we clapped the rhythm. Then we sang the notes to scale and brought in the rhythm by clapping. Finally, we used the words of the song instead of the names of the notes. It was an interesting study and the kids enjoyed it.

After this preparation we were ready to continue singing songs we already knew and learn new ones. We did a lot of singing during the year and chose songs that were enjoyable. When studies became boring, it often provided a good break to stand up and sing a lively song. We learned songs like "Allouette" in French or "The Kelligrews Soiree", which was more to the boys' liking. The older boys had trouble with their voices, so whenever possible they would play out the action of the song. A real favourite was "The Raftsmen", which is made up of action. While the rest of the class is singing, the boys "pack their grub, row away in their canoes, complain about the food, chop down the trees, and at the end of the year collect their pay". One of the girls would take the position of a clerk and hand out the money. Then the boys came home to meet their ladies, who were waiting to greet them with a kiss. This part usually broke down as boys don't like to be kissed, but it gave the girls a chance to chase them.

We did a lot of work with short plays, from books or plays which the pupils wrote themselves. One play had mother and daughter in the kitchen baking cookies. The two boys are outside fooling around. Then they smell the cookies baking and sit down under the kitchen window.

When the cookies are done mother puts them on the window-sill to cool. Before long the boys take down the cookies and start eating them. When mother and daughter realize what is happening they rush out to get the boys. The rule was that if the boys could get out of the classroom and into the hall before getting caught they were safe, but if the girls caught them they had to come back and wash the kitchen floor while mother and sister are watching them. The production was always hilarious.

I usually took a few minutes everyday to read a chapter from an interesting book, like *Tom Sawyer*. If well read, this provides a good distraction. But sometimes we needed something more physical. I had a strong twine stretched across the middle of the classroom, and in a cupboard we had three balloons, blown up. When I gave the signal "Get out the balloons", the first person went for them and in seconds the kids had separated into teams and were punching the balloons across the line, me included. After three minutes of lively action I called it off and we were ready to get back to our studies again. There was never any trouble settling down.

Art classes also became a major event. I am poor as an artist but I had collected many super ideas from other teachers and that was all we needed. Pattern making is one form of art we started from simple steps and worked up into complicated designs. The kids would easily pick up my ideas and develop them into their own forms. In other lessons I would just put up a few examples illustrating some technique, and ask them to use this technique to draw their own pictures. They were always careful to create their own pictures and not copy what I had put up. In contrast, in a white classroom I have had half of the pupils just copy the example that I put up for them to look at.

Bloodvein in the North was a different experience. Our resources there were limited so we took advantage of whatever we had. The school was situated beside the Bloodvein River and in fall when the water froze we had an excellent surface for skating. The Mission provided skates for all the kids and when recess came we put on our skates and went out on the ice. It was fun and recess usually took us half an hour, but it was worth it. Once the snow came, the fun ended.

It was a practice in Indian schools that we always provided a bowl of soup for each pupil at lunch time. Evidently they got little to eat if they went home. The soup came from a large tin but it was good hearty soup. This took up the first half of the lunch hour. Then we had to take turns at playground duty during the last half hour. When I was free I mostly used the time to prepare for afternoon classes, picking up AV equipment, films, etc. The result was that I had little time to eat lunch myself and I slowly got out of the habit. The same thing happened with recess break. While the other teachers gathered in the staff room I used the time to prepare for classes or correct assignments. I have already discussed the problems my superiors had with me on the political level but they seldom had any complaints with my work as a teacher.

In case you think I am trying to create the impression I was a very successful teacher, I will relate another anecdote. My Grade 9 Social Studies class at Oxford House was a small group, about 12 students, an ideal group. I felt relaxed when I entered the classroom and I enjoyed teaching them. That is, until one day in wintertime. They suddenly decided they had had enough of me. At first I was shocked, then I realized they had me in a corner. The boys had a way of disturbing the class that I could not control. On thinking it over I suspected they were tired of the sound of my voice, and it is true I was doing too much talking with them. I discussed the problem with the Principal, the only time I have been forced to do that. I changed my method of teaching completely and stopped talking. I made up assignment booklets so the students could study on their own and I settled down to correcting their papers and helping them personally where needed. I was deeply disappointed with myself about my inability to handle this class.

Now I shall tell of an experience in a white school. I was teaching literature to a Grade 10 class consisting of 56 students, It was a handful, absolutely all I could handle. A number of the students were exceptionally bright. Two years later, on finishing high school, several of them won top Manitoba awards for excellence in their studies. The first exam time came and good students are always worried. The exam paper I set was difficult. The day after the exam the students discussed the questions and found they had answered them very differently. They came to me and wanted to know who was right. I still had not corrected the papers but I told them the questions could be answered with a different approach and it depended on how well they developed their arguments. The day I handed back the papers they were eagerly waiting to see what I had done with them. It was only after they saw their marks that they believed what I had told them. Literature is not judged on the basis of right and wrong but requires a much deeper understanding.

However, not all the students in the above class were bright. About a third of them had been automatically promoted grade after grade up to Grade 10, which was the policy in that school. They could not cope with the work I was assigning to the class. I also taught their German course. A group of the boys came to me and begged me not to force them to do all of the assignments I was giving to the class. They said they just couldn't understand the work. I thought about it and realized it was true. They should never have been promoted to Grade 10. I told them to do what they could and we'd leave it at that.

My conclusion consists in repeating what I have said before: children love to work, but they need a bit of inspiration and understanding, and they must be allowed to express themselves. Above all, the teacher should treat them as equals.

BOBCAYGEON

Bobcaygeon is a scenic tourist town about 100 miles northeast of Toronto. It is located 22 miles northeast of Lindsay and about 35 miles northwest of Peterborough. The village is built on three islands situated between Sturgeon Lake and Pigeon Lake, and extends its borders on the north and south shores. It was on the north shore of Pigeon Lake within the village that Norah's cousin, Reg Blyth, bought a house including two lots with lake frontage rights, around 1948.

Reg's parents took Norah in when she became an orphan at age ten and she grew up with Reg and Alan, her other cousin, as brothers and sister. Reg died at the age of 57 with cancer in 1959 and Norah inherited the property. Family ties were very important to Norah, and for her it continued to be Reg's property for many years. Reg had hired Fred Jones to take care of the place and he continued to do so after Reg died and even after our marriage. He was paid for his work, but for him it was a privilege that he could still continue to serve Reg Blyth. All the people I have met who worked for Reg felt the same way. He developed a high spirit of loyalty in all who were associated with him. He had a strong personality and a very powerful mind, according to people who knew him. He was a civil engineer and became a bridge contractor, becoming one of Canada's top bridge builders. He built the Thousand Islands bridge across the St. Lawrence River at Ivy Lea, which is Canada's longest bridge.

Bobcaygeon is a popular area for Toronto people, where they love to spend their free time boating, fishing and enjoying other tourist activities. When Norah and I were married in 1976 we both gave up our jobs and planned to retire to Bobcaygeon. However, we first spent a year at the University of Manitoba and then a year at the University of Paris, just living at Bobcaygeon during in-between intervals. Norah found it difficult to let me become part of her Bobcaygeon property on account of its connection with Reg Blyth, although I had discussed this problem with her before our marriage. It continued to affect our relations for some years. Fred Jones took a more realistic attitude and I soon established good relations with him.

Norah's property consisted of two lots on Pigeon Lake at 131 Riverside Drive, an upper-class area. The place has a large, impressive entrance with a wide, double-winged iron gate leading into a circular driveway. The house is L-shaped, about 40 by 40 feet, with a large stone fireplace in the centre of the living room. It has a lot of windows: six single, three double, two picture and a bay window. Besides the fireplace, it has electric heat in every room plus an oil heater in the living room. It also has two washrooms.

Besides the house there are three other buildings. The boathouse is situated at the end of a 25 foot dock, about four feet below the level of the lot. The second building is a split-level affair. It is called Mike's house because Mike, the former family cat, used it as his domain. Its back side comes up to the east edge of the lot, which borders on a fire lane leading to the lake. The lane served to give fire trucks easy access to a supply of water. This lane is lower than the lot level so the bottom part of the building is used as a garage with entrance from the back lane. When I took over, this part was filled with logs and old lumber, enough to supply the fireplace for many years. The front door of Mike's house is even with the lot level and opens into a room with two built-in beds. It also has an oil heater and sink. Stairs lead up into a higher level which is also intended to be a bedroom. Mostly we used the building for storage purposes.

The third building is just as complicated. First of all it is a garage. Here the ceiling opens up and there is a storage area under the roof piled up with doors, lumber, and wood panels for closing up the house windows during the winter when it is not occupied. Walking through the garage part we come into a small workshop. The building also contains a bedroom and laundry room with entrances from the side. The laundry room has a shower, sink and toilet. The bedroom has double-decker beds; we always put fresh cedar branches under the mattresses every spring to give the beds an aromatic smell.

But I must not forget the gazebo, a quaint, six-sided wood structure with screened windows all around. It has a lovely location under the trees. Here we have enjoyed many happy lunches and dinners together. Often we brought out our barbecue and prepared our meat on the charcoal fire. It was an idyllic spot.

The lot is a good size, with a large lawn to care for. I counted over 90 large trees on it and had over 60 smaller trees, of which I kept a record of their growth. There are cedars, pines, spruce, birch, oak, junipers, mountain ash, maple, apple, elm and other trees. There is also a fine row of lilacs and about 200 feet of cedar hedge. The trees need a lot of pruning and respond well to this care. Many of the small trees have to be sprayed to kill insect infestations and the hedge needs a lot of trimming. The lawn has to be fertilized and the weeds removed, and it has to be treated to kill the white grubs or else the skunks come in spring to dig it up to get the grubs, ruining the lawn at the same time. It took a lot of work to keep the place in good shape, but I loved the work. When Norah saw the work I was putting into her place she began to accept me as "belonging".

For the most part Bobcaygeon is sitting right on limestone bedrock. Our place had three to six inches of soil on top of the rock, with a few areas of greater depth. A lot of the soil was only sand which had been brought in as cheap landfill. About every other year I bought a large truckload of topsoil which I slowly spread around to improve the soil. The soil was too poor for good plant growth and bedrock drained off the moisture very quickly. In summer we usually had several sprinklers going all the time. We took the water from the lake. If the soil had been better I would have gone into a lot more horticulture, something I truly enjoy.

We spent a number of years at Bobcaygeon, staying the whole year except when we were away travelling. There were many things to do to keep us busy. Across the street from our place in those days, there was open bush, with rugged terrain and large gravel pits. In summer it was an interesting area for walking, in winter we made ski trails all over. Lately the area has been taken for residential development and all our trails are gone.

We had a canoe and motorboat which we used a great deal on the river and lake. During the first years we used the boat to go downtown to do our shopping. Later there was too much traffic and we could find no place to dock our boat, so we only went for the trip. Pigeon Lake was sort of L-shaped, extending south and east for about ten miles, but full of islands further east. In the middle, across from us, was a large island which we often circled. It was common to see loons on the lake, and in the evening we often heard them from the house. We also had a beaver family living under our dock one summer, which did not please us at all. Beavers can do a lot of damage but fortunately they left our trees alone.

We had an old-fashioned canoe made out of wood. It was excellent for exploring along the shore. It was delightful to spend a peaceful hour or so on the canoe, seeing what the neighbours were doing. On the west side of the lake was a large area of reefs through which we often threaded our way, and mostly got stuck, as well. Further along there was a small creek which was almost adventurous to follow into the bush.

The village itself is an interesting place, consisting of three islands between two lakes. The Trent-Severn Waterway, which links Georgian Bay with the St. Lawrence River, goes through the centre of the town where one of the locks is located. We often stopped to watch the boats go through the lock. The bridge at the lock is a swing bridge, so that it opens up to let the larger boats go through. To make the bridge easier to open, it is single lane for traffic. This results in many traffic tie-ups. Formerly, the main highway passed over this bridge but later the highway was re-routed to the edge of town and a proper bridge was built over the canal. It was built by Reg Blyth.

Slowly Bobcaygeon changed from a tourist town to a retirement place for Toronto people. Large residential projects were started and continue to grow. They are very attractive and unique. One large area is built on bedrock and has a fantastic array of rock walls and other rock structures incorporated into the area. It is an interesting tour, to drive around Bobcaygeon and see the residential areas. People are selling their old houses in Toronto and buying new and more attractive houses here for half the price. It is a nice way to retire.

Bobcaygeon is located in the middle of the developed part of Ontario, which has a tremendous number of picturesque places to see and exciting things to do. From Ottawa to Windsor, and from Niagara Falls to Sudbury, it was all within easy driving distance for us. We did a lot of travelling within this area and fully enjoyed it. Norah had friends in many places, and we both enjoyed sightseeing and spent many hours walking wherever we went. We were both more interested in nature than in concerts, although we did not neglect the latter.

However, there was something lacking, as far as I was concerned. I found it difficult to become socially involved in Bobcaygeon. We had many visitors come in, but they came from further away and it was not like neighbours you saw more often. We knew a number of people at church, we joined the Horticultural Society, and we took part in community affairs at the arena. We tried to go to everything that was happening, but I still felt lonely because I was not making close friends. Partly it was my nature, but I was also thinking of our future. We were getting older, but most of Norah's relatives and friends were older than we were, which meant we would end up alone. Norah saw I was troubled, and she agreed we would spend the summer at Bobcaygeon and the winter in Winnipeg. This turned out to be a good compromise. Summer was the best time to be at Bobcaygeon, as winter was slushy and humid. Winnipeg is drier in winter, and I could continue with university studies. Norah did that as well.

Summers at Bobcaygeon continued to be lovely. When we were alone we sat at a smaller table in the living room for our meals. Here we looked out across the front lawn to Pigeon Lake. We used to watch the robins pick up worms on the front lawn. On the lake we could see the boats going along the waterway. This part of the lake was a popular area for sailboats as well. At this table we had our Bible reading and prayer in the morning after breakfast. We spent many happy hours at this spot.

Our favourite spot in the evening was in front of the fireplace. We always lit a fire except during hot weather in the summer. We both loved to sit and read and passed many happy evenings together here. When visitors came they always joined us in front of the fire.

Slowly Norah's health started deteriorating and she had to visit the doctor more frequently. Then we found she had osteoporosis and had to be more careful with her activities. She had to stop cross-country skiing and hiking on tough terrain. Once she slipped on a small rug and fell; I decided all scatter rugs had to be taken out of the house.

Slowly her walking became more risky, until one day it happened. She had gone to visit our neighbour across the side lane, and I was worried about her. The house had a number of steps going up to the front door. Often the neighbour lady was in the back, which meant going along a sidewalk made of rough stone and up some steps with rocks piled up. After Norah had been away for half an hour I went over to check and found her lying on the side steps, hurt and half-conscious. She could not get up, so I got help. Between two of us we got her back home.

I realized I would have to be with Norah at all times because we had steps around the house as well. Her Alzheimer problems were also developing. Altogether I found myself in a very confused state with our lives. I was suffering from a severe skin disease which came close to breaking me down; the doctors called it neurodermatitis but could do little for it. It was difficult to know how we would be able to manage our lives. I decided we had to leave Bobcaygeon. We left to settle down full time in Winnipeg. Norah never saw Bobcaygeon again. In fact, when her Alzheimer afflictions developed, Bobcaygeon completely slipped from her mind. She showed no reactions at all when I showed her pictures of her beloved home. I had not thought it possible she could ever forget Bobcaygeon.

Those days were not without problems and disagreements; that is part of the human equation and the environment in which we live. But we learned to understand each other and adjust to our unique personalities. The environment caused us many problems and much work, but the more effort we put into the place the more attached we became to it. In Winnipeg it was easier for us to take care of ourselves and this became the deciding factor in our move. Those were happy days we spent in Bobcaygeon!

PARIS

I did not go to Paris as a tourist in 1974; I went there to reside. There is a great difference between the two. I did not want to be stared at as an American, I wanted to become a citizen of Paris, and to some extent I succeeded. How could I tell? When other Parisians stopped me on the street to ask for directions, I knew they regarded me as another Parisian. Sometimes I could help, sometimes not; Paris is a complicated city and often it is difficult to find the address you are looking for. Frequently you have to ask several times before you find it.

You realize very soon after arriving in Paris that you have entered a different culture. The first time I went shopping in a large department store had me badly confused. I found what I wanted and took it to a sales clerk. She took the article, gave me a sales slip, and told me to go and pay for it and pick up the purchase later. I didn't know what to do. When she saw me hanging around she came back to me and showed me where to go and pay and told me to bring back the receipt. This I did, and she gave me my parcel when I returned.

There was a six-story bookstore on Boulevard Saint Michel where I frequently went to buy books. They only had one place in the whole store where you had to pay, and you left your books at the counter where you picked them up. You only took possession of the books after you produced the receipt. It was also common practice to have your shopping bags examined when entering and exiting a store. In some places you had to leave shopping bags at a special counter at the entrance. Ladies' purses were also subject to examination.

When it comes to eating, Americans and Canadians have rather queer habits compared to the French. Americans have no sense of the time of day; they eat whenever they feel hungry (which is most of the time). I have found myself at three o'clock in the afternoon looking for a place to eat, after missing lunch, and couldn't find an eating place that was open. Grocery stores were closed too, even large supermarkets. Parisians eat at regular mealtimes and the restaurants close up to prepare food for the next meal. Grocery store people want a break in the afternoon, so they close shop. Parisians have well-defined habits for eating and grocery shopping. The changes that happen to a street during the day are amazing. At 3:00 p.m. the street looks dead; all the windows are barricaded with shutters or doors that come down and close up the shops. At 6:00 p.m. the whole front has been opened up and counters with food for sale have been pulled out to half cover the sidewalk so you can hardly walk past, with customers crowded all over. They shop for fruit, vegetables, meat and bread just before supper so they can prepare a fresh meal. We learned to do the same. Their apartments are small and so are their fridges and kitchens; they have little storage space in their homes.

The first time I flew to Paris I left from Montreal, where I had spent several days. Montreal is a fun-loving city. At 9:00 p.m. it comes to life, the streets fill with people and merry-making goes on into the night. I expected the same thing in Paris. Was I shocked when I found that by 9:00 p.m. the streets were dead, no one was about, and store fronts were closed up with large metal shutters! It was a great change after Montreal.

Later I found there were areas open in the evening for entertainment, theatre, concerts and movies, but they were often well hidden. One street I remember was wide open in the evening but when I returned the next day it was all closed up, so it was impossible to identify the activities I had seen the night before. I discovered there was a cinematheque showing special movies at reasonable prices, mostly frequented by students, just below the Palais de Chaillot. The place was well hidden, at the end of a curving path into a heavily treed spot. There were many people coming in but no indication by way of signs that the place existed.

The famous Left Bank has its own character. There were more activities here at night. The streets were dark and poorly lit. An area crowded with eating places was open late into the night. Walking past on the sidewalk, looking in through the windows, they looked strange inside. They had a Bohemian atmosphere, were cramped for space and, being poorly lit, I could often see the charcoal fires of the barbecue on which they were preparing the meat courses for their hungry customers. It seems many people have little time to eat during the day, so they spend the night catching up. In Winnipeg I would have felt scared to walk these streets; in Paris they seemed quite safe and no one ever bothered me. There are areas of Paris that are notorious for their immoral night life, like the Pigalle. I never ventured there at night and I think it was mainly intended for tourists. Another part I avoided was the Arab district, which was famous for its criminal gang activities.

Another item we had to get used to were the French washrooms, or toilets. French people are different from us. I believe they don't need to use the toilet between the time they leave home in the morning and return home at night. (We need to go more often.) Public washrooms are scarce. When I was there the first year they still had a few of the old-fashioned urinals on the streets for men to use (as if women didn't have to go). They usually had a wall behind them to provide some privacy, but I have seen them beside the sidewalk on the wall of a building, all open. Today I believe this institution has disappeared.

If you find a public washroom it usually is large and well supervised. Mostly there is a woman in charge and you pay to go in. There are no problems in the washrooms. French women are famous for maintaining strict order and nobody fools around when they are in charge. Sometimes they have different sections for the men and for the women, but they don't have open urinals so it doesn't matter if they have both sexes in the same area. The problem that arises is the national shortage of paper, and it is most acute in the washrooms. I learned to always carry extra paper with me and save any napkins or tissues that I got my hands on. It became a habit. The same held for sugar cubes. Even though we didn't take sugar in our coffee we always took them when they were offered.

Telephones were another problem, and it took me a long time to learn how to handle them. Public telephones belong to the business in which they are installed and to use them you have to buy special tokens from that business. You cannot use these tokens in any other phone. That is why phones would seldom work for me, until I finally discovered what was wrong. Long-distance calls were even more trouble. For these I had to go to a telephone company centre. I told them whom I wanted to phone and they made the call. As a rule, I had to pay for the call in advance and then check after to see that it was correct. When they got an answer they directed me to a row of booths but I had trouble understanding which one they wanted me to use. For calls after midnight, which was often necessary when calling Canada, there was only one place in Paris where they could be made. The experience in Paris helps me to appreciate our phone system in Canada.

A basic trait of the French character is that you must not change or improve your environment. As we wandered through the countryside of France we were often shocked to see houses falling into disrepair, plaster falling off, outside walls in shabby condition, and buildings left unpainted after the old paint was all gone. To them it is sacrilege to fix up the houses to look like new again. Cleanliness was more important but far from what we saw in Holland. In contradiction, landscape gardening had to be beautiful and perfectly laid out. French gardens are faultlessly geometric, ordered and clean. Formal is the word, in comparison with English gardens which are informal, well kept, but have no geometrical order. The French culture is the opposite of the American "throw-away" society. Furniture is well built and passed on from parents to children. The same goes for houses and apartments. The people value what they have and replace articles only when they cannot be repaired.

Paris has a vast number of underground halls and tunnels. I believe many of them resulted from underground quarrying to obtain stone to erect new buildings on top. Some of the areas of Paris are actually in danger of sinking down into the abyss below because the structure of rock left below is barely able to support the weight of the buildings erected on top. The subway system makes use of some of these tunnels. One of the large caverns is about a mile in length. They had plans to build a large shopping centre underground there.

In 1875 the problem of overfilled cemeteries in France came to a head and the solution was to use the empty underground spaces of Paris. Cemeteries from all over France were emptied and the skeletons were deposited underneath Paris. I believe the Revolution of 1789 accelerated this operation because many cemeteries suffered destruction during the fighting and many streets were widened to allow fast movement of armies. The work was done carefully, with due respect for the skeletons.

On my first venture into the catacombs I was warned to be ready for a gruesome sight and to wear good shoes and bring a light. We had to come at a set time and were admitted as a group. Then the entrance was closed and we were guided through. We went down for a distance and then followed damp, dark tunnels for about 15 minutes with no lighting. It was scary! Then we came to the skeletons. The bones had been carefully sorted out. Skulls had been piled up in one section, about six feet high, and carefully laid one on one to form a clean horizontal wall. On the inside they may just have been thrown in but I did not care to look. The same thing was done with the other bones; sometimes they were piled up in neat, intricate designs. A number of altars had also been built. There must be at least a million skeletons in this subterranean vault. It was gruesome—and sickening. I was glad when we finally got out. When Norah and I went down two years later the tunnels had some lighting but the sight was just as hideous. Don't take the tour if you are faint-hearted.

The Paris sewer system also makes extensive use of the underground tunnels and is open to public tours. Norah and I took this tour. It was not as dramatic as the skeletons, although the smell was worse.

Another aspect of French culture is the great emphasis on professionalism; the aim at perfection in all the arts like music, painting, theatre, ballet and concerts. People don't hang around, they get involved in developing their talents. Instead of having only one good orchestra they have 100. The same goes for the theatre and other forms of cultural expression. The quality of performances was always excellent. They published a small booklet every week for one franc, listing all the events open to the public. The copy for March 15, 1978 has 140 pages filled with ads similar to the classified section in a daily newspaper. There was never any reason to sit at home wondering what to do, and most of the entrance tickets were very reasonable.

My first year in Paris I was single and lived at the Cite Universitaire in an area of 40 hectares occupied by student residences, official buildings, restaurants, cultural and sports facilities, and other amenities. It has 37 residences, each founded by a different nation, including a Canadian residence, but all controlled by the French government. The French bureaucracy is always arrogant and disdainful of those underneath. This results in frequent student activities challenging the bureaucracy. One Sunday morning I woke up to the call of marching music that sounded a rebellious note. I went out and found students gathering for a march on the Spanish residence, so I joined them. It had been closed for some time on account of insubordinate activities. The march ended with a lot of verbal tirades but that was all. A couple of weeks later the drums called again but this time I did not join the march. I heard later on the news that they had broken into the building this time and ransacked it, but the police had arrived and arrested a number of the culprits. The Canadian residence was also in a state of revolt the last half of the year. The students refused to pay their monthly rents and the Canadian Embassy had to intervene. I was glad I had been put in the Cuban residence; it was a quiet, peaceful place to live.

"Anti-something" demonstrations were popular in Paris and the government could not take them for granted. They had to be prepared for violence. Once I just happened to come upon an anti-nuclear march, so I joined in with the crowd. I noticed there were many truckloads of soldiers parked only a block away from the demonstration route. The truck licences showed that they came from country points. Evidently the government did not trust Paris soldiers to handle a Paris march if it became ugly. The demonstration easily had about 100,000 protesters. It seemed very peaceful to me but the papers reported the next day that there had been one violent incident. Another time, the Communist Party had a huge demonstration which paralyzed Paris for half a day. I took part in this march. It was very well organized. They formed a solid block of protesters filling a main thoroughfare right across Paris. Our university section had a specific spot in the long stretch of people. It was a hectic rush trying to get into place for the high moment of the demonstration. People from all over the city were flocking towards their place in the event and it was evident the whole city came to a standstill. However, it was a peaceful affair; the Party was only flexing its muscles and demonstrating the power it had. There were at least 600,000 people involved in the demonstration.

In 1978 Norah and I went back to Paris to study for a year and we had to find private accommodation. We joined the APLI, a church affiliation, and Madame Bouteiller helped us find a place to live. We moved into a one-room suite at 42 rue Damremont in the 18th arrondisement, a middle-class section of Paris. We were on the eighth floor of a good apartment building. Some of the suites were rented but many were privately owned. There was no elevator and we had to walk up to the eighth floor; we soon got used to it. Our one-room suite had everything we needed, although it was only nine feet, six inches wide, and about 17 feet long. It had a large window facing the inner court of the building and a skylight in the bathroom. It had a sink, small stove and fridge, table with two chairs, bed, wardrobe and some shelves. The washroom included a shower. We also had a TV sitting on top of a decorative fireplace and a telephone. What more could we want?

I will describe some of the parts of Paris that appealed to me. Originally Paris was built on an island in the Seine River, which enabled it to be highly fortified. Today this part is called the Cite de Paris and is still the highlight for any visitor. It contains the ancient Palais de Justice with its wealth of history, plus La Sainte-Chappelle, a beautiful church. The Police Department still has its headquarters on the island. But most important is the huge church, the Notre Dame, probably the most visited spot in Paris. We have gone to church services and concerts there, or just to explore. It is exciting to go up to the top of the towers, walking up the spiral staircases, especially if you have read the stories by Victor Hugo relating the events that happened there.

Crossing the bridge to the north mainland and turning to the west, we soon arrive at the world-famous museum, the Louvre. It is easy to spend the day there without running out of things to see. It is also a complicated building. I remember being lost in it and not finding my way out, but when the bells announced closing time I just followed the crowd to the exit. I remember spending a day there with Norah. The most exciting part was getting something to eat at the cafeteria. It was a shmozzle like I've never seen in America. The seating area was in complete disorder. First Norah and I checked out what was available and decided what we wanted. Then Norah went back to try and grab a couple of chairs; meanwhile I waited in line to get the food. Going back with my tray of victuals I searched the area for Norah. Luckily she had a hold on two chairs; now we had to get our tray onto a table. If there was a vacant spot on a table you took it regardless of who else was using the table. Finally we settled down to enjoy the typical French ambience and the food. It was an exciting adventure, the food was good and, it was worth it.

From the centre point of the Louvre going west, we find the Route of Triumph. It passes through a large park area of lovely gardens called the Tuilleries bordered by famous art galleries, through the Place de la Concorde which is the world's largest traffic circle (about 25 acres), and into the Champs Elysees, Paris' most famous street, ending at the Arc de Triomphe. On the north side of the Louvre is the Palais Royale, northwest we can see the celebrated Opera, and north of the Tuileries is Place Vendome.

We have spent wonderful days in this area, walking from the Louvre to the Arc de Triomphe built by Napoleon. It is the elite district of Paris which celebrates the glories of its history. The Arc de Triomphe also is a vast traffic circle, but fortunately they have underground pedestrian walkways leading to it so you can approach it safely. Pictures fail to give a sense of the size of the monument and the surrounding area. We climbed up to the top of the arch, which gave us a solid impression of its size.

To see an ancient castle we visited Chateau Vincennes, dated to the 14th century. The castle is impressive, especially the dungeon. History is written all over its walls, and you can feel it with your senses. It makes the old stories of the knights become real and gruesome. Attached to the castle is the forest of Vincennes, a huge area of parks, gardens, zoo, racetrack and more. We enjoyed visiting this place.

On the other side of Paris is the Bois (Forest) de Boulogne, about two and one-half miles long and over a mile wide, an enormous park area with many different attractions. The French don't leave an area wild, they develop it, and they make full use of their imagination in so doing. I have spent many days alone, and later with Norah, hiking through this area and enjoying its attractions. We took a lunch along so we could sit down and eat when we were hungry. My favourite spot was the Bagatelle, a special area where we had to pay admission. It had many beautiful attractions but the Roserie was tops. It is the largest and most gorgeous rose garden I have seen.

One day when Norah and I were roaming around northeast of the Louvre, we came into a large open area. It was the location of the former wholesale vegetable market which had been moved to the north of the city. As we looked we saw a huge monstrous sort of building, or was it a building? It could have dropped down from Mars. Nobody had ever talked to us about something like this. French people hate to admit that such things even exist in their city. We sat down and rested for a while, wondering what it was. It was made of metal and glass, with queer pipes in odd places, and it was large. There were signs on it which made no sense. We decided to approach it and, finding a door, we entered. It was some sort of an intellectual, cultural arts conglomerate, with weird art and nonsensical doo-jiggers all over. In the centre was a large monster made up of wheels, levers and other odd gadgets, dropping marbles from one spot to another, just keeping itself going without accomplishing anything, a contraption like I've seen in other places, only 25 times as large. Indeed, it is a true monument to modern art and intellectualism! Our city map showed the area was vacant; even map-makers were ashamed to print it, but we found out later that it is called Beaubourg, and that we were not just having a nightmare during a clear sunny day.

Going west but staying close to the Seine River, we come to the Palais de Chaillot. The palace is made up of two identical but facing wings, with a large terrace between the two parts. Between the palace and the river is an area of gardens and trees and a large pool with fountains. It was in among these trees that I found the cinematheque I mentioned earlier. Looking across the Seine we have a full view of the Eiffel Tower set in a park area almost a mile in length, ending at the Military Museum. We have often strolled through this area, but one day we decided to go up the Eiffel Tower. We went early to get there before the place opened but already there was a long line-up ahead of us. We took the elevator but the tower is built in three parts, so that meant going through three line-ups to get to the top. It was almost lunch time before we got to the top. There were eating places and a restaurant on the first level up. We had a tremendous view of the city from the top, and it was worth it.

Now I want to take you to St. Denis on the north side of Paris. Its first church was built in A.D. 475, marking its importance in early ecclesiastical history. Here, in the 12th century, was built the first large Gothic church, the Basilique St. Denis. It started the era of Gothic church buildings which spread through Europe. Walking through the building we easily sensed its age and historical significance. It is the burial place for royalty, who are honoured with their tombs and royal sculptures. The crypt is full of tombs: majestic, overwhelming, loaded with pride, and deadening to the senses. It was good to get out into the open, but the impression was unforgettable. St. Denis has another attraction, a famous theatre. We have seen a number of plays there.

The Opera is the pride of Paris. It is a magnificent building, described as the largest theatre building in the world. It has an open oval interior, with row upon row of loges all around the inside wall. The floor space is filled with seats. The ticket prices are high and I have only been to it twice. The first time I went with a group of Parisians who had rented a loge. It was located on the side, so we did not have a direct view of the stage. We could hear the music without trouble and we took turns sitting at the front. The second time, I went with Norah and we sat in the centre on the floor level. It was a grand experience.

Norah and I have been to many musical concerts and theatre productions while in Paris. There are a great number of people involved in these two cultural activities and it is necessary for them to practice their skills in public. As a result ticket prices are low, and places where performances are held are mostly unpretentious. Music concerts are often held in churches. The main problem is that frequently it is hard to locate the places. I remember one theatre performance given by a railway workers' union. It was held in the railway station complex, which occupied several city blocks. The offices were closed in the evening so we walked around until we saw others going in the rear of the building and we followed them. We could never have found our way in alone. Finding the place was almost as exciting as the performance.

After spending two years in Paris I got to know it well, better than many Parisians and better than I know my hometown Winnipeg, but I realize there is much more to discover in Paris.

FRANCE AND BEYOND

Travelling is easy when you live in Paris. In summertime 1972 there were 260 trains leaving Paris every day. If I wanted to go out of town, I just checked which of Paris' six railway stations had the train that went to my destination and then I went to the station. There was seldom a long wait for the right train. There were many bus tours going out of Paris as well. The RATP, the Paris transportation authority, had an extensive network of day tours leaving Paris in buses. In 1978 they listed 73 half-day tours and 49 full-day tours, on the weekends from March to October. Most tours were repeated once or twice each month. The day tours left at 7:00 a.m. and returned around 11:00 p.m. This enabled them to go long distances, covering about half of France, plus Alsace and Belgium. The railway system also offered many organized, longer tours, not only in France but all through Europe. Besides these there were many private tour companies that offered a variety of excursions.

My first excursion was a tour bus trip to Amsterdam, which I took together with my friend Takayuki. It was cheap because we travelled during the night. When Norah was with me we made a trip to Amsterdam spending several days there. We stayed in a private family home, which was a popular thing to do. While there we took a tour into the countryside during tulip time. It was an unforgettable experience, seeing the tulip industry in its various operations: growing, selling and advertising. I recommend tulip time in Holland for anyone who can make it. We also visited the world's largest diamond factory and saw how diamonds were made from the rough rocks.

Another time I took a weekend tour to Heidelberg, Germany, this time by train. It was a low cost fare for the train because we travelled during the night. It also meant I only had to get a hotel for one night, which made it an inexpensive excursion. However, I was soundly fatigued by the time I arrived back on Monday morning. Heidelberg, with its great German university made famous by its poets, is a fascinating city.

I took many day tours offered by the RATP, including the coastal towns where the Allies landed during the war; Mont St.Michel, the grand rock fortress off the mainland; Dieppe; Etretat; Strasbourg; and the valley of the Loire River with all its castles. I loved tramping through the old castles because they made the history of the Medieval Ages come to life in realistic fashion. In your mind's eye you could see the knights in their gleaming armor coming up the spiral staircases as they captured the castle. These tours were popular with the French people and they demand value for their money. The tour prices were reasonable and they gave us excellent service.

Versailles, the magnificent palace built by King Louis XIV, his crowning achievement, is only a short distance out of Paris. I have visited it alone and also with Norah. We could reach it either by bus or train. The palace is 500 metres long, and the park area behind it contains about 100 hectares of surface. The park area has an array of gardens, fountains and canals, plus a number of other buildings. Its great halls are covered with the best in art and sculpture. The disturbing factor is that the whole of France was groaning in misery in order to pay for the King's extravaganza.

The year when Norah was with me we did more travelling, as we had more money. During the winter we took a three-day bus tour into Germany to see the Black Forest, which is praised by German poets. When we were up in the mountains we came into a real snowstorm, almost a blizzard. It made us feel right at home. Europeans are always excited when they see snow, as it's such a rare experience for them. The next day we were in Freiburg, a city famous for its spas but it was not warm enough for swimming. On another occasion we took a tour to Munich with the SNCF, the French railways. This included a stay at one of the best hotels in Munich, which made us feel important. We went to visit the sports complex where the Olympic competitions had been held recently. As usual we walked all over the city, enjoying to the full its quaint Bavarian atmosphere.

For Christmas we took the train to Nice, where we spent a week. Our tour included a trip to Monaco, the gambling capital of the world. We didn't gamble, we just watched others; it was saddening to see the looks on their faces. But gambling wasn't everything we saw at Monaco. We visited an exotic desert garden with the largest cacti I have ever seen in a non-desert environment.

The high point of our stay there was Christmas Eve. At 9:00 p.m. we went to the Anglican church for their Christmas celebrations and then we went to the Catholic church for Midnight Mass. It gave us a real Christmas experience in a country where, normally, Christmas gets no more attention than the birthday of one of its minor poets. One of Norah's favourite artists was Chagall, who interpreted many Biblical passages in his paintings. The art gallery in Nice is the best place to view his paintings and we passed an enjoyable time viewing his art.

Walking around the ancient part of the city one day we came to a small soap shop. The owner claimed their soap was made with real olive oil, so we bought a bar. It turned out to be the finest soap I have ever tried, so next day we went back and got a good supply. One day we took a tour to Genoa, Italy, following the coastline. The coast is bordered by a high ridge of mountains traversed by three sets of highways. One route stays at the bottom following the shoreline. The second road follows a line about half way up, and the third stays on top of the ridge wherever it can. It was a fantastic scene driving these roads. Another day we took a tour north into the Alps to watch the skiers. They were skiing on the north side of the mountain, but the south side was almost bare of snow. The road going into the mountains was narrow and often had a sharp drop on one side, but that did not keep the drivers from going over the speed limit.

When spring came we took a bus tour through southern France. A seven day tour starting on April 9 took us through a fascinating part of France. The first day we arrived at Le Puy, which has a church built on top of a sharp rock sticking up about 100 feet over ground level. On the third day we arrived at Carcassonne, a small ancient city complete in itself. It still has its ancient walls intact all around the city and no new additions have been made. It looks like it did in the Dark Ages. Then we came to Lourdes, the world-famous city for healing miracles. The main healing services took place in what is actually a large cave area. The town was filled with sick people coming for healing. It was unbelievable; the people we saw in wheelchairs and walking with canes. Despair hung over the place because there were few signs of miracle healing. The town itself was a real tourist trap, filled with souvenir shops.

The last highlight of the tour was a visit to the extraordinary town of Rocamadour. It is situated on the side of a steep precipice, facing a river valley. It looked almost like a picture hanging on a living room wall. When we arrived, our guide and the bus driver got into an argument. The driver said we could drive up but the guide said we couldn't, so we got off and took an elevator up to our hotel, halfway up the precipice. When we got up the bus was already there; the driver knew what he was saying. Our hotel was of very old-fashioned construction, with a delightful charm. It was a thrill to spend a night there, perched midway in the air like in a bird's nest.

We also took a seven day trip to Denmark that spring. The first day we arrived at Cologne, Germany, and stayed for the night. The cathedral at Cologne, built of black stone, is very impressive. The city is located on the Rhine River and we loved to watch the boats on the river. The next day we got to Hamburg. It is one of Europe's largest port cities, although it is located 130 kilometres from the ocean. We rented a boat to take us around the harbour and were truly impressed with the activities we saw. There was a lot of boat building and repair in progress, as well as the usual freight transport.

Then we continued on to Copenhagen, which included a long ferry trip. Norah had a friend there and we managed to visit her. We also saw the palace where the story of Shakespeare's play, *Hamlet*, is said to have taken place. On a promenade along the waterside we saw the famous sculpture, The Siren. On the way back we stopped at Odense, where we saw the house in which the famous author Hans Christian Andersen had lived.

Travelling through different countries like this one always meant a variety of different meals and dining became a real adventure. At one hotel in Denmark we were treated to a lovely smorgasbord. To most of our French co-travellers that was a new and strange experience. They helped themselves to a moderate serving and thought that was it, being well-mannered as they naturally are. Then when they saw others going back for second helpings they took the hint and followed. Then they took full advantage of this new opportunity for repeated helpings. They ate enough to be sick for three days. We had a similar experience at a restaurant in Germany. First they served everyone an individual pot of baked beans with pork. We thought it was the main course, but it was only the hors-d'oeuvre. It was followed by a very substantial main meal. We all ate too much but it was delicious!

Our most extensive tour that spring, and our last, if I remember correctly, was a trip to Spain with AIRTOUR. We arrived in the evening in Madrid by plane and almost got lost in Customs. As visitors we had to go through about five different procedures before we were allowed in. We had to take a bus from one office to the next and always had to line up without knowing what was happening. We just followed the crowd which became smaller at each point but somehow we managed to get through to the end. It was midnight by the time we got to our room at the hotel and were we hungry! To our surprise,we found two hearty bag lunches in our room, enough to last for a whole day. We did not eat too much because we had to leave for the airport the next morning at 6:00 a.m.

Things changed when we arrived at Torremolinos. We stayed at a truly palatial hotel, really grandiose, situated on the ocean, and the weather was sunny and warm. My memory here depends on my stomach. They had a smorgasbord setting for breakfast with huge supplies of food, especially fresh fruit. I love fresh fruit for breakfast. We could also take the food back to our room to eat there. Norah was watching two German tourists while we were eating our breakfast. She noticed they were walking out with their plates piled high with toast, almost a loaf of bread on each plate. I told Norah that German bread is always soggy and clunky and this bread was like a gift from heaven for them.

While in Spain we visited Malaga, Grenada, Seville and Cordoba, cities built by the Moslems during their occupation of Spain. We immediately noticed a sharp change in the architecture of the buildings from that in northern Europe. Decorations are of intricate geometric design and domes replace the Gothic features.

Our tour guide took us to the gypsy area of one of the cities. The place was actually built into a cave on the side of a mountain. We saw the gypsies perform, a troupe of young women who entertained us with some colourful dances. At the end we applauded and a few people threw in some change. I had some change in my pocket so I gave it to the nearest girls. Bingo! The rest of them mobbed me, asking for more money. I didn't have any more change, and I had difficulty getting away from them.

The cities we visited were wonderful, but the place I remember best is Ronda, a village set in the clouds, on a high prominence of rock overlooking a deep valley from a steep precipice. It was so natural and awe-inspiring; I wish I could go back there again.

When Norah and I left Paris we went to England for a week before flying to Canada. We spent only a few days in London and then went south to Lewes to visit Norah's friends, the Sheppards. We had an interesting stay with them as they drove us around to see the countryside. They have also visited us at Bobcaygeon since then. Then we went to Exeter in the west end of England for a few days. This is where Norah worked in the hospital for a year when she was young. She still remembered the city from that time.

We took full advantage of the time we spent in Europe and did many interesting things. However, we spent little more money over there than we would have spent if we had stayed at home. Our purpose was to understand the new cultures of the peoples we met and enjoy living as they lived. Norah and I both shied away from expensive living and entertainment out of a deep sense of the true values of life. Most of the things we did were reasonable in cost, within reach of most people, but they did require some careful planning and the willingness to take chances, which is often the most exciting part of the adventure.

TEACHING ON AN INDIAN RESERVE

Thinking back about the native children I have taught, I realize many of them suffered under serious handicaps. I have had young children come to school in the morning practically stoned from sniffing gasoline. I just left them alone because I realized they could not operate mentally. Many children suffered from smoking, alcohol, poor diet and family situations that were inflicted upon them. From the ages of six to ten years my pupils generally were bright mentally and eager to learn. I could not tell they were mentally handicapped. After that their mental abilities suffered badly due to the lifestyles under which they lived. In comparison, in white schools, I see many children who apparently are mentally handicapped from birth, and cannot learn normally. I have been puzzled by this difference.

Children want to be respected and it solves many problems when we can do this. The first day of classes is always critical and difficult. In this particular case I assigned all the pupils to desks before they came in. Their names were written on a piece of paper stuck to the desk. That way there is order in the room as soon as the pupils enter. Some changes have to be made but that depends on various factors. One of the older and taller boys found himself sitting towards the front among some girls. He asked me to be moved to the back of the room. "All right," I said, "if you will cooperate with me and behave. Where do you want to sit?" He chose a seat in the back and cooperated with me to the end of the year. I was happy with him when I had him, but in later years he became a serious problem.

My teaching usually aimed at motivating pupils to think and this requires discussion. After a while pupils catch on and are open and frank with their arguments. Reading classes are a good opportunity for discussing the stories we read. One day we had a question that raised many different opinions. As usual the pupils carefully observed my facial expressions, tone of voice and words I used, to pick up hints to the right answer. The boy who had asked to sit in the back raised his hand and we listened to his answer. "Well," I said to the others, "what do you think of that?" The clue was that I disagreed, but my purpose was for the class to think on their own. Slowly the argument developed and drew nearer to the answer from the boy in the back. Finally we concluded he had been right all along. For him it was a victory that he seldom experienced, he was right and all the others were wrong. He cherished that day in his heart. I knew he was the key to the behaviour problems of the classroom, and if I won him over I had won the battle. It worked.

Teaching on the reserve meant living on the reserve, and this included many problems. Teachers were expected to take part in community activities. I was generally involved in most activities on the reserves where I taught, more so than most teachers.

Popular local activities were cribbage and bingo. The natives loved to play cribbage and so did my Principal, but I found it hard to maintain an interest in the game when I found myself losing all the time. Bingo was a little easier for me, but I never won. It was weird how the Indian people always won and the white people always lost. Possibly it depends on how much you love the game.

Some activities were held in the school, but this was not very satisfactory so eventually a new community hall was built close to the North Shore School where I taught. They had an opening ceremony when the hall was finished and teachers were expected to attend. I went but only a few teachers came. It was supposed to be a big dance and they had live music to accompany the dancers. The front part of the hall was well lit up for the dancing, but the back part was darker and that is where most of the men stayed. The entrance door was also in the back. Probably the men had brought some beer along because soon there was continual fighting and yelling in the back, while we were dancing in the front. How were we finally going to exit where all the fighting was in progress? The ladies I was dancing with most likely had husbands in the back who were watching me. Ladies love to dance and the men prefer to drink beer and fight, but that doesn't mean they are happy to see their wives dancing with someone else. It was, at best, a risky situation for me. And what about my car outside? Would it be smashed up? I worried a little, but I was used to these situations and seldom showed fear. I faced many risky situations while I worked on the reserves. The fact that I took part in activities brought me into many difficult situations. I don't remember how the evening ended but I did get out and back to my hotel safely.

Another big event at Fort Alexander was the celebration of Canada's centennial birthday in 1967. We held a lot of money-raising events to raise money for the Band. Bingos were always popular, but we also set up a gambling machine with a roulette wheel. The players with money on the spot where the wheel stops are the winners, the others lose their money. One day we had a group of wrestlers in from Winnipeg.

During my last year at Fort Alexander I started to withdraw. The political climate was becoming dangerous and the Indians were antagonistic against our union, the PSAC, in which I was active, even though I used my influence in their favour whenever I could.

It was in this year, 1973-1974, my last at Fort Alexander, that the following incident occurred. They put on a large Christmas concert at the

South Shore School. I had always attended but this year I didn't. I taught at the North Shore School so I had a good excuse. My friend Terry went. They charged admission so they had a native lady sitting next to the door to collect the money. Towards the end of the concert this lady had seen a group of punks outside gathering at the door and guessed what was happening. She grabbed the cash box and escaped by way of the back door. The boys were armed with baseball bats and, having missed the cash, they stayed at the front door and beat up anyone who came out, with the bats. My friend Terry had left just before the incident started. It was an unhappy ending to the Christmas concert. I was glad I had stayed away. One of the boys involved was my friend, the big boy in the back seat of my class.

As a result of the above incident I became increasingly nervous about driving through the reserve. One of my friends had a bullet hole in the side of his car, having been shot at while driving through the reserve on Highway 11. Our local service station manager was in the hospital for two days after he was attacked by natives when he went out to tow in a car that had been involved in an accident with natives. A scary trick the natives used was to roll logs onto the highway, pour gasoline on them and set them on fire at night. It was a grim situation for the motorist to face a wall of fire and know there were punks in the ditch waiting to attack him if he stopped. It has not happened to me. The result was that I started taking the local road through Stead when driving to Pine Falls. It was a poor side road then, but it has been upgraded since and today is the main road to Pine Falls and further north. It takes the outsiders off the road through the reserve and leaves the Indians free to attack their own people, which happens a lot more than attacks on white people, sad to say. They are not kind to each other.

"Do-gooders" from the city and beyond were often present on the reserve for various purposes: educational activities, charities or just sightseeing. They were serving their own short-sighted ends, and using their influence in the news media to protect the poor Indian from the awful White Man. To us they were a nuisance because they formed "noisy" opinions simply by spending a few hours on the reserve. "Do-gooders" never lasted if they had to spend more time on the reserve, like the teachers and nurses did. The Indians themselves made sure they didn't last because they did not like their paternalistic attitudes. The Indians made full use of them to further their own interests through the political leverage they gained from the favourable news media coverage, but privately they laughed at the "do-gooders" and called them "stupid whites".

One incident stands out sharply in my memory. Indian Affairs brought in a dentist from Montreal to check the teeth of all the native children. He immediately took a very superior attitude to us teachers, and criticized us high-handedly for the way we treated the Indians. As he did not have his own car I was told to take him along to school and back. That meant I had to put up with him twice a day. Another complaint he persistently talked about was the uncooperative behaviour of our white women. He clearly expected that when he wanted a woman for the night they would be only too glad to volunteer. In Montreal he had no trouble with the women. Here the women were too ignorant to know what their purpose was. On top of that he was usually late in the morning. I had other teachers I picked up and we needed to get to school in time. Finally I decided that if he was late again we would leave without him. Sure enough, he wasn't on time the next morning, so we left without him. But this time the Indians beat me to it. I learned in the evening that the Band had expelled him from the reserve. They couldn't stand him either, despite all his pro-Indian talk. It was a happy ending!

There were always a number of teachers on the reserve who did not have cars and thus needed rides. The officials counted the number of cars available and then determined whom we had to pick up. They didn't ask, they told us. It was a bit high-handed but we realized it was necessary for us to cooperate. For me, it was a special problem. My eyesight has never been good enough to pass a driver's test; I have always obtained my licence by special permission. It has always been risky for me to drive long distances at night. However, the fact that I had a car precluded me from asking for exemptions in driving on account of my eyesight. There were no restrictions on my driver's licence. We have had occasions when I have had to drive as far as 200 miles at night after a strenuous day of teachers' in-services, when I really felt guilty about my responsibility for my passengers. Fortunately I always brought them safely back home. I believe God took good care of me in these situations, and I was not alone.

Another incident was less serious and thus more enjoyable. We were a group of men seriously interested in fishing and we often drove or flew out to the best fishing spots. We heard of a good place at Wallace Lake, so we decided to try it. Today that area is well developed with good roads, but not so at that time. The Principal had used his car on our previous trip so he suggested it was my turn. We were all right until we reached Bird Lake but then the road deteriorated badly. It was mostly bare rock and the bottom of my car was continually dragging on the rock. Too bad, my passengers said, it's your car! But then they soon realized they depended on my car to take them home. So I stopped and the others got off to lighten the car and walked on foot for about a mile, while I slowly drove on the rocks. The road was not intended for cars. We made it safely there and back, but it was hard on the car. I think the Principal had planned our trips carefully to go easy on his own car.

NORAH

When Canada became a bilingual nation and a knowledge of French became a valuable asset, I decided to get involved. My secret ambition had always been to study French, so it was no imposition for me. I began my studies in Winnipeg at St. Boniface College and at the University of Manitoba. However, I knew there were more romantic places to study French and it wasn't long until I was registered at Laval University in Quebec City for the Summer Session. That is where I met Norah. I spent the summers of 1971, 1972 and 1974 at Laval.

I believe it was in 1974 that I first took note of Norah in a serious way. I had gone along with a group of ladies on an afternoon excursion to a special tourist spot. While everyone was sitting and talking I noticed Norah was interested in going for a walk. So I joined her and we went for a hike. We have done an immense amount of walking together since then. We have travelled together in many countries and in Canada from coast to coast, and everywhere we went we have roamed around on foot together in the cities, parks and countryside. In winter we went cross-country skiing. It brought us together and kept us together.

Norah was born in 1915 in Clive, Alberta. Her father was a Methodist minister and from him she received a legacy of Christian faith which stayed with her throughout her life.

Norah grew up under difficult circumstances, becoming an orphan by the time she was ten years old. Her mother died first, after which she lived for some time with an aunt in California. She returned to live with her father and when he died, an aunt in Arthur, Ontario took Norah and her brother and cared for them until they were on their own. Here she became part of a family. Her aunt had two sons, a few years older, who accepted her as a sister, a relationship which lasted throughout their lives and had a positive influence on Norah.

Becoming an orphan early in life made a lasting impact on Norah's character. She had a need for security, and even when she became well off she still felt insecure. On the other hand, it also made her sympathetic and willing to help those who were in difficult situations. The religious faith she inherited from her father, and the feeling of insecurity from her childhood, were two important factors in moulding her personality.

The third and possibly the strongest influence in her life was her older cousin, with whom she grew up. Reg Blyth was a very enterprising and capable civil engineer who went into bridge construction and became one of Canada's leading bridge contractors. He was aggressive in his work and this brought him wealth and a place in the upper-class society of Toronto. He shared both freely with Norah.

Norah got her Bachelor's degree in Home Economics from the University of Toronto. She worked as a dietitian in hospitals in Essex, England, Montreal and North Bay, Ontario.

Her cousin never married. When he became established he needed a housekeeper to entertain the many guests he brought home. Norah took this position; she was a dietitian and had a lot of experience in cooking. He lived in Rosedale, Toronto, a community created by the upper middle class of Toronto and designed to stay exclusive. This set the style of living to which Norah became accustomed but it did not change her humble, generous personality.

During her lifetime, Norah's travels took her all over the world. Much of it must have been paid for by her cousin. After he died in 1959, Norah took a job with the Department of Agriculture working as a seed analyst, where she remained until we were married in 1976. However, when I got to know her she was working part time, taking the summer off so she could travel.

We got married on April 1, 1976, while I was teaching with Indian Affairs at Oxford House in Manitoba. I resigned from my job at the end of the school year and never had time to look for another job after that.

The first year we were married we lived in Winnipeg and registered at the University of Manitoba to continue our French studies. The next year we moved to Paris for a year of studies at the University of Paris. I had already spent a year at that university before our marriage and Norah had been in France at smaller universities for several summers.

After that we settled into Norah's lovely home in Bobcaygeon, Ontario, located on Pigeon Lake. We stayed there for several years. We found small-town life not quite satisfactory so we moved to Winnipeg for the winter and returned to Bobcaygeon for the summer, a practice we kept up until Norah's health forced us to stay permanently in Winnipeg.

Southern Ontario is beautiful and interesting, and we have travelled around from Ottawa to Windsor, from Niagara Falls to Sudbury. Travel continued to be a permanent part of our lives. We motored across Canada from Newfoundland to Vancouver Island, we flew to Florida, we visited friends in California and we loved to go hiking in the Canadian Rockies. In 1980 we took a tour to China which included the Philippines, Hong Kong and Japan.

To Norah, her home at Bobcaygeon was truly HOME. She liked it the way it was and wouldn't have anything changed unless it fell apart. The way Reg Blyth had left it was the way it had to be. This posed difficulties for me. The caretaker, Fred Jones, who had been hired by Reg over 17 years ago, recognized me as the new head of the household and this gave me a chance to settle down in the place and become more than just a visitor. Norah had entered upon a risky venture when she married me, her first marriage at the age of 65, and I realized I had to give her a "big chance" to help her make it. Her only relatives had tried to stop our marriage even on the morning before it took place. I did not know about this until after her death. I can now see that I needed to give her all the consideration I could, but I must admit that at times I felt rather dissatisfied. Regardless of problems between us I took excellent care of her property and made changes very slowly, one small step at a time, and always discussed everything with her. Whatever she wanted to have done, I saw that it was done. Slowly she started to appreciate my work. I kept the place clean, I pruned the trees, I cleaned out weeds and improved the driveway, among other things. It made her feel that she had made the right move in marrying me. Today when I look at photos of us together, I always see her looking at me with an approving smile. My efforts were not in vain, I am happy to say.

Norah always loved to do new things; life was an adventure to her. She had never slept in a tent, so we bought a tent and headed out to Ottawa. It may have been our first night in the tent, close to Ottawa, when we woke up in the morning to see the sunlight on the tent walls. It felt great, but then it turned dark and raindrops started falling. Norah was scared. She wanted to get up in a hurry, take the tent down, and get into the car. I restrained her and told her we were staying right in the tent. The thunderstorm was over in half an hour and the sun came out again. We were still dry, the new tent had proved itself, and Norah was now an experienced tenter.

Norah also had her own ideas about what she wanted to do. She picked up an interest in native rock art and we searched out a number of interesting rock art locations in Ontario. One amazing example is found in Bon Echo Park in eastern Ontario. The drawings are made on a sheer cliff, about 25 feet above water level, for a distance of hundreds of feet. Another place was at Agawa Bay in eastern Lake Superior. To reach it we had to go through a spectacular canyon about five feet wide, then onto a narrow ledge beside a high perpendicular cliff. Here we found red rock art on the rising stone wall. Then we went to Clearwater Bay in Lake of the Woods to see a very different site. This had a deposit of gravel over it with trees growing on top, but part of it had been eroded away to reveal rock art on the bedrock beneath it. The art also extended below the surface of the water. These were actually carvings in the rock. We have also visited the greatest display of native petroglyphs found in Ontario, at Stonyridge off Stony Lake. These have been covered by a glass building to protect them. These are made on the bare rock floor and measure about a hundred feet in width. We also visited the Indian mosaics in Manitoba's Whiteshell Park, but these have been badly disturbed.

Norah loved flowers and plants, so every spring we visited the nurseries and bought twice as much as we could possibly use. It is a common practice, and the nurseries bless us for it. We also planted many new trees or transplanted what we already had. We had about 65 small trees of which I kept a record to see how much they grew each year. We had over 90 tall trees on our property besides the small ones and they needed a lot of pruning every year. Both of us loved working outside and we shared the work inside as well.

We took part in many community activities. The local arena was used for hockey and skating during the winter, and we took part in the skating. In summer there were many affairs at the arena with the Fiddlers and Tap Dance Festival at top place. In winter we went to Fenelon Falls for square dancing, and in the summer to Lindsay for swimming at the Community Centre. I took lessons in woodworking and furniture refinishing, and Norah took lessons in her own interests. My lessons enabled me to refinish a large part of the furniture in our house. There were small towns all around and we took part in many of the happenings they offered.

Norah was a generous and hospitable person. Her cousin Reg had taught her how to entertain people and she was used to having people coming and going at all times. She had many friends in many places, and she kept in touch with everyone by sending out cards at Christmas time. She had over 100 addresses on her card list when we were married and I still have about 50 of them on my list now. We had visitors coming in from places in England, the U.S.A. and all over Canada. We were well prepared for them. Besides three bedrooms in the house, we had two other buildings with sleeping arrangements, plus a couch in the living room. Visitors could use our boats, go swimming or just laze around the lawn. The village of Bobcaygeon was a very scenic place to see as well. While Norah spent a lot of time in the house preparing food the visitors could do as they pleased. In the evening we gathered in front of the fire in our large stone fireplace. It was always a time to be remembered. When Norah developed osteoporosis and arthritis we had to cut down on visitors, but this almost happened by itself because they were all getting older.

We did a lot of visiting in return. Her relatives lived in Guelph and she had many friends in Toronto and other places like Perth, Arthur, Aylmer, Fergus, Grand Valley, Cambridge, Kingsville, Windsor, Mount Forest and Ivy Lea. Every year we made a trip to the Stratford Theatre at Stratford to see some Shakespeare plays. It is the top theatre in Canada and draws many American visitors.

There are many other things to see in Ontario: Algonquin Park with its display of original timber logging machinery is fantastic; Canada's Wonderland tries to rival Disney World; Empire Loyalist Village and Canada Village take us back to pioneer days. At Sudbury we went down into the mine to see mining operations. Point Pelee Park is the southernmost part of Canada and a main point for Monarch butterfly migration in spring. We took a ferry trip from Manitoulin Island across Lake Huron. In Toronto we saw highlights such as Ontario Place, Toronto Island, the C.N.E., the Science Centre and the CN Tower. Of course, I must not forget the world famous Niagara Falls. Our life was filled with work, friends, travel and interesting activities.

Norah was a modest, unassuming but confident person. She never used cosmetics, not even lipstick, and she never had hairdos or expensive jewellery. She bought good clothing, not to show off but to use. She was not talkative but people listened to her when she spoke. She was willing to accept responsibility but she did it quietly. I did not know she had become a member of the Church Board at Bobcaygeon until I saw her name listed in the church bulletin. She was generous in giving to charities and to people in need, but she made no fuss about it. People who knew her from the past respected her highly, but new friends often regarded her as ordinary because of her unassuming character.

Norah's example has taught me a better way of life.

FISHING

It was during my stay at Pine Falls that I learnt to fish. I had tried it before but there were very few fish dumb enough to get caught by my greenhorn techniques. At Pine Falls I fell in with a group of experienced fishermen who were willing to help me learn.

Fishing depends more on intuition than on ability. Fish are smarter than we give them credit for. We were usually a group of four, with me being the sole greenhorn. The first year we fished together the others were hauling in the fish while I hardly even got a single bite, although I was using the same technique and bait as they were. The fish wouldn't take the hook of an inexperienced fisher like me. The second year I began to catch some fish, and the third year I frequently caught more fish than the others. The fish now considered that I had enough experience to be worthy of being taken by them. Fish think it an insult to be caught by a greenhorn.

Most of our fishing was on the Winnipeg River. They had already marked a choice spot on the surface of the river by using a large rock to anchor a car tire floating on top. We spent many pleasant hours here in our boat pulling out the fish. In later years I often went alone to the dam to fish. I went in the evening just before sundown, the peak time for fishing. In an hour I could often catch as many fish as the others who had been there all day. One time I slipped on the slimy rock and fell into the river. I had to drive back home wet halfway up to my head.

Fishing for goldeye is a real art, and one of my friends was an expert at it. For this we went up on the power dam, right in line with the water rushing through the generators. It required the right size of hook, the right bait, and a float attached about six inches above the hook. Then we cast the hook into the water just where the foaming turned calm. You watched the float and when it ducked down under water, you gave the rod the right jerk and you had a goldeye. It took a lot of skill. My friend packed his deep-freeze with goldeye. In early spring he cured them in his smokehouse. Fresh from the smokehouse, with the warming winds of spring upon the snow, goldeye are delicious.

One spring we were fishing for trout. The best time for trout is in spring when there is still ice on the lake. We only had one boat, so some of us stayed on shore. The fishing was slow and after a few hours the fellows with the boat came back. The shore where we were docked was solid rock with a straight edge going down. In fact, the surface rock protruded like an overhang over the main rock formation. While we were talking I kept my hook in the water close by. Then I thought I felt a tug on the line, but nothing more. I tried to pull my line in but it was stuck. It seemed that my hook was receding in the water. There could be a fish on the hook, hiding under the overhang of rock. I got into the boat and had one of the men pull away from the shore. This would pull the fish out from under the rock. Right! As soon as the boat moved away from the shore I pulled the fish out from under the rock and the struggle began. The fish churned the water into foaming waves. It was a good-sized fish and it put up a real fight, but we ended up eating him.

One time we flew out to a northern lake where they had boats we could use. There were many fishermen flying out but there were still a lot of fish left in the lake. We caught various kinds of fish, but mainly northern pike, over two feet long; we didn't take smaller fish. These pike put up a real fight and it might take almost half an hour to bring a fish into the boat. The most difficult move a fish can make is to pass from side to side underneath the boat. It usually breaks the line. This is what a large pike did to me, taking along one of my best spoons. However, only a few minutes later one of the other fellows had a bite and managed to pull his fish in. It was my fish; he still had my spoon in his mouth, so I got my spoon back. We caught so many fish that day that we filled a number of black garbage bags with them. When the plane returned for us at the end of the day the weight of our catch was too much for the plane, so we left some bags of fish behind. The plane returned later to pick them up, but one of the plastic bags broke while loading and so part of our catch was lost. Does it sound like a "fish story"? Well, it is a fish story all right.

Some of my fondest memories are of going fishing with my sons in the Whiteshell. Most of the fishermen go out with their powerboats and are limited as to where they can go. Instead, we got a light rowboat and went up the small creeks. Sometimes we had to pull the boat across a beaver dam but we enjoyed doing that. We faced many obstacles on these small streams, but that was just like exploring the wilds. There were always fish in these places, although most of them were small. Fishing was really only an excuse on these trips; what we enjoyed most was the adventure of all the obstacles and being away from the motorboats.

One of my friends from Pine Falls was basically a good, law-abiding citizen; that is, apart from the subject of fishing. But he has been guilty of breaking the fishing regulations all his life, and I suspect his deep-freeze will still attest to this statement. I still remember the time we were fishing at the mouth of the Manigotagan River well before the fishing season opened. This is when the fish are most plentiful. It was at a scenic part of the river with continuous waterfalls, making it a risky adventure. I didn't have a fishing rod with me, so I stayed close to the highway to warn him in case any law enforcers happened along. None ever did. Was I an accomplice in breaking the fishing regulations? I am afraid that my conscience was not too clear at this time. However, this friend of mine had many law-abiding adventures as well.

Every spring the silver bass would move down the Manigotagan River into Lake Winnipeg, and then the fishing was excellent for a couple of weeks. We had a nice spot not far from the mouth of the river, a small open spot in the bush. It was an earth bank with a steep drop to the river. At the bottom were a couple of rocks, just enough to stand on to pull the fish in. We could not pull the fish in from the top, we always had to slide down and try to climb up the bank with the fish in one hand, Once we were there after a hard rain and the bank was slippery. We were very tired that evening. For bait we used worms on a pickerel rig with a float attached. We cast out the rig and then sat on the bank and watched for the familiar tug on the line, telling us that a fish is looking at our bait with serious intents. It doesn't take the fish very long. Sometimes they manage to get the worm off the hook, sometimes they are just playing with the hook, and often they manage to get loose after being caught, but it always meant sliding down the bank and back up again. If the fish stayed on the hook it was a fight trying to get him in, myself perched at the edge of the water with little to stand on. Most of the fish were big, from two to ten pounds, and put up a good struggle. A pickerel rig has two hooks on it and one time I caught two fish at once. We usually ended the day with at least 12 fish each. During the day we would build a fire surrounded by rocks so we could put a grate on it, which I kept in my car. Then we filleted some fish and cooked them on the fire. This was our lunch.

Another time I went out to this spot with Albert my son, and Kenny my grandson, but it was after the silver bass season. We were getting a few nibbles but no fish. Then Kenny called out that his hook was snagged on something. I took hold of his fishing rod to size up the problem, but I thought it might be a fish. I told Kenny that most likely he had caught a big fish and it was lying on the riverbed, too heavy to be pulled in. As we played around with the line it moved further out and I was sure it was a fish. Slowly we got the fish activated, but he did what he wanted. He was too big to be controlled and too heavy for the fishing line we used. He became more active and Kenny fought with him for over half an hour before he could finally pull him in. It was a catfish weighing over 15 pounds.

Pickerel are our preferred fish, but if we can't find pickerel we will go after pike; they usually are bigger and more of a challenge to get into the boat.

Another adventure, on a large lake, involved a different friend. It was a warm sunny day and we weren't getting any bites, so we headed for the part of the lake covered with reeds. Pike love to lie among the reeds on a sunny day and enjoy the warm water. I had cast my hook way out among the reeds like a fool, and my hook was badly entangled among them. So my friend paddled out while I looked after my line. As he rowed the boat among the reeds, I looked down beside the boat and there at the bottom was a three foot pike lazily sunning himself. Too bad, but I had to get my line unstuck first. After I had my hook out of the water I told my friend to row back and see if the fish was still there. Sure enough, he was there in about four feet of water. I dropped my hook down beside the boat and the pike snapped it up just like magic. We had him, but not in the boat. He started sailing around among the reeds just like wildfire, and it took everything I could do to keep my line from being entangled again. If you catch a small fish you can just lift him up with the line, but with a heavy fish this is not safe. With the silver bass I could put my forefinger into his gills and lift him up, no trouble. But you can't do that with a big pike, he bites. You need a big net to take him, but we didn't have a net. We always had a pliers along to take the hook out of the fish's throat. We also used the pliers to take the fish out of the water. Open the pliers wide, grab it by the centre, and push one arm of the pliers into the gills of the fish, like I used my finger with the bass. This is what I usually did instead of using a net. When the fish was tired out and close to the boat it only took a few seconds to pull him into the boat with my pliers. But here I couldn't do both, hold the fishing rod and use the pliers. The fish was too big and active. I asked my friend to use the pliers but he had never done it before. When I got the fish close by he grabbed the lips of the fish's mouth, like you hold a bolt with the pliers, but he could not lift the fish out of the water that way, it was too heavy. I tried to tell him how to do it but the fish kept me busy and my friend did not understand. Finally the fish swam underneath the boat to the other side and snapped the line. That was the end, the fish had won. We had spent about an hour among the reeds and were quite tired out.

Bobcaygeon was another challenge. Here I was a greenhorn again and I never got past that stage.

Opening day of the fishing season used to be a grand affair at Bobcaygeon, located between two lakes connected by a river about a mile long. The day begins at midnight and the fishing season starts in the first minute after midnight. At that time the power dam, bridges, riverbanks, and shores of the lakes are crowded with people holding onto their fishing rods. When the sun came up we could see about 100 boats on Pigeon Lake. You would think that all the people of Toronto had come out to Bobcaygeon. Later they changed the fishing laws and the affair was more subdued.

However, going back to the good old days, I remember one morning of the season's opening day. I got up just after sunrise. It was a heavenly morning—sunny, quiet, without a bit of fog on the water. I went over to my neighbour's place which was closer to the river. For a while I had no luck but then I caught three fine pickerel in a row, and that was it. When I got back Norah was up, ready to fry the fish for breakfast as soon as I had filleted them. We had a lovely breakfast together.

I never really became a fisherman at Bobcaygeon. Oh yes, I usually had my rod along when we went on the lake and I kept the line wet, but I didn't know what I was doing like I did in Manitoba. Occasionally I caught a fish, more by accident than by skill.

On another occasion my son Edward, my friend Bill from Toronto and I decided to go fishing at Rice Lake, north of Toronto. Bill knew about Rice Lake and its reputation as a fishing spot, but he was no fisherman. We hired a boat and went scouting around the lake. We didn't know what we were fishing for or how to fish. We caught some small fish about eight inches long, but we threw them back. Seeing we found no other fish we started to keep them so we wouldn't return empty-handed. When we got back to shore we were sort of ashamed of our catch, but when the other fishermen saw what we had they were amazed at how well we had done. We were suddenly sorry we threw the first ones back. You never know in life!

MY EDUCATION

I learned to read well after only a few years at school and I have loved reading ever since, always looking for a variety of subjects and not afraid to read books that are considered dangerous. The more a person reads, looking at different viewpoints on a subject, the better one is able to discern where the truth lies. However, the truth is usually contained in paradox and conflicting opinions, rather than in clear dogmatic statements.

In my school days in the one-room elementary school, libraries were small. We had one shelf of good books and I read most of them. They were fiction by authors we would today regard as classical writers, books that have become part of our literature. In contrast, most of the fiction in school libraries today rates little above the typical "drugstore novels", which are dated by the trend to relate to contemporary issues and thus drop out as soon as the fashions of the day change to new whims of expression. The trend towards "naturalism" in this century has almost eradicated the possibility of literature being created.

The books I read gave me a taste for literature, which has led me on from English to German, French, Latin and Greek literatures. It has been a wonderful life of discovery and adventure, and has brought me into a knowledge of many great people of all ages. Another book that has kept my attention throughout my life is the Christian Bible. It has had a greater influence on me than any other book because it has revealed God to me.

Buying books was difficult in those days. Not only did we not have money to buy them but we had no access to bookstores, either. My Dad helped the situation a number of times by obtaining a "travelling library", a case with about 25 books, from a library in Winnipeg, the books to be made available to the community. This helped.

My parents noticed my interest in reading and made it possible for me to get my high school education by sending me to Steinbach to attend school. Their decision started me on a course in life which has made me what I am. What would have happened to me without high school? I can't imagine the answer to that question. I had a few rebellious tendencies in high school, mainly against good literature like Shakespeare, but that did not last long. Only a few years later I found myself reading Shakespeare for enjoyment in my spare time.

My teenage days were difficult years, and I spent my time and energy trying anything that could lead to a job. Later, when I had obtained work with the Winnipeg Post Office, the desire for more studies came back to me.

In 1943 I began a business course with the Russell Institute of Winnipeg. It cost me five dollars a month. It prepared me for the accounting course I took later. In 1944 I enrolled for a correspondence course in radio servicing through the Manitoba Department of Education, given by the American School in Chicago. Taking a technical course by correspondence did not make much sense so I also enrolled with the Radio College of Canada, Toronto, for Applied Radio and Electronics. With this I received a package of radio parts and built my own radio, the way they were built in those days. The radio worked quite well. At the end of the course I went to Toronto, where I spent two weeks in their laboratory to learn actual radio servicing. They also introduced us to television a year or two before it came into operation on a public scale. Television was based on a very complicated system of mechanical synchronization at the beginning. This was 1947.

In 1944 I rented a typewriter and bought an instruction manual so I could teach myself to type. This skill has been useful to me throughout my life. I did not acquire a professional speed, but it enabled me to type dozens of essays for my university professors and today it helps me operate my computer.

In 1946 I started taking accordion lessons with Kent's Accordion School, using an old instrument. In 1947, when new accordions came on the market after the war, I bought a new Sonola, made in Italy. My musical abilities are clearly limited but I enjoyed that accordion for many years. In 1992 I finally put it in the garbage, having worn it out completely. The instrument meant a great deal to me.

The next few years passed by quietly; the children took up a lot of my time. However, in 1957 I began with serious studies: I registered with the University of Manitoba and took Calculus in evening school, my first attempt at university studies. I did very well, with a mark of 91, and continued by taking two courses at summer school in 1958. To do this I used my holiday time plus an extra two weeks without pay. My wife Helen was working full time now so we couldn't travel anyway.

Then in September 1958 I enrolled with the Society of Industrial and Cost Accountants. The lectures were given in the evening but the course was heavy and required a lot of study time. I took two years of a four-year course and acquired a wide knowledge of the accounting field. However, the course required that I should be employed in accounting work to gain practical experience with the studies, and I realized I was going nowhere. I got an offer from the Post Office to transfer me to Ottawa, but it was not specific. I dropped the studies after two years of above average marks in the exams, which were gruesome four-hour affairs.

In 1960 I resigned from the Post Office and registered with the Manitoba Teachers College. It took me into the exciting profession of teaching, full of problems and pitfalls for a person now 41 years old. I wouldn't advise anyone else to try it because you need to be young to cope with the vagaries of youth.

Besides the accounting studies, I kept taking university courses through the Extension Department. In May 1963 I obtained the B.A. degree. Then I was admitted to the B.Ed. program and graduated in 1965. The next step was to enter the Master's program but here I was faced with a dilemma. I had to choose my major from the courses I had taken for the B.A. degree and German literature was the only one in which my marks were high enough for me to continue. I was not interested in German and it took me a year until I could make up my mind to major in German literature. However, I did make that decision and never looked back. I thoroughly enjoyed German literature. In Graduate Studies I had some advantages. I was working on Indian Reserves now but I could come to Winnipeg on Saturdays, so my professor scheduled classes for Saturday morning for his graduate students. In another year, when I could not come to Winnipeg regularly, he assigned me studies and I worked at home, just turning in my assignments. My Master's thesis took a lot of research. I spent my Christmas and Easter holidays at the university working on research and finally graduated with the M.A. degree in October of 1973.

I wasn't far into my teaching career before bilingualism rose to the forefront of national politics. Obviously a good knowledge of French would become an important job factor, and in some areas even a necessary qualification. I wisely decided to accept the challenge. As I was now working on Indian Reserves, outside of Winnipeg, this presented a problem. Nevertheless, I started taking French through the Correspondence Branch of the Department of Education in 1968 and continued for four years. I had always nurtured a secret desire to learn French so I was happy with the new challenge I faced. French studies have taken me to many different institutions of learning over a period of 20 years.

In the summer of 1970 I took my first course in French Conversation at St. Boniface College and here I faced the real task of learning the language. So far I had only studied the grammar; learning to speak the language was a whole new challenge. I was back there in the summer of 1973 for more conversation. I found that French people I met outside of the school were not at all interested in helping students learn their language.

The summer of 1971 took me to Laval University in Quebec City for French studies and here I faced a rigorous regime of studies coupled with a French environment. The University had also organized an interesting program of recreational activities and I found my summers in Quebec

City both enjoyable and exciting. I went back there the summers of 1972 and 1974. It was there that I met another student who later became my wife, Norah Bradley.

By 1973 I was seriously involved with French, so I resigned from my teaching position with Indian Affairs and spent my first full-time year studying French at the University of Manitoba. One of the courses was taught at St.Boniface College, a heavy course that demanded a lot of work.

In 1974-75 I went to France to study at the University of Paris III. Actually I took classes at Centre Censier, a branch of the Sorbonne where foreign students at the beginner level were taught. They gave me very little credit for my French studies in Canada. One of the students I met introduced me to a German Professor from behind the Iron Curtain, and he allowed me to take a German course he was teaching at another Paris University. The subject of his course was the Don Juan story as dealt with in the literature of different countries. It was an interesting contact with the Communist world. The campus at which I took this course was a unique place. It was the new Science University, less than ten years old. It was built in pods, each standing on pillars above ground level, with seven rows of pods and each row having seven pods (if I remember correctly). Seven times seven equals 49 separate buildings each standing on its own pillars, an impressive sight. They were all connected by elevated crosswalks going in each direction. Despite the fact that they were almost new they were already dilapidated on the inside. In the morning the ground level was usually white with scattered Communist propaganda leaflets handed out on the street corners. There was seldom a morning without a dose of propaganda.

Realizing that I was not gaining much with the studies I was taking, I decided to take some language studies on my own. The French government held exams for foreigners so they could get official standing for their proficiency in the language. I obtained the required information and then studied at home. I received a passing grade for the Certificat Pratique de Langue Francaise, 1° Degre.

Together with my studies at Centre Censier I was allowed to register for another course at any other of the Paris universities. Adventure always seemed to be my rule so I registered for a class in Folk Dancing at a university in the area of Denfert-Rochereau. Classes were held in the fourth level underground in the evening. As ever, just finding the place was an adventure in itself. It introduced me to a new environment and a new circle of people. We studied the folk dances with their music, from different peoples around the world and from different time periods. We also practiced the steps to the music. The dances varied greatly. American dances are mostly fun and physical. Many of the others were serious religious dances and could be very moving emotionally. I especially remember the ancient Hebrew dances, probably what the people of Israel sang when they had been taken captive to Babylon. I was so moved I could hardly keep from crying while doing this dance. I have since tried to get the music for these ancient Hebrew dances but the music available here has been modernized and has little emotion left.

Walking down to the fourth level I often passed by a band made up of African blacks who were practicing rock music. The music was of high professional quality with deep emotional content. I was very impressed with it. In comparison, the rock music we hear on American TV and radio is just frivolous and of low musical ability.

I must relate another event that was rather shocking. It was exam time and the procedure followed in our literature exam was unorthodox. Our Professor took us in one at a time. In the first room was a table with a pile of folded-up paper pieces. On each piece was the name of an author or title that was on the Course. When you came in you picked a piece of paper at random and then sat down for about five minutes to consider your topic, while she questioned the previous student in the next room. I was fortunate, I had picked an author whom we had studied in class, and whom I knew well. The next student, a friend of mine, picked a minor author who was mentioned in our course material but whom we had never discussed in class. She could remember nothing about the author. She got a zero in the course, although she was an excellent student, and I got a high mark. If I had made her pick I would have received a zero. We thought the exam was most unfair.

University life in Paris clearly lacked self-discipline. Students attended classes when their social activities or other interests permitted. There always was a core of dedicated students in each class, but the stragglers were quite evident. Many of these were involved in various political activities such as Communism, Islamic fanaticism and anti-U.S. propaganda. The knowledge I gained there from “rubbing shoulders” with people from many countries certainly colours my opinion about the political events we see on TV today. I finished my studies at the end of the year with the mark “Superior”, following the exams.

In the spring of 1976 Norah Bradley and I were married. We had both resigned from our jobs so we decided to spend our first year studying French at the University of Manitoba. I was admitted to Graduate Studies at the Pre-Masters level of the Arts program in French. I found the studies demanding and felt my abilities were slipping. To write good French at the level of a Master’s thesis requires the appropriate expression for every statement that is made, and my memory was not capable of doing this at my age. I ended the year with good marks, B or B+, but I did not feel I could cope with writing a Master’s thesis. It was the end of my French studies at the University of Manitoba.

Norah had been to France to study at Tours during the summer session, but she wanted to go back to Paris for a year like I had done.

Accordingly, we registered with the University of Paris and went to France for 1977-78. This time Norah took classes at Centre Censier and I was admitted to classes at the Sorbonne.

Here I found myself in a typical French university situation. The buildings were crowded, especially the areas where we could get a coffee or snack in between classes. Facilities definitely were poor. I had a lot of research to do and it was difficult to find an empty spot in the library to sit down. We were not allowed to enter the stacks but had to order the books we needed, which was often a confusing affair, working from the card catalogue. However, not far from the University was the Palace of Luxembourg with its lovely large park area. It was a favourite spot for the students to go out and relax. I have spent many hours there. Further off was the large Jardin des Plantes, a botanical park with an impressive museum of zoology next to it.

At the Sorbonne I experienced an atmosphere of liberal intellectualism that was overly pervasive; it was stifling. It was not contentious but infiltrating in a warm manner. In general, the irreligious academic attitude was repulsive to me. I started the year with about seven courses and slowly dropped courses so that I was only attending about two or three classes at the end. I don't remember if I wrote any final exams or not; I have no statement of marks to show that I did. It was truly a year of enlightenment for me. However, I got to know enough local French people to realize that the atmosphere I experienced at the University did not truly represent the nation as a whole. I had a similar experience at Laval University in Quebec City where the independence movement was rife, but not truly representative of the Quebec people as a whole. Universities have their own characteristics.

Again, during my second year in Paris, I studied for a government exam on my own. I obtained Diplome d'Etudes Francaises, 2° Degre, with a mark of "Assez Bien", or "almost good". It did not involve indoctrination, which was the goal at the University, but was a true estimate of scholarly achievement.

The end of my French studies did not mean the end of university for me. We moved back to Winnipeg for the winter of 1982 so I was able to register at the University of Manitoba again. This time I chose to study Linguistics. I took two half courses during the Regular Session of 1982-83, and again the next year. The study area intrigued me but I felt the courses being offered did not satisfy my expectations, so I switched back to languages. In 1984-85 I took Elementary Latin and continued the next year with Latin Authors. I found Virgil fascinating. I think he is the most capable poet I have studied, even surpassing Shakespeare. I should have continued to study Virgil the next year so that I could read him fluently, but it was not to be. As the course in Virgil was not offered the next year, I switched to Greek Studies.

Someone had told me that Classical Greek is easier than Latin and it influenced my decision. I am glad I started with Greek but found the information I had been given was totally false. I spent four years with Greek, going up one level each year. The vocabulary of Greek authors is much greater than that of modern authors. The language is complex beyond comparison with the English language. For instance, the inflection of verbs is almost limitless, with a single verb having as many as 150 different forms, some of them showing no recognizable similarity. This includes most verbs.

I did not study the Koine Greek of the Bible, but it is relatively easy after studying the writings of five centuries of Greek authors. Still, when I read the letters of Paul in the New Testament I find he keeps on introducing new words in almost every verse, from beginning to end. If you look at the English translation you find the vocabulary used is definitely limited in comparison; the same words are used over and over again.

When Norah became afflicted with Alzheimer Disease I had to leave my studies so I could be with her. At the same time, my eyes were weakening and I found the Greek script very tiring on my eyesight. My official studies have come to an end but there is still much reading I can do, and I hope to exercise my brain to the end.

LAVAL UNIVERSITY—QUEBEC CITY

I knew before my first trip to Laval in 1971 that I could expect a new cultural experience in Quebec. I was not disappointed. I realized from my friendships with Francophones in Manitoba that they had a different personality. Most English-speaking people have trouble understanding this. The francophones here were not interested in helping students to speak French, they couldn't stand listening to French poorly spoken. How would the Quebec people respond?

I registered for the six-week summer session at Laval at the beginner's level, and chose to take accommodation with a local family. I drove out by car and spent a day or two in Montreal to see the city. Montreal is an intriguing city and I enjoyed wandering around and seeing the sights.

What I soon noticed in Quebec was that the highway signs were based on a different system than I was accustomed to. Ontario highways have a system that is easy to understand; anyone can successfully navigate the famous 401 without trouble. I found Quebec highway signs misleading, and often they appeared too late to change lanes. The result was that when I left Montreal I took the wrong exit and was bound for the U.S.A. instead of taking the south shore highway to Quebec City. I finally got off the route and headed cross country to find the highway I wanted but it resulted in my reaching Quebec City a few hours later than I had intended.

Once there I had to find the home where I was staying. I couldn't locate the street so I stopped and asked a couple, who were standing on their lawn, for directions. They both talked at the same time, faster than I could understand, and waved their hands as well. However, I understood enough that I managed to find the street I wanted. Quebecers talk with their hands as much as with their lips and at too great a speed for students to understand.

The home to which I had been assigned belonged to an elderly lady. She served me breakfast in the morning and then at night spent about 15 minutes talking with me. She was a nice lady but gave me very little practice in speaking French. In succeeding years I stayed at the university residence and did much better.

Laval University was originally situated in the old part of Quebec City where space was very cramped. After the war a military air force site on the edge of the city became vacant and Laval University obtained this land to build a new campus. It was an excellent opportunity, given the large size of the area and the fact that a whole new university could be planned from the start. They evidently had sufficient funds available and built a well-planned campus. It was a joy to study at this university.

My experience with French culture, whether in France or Quebec, is that they are excellent planners and organizers. In France I admired their railway system and the new Paris suburbs. At Laval I found the careful planning that had built the campus had also organized our studies and the free-time activities for the rest of the day. It gave us a positive introduction to the unique culture of Quebec, which stands above anything we find in the rest of Canada.

Students were warned at the beginning that anyone speaking English on campus would be expelled without further notice. It worked. The only way to learn a language is to be forced to use it. The students were interested in learning French and faithfully obeyed the rule. There were many Americans and Mexicans with us Canadians taking French.

During the first week they had a special welcome evening for the students as a group so they could mix and become acquainted. One event was a "mixer", very exciting, and involved all 150 students present. We had a large stage with 30 chairs placed in a circle and a band to play music. The students were divided into families of five persons, each group with its own family name. Mother sat on the chair, she held Baby on her knees, Father stood behind the chair, Son stood on her right and Daughter on her left side. Each person received a large card with the family name and position in the family. When the band played everybody got up and circled around the stage, trading cards as they passed by others, and one chair was taken off the floor. When the band stopped we looked at the card we now carried and then had to get our new family together, plus a chair for Mother. One family lost out with each round. It was a hilarious event and we came into contact with every student on campus. Plus I was part of the winning family and I have a photo to prove it. I was Mother and had a female Baby on my knees.

The studies were more serious and there was no goofing off here like in Paris. Classes started at 8:30 a.m. and continued with only ten minute breaks until finished. The first year I only had four hours of classes so I easily made it to the cafeteria for lunch. The second year I had five hours of classes and just barely made it to lunch. The third year I had seven hours of classes and that meant missing lunch, except for what we could get out the vending machines during the ten minute breaks. It was a steady grind and for serious students only.

I seriously considered staying at Laval for full-time study, which would have given me a much better standing in French. I even applied for registration in the regular session but the lure of Paris was too much for me.

Recreational activities were well planned, there was at least one event happening everyday, and when we had free time we went downtown to see the Old City with its stone walls. They had a number of bus tours going in various directions. One took us to an island, the Ile d'Orleans, where we saw the site of a well-known TV program, and had dinner at a unique restaurant. It had three floors of dining with the whole centre part open from the floor to the ceiling. A band playing on the second floor was visible from all three floors.

Another time we went to Baie-St. Paul for a folk festival. The whole town was taken up by the festival and closed to all vehicle traffic. People came from far and wide. As the day proceeded my friend and I realized we needed to find a washroom. We were in a school at the time so that should be no problem. We found a washroom but could not read the writing on the door, it looked more like Greek than French. Then we noticed there were women going in and coming out. So we looked for another washroom and found the same writing, plus women going in and out. We decided not to take a chance with the Quebec women so we postponed the matter. I believe we ended up going into the bush.

Our return in the evening almost ended in a worse crisis. The buses that brought us in had parked on the outskirts of town and the drivers told us to come back there at a certain hour. When the time came we went back to look for the buses and found they were gone. Fortunately we found someone who knew where they were. The drivers had moved them and parked behind a large building so they could not be seen from the street. A number of students never found the bus, so we left without them. You have to be ready for these tricks in Quebec.

One day we took a trip to St. Jean Port Joli. This town is famous for its wood-carving artisans and is well known throughout America through the medium of tourist information. All tourists stop and shop here. We saw many beautiful carvings.

On another trip we visited an old monastery, a quaint place. It had a good-sized canal laid out in the shape of a rectangle. There were about a dozen canoes there so we could paddle around the canal. One of them was called a "demon" because it tended to upset rather frequently. The girls had their suspicions about the problem and kept away from it. I was sure I could handle it so when it was free I got into it myself. I wasn't in it more than ten seconds before it turned over and dumped me into four feet of water. Fortunately I had left my jacket and camera on the bank. I was wearing jeans and it takes a whole day for jeans to dry out by themselves.

One of the trees beside the canal had a swing on it and by swinging full speed you could jump off and land on the other side of the canal. It kept the boys busy for awhile. Then it started to rain heavily, so we ran for shelter. It was also high time to look for a washroom. The monastery was a long narrow building with a washroom in the middle of each side, one for the ladies and one for the men. Washrooms did not have urinals, only closed closets. We soon filled the closets and then there was a knock on the outside door. It was a girl demanding we let her in, she had “to go” and would get all wet if she ran around to the other side in the rain. The boys refused to let her in but I don’t know what happened to her. I think the boys were tired of the continual presence of women in the men’s washroom. We ended with a dinner at the place but I wasn’t too comfortable sitting in my wet jeans and don’t remember what we had.

I spent a lot of time in the Old City, alone or with friends. Parking was always a problem so I usually parked in the “No Parking” areas. I hoped that they were reserved for tourists and I never had any problems. The Old City is wonderfully located on top of a high cliff, overlooking the St. Lawrence River. It was surrounded by a stone wall, much of which is still standing today. On the west side of it is the Citadelle, a queer kind of fort. It is sunken into the ground, but open, with a passageway all around. It can easily be entered by an enemy from all around. I never figured it out. Further west along the shore are the Plains of Abraham. They go down almost to river level, so General Wolfe never had much trouble pulling his cannon up the cliff. It is now a beautiful park area.

Beside the Citadelle on the side of the St. Lawrence River, they have built a walkway hanging onto the side of the cliff, which leads to the Terrasse Dufferin, a promenade high over the Lower City. The splendid Chateau Frontenac is just a little further up. It always was my ambition to stay in this hotel but I have never done it. Further north is a stairway leading down to the Lower City, or you could take an elevator down from the Terrasse Dufferin. Halfway down the stairway was a lovely restaurant in the side of the cliff. At the bottom of the cliff was a cave going into the rock. It had been used for illicit purposes during its historic past, but now is converted into a bar. It is all bare rock on the inside with only the furniture added. It was eerie and clammy in this cave bar. This lower part of the city was being restored to its original condition to convert it into a tourist attraction. It included an interesting church, Eglise Notre Dame des Victoires, where I have often knelt to pray.

The upper part of the Old City had many interesting shops. One restaurant featured the Quebec crepes, or pancakes, with hot apple cider. They used the crepes to make the main course and the dessert as well. We liked to go there to eat when we could afford it. One of the street alleys was devoted to artists who hung up their artistic works all along the lane to attract tourist customers. They were mostly sketches of Quebec and I bought a good number of them.

The officials working on the ferry going across the St. Lawrence were on strike but the ferry was still making its regular trips across the river. We could use the ferry without paying because there was no one to collect the fares. We frequently crossed over free to the city of Levis to explore that area.

Those were the years of the “coffee house”, an institution of the “flower children” and hitchhikers. The young people got together, strummed their guitars, and sang the popular songs of the day. It was boring, but it was a very important institution for the youth. At least once a week we had a coffee house evening. The group I was with decided we should make an attempt to put more life into the evening. We wrote a skit and acted it to demonstrate the problems we had with the French language. Each time we did it we received enthusiastic applause; it was a bright interlude amidst the boring strumming of guitars.

One afternoon I was sitting peacefully reading in a large assembly room, the name of which translates into “hairnet”, derived from the queer netting hoisted up around the ceiling. At the other end of the room was a group of young people. One of the young fellows walked over to me and noticed I was reading a book of drama. It’s what got me into trouble. “You are just what we need,” he said in French. “We are preparing a short play and need advice from someone who knows drama.” He trapped me very neatly. “We mostly just need your academic help in this venture,” he added. The end of the summer session was getting close and the students were putting on a great concert at the end.

There had been an article in the local newspaper poking fun at the battle of the Plains of Abraham in 1759. This had given the group a topic to work on. They had written it up into a play which ends with the two generals in a bathtub playing with a rubber ducky. The play was both serious and ridiculous. It could also be risky because the independence movement was boiling at the university among the professors.

As we were trying to work out the details we realized we needed more help. There was an older man standing further off. We sent one of the young girls over to ask him for a bit of help, nothing serious. How could an old man resist the charm of a young woman? He was soon helping us lay out the different parts of the play. Later I heard him say, “I was just innocently standing there minding my own business, how did I ever get myself involved with this?” I was a bit worried too.

The great evening came. Our biggest problem had been getting a rubber ducky. For a bathtub we had one of those outdoor children’s play pools with real water in it. We had some soldiers and dressed them as well as we could. I was General Wolfe and the young leader of the group was General Montcalm. I had the most risky part to play. Our play came on towards the end of the concert. The attention of the audience, which had a lot of outsiders in it, was diverted to the front where preparations were being made. Our scheme was to take the audience by surprise. The two generals came in from the rear, one from each side. Coming out of our corners we shouted taunts at each other, like "Down with the French!" as we cut across through the audience on our way to the front with our spears raised high. The audience was almost shocked. At the front the contention was about to come to blows between our soldiers when something intervened. In the end we were both sitting in the water playing with the rubber ducky, a ridiculous sight. The moral was that the whole French-English argument was silly as well. The applause at the end was almost thunderous. The generals had to go back to get dried and properly dressed. Some of my clothing had vanished, but I managed to get home as I was.

They had built a lovely Catholic church on the campus, and I enjoyed going to the service there. Some years later when I passed through Quebec I went to visit the church again and found the interior blocked off. A man standing there told me it was no longer a church, it had been converted into an archives building. A sad state, I thought, but it shows only too clearly where Laval University has put the Christian faith on which it was founded.

One of the persons I met at Laval was a fine Cuban lady by the name of Olga Ortega, about my age. She had attended university in Cuba when Fidel Castro was also a student there. Her father owned the leading newspaper in Cuba and supported Castro when he began his revolution against the government. Her father was wealthy and influential. When Castro's army had taken over Cuba he also demanded control of the newspaper. When her father refused, Castro sent in his soldiers, took over the press, and expelled her parents. In the meantime Olga had married a top Spanish diplomat, Mr. Ortega. This meant they moved around among the nations' capital cities, depending on where her husband was involved in diplomatic affairs. They had two sons during this period. However, it was a traditional custom for Spanish lords to have a mistress, and in this case it was his secretary. When Olga could no longer stand having another woman in the house she packed up her sons and moved to Miami, Florida. At the same time she also had trouble with her eyes and was slowly going blind. She came to Quebec mainly to get away from her troubled life and try to retain her sanity. We were both rejected by our spouses and suffering severe spiritual distress as a result.

Ste. Anne de Beaupre is the name of a church about 25 miles northeast of Quebec City, famous among Catholics for miracles of healing that occur there, much like Notre Dame de Lourdes in France. I put little faith in the stories of miracle healing but I needed to spend much time in prayer to relieve my troubled spirit. These great church edifices have an awe-inspiring atmosphere that lifts a person up closer to God. I visited many such churches in those days just to spend time in prayer. Remarkably, I was never alone; there always were other people doing the same. So I took a bus trip to this church just for prayer and a time of meditation with God. The Church was truly a place of prayer and it was one of the experiences that kept me together. The next year Olga and I made the trip together. We both wept as we prayed for our spouses.

While at Ste. Anne de Beaupre we visited the Panorama of Jerusalem. It is a huge, circular building about 100 feet in diameter. The inside wall is painted all around with a picture of Jerusalem and the surrounding area, depicting the story of Jesus. The floor level between the viewing platform in the centre and the wall is filled with lifelike scenes that integrate with the drawing on the wall. It is an impressive creation.

Norah also developed a close friendship with Olga on her own, and when we were married we found that we had a common friend. Norah and I kept up our communication with Olga through the years. Her sons are now grown up and doing well in life. The last few years she has been together with her husband again. She still writes her own letters, so she still has some eyesight.

I also had an experience with death while I was at Laval. We spent one Saturday evening at a Catholic institution where we had a special dinner. During the night I woke up at about 3:00 a.m. and felt horribly sick. It pained me to lie down, and when I got up I could not straighten up. I had to stay bent over with cramps in my abdomen. I was up and around in my room for two hours but it only got worse. I was staying at the university residence at the time. I knew there was a guard on duty downstairs, so if I was going to die at least I would not be alone. I got dressed and went downstairs. By 6:00 a.m. I could stand it no longer so I asked the guard to call a taxi to take me to a hospital. The taxi took me to Laval Hospital. I walked in alone to the emergency counter. The doctor was just writing up a report and asked me to wait a bit. I held onto the counter with both hands. The next thing I knew a nurse was taking me into a side room. She put the familiar thing around my arm to test my blood pressure. Then she took it off and wrapped it around tighter. This was beginning to hurt when she did it a third time. Then she ran out. The next thing I knew I was on a bed being wheeled away.

It was about 8:00 a.m. when I came to again. I saw a group of hospital persons standing around me. A doctor apologized that there was no one in the hospital who could speak to me in English. He explained to me that I was dying and they did not know if they could save me. I felt awful to be dying, and nobody even knew that I was in the hospital. Then I lost consciousness again. By 9:00 a.m. I came to again and I noticed there were only two persons beside my bed. Maybe the crisis was easing? Then a little later I felt something move inside my abdomen and the pain began to ease. Obviously there had been a blockage in my digestive canal. In another hour or so I managed to get up. By 12 noon they discharged me and I walked out alone, fully recovered. They gave me a document saying they had misdiagnosed me and advised me to take it to my doctor on my return home. They did not know what had been wrong with me. I suspect it was the meal I had the night before, but when I talked to the others who had been at the same meal none of them had had any problems. Twice in my life afterwards I have felt similar pains developing, but fortunately they did not become severe. I am always somewhat afraid when I eat a strange meal.

MY FAMILY

Albert was born on July 7, 1941, at the Steinbach Hospital, while we were living in a little house on 80 acres of land about six miles southwest of Grunthal. The cost for ten days in the hospital was $14 and the doctor's fee was $15. Can you believe it? Only $29 for having a baby! You'd think he was born in the Stone Age.

Albert's mother had a difficult delivery; it was hard on her and it also had an effect on the baby. Albert's health was poor for some years but later he outgrew it and became a healthy teenager. He was an active boy; he climbed up on a chair by himself at six and one-half months and started walking not much later.

By the time Edward was born I was working at the Post Office in Winnipeg and we lived in a two-room suite at 368 Spence Street in the rooming-house district. He was born at Concordia Hospital on November 10, 1942. He was a big boy, weighing over 14 pounds. Costs had gone up by now. The hospital charged us $24.20 for a nine day stay, but the doctor's fee was still only $15. It's hard to imagine how the costs for a pregnancy have risen since then.

Edward was a calm and relaxed boy; he saw no purpose in running all over when he could just sit and play. He was slow learning to talk as well.

A couple of weeks after Edward was born we moved to a small, new, non-modern house at 277 McKay Avenue in North Kildonan. Across the back lane was an open field, an ideal place for the boys to play.

We stayed in this house for six years. This period was marred by the fact that I developed asthma and almost became a "basket case". I survived and defeated the disease, but it was a tough time for me, and it must have been difficult for the family as well. I remember we did a lot of walking during those years. Behind us was a railway track built during the first World War to divert rail traffic past Winnipeg. It had a swing bridge across the Red River which opened during the summer to allow the S.S. Kenora to sail through on its Sunday trip to Selkirk. The railway line wasn't being used, so we often walked along the rails on Sunday afternoon to watch the S.S, Kenora sail through.

Six years later Irvin was born on March 20, 1948, at Concordia Hospital. Spring was early that year and the Red River started flowing before mother and son left the hospital. Helen's room was located so she could see the river from her window. The hospital charged $37.75 for six days and the doctor took $35.

With three children our house was too small, so we bought a lovely large house at 1329 Somerville Avenue in Fort Garry. There was still lots of open territory around, another ideal spot for the kids.

Irvin was a lively kid but good-natured. His older brothers were a bit rough with him at times and then I had to defend him. I remember one nightmare I went through with him. He became badly sick for two full days, and I was at home those two days while his mother was at work. He cried and tossed around in his crib for 48 full hours. He could finish a bottle of milk in one minute flat and then tossed it across the room. Fortunately we both survived the illness. For the rest I remember him as a peaceful boy.

About this time Dairy Queen opened their soft ice cream stores. It was a great event for the kids (and the adults as well). We spent many happy hours lining up for soft ice cream on hot summer days.

Then came the year of the Great Flood, 1950. Fortunately our house stood on a high lot but there was water all around us. I had to park our car on Pembina Highway and there wasn't much driving I could do. We had a wooden sidewalk on the street and it floated, so I put boards along it and nailed them down to keep the walk together so it would not float away. That way I could walk to Pembina Highway. Families had to be evacuated, so Helen and the boys went out to the country to live with the grandparents for about six weeks. Isaac Friesen came to live with me and we stayed in the house through the flood. Someone dumped a canoe down on the street in front of our house so we took it behind the house. Then we lowered a rope from the second floor bedroom and tied it to the canoe. In case we were flooded seriously we could evacuate with the canoe. After the flood I put the canoe out in front again and it vanished as mysteriously as it had appeared. It was a mysterious case!

Then our camping days began. At first we slept in the car. The back seat came down and opened into the trunk. That way Helen and the boys could sleep in the back and I slept in the front seat. Soon, however, we bought a tent and then we could sleep properly. We camped and roamed all over the Whiteshell and the Lake Winnipeg beaches. We also managed to rent a cottage for a week practically every year at Grand Beach, Winnipeg Beach, or Riding Mountain National Park.

Helen started with music by getting a guitar and taking lessons. Then I got an accordion, and later we bought a piano for the kids. They all took piano lessons but it wasn't always easy. Later they bought electric guitars, a banjo and wind instruments. Music in the home is a wonderful advantage and brings lifelong benefits. Albert became advanced in music and was able to organize, lead a band and prepare the music.

As Helen spent more time working out, I spent more time with the kids at home. It was at this time that I had the choice to go on the Clerk's Staff at the Post Office, which would have opened the opportunity for future advancement, but I turned it down because it meant working the evening shift and I would never be home with the children. My memory of these years has dimmed. I remember spending time pushing a baby carriage around on the sidewalk, but the boys didn't stay in the carriage too long. We also spent a lot of time with a softball and bat.

I remember one thing that was held against me for a long time. Albert could have started school when he was six, but his health was not too good so we kept him at home until he was seven. He and Eddy were always together and we didn't want to separate them, so we let them start school together. This gave the false impression later that Albert had failed a grade. He resented this. I'm afraid it was a mistake on my part.

The new house on Somerville Avenue didn't have a sidewalk going from the house to the street, so Albert and I decided to put in a concrete sidewalk. I think he was under ten years old at the time and neither of us had any experience with concrete. I made the forms and then mixed the concrete. Albert had the job of leveling off and finishing the surface. We each learned how to do our own job. By the end of the day we were both experienced. Later at the university Albert took up civil engineering and is today a specialist in concrete work. I believe his profession started on the day he did the finishing work on our sidewalk.

By the time Helen and I thought we were too old to have another child (she was 30 and I was 33), we were surprised to find that it was happening. Would it be a girl? After three boys it seemed too much to hope for. Helen seemed sort of embarrassed that she was pregnant again. We had gossipy neighbours and they loved to talk. The day came when she decided to put on a maternity dress. Why? To conceal the fact, what else! I told her that putting on a maternity dress was an advertisement to all the world that she was pregnant, the very opposite of what she wanted. Everybody would immediately know that she was pregnant. So she postponed the matter and nobody suspected what was happening. We went through the same argument three times, with the result that she never wore a maternity dress.

Finally, on the morning of July 13, 1952, I had to take Helen to the hospital. I stayed home from work to look after Irvin. We were out on the front lawn when a neighbour lady came over and asked why I was at home and not at work. I told her I had taken Helen to the hospital. She was surprised and wanted to know why. I expected her to know but she claimed she had no idea Helen was pregnant. Then another neighbour lady came over and also admitted she had not suspected Helen was pregnant. Helen certainly showed it, but if a woman doesn't wear maternity clothing everyone only thinks she is getting fat.

It was a happy surprise, it was a girl! Now we felt more like a family.

At this point there are five years in which my records are very sparse with entries. No new events were happening in my life. I conclude that in these years I devoted most of my time to our children. Helen was away working with outside jobs and it made sense that I should put in more time at home. This is also the period in which I learnt to do a lot of housework like doing the laundry, ironing, cooking and baking.

Marian grew up a quiet, well-balanced child, almost angelic. I spent much time on the sidewalk with her in the baby carriage. When she grew older we took long walks together. There was an A&W Root Beer place on Jubilee Avenue at the narrow one-lane bridge. I remember going there together with her to get a Root Beer ice cream float. They were delicious.

At this time we had a large garden across the back lane where the lots were still vacant. We grew a lot of vegetables, which meant a lot of work. Here the boys learned to work, hoeing the weeds and digging up the soil in fall. I worked with them but tried to let them learn work skills by themselves. When they grew up they became very independent persons; when I reflect on it, I realize it probably resulted from my way of training them. As soon as they were old enough they went to work on vegetable farms just a little west of us to earn their own money. My salary seldom did more than pay for essential expenses.

This was also the time they had problems with the Derhak boys. These boys came from a rough family, and were bigger and tougher than the other boys in their classes at school. They loved to fight and scare the smaller boys. Our boys often came home crying after having been beaten up by the Derhaks. I had always taught our boys not to fight but their mother took it into her hands to give them some different advice. I only heard about it later. The result was that the smaller boys at school ganged together and easily beat up the three Derhaks. Once they had been put in their place they tamed down and became more civil and the problem was over. I grant it was a good solution.

Irvin had two bad accidents when he was young. When he was about four years old he ran out on the street from between parked cars and was struck by another car. I heard him cry out and saw him run back to the house before he crumpled up on the lawn. Fortunately he wasn't hurt seriously. Some years later he had a bicycle accident which was more serious. I have to take the blame for it. I had fixed up the front wheel of his bike and knew it was not a safe job. One evening two of his friends came carrying him home. The front wheel of his bike had broken off and he had crashed head first down on the concrete sidewalk. He was semi-conscious and kept repeating, "What has happened?" When I explained what had happened to him he was quiet for a minute and then started repeating the same question again. We finally took him to Emergency at the hospital. It took until morning before he became fully conscious. I was always afraid his brain might have been damaged but there were no further problems.

Albert was quite resourceful when it came to finding summer jobs. He started out with the Dickie Dee Ice Cream Company, driving their ice-cream cart around on the street, selling ice-cream bars to the kids. It was a risky, tiring job. His next job was even more demanding. He was the newsboy on the passenger train, which meant selling sandwiches, drinks and papers on the train going between Winnipeg and Vancouver. He had to pick up his supplies and get them onto the train where the other workers had priority over him. He was only about 15 at the time. There was usually a stopover at the end of the run and he had to sleep in the railway coach parked some place. Then he had to pick up his supplies for the return run in a new locality. I don't know how he managed but he certainly learned how to cope with the vicissitudes of life at an early age.

When the boys were a little older and could look for a regular type of job, Helen and I thought it was our duty to help them out. We went along a couple of times when they applied for a job, but it didn't work. Our help was only a problem for them. They hinted they wanted to go it alone, so we stayed at home. They always found work on their own.

In July 1964, when Marian was 12 years old, the two of us took a four-day trip around Lake Superior in the new Comet sedan I had just bought. It was a most memorable event for me at a time when my life was starting to break down. We passed the first night on the north shore of Lake Superior in the tent we brought along. The next day we drove through Sault Ste Marie into Michigan as far as St. Ignace. We didn't want to drive further here but wanted to see the long bridge over Lake Michigan. We decided to take a bus over the bridge instead. Then from the south shore we took a boat to visit a famous island in the lake. We got back to the mainland just in time to catch the last bus taking us back to St. Ignace. By now it was late and we had trouble finding where we had parked our car. It was midnight by the time we found a camping spot. Taking risks didn't seem to worry me in those days.

The next day we drove through northern Michigan and Wisconsin. It was a very lovely drive, we admired the splendid maple trees we saw all over. At some places the tops of the trees spread right over the highway, closing it in overhead. We stopped just short of entering Minnesota, where we camped in a park for the night. We had selected this spot from the tourist literature but had trouble finding it. There was only one small sign on the highway and we drove past it three times before we saw it. Our last day home seemed like the longest day, driving through northern Minnesota and back to Winnipeg. I was getting tired and we were both hungry, but there seemed to be no restaurant in sight. Finally we saw a large house with a restaurant sign. We stopped, although it didn't look too promising. What a surprise! They served us one of the most delicious meals I have ever eaten. Back on the road again, we finally made it home to Winnipeg. The trip stands out as one of the most enjoyable events of my life.

Edward was always more interested in sports than in studies, and he managed quite well to hide his scholastic abilities from us until he entered university. However, he was not going to be left without recognition. He won first prize one year in the elementary school for having made the greatest improvement in his marks over the previous year. I think he planned this the year before by keeping his marks right at the passing level. I had the same accusation thrown at me one year when I won first prize for having made the greatest improvement in my bowling average over the previous year. Of course, it wasn't true that I had engineered this, it was just my good fortune.

Edward clearly proved his abilities when he obtained his first driver's licence. I had given him a few driving lessons before his sixteenth birthday, but I figured there was no hurry. I didn't know he went in on his birthday and made an appointment to have his test only a week after he turned 16. I felt guilty for neglecting him when I heard about it two days before the test. It was too late to help now. However, he came home after the test with a smile on his face. He had gotten his driver's licence with his first test.

It was the practice in high school that awards for top scholastic achievement were handed out to students when they finished Grade 11. Edward was on a high school-leaving course so we did not expect anything for him, but Albert was doing fairly well in his courses. I was working, so I could not attend the ceremony, but Helen went to see how her sons were doing. Imagine her surprise when Albert and Edward each won a first award. She was the only mother with two first award students and became a true celebrity that afternoon. Albert won the award for Physics, and Edward for Typing.

All four of our children turned out to be resourceful, hard working, and able to take the initiative in directing their lives. I will let them tell their own stories.

About this time my marital problems (my wife became involved with another man) and the alienation of the family began to destabilize my nervous system so that I could not perform satisfactorily. I lost two jobs and was forced to find work on Indian reserves. That further darkened my gloom. But I managed to hang together. My marriage with Norah did much to restore me. Our conflict with Alzheimer Disease worked to bring us closer to God, and my heart is looking up and away from the battle I have lost here on earth.

ALZHEIMER DISEASE AND NORAH

Norah and I had never heard of Alzheimer Disease. When troubles started we did not know what was wrong.

It happened one day that Norah could not find her way home in Bobcaygeon after going downtown for shopping. It was her hometown. When we went into a restaurant to eat she had trouble ordering her meal, she could not make a choice. She then ordered the same as I did. She had been an excellent cook, but now some of her cooking did not come out right.

Then her cheques started coming back because they were improperly made out. This puzzled her because she had never had that problem before. So I offered to help her with the cheques, and slowly I started to take over her affairs. She was getting to be very disorganized and was using cheque blanks which were no longer valid. When she started losing her Visa card the matter became worse. Then the Toronto Dominion Bank in Toronto turned her account into a joint bank account without her permission. It meant they were having trouble with her and wanted me to take over. The problems were becoming more serious.

As far as I could see she felt secure in herself; she did not suspect she was to blame for the things that went wrong. However, she must have been worried by what was happening in her life. I wonder what she really felt like.

How did I feel about the changes I saw in Norah? When she got lost in Bobcaygeon I was truly worried for I knew this wasn't carelessness. The reason her cheques were coming back was that her records were in a mess. We had moved and changed banks, and she had a lot of cheque books that should have been thrown out, but she wouldn't do it. When she let me help her with the cheques I sorted them out and put the invalid ones away in a safe place. When she couldn't handle something she would let me help her, and then slowly I put things in order.

When we got into a clash over the two thermostats in our suite it was a more serious affair. At first I thought she had turned them up by accident so I reminded her to keep them down. She just put them up higher. Then I told her not to put them up to 80 degrees. With my present knowledge I would never have done that. It is a serious mistake to give orders to an Alzheimer person. It had a very negative effect on her and I suffered the consequences for a long time. When an Alzheimer person does something wrong, don't order him around or tell him off. He doesn't know what he is doing, but his response to a negative word or action can be disastrous to relations with the caregiver. Regardless of what an Alzheimer person does, we must reply with positive and caring attention. Our problem with the thermostats took over half a year to resolve. I believe it also affected Norah's attitude to her husband for much longer. As it turned out it wasn't long until she no longer recognized me as her husband, so then I could stand aside as her caregiver and escape the "husband's" blame. It didn't help my conscience, though.

I had done a lot of work in the house for years, so it was easy for me to take over the household duties. When Norah needed more help with chores she couldn't handle, I just helped her and took over. This part worked out well.

Going out to shop or visit was more difficult. Norah's other illnesses, osteoporosis and arthritis, were changing her body and this made it necessary to buy new clothing for her. She had trouble making a choice, but she did not want to be shown what she should take. Between the saleslady and myself we often couldn't manage to select the clothing for her that she needed. One time after Norah had been in the fitting room for some time, I asked the saleslady to go in and check. She found Norah undressed, sitting on the floor with the contents of her purse spread around her on the floor. She got Norah dressed and brought her out, and we gave up on making a purchase that day. Once Norah was out of the store she completely forgot what had happened and we cheerily went on with our day. However, I never knew when something like this would happen. Frequently problems arose when she had to go to the washroom in a public place. She would go in and forget to come out again. Then I had to get help from other ladies or go to a saleslady for help.

One day we went to visit some old friends of ours. The evening was pleasant and Norah seemed to be almost normal. When I suggested it was time to go home, trouble began. Norah stated she was at home. When I asked her where she was going to sleep she went through the house and showed me the bedroom and bathroom. That was all she needed. She had seen them during the evening and taken note. It was with difficulty that we got her to put on her winter coat, and then we had to forcibly take her out of the house and into the car. As soon as we were on the road she was back to normal again.

A number of incidents happened at St. Boniface Hospital. One time when she was seriously ill I got the ambulance and had her taken in to the hospital. They kept her in the Observation Unit for eight days before they found a bed for her. I came in one Saturday morning when the O.U. was almost empty. It is a long room, open in the centre with a table in it. This is the organizing area for the staff. There were about five staff members sitting at the table and talking. Because they try to empty the O.U. for the weekend there were only about two patients left in the place. I saw Norah on one side, sitting in a chair. She was tied to the chair, arms and body. She was almost naked, wearing only the light hospital gown coming down to her hips. Her bare feet were on the cold floor. She was shivering all over, her feet, legs, body, arms, and face! I asked for some clothing but the nurses said she was all right. I had never seen her shiver like this before. I had brought her some warm clothing the day before. It was lying on the shelf behind her untouched. First I put the booties on her feet. Then I put a woollen robe over her shoulders, and a blanket over her knees. Some time later one of the girls came over and looked after her. I was so mad I didn't dare talk. If I had had a camera with me I would have taken a picture of the staff sitting and talking, and of Norah tied up and shivering. I would have taken them to our lawyer and sued the hospital. As it was I was helpless because I was alone. With the talk that went on I gathered that Norah had escaped from the O.U. and caused trouble for the staff. Also, she had been awake all night and been a nuisance. So, they tied her to a chair and let her suffer, almost naked. They were punishing her like a common criminal. They ignored the fact that she had Alzheimer Disease and had no idea what she was doing. Alzheimer Disease should have been marked on her chart because she had already gone through a lot of testing at St. Boniface Hospital.

Over the weekend I wrote a letter to Norah's lawyer explaining the case. On Monday morning I dropped off a copy to Norah's doctor and then took the letter to the lawyer, and asked him to look into the matter. I heard no more about it but Norah's care improved, and they kept her in the hospital about an extra ten days to make sure her pneumonia was all cleared up before she went home.

Another time they took Norah to St. Boniface Hospital for a week to do some testing. It included withdrawing some spinal fluid, a fairly complicated test, and they did not manage on the first try. That meant she would have to stay another week. Actually the test could have been done in one day and not two weeks if they had any proper organization at all. I checked this out with my son, Irvin, who is a neurologist and does the same kind of work. I noticed Norah was sitting around in the corridors endlessly through the day, waiting to see doctors. It was so boring I couldn't stand it myself, so I cut down my visits. It was just like hell for me waiting around in the corridors all day. And what about Norah? St. Boniface Hospital was hopelessly mismanaged! On Friday, at the end of the first week, I told the Head Nurse that I was taking Norah home. She didn't approve but she let me sign the necessary paper and I took Norah home. I didn't want Norah to spend another week like that in the hospital just sitting around in the halls waiting for doctors who couldn't get their work done anyhow.

It was a different hospital stay when I came to visit Norah one day. As I came into her ward I noticed there was a sizable crowd gathered at the Head Nurse's desk. Then I heard the Head Nurse talking with Norah.

Norah claimed her husband had been killed and that she was going out to do something about it. Evidently she had already been out of the ward and someone had brought her back in. However, you can't just do nothing when your husband is killed. Then the nurse saw me coming and said,

"Here's your husband. See, he's coming to visit you."

She took one look at me and replied, "That's not my husband."

"Well, who is it then, if it's not your husband?" the nurse demanded.

"It's Daniel," Norah said, not sure of herself.

"Well, Daniel is your husband," argued the nurse.

"No, he's not," said Norah.

It had gone on long enough, I thought, so I took Norah's arm.

"Come with me. We'll do something about it," I said. We walked up and down the hall several times and it was over. Norah forgot all about it.

I wasn't her husband, but who was I? One day at home in the living room, she had not looked at me for some time. Suddenly she looked around and saw me there.

"Who are you?" she said, surprised to see someone in the room.

"I live here together with you," I replied. This didn't seem to mean anything to her.

"What's your husband like?" I asked her. She frowned a bit, but couldn't answer.

"Is he mean to you?" I asked.

"Yes," she replied. She frequently objected to the fact that I did not let her go out alone anymore.

"But what about Daniel? What is he like?" I tried again.

"Daniel is nice," she said, and her face brightened up. The difference between the two was clearly evident. After all, Daniel did lots of nice things for her, compared to her husband.

The next question I should have asked is, "But who am I?" I am sorry I never got down to this question, although I had many opportunities. Now I will never know!

Why we left Bobcaygeon relates directly to Norah's illness. Decisions are hard to make, but in my experience many decisions result from events as they occur. It was a pleasant summer day at Bobcaygeon and Norah decided she would go to Mrs. Bolton's place across the side lane. At this time osteoporosis and arthritis were a greater threat to Norah's safety than Alzheimer Disease. Thirty minutes after she had left I went over to check on her to see why she wasn't coming back. There were about eight steps going up the front door. Often Mrs. Bolton was sitting behind the house, which meant going up a crude stairway made of flat rocks. I went to the front door and got no answer. Then I went to the side and saw Norah lying on the rocks, hurt and barely conscious. We had a visitor at the time so I ran and got her; between the two of us we managed to get Norah home. I realized there were too many safety hazards around the place and help was not easy to get. It was much safer for us to be in Winnipeg. The result was that we settled down permanently in Winnipeg.

One day the mailman brought a letter that caused an immediate crisis. It was an invitation from the University of Toronto to a special reunion of graduates of Victoria College. I told Norah her state of health was too poor to risk the trip. No use! Then we went to her doctor and he told her the same thing. I told her I wasn't going along. The next day she came home from the travel agency with her plane ticket. It was evident she was going. I phoned her cousin in Toronto and asked her to look after Norah for the four days she would be there. When I took Norah to the airport the ticket lady noticed her condition and got a wheelchair and an assistant for her. They did the same for her in Toronto and in Winnipeg again on her return. It seemed God was taking care of her, as every provision was in place. Norah had a great time in Toronto and was on the go almost day and night, completely tiring out her cousin. Alzheimer persons have marvelous strength when they need it. I breathed a sigh of relief when she was safely back home and thanked God for His care. It was the last "great" event for Norah in her life, and after she was safely back home I felt happy that she had gone. About two months later the police picked her up on the street, unconscious and badly bruised, and took her to Emergency. After that I knew I could not let her go out alone again.

In September Norah had gone to the University of Winnipeg, just a block away from our place, to register for some courses. She came back for lunch at noon and said she had to return to the university to finish registering. Something seemed to be wrong. I did not realize at this time that she was getting hopelessly mixed up when she did something like this. It was almost 5:00 in the afternoon and she wasn't back. I phoned security at the university and asked them to make a search for her. Half an hour later they called back saying they could not find her. I was worrying trying to decide what I should do when the phone rang. It was the police saying they had picked her up on the street and taken her to Emergency at St. Boniface Hospital. So I drove over to the hospital. She was conscious but her face was covered with blood, she had two very black eyes, and three teeth were badly damaged. She did not know what had happened. It was difficult to imagine how her injuries could have resulted from a fall on the street. It was now evident she could no longer go out alone, and I had a solid excuse for keeping her in. But at what a price! It was a difficult matter. I had already discussed it with our lawyer who warned me that Norah had her civil rights unless there was sufficient cause for them to be curtailed.

The decision not to let Norah go out on her own greatly heightened the tension between us. She openly accused me of keeping her imprisoned. It severely tested my strength of character, but it also tested my ability to keep from being outwitted by her. She was a sharp escape artist. I had an alarm hanging on the doorknob which went off as soon as it was touched, but sometimes she managed to get past it. One morning at 7:00 a.m. she got out while I was shaving. It took a couple of hours until a security officer from Portage Place brought her back after I had looked all over. Another time she got out of the building in the middle of the night and Kiwanis security brought her back. Her conscience bothered her about it and she woke me up in the middle of the night to tell me about it. A number of times the residents of our apartment block brought her back because they knew she was not supposed to be out alone. She was usually up all night and had lots of time to try things. How could I sleep? When I was completely exhausted it was impossible to stay awake.

"Why keep her in?" you ask. "Why not go out together?"

That is what we did. We went out a great deal, driving to many interesting places in Winnipeg and outside of the city. My eyes were a problem because I was not getting enough sleep, and often I made it back with my eyes half closed. Walking was easier for me and we walked a lot, but often Norah was not strong enough to walk far.

It might be 10:00 p.m. when she decided she had to go to the bank. She believed I was only being difficult when I told her the bank was closed at that hour.

The following is a typical story. She decided she wanted to go out, so we went. We didn't walk too far before she was tired. So we turned back to Kiwanis Chateau.

"What do we want here?" she said, as we came to the entrance of the building.

"This is Kiwanis Chateau, where we live," I replied.

"We don't live here," she said. However, she came in reluctantly.

"Is this where we live?" she asked as we got into the elevator.

When we came to our apartment she asked again, "What do we want here?"

She came in very hesitantly. Then I asked, "May I take off your coat?"

"No, I don't want to stay here. This is not my home," she replied.

I got her to sit down at the table while I made her a cup of tea and put the Globe and Mail in front of her. Slowly she settled down, but she kept her fur coat on for the night. That was okay with me because I knew she would be up and around as soon as she figured I was asleep in my bedroom. At least she would be warm as she roamed around during the night. We faced a lot of problems no matter what we did.

I was not coping with the symptoms of Alzheimer Disease because I did not understand what was happening to Norah. I was close to having a nervous breakdown. One morning my limit had been reached and I could not cope with Norah any longer. Wisely, I got help in and left the apartment. I walked the streets until 4:00 p.m. that day, struggling with myself. It took half a day for me to cool off and half a day for me to see through my problem. Obviously Norah was incapable of changing. Only I could change, and I would have to change. The solution took some time to sink in, but I was desperate and I knew it. I went home with a smile on my face, maybe somewhat forced, and I smiled at Norah no matter what she did. It worked on her and it worked on me. The tension lessened and our relationship improved. Then I learned to fuss around with her, to say silly things no matter how serious the situation. That worked even better. It changed the subject and made us forget what was troubling us. It let us smile a little instead. The system works wonders with an Alzheimer person, and I have a hunch it might even work with ordinary people.

My new philosophy of dealing with Norah was successful and changed our lives. Slowly but surely we learned to enjoy ourselves together.

She was back in the hospital again in December 1991 for the last time. After a couple of days, Vista Park Nursing Home phoned that they had a bed open for her, but she had to come within three days. It was doubtful if the hospital could release her that soon. However, I immediately went to the nursing home to bring in Norah's clothes, and I paid them for the first month. This was an excellent move on my part. They now waited until Norah could come. Then, on the day Norah was to be released, just before the departure hour, I was walking in the hall with Norah. She turned around sharply to look at something and crumpled down on the floor. When they examined her they found she had broken her hip. That meant another three weeks in the hospital. If I hadn't paid the nursing home we would have lost the room, but now they kept it.

Norah's hip healed but she never walked again. She had lost the concept of walking due to Alzheimer Disease. We tried to get her to walk but she had no control over her legs. She was now permanently in a wheelchair. This changed her whole personality as she moved into another level of the disease. She now accepted her situation. Her self-confidence returned. The staff joked around with her and she responded in a bright fashion. She could only repeat words but sometimes she changed them a bit to make them more effective. The way she accepted her life and made the best of it has become a source of inspiration for me. She was neither grumpy nor bitter nor negative. I pray God that I may be the same.

The nursing home was a new challenge for our relationship. Norah no longer knew me as her husband or as Daniel. I was just a person who came, did things for her, and left. But it didn't matter. I learned to do things with her: reading the Mowgli stories or poems by Drummond like "Leetle Batiste"; looking at the many picture books we had; playing with a sponge ball, or letting her play with a small keyboard. Sometimes she played tricks on me. We were sitting downstairs looking at a picture book while she was drinking a coffee from the machine. She was reading the words on the paper cup. While I said a few words to a nurse walking past she turned the cup upside down to read what was on the bottom. The coffee spilt all over the picture book. She did a similar thing a number of times. It made me wonder about her cognitive ability.

Our best times together were when I took her out on the wheelchair. It was a form of adventure, and she had always liked adventure. In fair weather I pushed the wheelchair for long distances on the street. Often we stopped to have a treat some place, like a banana split or milk shake or salad. But on Saturday mornings we took HandiTransit and then we travelled further. We have visited Assiniboine Park, The Forks, Museum of Man and Nature, Art Gallery, Convention Centre, Taste Manitoba, and so on. We enjoyed ourselves together, and now I miss the good times we had. Then on October 5,1993, when I had her almost ready to take out, she took a seizure and in an hour she was gone.

AT NORAH'S GRAVE

This Sunday, early in the morning, I went to Norah's grave.

With tears in my eyes I remembered the sleepless nights and the days of turmoil, and I wished I could have them back again, just so I could once more put my arm around her and tell her I loved her. Life is so lonely now!

During those days of turmoil I longed for peace to reflect and to compose my thoughts. It would have helped me understand the ravages inflicted on Norah's soul by Alzheimer Disease.

Here at the grave it is peaceful, but now it is too late.

As I leave the grave the cold wind in my face brings back to me the reality of life and I drop my "wishing".

I long for the quiet faith in God that shone through Norah's life in her better days, and which once again was visible in her face the last year of her life. May it also be evident in the years that remain for me!

As I look around me I see other "Norahs" who need a touch of love. As I take their hands, as Norah would have done in my place, I am again touching Norah, and peace comes into my heart.

THE ROCKIES AND ME

One of the greatest joys of my life has been camping and hiking in the Rockies. Hiking on the mountain trails requires a healthy physique and a sound heart. When the ascent becomes steep it doesn't take many minutes until my heart is beating at top speed. Then I stop for a minute to catch my breath. As I keep going up, the view around me continues to change endlessly. This is one of the inspiring aspects of the mountains—the ever-new perspective of the scenery around you. Back down in the campground the tired muscles of my body have the relaxed feeling of having succeeded in a challenging task. The air that fills my lungs is pure and fresh and soon revitalizes my body, together with a generous supper cooked on the big cast-iron stove in the outdoor kitchen. A good night's sleep under the evergreens finishes the exciting experience of the day.

Nostalgia fills my soul as I try to write about the days and weeks I have spent in the Rockies. I have been there on different occasions with Helen, or Irvin, or Bill, or with Norah, and have always felt a closer than usual friendship with my companion under the influence of the mountain environment. I have also frequently camped and hiked alone, but I realize it is better to have a companion in case a misadventure occurs. It is also true that sharing happiness doubles it.

My earliest memory goes back to a time when Helen and I were tenting in the Lake Louise campground. We had done some strenuous hikes during the previous days and this day we were resting up, spending the afternoon at our campsite. We were sitting at the table talking, when suddenly we looked around. There we saw a huge bear slowly walking across our lot, between us and the tent. What should we do? Nothing! The bear was harmlessly crossing our camping spot. That's all!

Another experience was different. I was camping in the same campground but this time I was alone. It was getting dark, and I was in the covered kitchen cooking my supper, along with a number of other campers. I had been out on the trail all day. I noticed the rumble of a commotion spreading over the campground. Strange! Then some kids came and asked their mothers for flashlights and then disappeared. There were no kids left at all now. Then someone came in with the explanation. The kids had seen a bear crossing the campground and were chasing him. They needed the flashlights to find him in the dark. In ten seconds flat there was another wave of commotion sounding across the campground. This time it was the mothers running out to bring back the kids.

I had been on the trails before, but it was when Irvin and I went out together for the first time that I got into real hiking. He had driven through the Rockies with his friends before, but they didn't want to hike—it was too much like work. He made me promise that this time we would go up the mountains. I agreed but said we needed to use restraint. So much for that! We went up, far past the end of the trails on several hikes, and I was in the lead as often as not. We tackled Cascade Mountain from both sides and stopped short of the top only because we needed daylight to get back down again. When you get higher up on the slopes you always find they are steeper than they look. At C-Level Cirque, where we did some tough climbing, we certainly found that was true.

The Plain of the Six Glaciers, heading west from Lake Louise, has a trail I have often taken. It is very popular because you can see the Victoria Glacier ahead of you all the way. Occasionally you can hear the crash of large chunks of ice and snow falling down the steep precipice in front of the glacier. Going past the Tea House the path leads further, on top of a wall of rock. The side drops down sharply, over 100 feet, at an angle of about 80 degrees to the glacier below. This valley has been gouged out by the moving glacier below. Looking down I saw a father with his eight-year-old son walking on the ice of the glacier. Well, if the kid can do it, so can I. Going down was easy, too easy. The ice was perfectly safe to walk on, it was crusted with sand and gravel. But then I had to get up again. The top part of the climb was almost vertical. I made slow progress until my head was only about six feet below the top, but there I was stuck. I was holding onto a root with one hand and was supporting one foot on a rock sticking out on the side. I couldn't spot anything strong enough so I could pull myself up higher. Indeed, I could hardly keep myself from sliding down. I sweated, not knowing what to do. How could I pull myself up the few remaining yards? I finally found something to hold onto which enabled me to reach the top. For a while I was in serious trouble. The next time I went down a rock slide of fallen talus. This wasn't much better because the rocks were piled at a steep angle and were just waiting to start tumbling again.

Another summer I was travelling with my friend Bill. He was the one who had been an undercover Communist agent at the University of Toronto. One day we crossed over into B.C. just north of Lake Louise. When we came to Mount Revelstoke we were impressed with the view of the mountain. We found out there was a road leading up to the top, about eight miles one way. I thought it was a good idea to drive up, so we started. Then I noticed Bill huddled up in the corner of his seat and holding himself together as if he was mortally afraid of something. I asked him if I was driving too fast.

"Yes," he said.

"Do you want to drive?" I asked him.

"Yes," he said, "but I'll be driving at two miles per hour."

That would take us eight hours and I wasn't ready for that. Then he blurted out,

"You Christians are lucky, you have another life to go to when you die here, but for us atheists, when we die, that's the end."

He was so dead serious that I could hardly refrain from laughing, but I controlled myself. I drove up to the top, but slowly. Poor Bill; life is tough on atheists.

Norah and I did a lot of exploring around Jasper, but did not go on all-day hikes. We visited the large C.N.R. hotel, Jasper Park Lodge, and Norah could remember staying there with her parents as a young girl. There is a lot of interesting scenery in the vicinity of the town, like Maligne Canyon and a row of lakes across the river from the town. We drove up to the top of Marmot Basin, a large mountain which is flat on top. We visited Medicine Lake, which disappears at a certain time of the year, and also Maligne Lake, which is very popular with photographers. Then we planned a hike to Mount Edith Cavell together with Ed and Diane, who were in the vicinity. It is south of Jasper. We drove out there in the morning and waited for them. When they did show up they both had excuses. Ed had a sore thumb and needed to see a doctor, and Diane had some shopping to do. Good, Norah and I went out alone. We hiked to the foot of Mount Edith Cavell; it is a beautiful trail.

One summer I was travelling alone on the way from Edmonton to Jasper. I planned to stay at Miette Hot Springs for the night. My car was getting old and the motor had very little compression left. I had quit my job and had no money to spend on the car, but was going to drive as far as it would go. The road to Miette was uphill all the way and my car started slowing down. Slower and slower it went. When I reached Miette I drove into the camping area and stopped at a tenting spot. By that time it was hardly moving. I got my tent permit and then tried to start the car again, but it wouldn't do a thing. What would I do now? I decided to worry about it tomorrow. I put up the tent, cooked supper, and had a good night's rest. The next day the car started just as usual. No problem, and the road was downhill all the way to the highway.

My first year out with Norah we were hiking in the Lake Louise area. We walked up to beautiful Lake Agnes and had something to eat in the rustic, log Tea House. Then we circled around the foot of the Big Beehive to get into the Plain of Six Glaciers. Here the trail leads onto a walk hanging on the side of the vertical face of the mountain. I pointed out to Norah the vertical drop falling hundreds of feet down. Norah was sore at me because she said heights made her sick and I shouldn't bother her. She felt dizzy looking down. I said I was sorry and apologized to her. The next summer we went back to the same spot. This time the height didn't bother her at all. She was used to it now after all the hiking we had done.

One day Norah and I went up Sundance Canyon; it is situated southwest of Banff on the east side of Sulphur Mountain. It is a small gorge that has a tiny stream of water tumbling down in a fascinating display of scenery. We had reached the top and were following the path on the low summit of Sundance Range. We had some cinnamon buns along and started eating them. The smell attracted a group of mountain sheep and they let us know they were interested in the buns. As they circled around Norah I took advantage of the situation to take an interesting photo of Norah surrounded by sheep. Norah was scared but the photo was more important right then. It only took me a minute. She was sore at me for not protecting her but I knew the sheep wouldn't harm her. I still have the photo.

I had some interesting times taking the trail that leads from Moraine Lake through Larch Valley to Sentinel Pass. The pass has an altitude of 8566 feet, a pretty good climb, and often had snow flurries on any summer day. The hike starts with a steep ascent from Moraine Lake, then meanders in Larch Valley for a good stretch, and ends with a steep climb to Sentinel Pass. From the top you look down on a long, steep stretch of talus, where the trail seems lost among the rocks, and into Paradise Valley, a long wide valley that appears to be relatively flat. I wanted to go down the trail through Paradise Valley, but it meant I would reach the road a good eight miles from where I parked the car. It was too much.

Norah and I took the trail to Sentinel Pass one day and ran into heavy rain when we reached Larch Valley. We were not fully prepared for rain. We crouched together under a clump of trees and kept from getting too wet, but when the rain stopped we thought it was wise to go back down. On another day we made it to the top.

The summer that Bill was with me we decided we would hike through Paradise Valley and up to Sentinel Pass from that side. We would still have to walk to the car but it would be downhill. Hiking through Paradise Valley was scenic, especially the area of the Giant's Steps, and not too strenuous. As we approached the ascent to Sentinel Pass I noticed Bill was getting worried. Then we saw three girls coming down the trail, giggling. I mentioned to Bill that the trail must be okay as the girls seemed to be happy. Bill replied that the girls were laughing because they had been scared out of their minds coming down. He said he wasn't going up, he was taking the trail back. I looked up at the trail and considered how often I had wanted to take that trail. I was so close to it now that I decided I would go it alone. Bill was going back to the car so he could drive to Moraine Lake and pick me up.

The trail going up was all on bare rocks and not well marked. Halfway up it crossed laterally to the other side and here I lost it. Now my progress slowed down. I could easily see the pass on high, but it was still about half a mile up, and every step I took the rocks slid down under my feet. On top of that the sun was hot and I was carrying a knapsack. It got worse. I had to go down on my belly, crawling along to keep from sliding down. I was gaining very little in distance. Finally I realized that the trail must be on the other side of the slope, so I worked my way to the right and finally found the trail again. It had taken me hours to do a good mile of steep slope. I came very close to complete exhaustion on that slope. But I made it!

Years later I went up to Sentinel Pass from Moraine Lake, together with Irvin and Gerald. We started early in the day and when we looked down into Paradise Valley we decided to take the trail down. Irvin's eyesight is better than mine and we managed to stay on the trail. However, we found it a grueling hike, even going down.

My faithful old tent became even more so, from use. It gathered up droppings of gum and resin from the trees, sooty smoke from the campfires, and perspiration from the sleepers inside. As a result, it was perfectly waterproof. I was tenting one night in the campground at Lake Louise, and it rained heavily all night. There was no point in getting up early because all the trails would be soaked. When I peeked out of my tent the sun was shining—it promised to be a glorious day. Then I looked around and saw confusion all over. People were spreading their sleeping bags, clothes and other belongings out to dry. My neighbours from California had brought an expensive modern type of waterproof tent. The rain had completely soaked through the tent and all their belongings inside; they did not have a dry spot left. They looked at my shabby old tent and marveled that I was completely dry. So much for advanced technology. I suggested that we heat up the stoves in the outdoor kitchen to help dry out, but they said there was no wood left. I knew where to get wood so I got in the car and went for wood. I was the only one who had an axe so I took over the facilities and soon had fires going in all the stoves. I also had a long rope to tie between trees so others could hang up their blankets to dry. Of course, everyone was hungry and breakfast was next on the agenda. By noon most of the campers had breakfast cooking on the stoves and were starting to eat a well-earned meal. The sun stayed out and it turned into a hot day, excellent for drying out tents and bedding. Everyone admired my "lovely" tent. They also vowed to keep an axe in the car for future emergencies.

HOW I CONQUERED ASTHMA

My cure may not work for all people but it cured me from asthma in a miraculous fashion. It involved no medicine or money, just a couple of years of misery and self-denial. My disease was at the stage where I realized that death was not far off; this gave me the strength to go through the difficult process that cured me of asthma. To understand what happened to me it is necessary to see how I acquired the disease. I am looking back 50 years to the time when I went through the crisis related below. I have never had a recurrence of asthmatic symptoms after the several years it took to get it out of my system.

Asthma is a disease associated with nervous problems. I am a nervous person and it is no surprise I developed the disease. It was during World War II and I was in my twenties; there were many reasons for me to be suffering from nervous tensions. I grew up during the Great Depression when jobs were impossible to find. The war opened up many jobs and we moved into the city where I found work in the Post Office. The change-over from country to city life in itself was a strain on both my wife and me. The fact that my name was of German origin, working in a British establishment like the Post Office, brought on real mental persecution. I had failed the first military physical when I volunteered for active service, but with each call-up the standards were being lowered. I had obtained my job on the condition that when peace came I would have to relinquish it in favour of the men who had left the Post Office to join the army. I was not in a happy situation. On top of this, I was put on the night shift at the Post Office and I never adjusted to sleeping in the daytime. After two years I got back on days but by that time I had become frail, sick and was coughing badly.

The doctor told me I had asthma and gave me medicine but it did me no good. I changed doctors but his medicine was no better. I started taking time off from work until I had used up all my sick time. My health was deteriorating and I was getting weaker. I noticed my wife was beginning to make plans about how she would be able to care for our two children and herself after I was gone. And then the crisis developed.

It was in the middle of winter, the weather was stormy and cold, and I had a mile to walk to the streetcar to go to work. Walking in the severe cold the coughing becomes uncontrollable, it has a choking effect that takes away a person's breath. The crisis lasted three days, as the temperature dropped and the wind got stronger. I had trouble walking the mile the first day and realized I was losing the battle. The second day the coughing choked me so I had to open up my clothing and bare my chest in the bitter cold to keep on breathing. I realized that it was my last day. I didn't eat anything that day. I was on shift work and my hours started at 12:30 p.m. My work was relatively easy at this time, the easiest job I have had in the Post Office. I didn't eat or drink anything the next morning before going to work. I knew I would never see my wife and children again. Doubtless someone would find my body on the road going to the streetcar, choked to death by the asthmatic coughing. We barely looked at each other as I left the house.

The wind and the cold were worse but nothing happened as I walked to the street car.

I shuffled through my day's work and never coughed once. Something had changed. I also knew my stomach was completely empty. There was no food, liquid or gas in my stomach. As soon as I had something to eat the coughing started again.

I had found the key to my recovery.

I had to eat to get energy to do my work, but as soon as I ate the stomach became enlarged and pressed on my lungs and the coughing started. I would eat for a day or two and then I would fast until the coughing stopped again. It was a heartless battle for a couple of years but I was making progress.

The food I ate was also a key factor in my recovery. I had to avoid foods that form gas in the stomach. Gas increases the pressure on the lungs and is a key factor in the disease. *To avoid gas I ate only raw, uncooked foods*. My diet consisted of raw vegetables and fresh or dried fruit. As time went on I could eat hard-boiled eggs and cold ham. It was easy to experiment with different foods because the reactions of my lungs always gave a clear signal as to what I could eat.

After several years my strength returned and the asthma was gone, but it took many years until my weight was normal. In the meantime I had developed healthy eating habits, which are an important factor for good health. Over the years I have subjected my lungs to severe tests but I have never again had asthmatic attacks. I have worked in the wheat harvest, on the combine or hauling grain from the combine until my lungs were filled with dust, but I had no spasms. I took up woodworking, especially wood-turning which creates a lot of dust, and got my lungs filled with dust until I could hardly breath, but I experienced no asthmatic spasms. I have been completely cured of asthma for over 40 years.

Suggestions

1. Diet is very important to eliminate gas in the stomach. Anything pressing on the lungs will cause asthmatic coughing. My diet of raw

uncooked foods is a good guide. *Avoid starchy foods*. Digestive systems vary greatly and you need to experiment with different foods.

2. Nervous problems are usually the basic cause of asthma.

3. Doctors generally are against fasting, but it is one of the best cures for most illnesses, *not all*. When the stomach is empty the body can use all of its resources to fight the disease instead of having to digest food at the same time. Think it through.

MY EXPERIENCE WITH CHURCHES

My life has been greatly enriched by the privilege I have had of working under, and worshipping with, churches of different denominations. It has not been a matter of jumping from one church to another; it mostly resulted from job changes, marriage or travelling. It has greatly broadened my perspective in the area of religion and taught me to appreciate and accept people of different faiths.

Being born in a Mennonite family, it was normal for me to grow up in the Mennonite faith and become a member of that church. Thus on June 16, 1939, I was baptized and became a member of the Bergthaler Church. For me it was a real spiritual experience, but for many it was merely a matter of becoming part of the community. You could only get married in the church, and the ministers would not marry a couple unless they had been baptized. So when young fellows started "going out", they were forced to think of spiritual matters. There was no other way, and it had a civilizing effect on many of the wild young punks. It also meant that, for many, the matter of "getting saved" was just a prerequisite for getting married.

We lived in a part of Manitoba that was just being opened up and during my younger years we did not have a local church in our community. My religious experience began with the Canadian Sunday School Mission summer camps at Gimli. It probably was the summer of 1930 when I attended my first summer camp, after having memorized 500 Bible verses. Reverend J. Lloyd Hunter was in charge of the camp at that time. He loved children and knew how to work with them. He had a tremendous influence on all of us who came under his direction. I was one of them. The Bible became a real book to me, not just a place to find appropriate verses to support the required church doctrines. The church has never been able to convert me to its way of using the Bible.

The experience of the C.S.S.M. summer camps brought me to an early acquaintance with Elim Chapel on Portage Avenue in Winnipeg. The church was the gathering place where we met for transportation to and from the camp. Prominent persons from the church were among the founders of the C.S.S.M. and through them the church obtained a high place of importance in my memory.

The main feature which set the Mennonite church apart from all others was the doctrine of non-violence. It required its members to refuse military service, which resulted in frequent persecution by militaristic governments. The doctrine also forbade violence on a personal level and required its adherents to live in peace in their community. The latter requirement was broken more often than the first one. After all, no one really wants to go to war, but it's not easy to get along with your neighbour. When I volunteered for active overseas military service on October 23, 1943, my membership in the Mennonite church was canceled. I respect the Mennonite Church for being faithful to its doctrinal position.

On November 8, 1941, we moved to Winnipeg and it became our permanent home. It took some time for us to find a suitable church but we slowly settled down to Elim Chapel, an independent evangelical church. It was organized on the positive doctrine that if you were a born-again Christian you were a member of God's Church, and consequently also a member of Elim Chapel, with all voting privileges. It made sense to me from a Biblical viewpoint, but I have never met another church with the same policy. We were out of our class at Elim; we were poor, but there were some other poor people besides us. Here we brought up our children. Sometimes they were a bit too noisy, but we insisted on taking them into church with us at all ages, and I believe it was a wise practice.

In 1944 we became involved with the Church of God from Indiana, as a result of listening to their radio broadcasts. They sent Reverend Heffren to Winnipeg to start a church here and we worked with them, but we did not leave Elim Chapel. I don't remember much about them, but they had the usual belief that they were closer to the real truth than other churches. After about a year their work in Winnipeg collapsed.

There were few young people at Elim Chapel and when the boys grew older they started to get involved with youth from other churches. Alliance Church on Furby Street was a popular place for them so we transferred to this church. Alliance had a more spectacular approach to the presentation of the Gospel and this had often attracted family members to go to their worship services. It was a vibrant church, but it also had problems. In 1966 I withdrew from membership there when the minister condemned Helen for her marital problems. I thought she deserved more help than that. This left me without church membership until 1984.

On November 17, 1964, I took up a teaching position at Bloodvein in the Mennonite school. The Mennonite Mission had invaded Catholic Bloodvein Indian Reserve and managed to convert half of the reserve to the Protestant faith. They had started a one-room school the previous year. This year they had received the blessing of the Department of Indian Affairs who were now paying for two teachers, including me. The Mennonite missionary was the other teacher. Thus I was again involved with the Mennonite church, working under them. The warfare between the two churches at Bloodvein was such that we had to be careful when crossing the boundary line between the two. It took me some time before I felt safe to cross over into Catholic territory. However, by the end of the year I was well respected in the Catholic area too. I remember one evening in the end of June when I had walked over to the Catholic domain to bid farewell to my Catholic friends. I met the Priest and he walked back with me as far as the boundary line. Being a Catholic official he did not venture to cross the line. We had a serious talk together. He asked me frankly for my opinion as to why they had lost half of the reserve to the Mennonites. This required serious thought on my behalf. I said that one of the reasons was that the Catholic services were too rigid, allowing little opportunity for individual expression. They should have other services besides the Mass. Many people want more emotionalism. I have noticed that over the years the Catholic Church has given more opportunity to its people for emotional expression, as seen in the charismatic movement. My friendship with the Catholic people on this reserve made me realize that Catholics are normal, decent people, although in our churches we had often been led to believe that all Catholics are evil sinners and on the way to hell.

In 1965 I was transferred to the Indian Affairs school on the Hollow Water Reserve. Now I worked under the Anglican Church, which continued until the church lost its control of the schools some years later. Originally all schools were run by the churches, but the government got involved and started paying for school expenses in order to raise educational standards. Eventually the church was phased out. My experience with the Anglican church was good and I was happy to worship there. This was the year that the Anglican and United churches almost reached agreement to unite after years of negotiation. What stands out in my memory is that union would require all churches to adopt the new hymnbook. When the people realized they would have to give up their old hymnbooks and learn new songs they backed away from union and it fell through. I kept up on church news by reading the Anglican periodicals. To me it seemed a ridiculously arbitrary move to disallow churches to use the hymnbooks of their choice. I find that singing is the most important part of worship for me.

I still kept up my attendance at the Anglican Church for some years when I taught at Fort Alexander, even though it was no longer mandatory. Winnipeg was closer now and I spent many weekends there. I also travelled a lot during the summer. As a result, my church attendance became more sporadic and varied. During my travels I found that large Catholic churches are always open and usually had people who came in to pray at any time of the day. I had a serious need for prayer and this opened up a new avenue for me. The Bible says that "where two or three are gathered together in my name there I am with them", and I have often taken advantage of this promise when away from home. It has been a great blessing for me. In contrast, Protestant churches are only open when services are being held, and they always try to "button-hole" every stranger who walks in.

My association with the Catholic church slowly increased. At Fort Alexander School I was asked to teach Catholic religion and that gave me a certain status. At the annual conference of Catholic teachers I asked the Bishop how come they had an evangelical person teaching Catholic religion. He was speechless but promised to look into it. He never did. My last half-year at Pine Falls I attended the Catholic church at Powerview. During my summer school classes at Laval University I attended the Catholic church on campus. Then in 1975, when I taught school at Oxford House, I went to the Catholic church there for the full year. An important reason was that my best friends there were Catholic. Norah and I were married in 1976 during that school term and we stayed with the Catholic church until the end of June.

My marriage with Norah brought me into a more regular relationship with the church. She belonged to St. Luke's United Church in Toronto, so when we moved to Bobcaygeon we were both without a church. We started going to Trinity United Church in Bobcaygeon, occasionally. Then I told her we had to attend regularly if we were serious, so we became faithful attenders. Norah had her membership transferred to Trinity and I remained a faithful visitor. Norah became very involved with the church, and became a member of the Church Board. I was not too happy with the United Church, as I could not agree with the direction it was drifting, and I found that our local church was weak spiritually. With Norah's involvement in the United Church we got regular information from headquarters in Toronto, and it was discouraging and worse. However, we had an elite group of Christians in the church, about a dozen, who were faithful Christians, and this made it worthwhile for me. They were also the most active people in the church and thus indispensable to the minister, drawing him to a deeper faith. When in Toronto we always attended St. Luke's United Church.

While Norah and I lived in Paris we occasionally attended the American Church, an interdenominational church oriented to English-speaking foreigners. It was a unique experience. They had an interesting format of worship, regularly asking newcomers to introduce themselves and become part of the social group. They usually had a dinner together after the service, but it was necessary to register for it a week in advance so preparations for the meal could be made. Newcomers were invited to the dinner without previous notice. One Sunday we had a Baptist minister from Communist Russia at the service. He was from a government registered church, so he had to be very careful what he said. He spoke German but no English. This enabled me to spend some time talking with him. He made me understand that the situation of the church in Russia was perilous at its best.

The time came when Norah and I decided to spend the winters in Winnipeg and summers in Bobcaygeon. That meant we had to find a church home in Winnipeg. Years ago, Helen and I were still attending Elim Chapel when the church split and the part that left formed Bethesda Church. We visited Bethesda a couple of times but decided to stay with Elim. Now, years later, Norah and I decided to take a look at Bethesda again. The result was that in March 1984 I became a member of the church and Norah an associate member. This way we had memberships in two churches.

The best part of our experience at Bethesda was the Growth Group to which we belonged. We had about ten persons in the group, every one of whom had serious problems, except for Norah and I. One person's wife had been in a nursing home for many years with Alzheimer Disease. Another one's wife developed Alzheimer Disease while in the group and had to go into a nursing home. Then towards the end Norah had the same problem. One year our group took in a young single woman who was pregnant. She came from a United church in Toronto and had been sent to Winnipeg to have her baby. Our group tried to be of real help to her and give her the acceptance she needed. About a year later she went back to Toronto with her baby, in good spirits. We received positive reports from her later.

Then, out of the blue, the assistant minister took over our group and decided to make some changes, as if he could do anything he wanted with us. He gave it up a month later, but he had seriously damaged our group and it broke up altogether.

Several years before this incident the church hired a second minister to help with the workload. The two ministers could not work together, nor were they willing to practice any humility. It threw the church into a crisis. It made me ashamed that I had brought Norah into such a church. However, she coped with it better than I did.

Then, when Norah developed Alzheimer Disease life became embarrassing for me. People couldn't understand what was happening to her. Her behaviour often appeared to be sinful, but Alzheimer Disease is not a matter of sin. You can't deal with the person on that basis. She had to make regular trips to the washroom, but her back was too weak to continue walking down the stairs, so we finally had to stop going to Bethesda.

Then we went to the Salvation Army Citadel, just a block from our place. They had a washroom on the main floor. Not much later Norah was admitted to the Vista Park Nursing Home. Here they had a church service on Sunday afternoons, with different churches participating each Sunday of the month. We faithfully attended this service until Norah died. One of the ministers that came every month was Reverend Terry Hidichuk from Meadowood United Church. He took Norah's funeral service and gave me much needed help at the time. The result was that I started to attend his church. During the winter of 1994, my first year there, he preached a series of sermons taking a positive attitude on the topic of suffering in our lives as we follow Jesus. I was impressed. It was the opposite of what we had been given at the Bobcaygeon United Church. There the tendency always was to blame God for our suffering, instead of seeing it as leading to positive spiritual growth. However, I am still nervous about the United Church because I am only too aware of what has been going on at its headquarters in Toronto. I hope the local churches will remain true to the Faith. My other problem is I have to drive ten kilometres to the church and I will only be able to attend as long as I can keep my driver's licence. My eyesight is a real problem.

THE NUNS

They used to dress in black, go around looking very sober, and give everyone the impression they were uninteresting persons.

When I actually got to know them I found that the stereotype was completely false.

The two nuns at Oxford House had two motorcycles, two skidoos, a good motorboat, and a full set of tools that could handle any breakdown. They were doing more than sitting in church and praying.

I became acquainted with them at organized events which were held by the teachers. The nuns can play the piano and sing, and they appear to know all the songs that have ever been written. They loved to sing and the songs were always lively. Everyone joined in and had a happy time. Going somewhere on a bus was always an enjoyable experience if we had nuns along.

We made an outing to Wendigo Lodge several times when I taught at Fort Alexander. It is located north of Lac Du Bonnet on the lake of the same name. It is a tourist lodge with a large indoor swimming pool. We started the excursion with a healthy swim, followed by a delicious dinner. Then we gathered around the piano and the nuns kept us singing for hours. It was a day to remember.

An event that stands out in my memory took place in St. Boniface. We were about 60 teachers together for a party at the end of an event we attended.

When I arrived for the party I was stopped at the door by—yes, a couple of nuns. They pinned something on my back and gave me an instruction sheet. The instructions said the word on my back was part of a popular saying. I was required to find the persons with the other words to complete the saying. Then the group had to write a poem containing that sentence. Next we had to set it to music, and finally we had to get up on the stage and sing our song. The best performance would win a prize for the group.

It took a lot of running around to get a sentence together, and often it would be challenged by another group who needed one of our words. It took some time to finish the first step. Writing a poem was somewhat easier because usually there was a least one hopeful poet in the group. Making up the music was more difficult, and often the poem had to be rewritten. Then the performance on stage—this was the embarrassing part, trying to put together the voices, music and the metre of the poem. It provided lots of laughter and enjoyment for the listeners.

It gave us an evening of excitement and fun and was an excellent mixer. We learned to work together with whoever happened to be in our group. They had lots of food ready for us after we had finished our work. It was an evening that I remember with pleasant feelings and it had no morning-after headaches.

MY PRESCRIPTION FOR HEALTH

It is with some hesitancy that I venture to write on this subject. I have not always been in good health and the skin disease with which I have suffered for many years has shaken the confidence I had in my ideas on health. However, at this point, 1994, the skin disease is finally under control, and I hope the only things that will afflict me until my death have to do with normal aging.

I am now 75 years old and as I read the "Deaths" column in the newspaper I realize that many men are already gone by that age. When I look around me the situation I see is even worse. I see many men younger than me who are going down fast. I meet few men my age who are still active and able to perform the way I am doing.

I do not have professional medical qualifications, I am merely handing on the knowledge I have gained from my lifelong experience with the illnesses that have troubled me.

If your doctor gives you directions that are contrary to what I am saying here, listen to your doctor. He knows your condition best.

My Suggestions

1. Maintain a cheerful, positive attitude to life. It promotes the secretion of digestive juices and helps other glands to function well. It helps you keep a proper body posture.

It is difficult for doctors to treat persons who are moody, whiny or complainers. These persons have a psychological attitude that has a negative effect on body functions. On the other hand, a happy, positive disposition will cure many ailments.

2. Practice moderation in all activities, especially eating and drinking. Overloading and overtiring the body hinders its organs and glands from performing their functions.

Moderation is very important. The human body can cope with many abuses but it breaks down when they become habitual. Taking alcoholic beverages everyday, even in moderation, will doubtless lead to social and health problems. The "tough guy" who brags about his ability "to take it" usually has weak, sickly persons like me, older than he was, at his funeral. My body can't take much abuse, so I have to take good care of it.

3. Eat the kinds of food that agree with your body. If they give you indigestion change your diet. Uncooked, natural foods are the healthiest. Choose simple foods and avoid rich foods.

Never take medicine to ease an upset or acid stomach. When the stomach rebels it is telling you to change your eating habits. Usually the problem is you are eating too many starchy and fatty foods, and eating them too fast. Let your stomach get empty, drink lots of water, and change to uncooked foods until your stomach is happy. Nervous problems can cause ulcers, but a proper diet can ease the ulcers.

4. Get sufficient exercise and avoid the chesterfield. You need:

a. aerobic exercise to keep the heart in shape. The best and easiest aerobic exercise is skipping with a rope. It will speed up the heart in a minute. I can't do it anymore because my joints won't allow it. Now I use my exercise machine.

b. stretching and twisting exercises to loosen up the joints and to massage the internal organs.

In the morning I use a special set of exercises to wake up my body. They only take about 5 minutes. Clench your fists for a more strenuous effect.

a. feet apart, bend over, arms apart, swing arms as far as possible, 50 complete turns.

b. feet apart, stand erect, arms stretched out, swing arms from side to side horizontally, 50 complete turns.

c. feet apart, hands down in front, do the "shovelling" exercise, throwing the "gravel" as high as possible, 25 times to the right, and 25 to the left.

d. Alternatively, go out and take a run around the block.

5. Keep your bowels moving regularly and avoid laxatives, except as a last resort. If needed, add more high fibre foods and raw vegetables to your diet until your bowels move properly.

Regular bowel movements are more important for good health than is generally recognized. When serious bowel problems occur an operation may leave your body in a worse mess.

6. The body needs sufficient rest and sleep, but if you are gaining weight you probably are sitting around too much for the amount of food you eat. Keep more active!

Your mind and body both need rest and sleep but if you abuse them, both your mixed-up nerves and your mistreated body will ruin your sleep with nightmares. A positive attitude to your problems and your friends, and sensible use of your body, will help restore to you the sound restful sleep you need. Easier said than done, sometimes. You need to work at it.

7. Don't become dependent on prescription medicine if at all possible. Use pills intermittently so your body can recuperate from them. Medicine is more effective if only taken when most needed. If you take a drug regularly it usually loses its effectiveness over time. It is better to alternate drugs, or try going without them for a while. The doctor will warn you when pills have to be taken regularly. Sometimes you find that your body no longer needs them. This happened with Norah.

Half of the drugs that doctors have prescribed for me either had serious side effects or no effect at all. The doctor can't know how your body will react to a drug. Some drugs have been very effective on me, and others have worked very slowly, but I took them because there was no alternative.

8. Practice fasting when your body is overloaded with wastes it cannot eliminate properly. It is the best cure for illnesses that are caused by germs because they feed and breed on body wastes. A diet of fruit and lots of water may also provide a cure.

Fasting has been more effective for me than any medicine. It allows the body to cure itself. However, I don't expect it will cure cancer or deficiency problems. If your body is not getting enough iron or calcium, for example, fasting will not help. Partial fasting may be preferable in most cases. A fruit diet will provide needed sugar, and fibre for the bowels. Together with lots of water, it will have a thorough cleansing effect on the digestive system, blood, kidneys and lungs.

9. Watch body position when sleeping. Spend equal time lying on the right side, the left side and the back. It helps the heart to keep its normal shape.

I have found that regularly sleeping only on one side had a bad effect on my heart. When I made it a practice to change into different positions my heart felt much better.

If you have back problems ignore the above and do as your doctor advises you.

10. As much as possible, eat freshly prepared meals and avoid pre-cooked, packaged foods. They all contain additives to enhance colour, taste, and shelf life.

With most mothers working today, they are doing less meal preparation. As a result, children are eating more precooked, packaged foods. Manufacturers, in preparing these foods, are mainly concerned with shelf life and the attractiveness of their products; the health qualities are of secondary concern to the manufacturers. They use whatever additives they can procure to maximize their profits.

My Theory

Disease germs cause symptoms, but not the disease, they are the result of the disease and are helping the body clean up accumulated wastes.

When undigested food accumulates in the digestive system it rots and turns into chemicals that are harmful to the body. The kidneys, lungs and sweat glands may not be able to eliminate all the extra wastes produced and then the body becomes a fertile feeding ground for germs. The germs cannot feed on healthy body tissues. The germs produce symptoms that help to eliminate the wastes and thus keep the body from poisoning itself. By skipping several meals all the body's organs can concentrate on cleaning out accumulated wastes and thus restore the body to health. However, when the disease is at its height the body may suffer seriously; it is the price that has to be paid for cleaning the body of harmful wastes.

In the case of cancer and other chronic disease little research has been done to determine the causes. Probably psychological disorders, environmental pollution, and food additives contribute to some of them. Most of the research done today centres on looking for genetic connections. Genetic factors increase the probability of getting an illness, but they are determinative in only a very few diseases. It still remains to find the other factors that lead to the illness. Following good health rules is still the best insurance against disease.

My Own Experiences

In some cases the medical profession was very effective in treating me, and sometimes they failed badly. In the case of my asthma they were of no use to me. In the battle with my skin disease they gave me medicine that finally helped, but it took many years before I had any real relief. They called it neurodermatitis, which involved it with my nervous system and put it into an unknown category.

However there were other instances in which the doctors were eminently successful. When I was delivering mail one of my feet started hurting and it soon worsened so that I had to stay home from work. My wife helped me get to the doctor because I could not walk alone. The doctor examined my foot, took a bit of cotton wadding and taped it to the sore spot under my foot, and told me I could leave. I told him I would need a medical certificate to get sick leave until my foot was better. He told me I could go back to work right away. In disbelief, I got up and tried to walk. I found my foot was all right. I was amazed what an effect that little bit of cotton had on my foot. All that was wrong with my foot was a pinched nerve.

I always was sort of a sickly person, suffering from one cold after another, a never-ending affair. One time when I went to see the eye doctor I noticed the wording on his door which said, “Eye, ear, nose and throat specialist.” I had an immediate inspiration that he might have something to say about my colds as well. I mentioned it to him after he had finished with my eyes. He said he had just received samples of a new medicine. He gave me two small bottles and told me to follow instructions. They were chlortripolons, an antihistamine, just coming on the market at that time. They worked a miracle on my colds and had no side effects on me. My colds just disappeared. When I did have a recurrence I just had to take a pill or two and the cold was gone. I have had very few colds since then for the best part of my life. More recently I have developed sinus trouble, which is more difficult to treat. The antihistamines still help, but I have to take more pills. They are not as effective and make me sleepy or nervous.

Throughout my life I have had the occasional bout with rheumatism; no lasting effects, but at times it has put me out of service. Then a doctor prescribed Indocid for me. After taking the pills for two or three days my joints are perfectly well, beyond the expectation of the doctor. The prescription works wonders for me.

With respect to one’s general health I have found that the person himself is his own best doctor. We need to take responsibility for our own daily health, because it depends mainly on how we treat our bodies. Too many people think that they can mistreat their bodies as they please, and when they get sick the doctor will give them pills to take and they will be well again. It’s a very silly attitude to health.

What Is Disease?

About nine years ago when my skin disease broke out, my sinuses were soon healed and my rheumatic problems ended. Two years ago when my skin started to heal, my sinuses flared up again and I am beginning to feel my joints again. It is a queer situation.

When I was young, about 20, I developed a difficult skin disease on the shins of my legs. The skin turned into an open sore and slowly spread down the shins. Then when I developed asthma my shins healed by themselves. After the asthma was gone I was plagued by colds and rheumatism.

It seemed the disease could move around in my body at will. When I defeated it in one area it moved to a healthy spot and started all over again. It could also radically change its character. Disease is a difficult enemy.

HOBBIES

When I was younger I never had time for hobbies. My free time was spent with studies. I enjoyed languages and the literature that had been produced by different civilizations. People in other cultures are different and this shows up clearly in the literature they produce. German prose is pompous and serious, the French is terse and conditional, and the English is less restrained and more casual. But when I retired early I started to look around for a hobby.

At Bobcaygeon we had lots of trees of all sizes and kinds. I started working with the trees and I loved it. Until I appeared they had just been allowed to grow as they pleased, and they looked like it—unkempt. I started by cutting off droopy, low-hanging branches. We had a huge apple tree, about 20 feet high, and it was sending out sucker branches all over. I crawled up the tree with tools in my hands and cut off all the suckers, plus a lot of branches, to bring the tree back into shape. There was a lot of pruning to be done on most of the trees. Some trees were too close together, some were hanging over the hedge, and others needed to be pruned to give them a better shape. Trees respond positively to pruning; it invigorates them, and they produce healthier growth.

We transplanted two low spreading junipers to a location with more space. They were overcrowded and did well in their new spot. There was a vacant area on one side of our lot so we moved a number of small trees into the space to provide more privacy for our lot. Altogether we had over 60 small trees; I numbered them and measured their height every year to keep a record of their growth. We had a long evergreen hedge that needed a lot of trimming all through the year.

Because our soil was poor some of the trees suffered from insect infestation and others from insufficient plant food. We had several lovely pines that required special fertilizers a number of times each summer to keep them from dying. A week after I fed them they looked healthy again. The young oak trees especially had trouble with insects that ate their leaves. I had to spray them regularly during hot weather.

I loved working with trees, but would you call it a hobby? It occupied my spare time, but only during the summer. I slowly got involved with woodworking, starting with furniture refinishing. Previously I had experimented with paint removers but without success. Now I took a course in furniture refinishing from a true antique dealer, south of Lindsay. He taught his class how to remove paint from furniture and then refinish it the way professionals do. Each person had to bring along a piece of furniture and then work on it. It was a practical, hands-on course. It is dirty work. His instruction was thorough; he took no shortcuts and our work had to be perfect. I learned a great deal and refinished most of the furniture we had at Bobcaygeon.

What I wanted, though, was to make my own handicrafts. In our firewood I found some nice pieces of birch log. I also cut down an apple tree that was half dead. Then I carefully seasoned pieces of the logs. My first venture was to make small plaques from them. When the logs were properly seasoned I cut them into slices with a saw. Then I sanded both sides of a piece to the best of my ability. Then I wrote on the piece the inscription of my choice and covered it with liquid plastic. I did not achieve anything near a professional product because I had no one to teach me; I was mostly just experimenting. However, in Winnipeg I found an interesting slice of wood from the base end of a tree, and made a clock with it of which I am truly proud.

In the meantime I was taking woodworking classes in Winnipeg and decided to go into wood turning. Our house was small and I was cramped for room. The standard wood-turning machine is built to take pieces of wood 36 inches long, and was too large for the limited space I had. I hunted around and bought a new machine built to take 18 inch wood pieces. I was fortunate because it was on the market for only a short time. I brought some of the pieces of log, which I had seasoned at Bobcaygeon, to Winnipeg and made some interesting bowls from them. Mostly, however, I bought good lumber, laminated pieces together, and then put them on the machine and turned out whatever shape my fancy dictated. With the help of the woodworking classes I was taking I was able to do some fairly good work. Finishing the objects was an art in itself. To begin with, they had to be carefully sanded. Then I gave them from three to five coats of Varathane, with a careful sanding after each coat. The last coat is sanded with very fine steel wool, and this gives it a lovely finish. There are many stages of work involved in producing a finished bowl.

During all this time, however, I had my mind set on lapidary work. Rocks had always intrigued me and I wanted to work with them. I didn't know where to turn for information, or how to get started. Wherever I went I had my eyes open for information. Then one day it happened. I was in the Bobcaygeon Tourist Office looking through all the brochures when I picked up a small, rather drab looking booklet. It was issued by the Geological Survey of Canada and had all the information I needed. It listed all the lapidary clubs, and stores, across Canada. It was a real Godsend the way this booklet came into my hands.

The nearest lapidary club was in Peterborough, about 40 miles away. I wrote to them but got no answer. When I was in Winnipeg I had the same problem, that I could not make any contacts with lapidary clubs. Evidently the information in the booklet was out of date. However, I finally managed to make contact with the Rock of Ages Club and was on my way to another hobby. I looked up the Happy Rock Shop and Mr. Williams sold me the machines I needed and gave me valuable advice. At the Rock of Ages Club I got more instruction and soon I was cutting and polishing ugly rock and turning it into lovely jewellery. Actually I learned most of my skills by the "trial and error" method, with the help of a good instruction book. At the club I always carefully watched what the others were doing when they were working on the machines and learned a great deal. It is a joy to turn ordinary raw material into pieces of beauty.

ANECDOTES

Fire in a Teacher's Pocket

This happened in the Morris High School. It was a sunny peaceful school morning, just after 9:00 a.m. While we were singing "O Canada" during assembly, we could smell a touch of smoke. We were barely finished with O Canada when the fire alarm rang. We marched out in good order and lined up outside. Real fire alarms don't happen often and there was an air of expectancy in the group. (Both teachers and students secretly wish for a break from the other party, although they may not openly admit it.)

Above all, we were curious. What was burning and causing the smoke? It did not take long until the firemen came out of the school. One fireman carried the overcoat belonging to one of the teachers. It had volumes of smoke coming out of its folds.

The principal explained the teacher had been smoking his pipe and had carelessly put the pipe into his pocket with the lit tobacco in it.

Everyone burst into laughter. Poor teacher! He was sorely embarrassed by the event. It was pretty difficult to keep a straight face and refrain from laughing all that day. It still tickles me when I think of it.

Panties

Seeing as I have started in Morris I might as well stay there for awhile. A number of teachers were living in Winnipeg so we formed a car pool to share the driving. One of the lady teachers lived in Morris but she came along on Friday to spend the weekend in the city.

Friday being the end of the school week, we were always in a hurry to leave as soon as possible after school. This lady teacher, however, had to go home and grab her stuff to take along. The driver this time was a young single man. He tooted the horn in front of her place in a hurry to get going, and finally she came out holding onto a number of bags, and got into the front seat of the car.

All went well, supposedly, but trouble lurks just around the corner and preys upon the most innocent persons.

On Saturday he went to pick up his girlfriend to take her out. He glanced at the floor of the car just as his girlfriend was about to get in. What did he see? A pair of lady's panties! He quickly managed to push them under the seat before his girlfriend saw them. What a narrow escape! Where did they come from? The lady teacher on Friday had taken her laundry along to do her washing in Winnipeg and, being in such a hurry, it had dropped out of her bag.

I don't know what would have happened to the young man if his girlfriend had seen the panties. Would you have believed his story? I wouldn't if I were a woman.

On Monday, when he saw the lady teacher, he gave her a thorough lecture. She smugly replied that if he hadn't rushed her the way he did, it wouldn't have happened.

A Blizzard

We are still in Morris and again it is Friday afternoon, but in the middle of winter. The problem this time was worse than panties, it was a real prairie blizzard. And it was my turn to drive. What I did was one of the most foolish acts in my life.

In town it was difficult to judge how bad the storm actually was. We soon found out when we came into the open. The visibility was less than ten feet and I couldn't see the road in front of the car. Should we turn back and stay in Morris for the night? Common sense told us we should. There was a major intersection just a mile out of town so we planned to turn around there. But we couldn't find the intersection. There was no way we could turn around without losing our sense of direction and going off the highway into the ditch.

The passenger on the right could see the shoulder of the highway when he opened the window. He instructed me to turn right or left and so I managed to keep on my side of the road. I never saw the road myself all the way into Winnipeg. Halfway home a large truck passed us. Probably he could see better because he was sitting higher. I could see the rear lights of the truck so now I used that as a guide, but I had to stay very close to him, only about ten feet, in order to see his lights. If he ever applied his brakes we would have rammed into him.

It was a relief when we finally reached Winnipeg. Thank God we made it! It would have been wiser for us to stay in Morris for the night, much wiser!

Man with a Gun

This happened while we were living in our little house in Elmwood before we had the house rebuilt. The shed on the back was narrower than the house and the rear door was on the side of the shed. Thus it was set in from the main wall of the house.

I had the queer habit of going outside to enjoy a bit of fresh air before going to bed. It was a warm, quiet evening, but dark when I softly opened the door and looked out.

What did I see? About five feet away, at the corner of the main side of the house, stood a man with a gun, the butt end on the sidewalk. I had a strange feeling. What should I do? Was I supposed to be afraid? Neither of us moved. We both listened. Then I heard a call from across the street in front of the house and another call from a different direction.

"I give up," he said, and I noticed the gun was only a broomstick. Without looking back he marched away to join his buddies. They were grown-up fellows playing an adult version of "cops and robbers", roving over a large area hiding from each other. My opening the door may have alerted another player to spot the one who was standing close to my door.

I found it exciting but was without fear.

Pine Falls—The Front Middle Seat of the Car

People nowadays don't know what I am talking about unless they have been in the front seat of a rear-wheel-drive car. The front seat always took three passengers but the middle one had to cope with the hump, and there was no place to put your feet. Passengers dreaded it when they were pushed into it.

I was driving into Winnipeg for the weekends and taking passengers along. This time I had five teachers coming with me so I had a full load. Four of them were staying at Manitou Lodge where I lived, but I had to pick up the other girl at the townsite. The girl sitting beside me was muttering about being forced onto the hump as we were driving along the highway to pick up the last girl. I didn't know how I would handle the situation.

But I didn't have much time to reflect. There she was, standing on the highway waiting. And she had a suitcase. My luck! I stopped the car and headed for the suitcase. The girls could fight it out while I was putting the suitcase into the trunk. Can a situation ever change in the wink of an eye! This girl had other ideas. She got in from the driver's side and grabbed the seat on the hump. That changed everything. She wanted the seat beside me and she got it. Her action was very obvious and the first girl abruptly changed her view about the middle seat as she lost it. When I got into the car there was an air of tenseness, as if a bomb was about to go off. The new girl smiled and pretended a sense of complete innocence. It took a while before the dangerous quiet turned into an air of more peaceful calmness.

Living with women can be a volatile affair.

Gathering Bark on the Riverbank

While I'm at Pine Falls I will mention another incident. I have always been the kind of person who is not very conscious of the age of the persons I am with. Likewise, people often forget about my age when they are with me.

We usually had teachers without cars so I always picked up teachers to take along on my way to school. One of them was a young girl, about 21, in her first year of teaching. She was an excellent teacher, enthusiastic and always trying out new things.

One day she was working on a new art project and she needed a good supply of tree bark. Where could she get it? On the riverbank, I told her. The river was being used to dump pulpwood and there was lots of bark on the bank of the river. She asked if we could stop at the river and I said, "Sure, we'll stop and gather some bark."

There we were, on the side of the river, jumping around on the logs, stepping into the wet mud, gathering up nice pieces of bark. Suddenly she turned around to me and said,

"You're as old as my father. He would never do anything like this. I'm sorry for dragging you down here like this."

"Forget it," I said. "I'm having as much fun as you are."

I learned a lot from another lady teacher, a Francophone, who was quite a bit older than I was. She had no sense of age either. Whatever the teachers were doing, she was with the young people and had as much fun as they did.

It is wonderful to be like that.

Helen and a Stalled Car

This story goes back many years, to my first marriage. In those years we were relatively poor. We had a car but we did not have the means to keep it in good driving condition at all times.

Helen and I had gone downtown for some entertainment. We did not have the children along.

The car starter had been causing us some problems but the car started all right when we left home so we took a chance on getting back again. It was late in the evening when we returned to the car and when I tried to start it the starter would not kick in. What could I do? There wasn't a service station in the vicinity, and in those days they didn't stay open all night either.

"Well, what are you going to do?" Helen asked. "I don't want to sit here all night."

"I don't know," I replied.

"Then let me get behind the wheel of the car if you don't know what to do," Helen demanded.

I was only too glad to cooperate. But what was she going to do? I got out of the car and walked to the other side. She slid into the driver's seat.

She sat there and watched the rearview mirror. As soon as a car turned into the street she stepped out and flagged him down. She asked him for a push. He got out to see if the bumpers matched. Then he gave our car a push. It started easily and away we went, homeward bound. She had solved our problem without difficulty.

One thing about Helen, she was resourceful and ready to take over.

Free Chicken Feed

In our early years we had bought a lovely home in Fort Garry, had several children, a car and needed to buy furniture, but my income from the Post Office barely covered expenses.

We had a large garden area across the back lane where we grew vegetables. There was a lot of vacant land around our place at the time. We had a double garage on our lot, so we screened off part of it and kept chickens. Outside we screened off an area so they could go outside. This provided us with eggs and some roasting chickens.

However, chickens need to be fed or else they don't lay eggs. Chicken feed costs money. There was a railway yard north of us between Wilkes and Grant Avenues. Someone told us they parked grain cars out there and we could get some grain by sweeping the freight cars. So we went early Sunday morning with brooms and sacks to clean the grain cars. It was easy to open the cars and climb in. We had to crawl underneath the cars to get from one track to another. We managed to gather a couple of bags of wheat. As soon as the yard crew arrived we beat it. We didn't want to get run over once they started moving the cars around. They didn't mind us sweeping the cars for them.

It was risky business but we did it a number of times. It helped us manage. In those days poor people took quite a few risks to try and make ends meet.

Buying a House

When we moved into Winnipeg we lived in a single room. Half a year later we rented a small suite with two rooms. Finally, after a year in the city, we rented a small house in North Kildonan and now had a decent place to live, at least in our estimation. We had an outdoor toilet and had to carry water from a pump about a hundred yards down the street.

After a couple of years Helen and I agreed it was time to buy our own home, a modern house. However, as soon as we went to look at houses, Helen would refuse to consider the matter. The house we were renting was getting too small and we often discussed buying a larger house, but it was difficult to get Helen to look at a house, never mind make a deal. This went on for a number of years, during which time I looked at many houses.

Finally I got serious and had a salesman working on it. One day he showed me a house on Somerville Avenue in Fort Garry. It had no basement and was of poor construction, but the price was high. I said no deal. A week later he called me and said he had a special on a house on the same street. It sounded like sales talk to me but he insisted. Helen wouldn't come along so I drove out alone with him. I didn't feel very optimistic about it, after the house he had shown me a week ago on the same street. He assured me I would like this house. As we drove down the street I eagerly looked at every house wondering which one it would be. Finally he stopped at the best house on the street. At first I wasn't sure if he was just stopping here or was this really the house. He took me in and showed me the place from basement to the second floor. I had never dreamt of owning a house like this. It had many extra features, like hot-water heating, side-by-side windows, a double garage, a 50 foot lot, and it was only a year old. I told him I was sure Helen would agree to take it.

When I got home I was all excited and Helen had no chance to disagree. The salesman took us both to see the place and Helen was impressed with it. It didn't take long until we were living at 1329 Somerville Avenue.

I should say a few words about Helen. She had faced big changes in her life and it is true she had trouble adjusting to her new life. We were the first ones from our area who moved into the city. Her mother feared she would lose her religious faith by moving into the big city. She was only 18 when we were married and we had three children by the time we bought the house in 1948. Also I had gone through a serious conflict with asthma which lasted for several years and almost finished me. She certainly suffered under it as well as I did. Helen had faced many serious changes while still very young.

After awhile she came to like the house. It was more than we had hoped for. She also got used to the big city and has not regretted making the move.

"Where is He?"

Norah did not "wear her feelings on her sleeve". That means the depth of her feelings was not obvious. She liked to know that I was around and where I was. I could be in my room all evening and she in the other part of the house; that was all she needed. At Bobcaygeon I could be working outside all day, only coming in to eat; she was perfectly happy. Personally I needed more closeness than that. But sometimes her real feelings came to the surface.

Our property at Bobcaygeon was almost surrounded by a massive cedar hedge. In the centre of one side of the lot was "Mike's House", and on the left side you could squeeze between the hedge and building to go into the side road. I was working outside all afternoon one nice summer day when Norah came out to speak to me. She came to the right side of the yard but couldn't find me. I happened to be in the left side of the yard. Then I walked through on the left side of Mike's House into the side road and around to the right side of the yard. In the meantime she walked over to the left side. When she didn't find me there either, she panicked and started screaming. It seemed to her that I had vanished. When I heard her I walked over to her and calmed her. We had missed each other because we had walked around in a circle.

The fact that she was deeply disturbed the moment she couldn't locate me showed how much she depended on me, even if she normally did not show it.

Pruning Trees

As an old gardener I know how important it is to prune a tree when planting it, and how beneficial it is to the tree to keep on pruning it as it grows. But some people don't like to see a tree "butchered" when it looks perfectly attractive.

After we had bought the house on Somerville Avenue, Helen and I wisely decided we would plant a Manitoba maple tree on the front lawn. It is a tall lovely tree today. There were a lot of trees growing wild in the ditches so we drove around to find one. It didn't take us long until we found a lovely tree, about six feet tall. We dug it up and took it home.

It was time to make supper, so after we had decided on the spot to plant it, Helen went in to cook and I planted the tree. Then I pruned it, cutting off about half the branches. It didn't look beautiful after that.

When Helen came out after supper and saw what I had done she was upset, and mad. It didn't help when I explained the tree would have died if I had left it the way it was. She didn't believe me.

Only a year later when the maple was growing and was again beautiful in appearance, could I point to it with pride as the result of my pruning. Even then I am not sure if she was convinced. Next we planted a lilac bush beside the front steps of the house. We wanted to keep it looking pretty in a nice round shape, but after a few years it started spreading too much. We discussed it and decided the bush needed some pruning. So I cut it down to about half its size, so it had room to grow and become more compact. Again Helen was sorely upset when she saw what I had done. But lilacs grow very rapidly and they improve from pruning. It didn't take long until it was obvious I had done the right thing.

At Bobcaygeon I had a much greater job with lilacs. We had a lilac hedge about 40 feet long, ten feet high, and eight feet wide. The hedge was getting on in years and individual lilacs were beginning to spread out like separate trees. I told Norah the lilacs needed a severe cutting back. We took time to think it over and then decided I would cut the hedge down to a flat five feet. It was a big job and took me a couple of days. It looked cruel at first, but in two years it looked beautiful and it developed into a thicker bush. We were both pleased with it.

At the Blyth place in Guelph I came upon a different problem. They had a lovely spruce tree in the front of the yard about five feet tall. Evidently they had planted it carelessly, not pointing it straight up, and so had put a stake beside it to straighten it. This had only aggravated the problem. I noticed there were several kinks in the tree stem. It seemed that every year it pointed in a different direction and had to be tied to a new stake to correct it.

I sort of felt sorry for the tree. One year I examined the tree and found it had about five kinks in the main stem.

"You're torturing the tree," I said.

"What would you do with it?" Alan Blyth asked.

"Just take off the supports and give the tree a chance," I advised. I was talking brashly, for I was far from sure whether I was saying the right thing.

However, they took my advice and released the tree. A year later, when we went back to Guelph, I was somewhat nervous about that spruce. I was greatly relieved when we examined the tree and saw that it had corrected itself and was growing beautifully.

I did a lot of tree pruning at Bobcaygeon and it did not take long until Norah had full confidence in me.

Kneeling

The act of kneeling has gathered bad connotations over the centuries because captives were usually made to kneel in front of their captors before they were executed. Subjects were made to kneel before their sovereign and slaves before their master. It is clearly a sign of subjection and servitude. But not everything about kneeling is negative, I found it has positive aspects as well.

I became a letter carrier in January, switching over from indoor to outdoor work at the coldest time of the year. My clothes were not appropriate and I did not have a uniform at the beginning. I suffered a lot from cold that first winter.

Later an old letter carrier told me the best thing to do when a person gets too cold is to kneel down for awhile. Amazing, it works! However, it would hardly be proper for the postman to kneel down on the sidewalk some place. What would the people think if they saw him there? Then the Post Office brought in the street boxes where the postie picked up his extra bundles of mail. The boxes were low and it was almost necessary to kneel down to refill your bag with more mail. I found that a minute of kneeling down at the box usually restored warmth to my body. It is a good thing to know in case a person ever gets stranded in cold weather and is in danger of freezing.

However, if we look at the accepted connotations of kneeling, isn't it true that most of us would benefit from more humbleness of spirit? I believe so!

During my lifetime I have experienced how the attitude of the Church towards kneeling has changed. When I was young, people kneeled to pray. Today very few churches still have their people kneel to pray; maybe a few Catholic churches. I also notice that humbleness and humility are becoming rare among church people. Christians today are wealthy compared to those I knew in my youth. Wealthy people don't need to kneel to anyone, not even to God.

I find it is a wonderful experience to kneel down before God when praying to Him. Try it. Get your church to try it.

Premonitions

This happened many years ago when I was a young lad about 12 years old. I have forgotten the details about the event but I do remember clearly that my Mother got up that morning in a very agitated state of mind. She had seen a vision in a dream; I forget what she had seen, but it was very real to her. It signified to her that someone had died.

Who could it be? We didn't have a telephone in those days and communication was difficult. But we did have telegrams.

In the afternoon a messenger arrived with a telegram. Who would it be? It was my mother's sister, Gertrude. She had been working in northern Saskatchewan in a lumber camp and had died suddenly.

When the subject of premonitions comes up I find myself on the believer's side.

A Visitor from Moscow

It happened when Norah and I were living in our apartment in Paris on the eighth floor during the Christmas holidays. We were home during the evening when we heard a soft knock on the door. It was very unusual for someone to knock on our door.

I opened the door and saw a young man standing there, a university student from Moscow, as it turned out. He asked if we knew a certain Russian person, but the name meant nothing to us. The person had escaped from Russia and his relatives in Moscow were trying to establish contact with him.

We started talking, so I asked him in and we had a good visit together. He was from Edmonton and had been sent to Moscow to study the Russian language. Canada needed persons who could speak and understand Russian. He told us much about the situation in Russia. It was an interesting coincidence that brought us together. This was the time that Russian might was at its highest, in 1977. He was in a safe situation as a university student from Canada, but he could observe what life was really like for the Russian people.

It was an informative visit.

Problems that Appeared Unannounced

Norah and I did a lot of travelling while we lived in Paris. It was easy to take the train and go anywhere we wanted. As a rule, we knew the system well and had no problems, but when you feel that you know it all is the time when something unforeseen happens.

Norah and I had decided to go to a certain town south of Paris that intrigued us. It was just a day trip, but in France you can go a long way in a day. We bought our train tickets and off we went. It was a straight trip from point A to point B, or so we thought. That was all the ticket showed.

Fortunately, Norah liked to talk to strangers and so the people around us knew where we were going. The train stopped a number of times to take on passengers, but suddenly at one stop the people beside us said we had to get out. Why? Several of them were going to the same place we were. They got us out of the train in a hurry—trains in France don't stop long. They told us we had to change trains. We had to walk about a quarter of a mile to the next station to get the second train. I was shocked.

We had been given no warning at all that we had to change trains. We would not have gotten to our destination without the help of the people sitting next to us.

A similar but less serious incident happened to me while riding on the Paris Metro, or subway. I had taken line 13 and was going to St. Denis. Then I noticed, by watching the stations we passed through, that I was on the wrong line. How come? I looked at my map and realized that at La Fourche, line 13 split into two branches. So I took the subway back a distance, turned around, and tried again. At La Fourche the subway car opened on both sides and you had to know on which side to get out. I could see no sign telling me what to do, but I learned the hard way.

A Drunk Pedestrian

Times have certainly changed as far as drunk driving is concerned. At least at Christmas time. This story goes back over 45 years.

It was Christmas Eve, I had finished delivering my mail, and was standing on Portage Avenue at the east corner of Eatons. In those days on Christmas Eve, there were more drunk people on the streets than sober people.

I was watching a drunk person trying to shuffle his way across the street, going to the Woolworth's store. He was too drunk to recognize traffic lights.

"Watch where you're going!" one of the car drivers shouted to him.

"Yes, I better," he retorted, "with all you drunk drivers on the street."

I couldn't help but laugh, and the incident still tickles me.

In those days I didn't take our car out on December 24 unless I had to. Too many drivers were going around in circles and had no idea which direction was home.

We have come a long way from those days. Today the police have to go looking for drunk drivers, and even then they only find a few.

Lost in the Fog

People talk about being lost in a fog, but that usually refers to their mental situation.

This anecdote speaks of a real fog. It happened on a warm Sunday afternoon in 1965 when I was teaching at Bloodvein. We had spent the weekend in Winnipeg and had driven north to the end of the road. There I left my car and we had to cross the lake by boat. We noticed that the native who was supposed to take us across had had too much to drink, and we decided it was not safe to go with him. We managed to hire another boat and set off across the lake.

We hadn't gone far before we were enveloped in a thick fog. Before long we had no idea which direction we were going. It was an eerie feeling, sitting in the boat on the calm water and only being able to see a couple of feet ahead of us. We were lost and didn't know what to do. As a rule I always carried a compass with me, but on the previous trip I had put it into my back pocket and had sat on it. It refused to point North after that.

We sat around for awhile and then started moving in a direction we hoped would take us to land. Finally the fog opened and we saw land ahead. Not only land, but a long dock stretching out into the lake. None of the persons on the boat, including a native, had seen the dock before. It seemed we were in fairyland. We landed and walked to a shack not far from the dock. There we found a man who was hired to look after the dock. He told us we were on the north end of Matheson Island. So we stayed close to the land and got back to the south part, to civilization. We gave up crossing the lake that day and stayed at the Mennonite Mission for the night.

Monday morning we got up early and made our way across the lake. I was a little late for school but no one had even noticed my absence. When we asked about the drunk native, who was supposed to take us across, we found that he had crossed the previous day without trouble.

The moral of the story is "Don't sit on your compass," and if you do, get another one immediately.

A Deep Disappointment

I believe that I was about ten to twelve years old at this time. The sad feeling of disappointment I experienced that day remains even though the details of the experience are sketchy.

My parents had moved from the well-to-do West Side of the Red River to the poorer East Side. There were differences in culture between the sides, and my parents retained some of the West Side customs.

In those days boys did not wear long pants like their fathers did, at least not on the West Side. The people where we now lived were too poor to be concerned about such customs. The result was that all the boys I knew were wearing long pants and making fun of me for going with short pants. Peer pressure was vicious, even in those days. How I longed for long pants!

Then I heard my parents were driving to Winnipeg to do some shopping and I asked them to buy me a pair of long pants. I waited anxiously for their return in the evening. When they came they showed us all the nice things they had bought for us. They had bought me a number of articles of clothing, but *no long pants* .

I was shattered! I walked into the bush and sat down and cried, in the dark. What they had bought me was more than the cost of a pair of pants. I would have to face the teasing of the boys again, who knows for how long?

Life would be so much easier for kids if sometimes parents would listen to their requests.

"Turn on the Heater!"

This happened on a cold, cold day in the middle of winter during the years I was single. Betty (not her real name) and I had gone out for the evening and had enjoyed ourselves. But now it was time to go home and it was at least minus 30 degrees outside.

"I'll go and start the car first while you wait inside," I told Betty, but she was determined to come out with me. She wasn't afraid of the cold. She was a fine, sensible woman, but she was a bit proud sometimes. She was dressed lightly and only wearing her mink jacket to keep out the bitter cold.

I hesitated, but she knew what she wanted. I wasn't even sure if the car would start, it was that cold.

We hurried to the car; luckily it started.

"Okay, turn on the heat, I'm cold," she ordered in a shivering voice.

"Sorry," I said, "but the motor is cold, it has to warm up first." She didn't believe what I was saying as she struggled trying to keep warm in the frigid car.

"I've seen you turn a little button somewhere on the dash and the heat came on. Now don't wait, turn it on before I freeze," she muttered in a threatening voice.

"It'll take about ten minutes before the car warms up in this weather," I apologized.

"I'll tell my son about you when I get home," Betty retorted, and now she was getting angry.

I drove slowly so the motor would warm up more quickly. Actually, I had my hands full just driving the car. It was stiff as could be and the windows were badly frosted up.

Finally the heat started coming and slowly our situation ameliorated. Fortunately, her son wasn't home when we arrived at her house.

Next weekend he was home though, and all three of us were sitting down eating lunch.

"Well, Betty, did you complain to your son about what happened last weekend?" I asked her.

Her son sat opposite from us with a smile on his face. Betty felt embarrassed and muttered some words in self-defence, which I have conveniently forgotten.

We had some fine visits together.

"Where is Norah?"

After Norah had been taken into Vista Park Lodge on January 1, 1992, it took us both some time to adjust to our new situation. I was defeated and fearsome, not knowing what to do with life. Norah seemed peaceful but lost weight rapidly, to the extent that I feared she might die. However, half a year later Norah was gaining weight again and I was trying out new ventures, things we could still do together.

One interesting thing I discovered was that I could take Norah out in her wheelchair with HandiTransit at the cost of regular bus fare. The head nurse at the Home had to make arrangements 48 hours ahead, but that was not a problem. The drivers were courteous and the vehicle was comfortable. We were away from the Home about four to five hours, and that gave us ample time to do something. At first Norah was suspicious about where we were going, but once she realized we always returned to her place, she started to enjoy the trips. And so did I.

Norah had always loved adventure, and when she was on the bus she kept her eyes open all the way. She watched the scenery and the driver as well. Then when everything is going well, something unexpected happens.

This time we had taken a trip to The Forks. The weather was chilly but not really cold. I had dressed Norah warmly so we were able to spend some time outside in this lovely spot. There are a lot of interesting shops to see inside and we also went up the tower. In between we had coffee, and later a good lunch from the take-out places. Then we had to get ready for the return.

Fifteen minutes before the HandiTransit bus was due we went to the door to wait for it at the wheelchair stop. As it was chilly, I parked Norah some distance from the door so I could watch her and keep a lookout for the bus. The time came but no bus was in sight. We waited another 15 minutes and still no bus. It had never been this late before. I knew there were two stops marked for wheelchairs but I could not be in two places at once. So I phoned the HandiTransit office. They were confused about the matter and told me the bus should arrive soon. After another 15 minutes I phoned again and told them I was desperate. They discussed the matter for awhile in the office and then decided to send out another vehicle. I had spent about ten minutes on the phone.

Then I looked around for Norah and she was gone. I rushed around in the Terminal and couldn't see her. I was in a panic. Who would kidnap a woman in a wheelchair? Looking up and down I tried to collect my senses. I asked one of the sales ladies in a nearby shop if she had seen anything. She said someone had taken Norah out through the door. I rushed out to see where she was. There I saw a Unicity taxi equipped to take wheelchairs, and the driver had just loaded Norah into the back of the taxi. When he tried to collect the fare from her he realized he had a problem on his hands. She couldn't tell him anything. I arrived just in time to clear the situation.

No one had told me that Unicity taxi was doing some work for HandiTransit. I had been waiting for the usual HandiTransit vehicle and had no idea Unicity taxi might be coming instead. I was quite shocked by the experience. You never know what can happen next around the corner of life. We had many other successful trips with Unicity after that.

Clouds of Fire

It was a clear Sunday morning and I was on my usual drive to spend some time at Norah's grave. It was very cold with some hoarfrost in the air. I was driving south on Pembina Highway. When I looked to the east I was amazed by the sight I saw. The sun had just come up. The smoke from the chimneys was going straight up. Every time a cloud of smoke passed in front of the sun it turned into a fiery orange pillar. It was a gorgeous sight to behold.

I had never seen such a display before. There must have been something special about the atmosphere that morning because on another similar morning there was no such phenomenon at all.

Nature has wonderful revelations at times.

The News Media

This story goes back to about 1940, the time when our civilization was emerging from the Stone Age and Radio broadcasting was being developed. They were building a radio tower at Morris when a sudden storm came up and toppled the tower. A workman was killed in the accident.

In our district lived a couple with a large family, mostly boys. The father was a blind person and quite ignorant of worldly affairs. One of their sons was working some place but they did not know where.

A news media reporter visited them and informed them that it was their son who had been killed. The parents had no recourse but to believe what they were told. The next issue of the Free Press Prairie Farmer gave a full account of the accident supporting the story. They also had a picture of the young man in the paper. However, the photo showed a young man dressed in an army uniform. Their son had never been in the army, so the story started to unravel. A few weeks later the boy returned home for a visit, safe and sound.

Where did the news media get the story? Who knows! Since then I have come across more news stories that are far removed from the facts.

News reporters try, but sometimes the gremlins are hard at work as well.

Stuck in the Snow

There was a lot of snow that year in the town of Fort Alexander and very little snow clearing had been done on the streets. I still drove my big Meteor and had lots of experience driving on difficult road conditions. I knew how to drive in deep snow but this time the snow was too much for me. I wanted to get out of town and onto the highway but I didn't make it. My Meteor was stuck solidly. The back wheels were turning easily, suspended above the ground. The car was sitting on a small hill of snow which had been pushed up underneath the car.

It didn't take long until six young men came to my rescue. However, try as they would, they could not budge the car. In disgust they gave up and walked away, leaving me to my fate.

What now? I felt rather forsaken sitting alone in my Meteor on top of a snow pile. Somehow I had to get out of this predicament. From somewhere I remembered an old proverb, "When everything else fails, use your head." After all, God doubtless gave us our brains for a purpose.

Then something in my brain clicked. I got out of the car, opened the trunk, took out the bumper jack, jacked up the front of the car as far as it would go, and then pushed the car back off the jack.

Now the rear wheels were again on solid ground. I put the jack away, got into the car and drove off without trouble. I also blew the horn as I drove out of town to let everyone know I had managed to get the car out on my own.

It's amazing, the things you can do when you use your head. It's good for many things besides carrying a hat.

I have used this method again for getting my car out of the snow. It's a very useful trick and much less trouble than calling a tow truck.

More Snow Trouble

This time I didn't get stuck, but my Comet was immobilized. It happened in winter one Sunday evening driving back from Winnipeg to Pine Falls. It had been snowing all day and there was about ten inches of fresh snow on the highway. The weather was mild and the wind was calm. There was only one set of car tracks on the highway but I had to make an extra track when meeting another vehicle. Sometimes I chose to drive on my side of the road and made a new set of tracks. It was no trouble driving in the deep snow because it was soft and loose.

But soon I noticed there was something wrong with the lights, they were getting very weak. And then the heater gave no heat and the motor wasn't working properly. Obviously something was wrong and I would have to investigate. I pulled to the side and stopped.

I got out my powerful flashlight and opened the hood. I saw a sight I had never seen before. Can you imagine? The whole area under the hood was tightly packed with snow, every cubic inch of it. Driving in the deep snow, higher than the bottom of the car, it had pushed up in front underneath the hood. I found a large screwdriver and dug the snow out until the motor was visible again. Then I saw the snow had pushed the fan belt off its pulleys. That is why the lights had dimmed. I was getting wet and cold from the snow but continued working until I got the fan belt back in place. Fortunately the battery was still strong enough to start the car and soon everything was functioning again. Slowly the heater warmed me up again.

It was an unusual experience, but I managed to cope with it.

Hauling Potatoes and Other Trucking Stories

This happened during the war while we were living in Winnipeg. Both of my brothers were away from home doing alternative war service and the cordwood truck was standing idle at home. For my sister Anna, then about 20, and my mother the truck proved a real temptation. The spirit of adventure is innate in our family. They started using the truck for any hauling work they could get.

One weekend when I was home my sister had a job to haul a truckload of potatoes from Grunthal to the railway station at La Broquerie. The store at Grunthal had been taking potatoes in lieu of money from its customers. On Saturday morning I went along with my sister and helped her load the truck with bags of potatoes. Anna was worried because she knew the tires on the truck were in poor shape.

Anna stopped every few miles to check the tires and make sure it was safe to drive. It didn't take long before one rear tire was flat. So we took it off. There was only one tire left on that wheel so we piled the potatoes over to the other side of the truck to equalize the weight.

Before long the second tire on that wheel went flat too and our troubles were mounting. We jacked up the truck and took one of the tires off the other wheel and transferred it to the first wheel. Now there was only one tire on each dual wheel in the back. It was getting risky.

We were still some distance from La Broquerie when Anna realized that another tire was going flat. She stopped and we put the jack under that side of the truck. We couldn't drive further with the jack replacing a wheel. Anna then phoned another trucker to come and pick up the potatoes and take them to the railway station. She also managed to get one of the tires to a service station where they repaired it so we could drive home.

It was not a successful day.

Another trip was more successful. This time Anna and Mother were hauling cordwood. I went along to help them load the truck. It is a strenuous job to load three cords of wood onto a truck. This time Anna was worried about the starter on the motor.

We drove to a farmer's place, into the bush, and loaded the truck. Then Anna drove to the house where she paid for the wood. When we were ready to leave the starter wouldn't work and the loaded truck just sat there. What now? What does a young girl do with a large truck in a crisis like this? Mother made a show of heroism and said she was going to pull the truck. She grabbed the front bumper of the truck and gave it a mighty pull. She was just a small woman but sure enough, the truck moved, Anna put it in gear and the motor started. Unbelievable, but I saw it with my own eyes. I believe the truck was standing on an incline but it was still a miraculous feat, moving a truck with three cords on it. This is the extent of my knowledge of the trucking adventures of these two women, but a full account from them would make interesting reading.

The war years were adventurous times and more than slightly unusual in some aspects. Anna only had her car driver's licence, the truck wasn't licensed for hauling heavy loads, and I don't think it carried any insurance. With most of the men away to war, the authorities were only too glad to see a few trucks still on the road and made no efforts to check them.

Leaving the ladies, I shall now relate a trucking story which happened to my brother Walter. This took place before the war, I believe, and Walter may have been less than 20 years old at the time. He was just getting used to the truck he was driving.

At this time he was buying cordwood around home, hauling it west through Morris into the Red River valley where he exchanged it for baled hay, which he then took back to sell to the farmers at home. I went along with Walter on one trip in winter. Everything was going well. We got our load of cordwood out west, traded it for hay, and were well on our way back home. As we neared St. Malo., Walter noticed that the motor was not running properly. He decided to stop at a service garage in St. Malo. The loaded truck was too large to drive into the garage, but they opened the door and let the front part come in as far as possible so that it was warmer to work on the motor.

The service man found nothing wrong with the motor but when he turned it off he couldn't start it again. It was 6:00 p.m. and time to close the garage. They told Walter to take the truck out so they could go home for the day. Walter replied he couldn't move the truck until they got the motor running again. It was a pretty good argument.

The truck was halfway into the garage and blocking the door. However, the men had finished their time and wanted to close shop, and they were getting frustrated.

Then Walter remembered what Dad had told him. Dad had warned him this could happen, and all he had to do was open the cap on the gas tank to release the vacuum inside. Walter went and took off the cap, the motor started and away we went, with everyone happy.

To Swim or to Drown?

In 1961 when I took teacher training, the authorities insisted that every teacher should be able to swim. A few had certificates to show they had passed an acceptable level of fitness in swimming and the rest of us were booked at the Sherbrook Swimming Pool to take swimming instruction. I had spent many years at the YMCA taking lessons but had never passed a test.

Surprisingly few of the students showed any signs of ability in the water, so the shallow end of the pool was crowded with beginners. Because I had an air of confidence they put me into the deep end. Sorry, but I did not know how to tread water.

The Sherbrook Pool had an odd feature at that time. The water level was more than a foot below floor level. If a person was in trouble in the water he could not swim to the side and pull himself out.

They lined us up and one by one we had to dive into the pool and practice swimming skills. My turn came. I dived in and, because I could not tread water, it only took a few minutes before I was drowning. The lifeguard pulled me out and put me back in line again.

Before long it was my turn to dive in again. Into the water I went and it didn't take long until they had to pull me out again.

They put me right back into the line-up again, for the third time. Wait a minute, how many times do I have to go through this drowning process?

I think I've had enough!

I slipped away to the shallow end where it was safe.

This is all I remember about my swimming lessons, except that I never did learn to swim.

POETRY

I WALKED ONE DAY...

I walked one day where Jesus walked
Beside the Sea of Galilee (Sept.27,1994)
In the misty light of the morning sun
I heard His voice drifting over the waves:

"Blessed are the poor in spirit
for theirs is the kingdom of heaven.
Blessed are those who hunger and thirst after righteousness
for they shall be filled." Matt.5:3,6.

I listened as I walked, and then I saw
The crowds rejoicing at His words.
His voice was calm and quiet
But His words were hard to understand.

How can the poor in spirit
claim the kingdom of heaven?
And when shall righteousness prevail
sought only by a few?

But then He touched my eyes and let me see
a kingdom not of this world.
There women, men, and children walk
in the light that comes from His word.

I prayed that He would give me grace
to touch the lives of those I meet
With a humble caring spirit
and a touch that is warm with love.

At the School I work with children
Who are eager and full of life,
At the Home I work with old people
Who have lost their joy and their home.

I greet them all with a humble smile
Which tells them that I care
And I pray that they will see through me
The words of faith that Jesus taught

On the shore of Galilee.

WHAT NOW? (caring for an Alzheimer person)

She reached for her fur coat
With an eye on the door
"Oh, Norah,
Are you going out?"
I quietly asked.

"I am going to the bank,"
she said
In a decisive tone of voice.
"But it's nine o'clock in the evening,
And the banks are closed at night."

"You're just trying to put me off,"
she rejoined,
With a cool look in her eye.
"What happens now?"
I said to myself.

I changed my course and softly answered
"I'll go with you, dear."
I put on my coat and down we went
Together, as couples should,
To enjoy our life in peace.

The bank had vanished from her mind
As we walked along the street
The air was cold
And Norah's pace was slow
"Are you cold, dear, and tired?"

She nodded with a quiet look
I took her hand in mine
As we turned to go back home.
"It's been a fine walk,"
I whispered in her ear.

She was content
and happy to go back.
But all was changed
When we arrived at the door
of our apartment block.

"What do we want here?"
she asked with troubled voice.
"This is where we live,"
I tried to explain
But it meant nothing to her.

She hesitated, but came with me
"This is not my home,"
she objected.
"We'll take the elevator up
And then we'll be at home."

Norah was confused as I opened the door,
"What do we want here?"
she asked.
"I don't want to stay here
This is not my home."

What could I say to her?
I had no answer
I felt so helpless and so weak
As I looked at her…and she looked away.
Whatever shall we do?

"Let me help you with your coat,
We have to stay here now."
"No!"
she said, "This is not my home."
And she kept on her coat and boots.

"Sit down here while I make some tea."
She looked at the Globe and Mail
While in the kitchen I made her tea.
Then we sat together, drinking tea
as we warmed our hearts in peace.

"It's time to go to bed,"
I suggested quietly.
Her fur coat and her boots stayed on
As unwillingly she laid down to rest
And I went to sleep in a separate room.

In the middle of the night
I woke up and looked around the house
Norah was sound asleep on the living room floor.
I covered her with a blanket
And left her to sleep till morn.

LORD, HELP ME TO CARE FOR NORAH
SHE SUFFERS MORE THAN I

NORAH ESCAPES

It was seven o'clock in the morning
And we were both up
After a restless night.
Norah seemed to be tired now
Maybe she will sit down and sleep.

I spent some time in the washroom
Thinking Norah was safe.
The noise of the electric razor
Deafened my ears for a while
Made me feel there was something I had not heard

I rushed into the living room—The door was open, and
Norah was gone!
I had not heard the alarm
Which always hung on the door.

Where had she gone?
Our block has eighteen floors
A walkway takes us to Portage Place
The U. of W. is only a block away
And the streets lead in four directions.

I hesitated, I was panic-stricken
If I could only think
And do the wise thing
Maybe I could anticipate her direction,
But my mind didn't work at all.

First I went down to the lounge
She might be there
No luck!
Then I dashed outside to look around
Hopeless—I didn't know which way to turn.

Portage Place is probably where she went
I sighed hopefully.
Down the long hallway I went
Which leads to the overpass
And into Portage Place.

All through the upper level I walked
And then I searched the main floor
All the shops were closed
Only a few stragglers were around
And no Norah!

Maybe she has gone back on her own
I raced back in hope
No, the suite was still empty
Maybe I'll find her outside
So down I went to the streets.

It was no use!
It was hopeless for me to look outside
I could never find her myself alone
In the maze of downtown streets
So back to Portage Place I went.

I searched through both floors
But all in vain.
Poor Norah, she had no sense of time
She didn't know why the shops were closed
And she had no memory of "home".

Back home I tried to think
To recollect my senses.
What could I do?
Call the police, my only resource,
But then, a knock on the door.

A security guard, from Portage Place,
He was bringing Norah home
She had fallen asleep on a bench
On the second floor of Portage Place
Waiting for the shops to open.

Asleep, she had fallen off the bench
And bruised her arm
Someone had walked her to the security office
And a guard had brought her home.
Thank God for the kindness others show.

Norah felt embarrassed by it all
And couldn't understand
Why all the shops were closed.
We ate breakfast together
And tried to calm our shattered nerves.

Her purse, where had she left it?
I phoned the security office, Maybe?
Yes, her purse was there
An honest person had brought it in.
Thank God for honest people.

Norah felt more humble than usual
And I was happy to take her hand
As we walked over to get her purse
Knowing we faced many more sorrows
But ready to stay together, to the end.

An Alzheimer person does not know what s/he is doing, and is often driven by wounds or crises suffered far back in her/his lifetime. We may have no idea what these are.

IMAGINE

What do I see?
Strange pictures floating in my mind…
What happened to my …?
No, where am I?
I want to go home.

Wait, what is that man doing here?
Why doesn't he help me?
Now he's gone, where is he?
No one comes to see me any more!
I want to go home.

What is that noise I hear?
Dishes, yes it sounds like dishes.
What are dishes?
Why doesn't the noise stop?
I want to go home.

There is that man again.
What is he putting on the table?
A table—what is a table?
Why don't I know what is going on?
I want to go home.

He is calling me,
"Norah, lunch is ready,
Come and join me.
Waffles and maple syrup."
I want to go home.

Maple syrup—I know what that is,
But my mind is getting dark.
Why is that man talking to me?
I am scared,
I want to go home.

Now he is taking my arm,
He is holding me close,
He is talking softly to me,
I don't want to go,
I want to go home.

That man is helping me sit down at the table,
I don't know what he wants.
Maple syrup? no, the Globe and Mail…
The T.S.E. is falling, it says,
Let me look at this.

"Here is your tea, and some lemon."
Have I seen his face before?
Waffles and maple syrup…
No, let me read the T.S.E..
Oh, these waffles are good
and I love the tea!

IMAGINE yourself in Norah's predicament. She no longer recognized her surroundings, her husband or her friends. She had no sense of the time of day or night. She had no idea what to wear or how to dress. She knew she had to hide her pills, her glasses, her wallet and all her credit cards. Why? Who knows? She knew she had to go to the toilet sometimes, but didn't know where it was or what it looked like.

She did remember the Globe and Mail newspaper which had always been important to her.

Home? She had lived in many places in her life and they had all vanished from her memory. The desire "to go home" is innate to the human being, but Norah had no home…

The caregiver will have a better understanding of his/her responsibility if he/she can sense what is happening to the person he/she is caring for.

"I REMEMBER"

I remember our last day
It came without warning
Norah seemed to be doing fine
As we enjoyed our days together.
Norah and I

I arrived at the nursing home early that day
On a quiet afternoon
Norah was still asleep in bed
But she was talking in her sleep.
It seemed strange

It was a day in early October
But not too cold to go outside
On the sidewalk for a walk
With Norah in the wheelchair.
Norah and I

She needed to be warmly dressed
October air is chilly
I carefully put extra clothes on her
And had her almost ready to go.
Norah and I

But we never got out of her room
She gasped one tragic shriek
And that was all
Life on earth was ended
For Norah and me.

CHRISTMAS

It came upon a midnight clear
as the shepherds were watching their sheep,
The song of angels burst all around,
"Christ the King is born this night!"
Where?
In Bethlehem.

We searched in Bethlehem
and found the baby in a barn
with His parents.
Could this child be a King?
We can't be serious about this event!
But three Magi from the East came and worshipped Him!

The ages have rolled past
and the world picks its kings among the mighty.
But a "chosen few"
read in God's book
how Christ walked among the poor, the sick and the rejected.
He healed them, comforted and fed them,
and the "chosen few" accept Him as their King.

Now the world has adopted Christmas,
the day that Christ was born
and made it the greatest holiday of the year.
With feasting and merriment
giving presents to each other
forgetting
Who was born that day!

I remember
years ago
standing on Portage Avenue, next to Eatons
a man was drunkenly shuffling across the street.
"Be careful, there," called a driver from a passing ca
"I better," he replied,
"With all you drunk drivers on the street!"
The scene has changed.
Today we see
less drunkenness on the streets.

And then came
the office parties.
NO WIVES ALLOWED
Married executives drunk with secretaries on their knees.
What a Christmas scene!
But now they are gone...
The feminist movement played a major role.

And now
Look at the shopping mall parking lots!
I can't find a place to park my car.
I have to
buy presents for...and...and... ... ...
Oh! what will I do?
Where can I park?
December 25 is so close
And then I reflected
WHAT AM I GIVING HIM?

Wars have taken their toll
Millions have died in our century
Human life was expendable for the cause of war.
But today
the feeling grows that life is more important than war.
From where
comes this new sense of values?

Hatred and strife
still rule in many parts of our world and cause
endless death, starvation and suffering.
Vengeance and greed
are the norm where the message
of the King of Peace
is unheeded.

Today
A new spirit is moving in the Western world,
of concern, matched with money,
for the hungry, the cold, the suffering
in distant places,
and even
for those in our own home town.

Have we caught the vision
of the King of Peace?
Whose hands touched the sick and the hungry.
Has He touched my spirit?
Will I seek to follow Him?
or will I look for a parking space at the mall?

Lord, help me
so to celebrate your birth
as you taught us while you were on earth,
not only on December 25
but all the year through!

A CAREGIVER'S CHRISTMAS

Cold and cheerless the day had come
While people everywhere are rejoicing.
My wife is sitting on the chesterfield, eyes closed.
My wife?
What is left in life for us?
BUT…from somewhere I hear strains of MUSIC!

Is she my wife?
I look at her
and see only sadness on her face.
That MUSIC… it beats at my heart.
I walk to her side,
Something is pushing me!

Her hands are disfigured with arthritis.
I kneel down in front of her
and take her hands.
"Your hands are beautiful," I whisper.
She opens her eyes
and she smiles.

She hasn't smiled for a long time!
"It is Christmas today," I tell her
and
"Yes, I know," she says.

"I'll make us some hot chocolate,
and I bought some Christmas cake."
Her heart was moved,
and I could see she was happy.

I brought out the old picture albums
and we lived again
the things we had lived before.
That MUSIC now swelled in our hearts!

We found more music on radio and TV
We phoned our children in St. Paul and Red Deer
And a friend called us to say
"Merry Christmas".
In the evening I read her a storybook
She had saved for many years.

The day has ended
so quickly
When you are happy together!
"Merry Christmas!" she whispered,
and I kissed her.
It all started with a bit of MUSIC.
SHE IS MORE THAN A WIFE TO ME!

THE CROSS OF JESUS

When Jesus walked the dusty roads of Judah
Or sat beside the Sea of Galilee,
He drew the people to His side
with thoughtful teaching
and words that touched their hearts.

The words He spoke led to the cross
Outside the wall at Golgotha
Not His sins
But mine, that nailed Him to the tree!
On that dreadful day.

"Take up my cross," He said to me
"and follow in my footsteps."
I read again the words that Jesus spoke
When He was here on earth,
And answered, "Yes, I'll try."

Cleanse me, O Lord, from sin and doubt
That I may serve you with clean hands
That others may see you
in my words and deeds
and look to you in faith.

The path I walk is rocky
With cloudy mists and hidden traps
I need your guidance and your care
And some friends
to share my joy and pain.

The cross of Jesus that I carry
And the suffering it involves
strengthen me.
They create in me a new person
growing in His Word.

As I walk the path that Jesus taught me
I leave behind my selfish will
When I see the pain that others suffer
Lord, help me to understand
and walk with them the "extra mile".

THE CROSS OF JESUS—2

"Follow me," said Jesus
To Peter and Andrew, James and John
In a voice that drew them
Away from the humdrum cares of life.

He did not promise them glory
In fighting the ruthless Roman regime
Or the wealth that could be made
In the grasping world of trade.

NO, war and revolt
Were not in His plan
And in the riches of worldly wealth
He showed no interest at all.

He was so different from other men
Was that why they followed Him?
What was He trying to do?
Without weapons, and without gold?

He gripped their hearts
And changed their lives
With the words He softly spoke
On the hill north of the Sea of Galilee.

With no sword and no gold
How could He transform this cruel world
With its hatred and greed
And brutal immoral deeds?

He taught men to love their neighbours
To be good to those who mistreat them
To obey their earthly masters
And to honour God above all.

What could He hope to accomplish with a program like this
In a world where evil rules?
His future seemed only to lead to defeat
As Jesus walked the road to the Cross.

The Last Supper marked the climax
When Jesus washed His disciples' feet
He left this example for all to see and heed
Before He went to the Cross at Golgotha.

Jesus bled and died on the Cross
To free all men from the bondage of sin
All those who look to Him
And follow Him on the path He walked.

The path of Jesus leads us to the Cross
He hasn't promised us heaven on earth
We have to leave our pride and the gold that we love
And humbly love our neighbours as Jesus taught,

While on this earth He walked.

This message of love has gripped the hearts of many
And curbed their evil selfish wills
It has changed their lives
And now they bear
The fruits of the Holy Spirit.

Lord Jesus, lead us
And teach us to walk in your footsteps
To bear the fruit of the Holy Spirit:
Love, Joy, Peace,
Long-suffering, Kindness,
Goodness, Faithfulness,
Gentleness,
Self-control.

THE GRIEF I CARRY

Norah has left me
and I am alone
with grief in my heart

Please don't annoy me with soft, soothing talk, and don't read Bible verses and pray with me.

If you want to help me, put your arm around me and cry with me, but please don't talk.

Quietly help me draw near to God

When God created us He gave us both
life and death

I can't understand these things
They are a mystery to me
They make me afraid

Then I remember Norah
The example she left me
and the lessons she taught me
They are still present with me

Her life was not in vain here on earth
where You prepared her for service with You
through all eternity

LORD, HELP ME TO CARRY MY GRIEF
DON'T TAKE IT AWAY
ONLY GRIEF CAN HEAL MY BROKEN SOUL

Grant that it may change my life
to help others carry their grief
and prepare me
that I may serve You here on earth
and then in heaven above.

I REMEMBER NORAH

I remember Norah
and the sleepless nights
when she was up all night
fussing around.
Would she get herself into trouble?
and when she was all tired out
where would she fall asleep?

She needed my care day and night
and I became so tired!

Now Norah is gone
and the nights are quiet.
I get up in the middle of the night
and look for her in vain.
There is no one sleeping on the floor now.

It is so quiet and peaceful now
and my heart aches
for the days when she was with me.

I remember lunch time
I made her the things she loved,
hot waffles and maple syrup
and black tea with lemon
just as she had taught me.

Sometimes
she ate her food with a smile
and my heart was glad

but on some days
her eyes were fixed straight ahead
they saw no food
and her ears were deaf to my words
and the waffles turned cold untouched
and my heart was troubled.

Now I eat my lunch alone
and think of Norah
and my heart aches
alone.

A baby is born
grows
and dies

That is our story
We don't understand it—we are troubled by it
and we don't have the answers

What is God's plan for us?
We look around us—we study our environment
our eyes reach far out into the cosmos—and we are amazed.

Everywhere we look we see purpose in the orders of creation. Scientists find that matter in all its forms is subject to laws and formulas, and even when these fall into chaos there is still purpose in disorder.

Such is life!
We can see the disorder in our suffering and pain, but not the purpose. Later we realize what God was doing with us—the suffering we passed through caused us to grow in strength and character, and kept us humble.

> When I was born a baby I was nothing; but then I grew through interaction with other people and with my environment. I struggled with my will and with temptations. I became a person, a unique human being. God gave me an intellect I could use to guide myself; sometimes I used it and sometimes I failed. Then God sent more suffering into my life. He wanted me to grow and become less selfish.

God used all the things that have happened in my life to make a better person out of me. I have failed Him often, but He has not left me.

And then I faced the death of my wife
I know that death is part of life
but I don't understand life—and I shudder at death!

One thing I know
When I consider all the work God has put into my life to make me what I am, He will not let His efforts go to waste. He has an eternal plan for me, and a place for me to take when He has finished with me here on earth
if I submit myself to Him.

I miss my wife Norah
my life has become empty

But I do not idly mourn. I had a lovely monument erected on the grave where the remains of her body lie, with both our names on it, and engraved on the bottom it says:

GOD HAS BLESSED US

I have faced death myself, I have seen my wife die. It is a very humbling experience. It has changed the priorities of my life. Ordinary fun and pleasure tend to make me feel sick. I can't stand the low "entertainment" that is ever-present on TV. Material things don't have the same value for me that they used to have. I now am more interested in helping others and in enjoying their company.

I don't understand death
I am only trying to fathom the meaning of life
and it is changing me into a different person
into a better person
I hope and pray.

I SLIPPED TODAY

I slipped today
and almost failed
my Savior and my God.

They were so rude with me
when they attacked me
Lord, I thank you
that I did not return their bitter words

Victory comes
when I do not talk back
and you helped me to keep silent.
Now I need your help
to heal the wounds
they inflicted on me.

Lord, I am so weak
and my love is so feeble,
You have told us to love our enemies
but these weren't enemies, Lord.
What do I do now?

Heal me now
and give me understanding
and increase my love.
My path is so dark
and I cannot see
but Lord, take my hand and lead me.

LESSONS I LEARNED FROM NORAH

Modest and unassuming
Norah was a quiet lady
Her words were few
and she seldom had to take them back
I admired her for this

Her eyesight was good
but she was colour-blind
in her relations with coloured peoples
a LESSON we all need

She had the wealth to stand among
the moneyed people in the crowd
but she made no difference between the rich and the poor
The first respected her
and the latter loved her
This is the hardest LESSON of all

Then her health began to fail
Osteoporosis, arthritis, Alzheimer disease
She suffered many years
but never learned to complain
I marvelled how she suffered quietly
and I pray that I may learn well
this LESSON that she taught so
courageously

LIFE IS A BURDEN
OR IS IT FAITH?

. . . .

Lord, I feel confused and lost
the answers are tangled up
in shadowy clouds of doubt and fear.

Then I remember
you also carried a burden
and your path led to the cross.
But, Lord
I feel so forsaken and alone
I grasp for your hand but
I need to hold a human hand.

There are so many questions all around me
Which way do I turn?
The paths are obscured with uncertainty
and I can't see where they lead.
Must I always walk by faith?
and not see where my path leads?

Lord, were we born to suffer?
Is that why you created us?
Then into my troubled soul
came some insight from above
I remembered Norah
and our life together.

You blessed us, Lord
with many happy times
but our wedded life was not always bliss
sometimes we even drew apart.

And then you sent us suffering
first Norah, then me, and Norah again
and we needed each other
and we suffered together.

In the end Norah suffered more than I
with the dreaded Alzheimer affliction.
In these last years of suffering
we drew closest together.
That is what you did for us, Lord!

I don't understand the human psyche
but I see that it grows through suffering.
Help me to understand, Lord
and walk in faith
the path you open up for me.

I am afraid, Lord.
Draw me near, and give me a hand
a human hand
and help me to grow
through the suffering
I still must face.

And then I felt His presence
He still cares for me
He is still shaping me
as I do the pieces of rock
with my diamond saw.

If I can grow through suffering
then let it be so, Lord
and don't neglect me like others I see
who idly sit and waste their lives.
No, help me serve you to the end
and bless me with suffering
your purposes to fulfil.

MY FAITH AS SEEN THROUGH THE SCRIPTURES

My faith is built on the teachings of the Bible, which have had a deep influence on my daily life. The words of Jesus have especially been important to me.

In the following quotation, the Sadducees confront Jesus with an important question, and Jesus answers them:

> "Teacher, which is the greatest commandment in the Law?"
>
> Jesus replied, "Love the Lord your God with all your heart and with all your soul and with all your mind. This is the first and greatest commandment. And the second is like it:
>
> Love your neighbour as yourself." Matthew 22:36-39.

Then the question arises, "Who is my neighbour?" Jesus answers this in the next quotation:

> On one occasion an expert in the Law stood up to test Jesus. "Teacher," he asked, "what must I do to inherit eternal life?"
>
> "What is written in the Law?" he replied. "How do you read it?"
>
> He answered: "Love the Lord your God with all your heart and with all your soul and with all your strength and with all your mind" and "Love your neighbour as yourself."
>
> "You have answered correctly," Jesus replied. "Do this and you will live."
>
> But he wanted to justify himself, so he asked Jesus, "And who is my neighbour?"
>
> In reply Jesus said: "A man was going down from Jerusalem to Jericho, when he fell into the hands of robbers. They stripped him of his clothes, beat him and went away, leaving him half dead. A priest happened to be going down the same road, and when he saw the man, he passed by on the other side. So too, a Levite, when he came to the place and saw him, passed by on the other side.

> “But a Samaritan, as he travelled, came where the man was; and when he saw him, he took pity on him. He went to him and bandaged his wounds, pouring on oil and wine. Then he put the man on his own donkey, took him to an inn and took care of him. The next day he took out two silver coins and gave them to the innkeeper. ‘Look after him,’ he said, ‘and when I return, I will reimburse you for any extra expense you may have.’
>
> “Which of these three do you think was a neighbour to the man who fell into the hands of robbers?”
>
> The expert in the Law replied, “The one who had mercy on him.”
>
> Jesus told him, “Go and do likewise.” Luke 10:25-37.

This is not a comfortable statement for us. The man in the parable is going down from Jerusalem, the city of God, to Jericho, the city of sin. He is not the kind of person we would want for a friend, but Jesus tells us he is our neighbour and needs our help, with personal attention. It is not an easy command but Jesus puts it into a strong directive.

In the next quotation Jesus deals with the subject of pride and self-righteousness.

> Also He spoke this parable to some who trusted in themselves that they were righteous, and despised others:
>
> “Two men went up to the temple to pray, one a Pharisee and the other a tax collector. The Pharisee stood and prayed thus to himself, ‘God, I thank you that I am not like other men—extortioners, unjust, adulterers, or even as this tax collector. I fast twice a week; I give tithes of all that I possess.’
>
> And the tax collector, standing afar off, would not so much as raise his eyes to heaven, but beat his breast, saying, ‘God be merciful to me a sinner.’
>
> “I tell you, this man went down to his house justified rather than the other; for everyone who exalts himself will be abased, and he who humbles himself will be exalted.” Luke 18:9-14.

Our personal pride is a difficult matter to deal with. We know we have the truth, and are convinced of our goodness, but Jesus stresses the humility of the sinful tax collector. Jesus puts humbleness of spirit into a high category.

In the last quotation Jesus takes up the question of those who witness to their faith with words, versus those who serve in a practical way without words.

> (Jesus said), "What do you think? There was a man who had two sons. He went to the first and said, 'Son, go and work today in the vineyard.' 'I will not,' he answered, but later he changed his mind and went. Then the father went to the other son and said the same thing. He answered, 'I will, sir,' but did not go.
>
> "Which of the two did what his father wanted?"
>
> "The first," they answered.
>
> Jesus said to them, "I tell you the truth, the tax collectors and the prostitutes are entering the kingdom of God ahead of you." Matthew 21:28-31.

Clearly Jesus is not satisfied when we make a verbal confession of faith. He tells us to put our faith into action in a practical way, with a truly humble conviction, willing to pick up those who have fallen by the wayside.